Praise for Marisa Babjak's debut novel *White Lies*

A passionate crusader for truth and tolerance, Paloma is the new worst enemy of the forces of hate. Marisa Babjak, Paloma's creator, writes with courageous heart and conviction, as rare in fiction as they are in real life. A fine first novel.~~Taylor Smith, author of *The Innocents Club, Guilt by Silence,* and *Random Acts*

One of the freshest voices in mystery fiction in over a decade! Don't start this book unless you have nothing to do. . .you won't be able to put it down. ~~Donna Harper, author of *Turn a Blind Eye*

This debut novel is hotter than Georgia asphalt on a summer's day! ~~Southern Journal

Marisa Babjak's compelling debut novel is packed with action, thrills, witty dialogue and sprinkled with liberal amounts of humor. She knows the South and writes you there!~~The New South Mystery Review

Don't miss Marisa Babjak's new hardcover forthcoming late Summer 2004

The Street Where Angels Fear to Tread
The Second Paloma Mystery
from *Low Country Publishing*
ISBN: 0-9675528-1-8

WHITE LIES

A Paloma Mystery

By Marisa Babjak

Published in the United States
By Low Country Publishing

Although this novel is based on historical facts, the story itself is complete fiction. With the exception of public figures mentioned incidentally, the names, characters, and events depicted herein are the products of the author's imagination. No resemblance is intended to any event or to any real person, living or dead.

Library of Congress Cataloging-In-Publication Data
2002108739
Babjak, Marisa, 1960–
White Lies / by Marisa Babjak
p. cm.

ISBN: 0-9675528-0-X

1. Paloma–(Fictional Character)–Fiction.
2. Mystery–Fiction
3. Hate Crimes–Fiction
4. Southern Culture–Georgia–(Rincon, Savannah)–Fiction
5. Southern Culture–South Carolina (Hilton Head Island)–Fiction
6. Computer Crimes–Fiction
I. Title

Carried By The Light, by Camilleri/Smith. Copyright 1990. Used by permission.
Strange Fruit by L. Allen, Copyright 1939. Used by permission.

Printed in the United States of America
First Printing, August 2003

10   9   8   7   6   5   4   3   2   1

This book is dedicated to the memory of four special people–
my grandparents (the real Sid and Kate), my friend Alice Carrillo, and
most recently, my father, Thomas Joseph Babjak.

Gran–my love of storytelling and crime show television was born in
your living room. *Eu sinto tantas saudades de você, mulher bondosa de
coração afável.*

Papa–salt of the earth, you possessed that rare quality of accepting
people just as they are–such a rare and wonderful gift for me. *Seus
rivais, seus sucessores? Não existe nenhum.*

Alice, dear soul, surrogate mom, voracious reader, and mystery fan.
You gave the best–your heart–and asked for nothing in return. *Minha
vizinha, amiga e madrinha – que sempre foi compassiva, prestativa,
divertida e amava ler mistérios, aceitando a todos que conhecia e
também sendo amada por todos, que compartilhou das dores e sempre
sofreu mais. Sempre terei você no meu coração.*

Dad, how can I sum up, in a few paltry words, a father's lifetime?
After giving me life, you gave me silliness in which to enjoy it. You
gave me the beach, Sinatra, the love of cooking (and eating).
I learned from you to take chances, go after what I wanted and to work
hard for what I loved to do.
I miss your cynicism, your stories. I'm *so* sorry you missed reading
mine.
I love you. Semper Fidelis.

*Papai, eu fui deixada aos tropeços, desconcertada, muda e cega. Eu
espero você saiba que tudo eu o quis saber. Agradeço-o por tudo, por
ser meu pai.*

The light in my world has dimmed.

Acknowledgments

To thank everyone who offered me encouragement and advice before, during and after writing this story is a monumental task. Many of these people are the women and men of the international mystery fan and writers' organization *Sisters in Crime*. I am astounded by their continued inspiration, creativity and advice. Special thanks to the Los Angeles and Orange County chapters!

The subject matter in *White Lies* would have been of much less significance if not for the book, *The Klan Unmasked,* which led to meeting the author, Stetson Kennedy. Thank you for modestly sharing your lifetime of daring and selfless acts against racism by the Ku Klux Klan and your continued efforts to promote tolerance. Thanks to the Simon Wiesenthal Center, its library staff and their Museum of Tolerance, all in Los Angeles, for their assistance in providing me with extensive research and background information; the Southern Poverty Law Center and the *Intelligence Project*, Montgomery, Alabama; The Center for Democratic Renewal, Atlanta, Georgia. The "lady locksmith," Elyse Rothstein, owner, *El Segundo Industrial Lock and Security,* brushed me up on lock picking with pink-handled tools. And thanks to my mom's friend, Rachael Buie–part of the inspiration for Aggie.

To the following mystery novelists whom I'm fortunate to consider my friends: tremendous thanks to Meg O'Brien, Earlene Fowler, Taylor Smith, all of whose editing talents and suggestions made *White Lies* a much better story. Noreen Ayres, Maxine O'Callaghan, Patricia McFall, Joyce Spizer, to name a few, answered millions of my questions and gave encouragement, and much more. Carolyn Hart, Karen Kijewski, Penny Warner–you might not have known how much you helped me, but I hope you do now.

Anna Devore, Claudia Peterman had the patience to critique my story from the infant stage and hung in there to the last word. Thank-you is most inadequate. Dorrie Lloyd, thank you for the last editing amid our various mishaps and adventures. Brazilian souls: the Pravaceks–Hans (by way of Chile), Vanessa and Suzanna, Los Angeles; Cristina Almeida, New York City. You all made your country come alive for me (meanwhile wasting a bit of government time) through its people, music, stories, food, language, dance and a fictitious little red-dressed, buck-toothed firecracker named *Mônica*. In São Paulo: real-life Mônica Akemi and Aldo Cvintal (thanks Aldo, for the *bostas*, et al.). I hope I got it right like a true *carioca*. *Muito, muito, obrigada, meus amigos!*

Debbie Cabeza, Los Angeles–thanks for trying–you know what I mean. Thanks to all at LCP! Southerners are known storytellers and I am blessed to be among the best: my family–the Hinely's, Babjak's, Gilmore's, and Wiggins'. Thanks for your support. Debbie Fox, Statesville, North Carolina–thanks for being a younger Aggie, the cross-stitch, and saving my sanity in Virginia. Phyllis Reynolds, Sachse, Texas–you are in my stories, in some form or other. Watch out for that extra crispy!

To my husband, Jim. Poor words for a monumental man. *Muito obrigada pelas sugestões, paciência, e especial amor.*

Author's Note

All the characters in *White Lies,* especially the bad guys, are figments of my imagination. The cities, towns and islands described are all very real. With the exception of parts of Rincon, Georgia, the buildings and historical information are exact and accurate. But as I was tasked to make up a story, I couldn't resist the chance to play God. So I rearranged things–like making the Savannah River a bit closer to Rincon, and added and took away other references. Change does eventually wind its way into small towns, even those in the slow-to-change South. I'm sure–in fact I know–a few of the places detailed in *White Lies* already have new names, different purposes. Some were kept in for sentimental reasons.

White Lies was written well before the September 11, 2001 terrorist attacks. Paloma's comments about security practices (or the lack of) at the Pentagon are coincidental. Before press time, however, I was able to update the hate crime information to reflect current situations and events. Klan activities, inside and away from their meetings, reflect fictionalized representations from documented sources. However, the Klan meeting procedures and recitations during the cross burnings in *White Lies* were taken in sections exactly as secretly video-taped during a Klan meeting in the Midwest.

All hate crime information detailed in this novel is from the following sources (except when the source is listed along with a specific fact):

The Klan Unmasked by Stetson Kennedy, reprinted 1991, Florida Atlantic University Press.

Klanwatch Annual Reports 1989, 1990, 1995, 1998, *Intelligence Project* website, Southern Poverty Law Center, Montgomery Alabama.

The Fiery Cross: The Ku Klux Klan in America by Wyn Craig Wade, 1987, Oxford University Press.

The Jim Crow Guide by Stetson Kennedy, reprinted 1990, Florida Atlantic University Press.

Southern Exposure by Stetson Kennedy, reprinted 1991, Florida Atlantic University Press.

Statistics and materials on racism collected by the Museum of Tolerance and the Simon Wiesenthal Library, Los Angeles, California.

Undercover video of Klan meeting, Kansas, 1996, property of the Federal Bureau of Investigation.

Contact the Author

Marisa Babjak can be contacted via the website for her business *femmes fatales* that sells unique gift items with an emphasis on mysteries. The address is: **www.mysterygifts.biz**. Due to various factors, including scheduling and health, the author may not be able to reply to each correspondence.

White Lies

A Paloma Mystery

by Marisa Babjak

Low Country Publishing
Charleston, South Carolina

black seas pitch and toss
'til you're unsteady on your feet
when they raise that fiery cross
together we'll share the heat
–Carried By The Light

The Black Sorrows
from **Harley & Rose**
St. Kilda, Australia, 1995

The Low Country

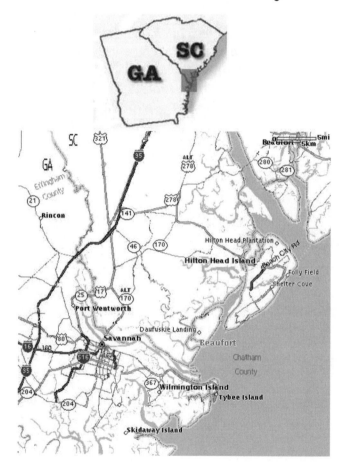

Prologue

The blow split his left cheek open. The force of the punch snapped his head back. It slammed into a hard and unmovable object behind him. Fear threatened to engulf him. The relatively carefree life he'd led until now left him ill-prepared for the confrontation he'd stumbled into tonight. To survive, he *had* to turn the fear into hostility. Hatred. He willed it to happen. He felt the indignation flow throughout him. Down into his fists, to summon up a dreadful depravity that swelled inside, so massive and forceful, that he should have been able to level mountains.

He heard the crunch a second before he felt it. His jaw shattered. One of them laughed while he choked on teeth and blood that flooded his mouth. He tried to cough it all up, but it was a weak reflex. Instead it spilled down his chin, and soaked into his shirt.

How long had the blows been raining down on him? How many bones tortured by angry, booted feet? He would fight every last one of them. Every fist, every kick. He blocked his mind away from the pain. He would not–could not give up. *I won't give them the satisfaction.* The young man became pumped up. For his survival.

He flailed out in a frenzy of punches and kicks, managing to inflict some damage. But he endured more than he dished out.

And then. Yes! He broke away! Adrenaline pumping, feet flying across the embankment. Airborne! He would run all night if he had to.

Out of the darkness it came. A slight tugging on his shirt. Then he was falling, crashing, tumbling in the weeds. His face was shoved down into the muck. Hands gripped his head and held it still. He tasted mud on his tongue. Fists and feet rained down on him. He was outnumbered, out hated, out reviled. They flung him roughly onto his back.

No! He almost yelled it out loud. When he saw what was waiting for him. Every cell in his body urged him to open his mouth, scream out his agony. Wrench the fear from his lips. Send it twisting through the foul night air.

So this is what these yahoos had planned to do with him all along. *No! No! No, no, no! Nonononono!* It was worse than any damage they'd done, or could have imagined inflicting. Seeing it there now in front of him–he could only focus on it. Stare at it. Not believing, but believing. It was as if reality became an entity that morphed and wafted in front of him while his thoughts became elusive and pulsating, as they undulated away from his grasp. He was a jerk-mode of confused emotions as he was confronted with a fear so real, so tangible, you could stink up the night with it.

Oh, please, not like this! He thought of his family–sister, brothers, mother. The dreams he had longed for throughout his youth–so many not even begun! His whole life ahead...only to come down to this. *This* way!

Had there been others? How many had been suckered like him?

Ha! It was quick and abrupt. Absurd. If he'd realized he'd done it just then, he'd have probably laughed again. But there was more on his mind. So much more. He didn't have time to reflect, and he could no longer be bothered with dreams. The blows kept coming.

"Stop," he wheezed. "Please. You can stop now. I'm already dead."

He took a few seconds to pray. But he didn't ask for God to spare his life, in a miraculous rush send someone swooping down to save him. There would be no miracles here. Instead he asked–begged–for a different ending to his short life. *If I have to die, God, please, not this.*

Anyway but this!

In the 1840's the Know Nothings, an anti-alien, anti-Catholic secret society, was formed. It's goal, lasting almost twenty years, was to provoke riots, inspire national suspicion and promote terror against German and Irish-American Catholics.

Chapter One

I'd set the timer on the bomb. When I was long gone from there, Baron Industries' financial structure would be destroyed. I'd created a daisy chain version that would go off in one part of the company at a time, slowly spreading its destruction like a virus. "Paloma, *são uma menina muito maá*," I said aloud to myself. A very wicked girl! "That's why I love you so." I blew a kiss for luck to my nefarious creation, packed up my materials, while I quietly sang, "Another One Bites the Dust".

I left the computer room, double-checking that the door with the electronic keypad entry system–which I'd quickly hacked into exactly two minutes, sixteen seconds earlier–locked behind me. Now to slip out undetected. At this point in the caper to keep my wits, I quietly hummed my finale, "You Dropped a Bomb On Me", even though I had to skip making the high-pitched whistle sound-effects of a falling bomb–my favorite part.

No one questioned my unescorted status as I left the building, the first in a long list of no-no's I'd uncovered during my assignment with Baron Industries. All visitors were to be escorted by an employee at all times. There were no sharp eyes to scrutinize my visitor's badge. I'd made a photo copy of a previous one, then reproduced it at home on my computer and color printer. I'd made a quick stop yesterday at Staples to laminate it and add a clip attachment so it could hang off my shirt collar and match Baron employees. Not a bad imitation of the real thing. Unless someone asked to see it.

I'd been snooping in the building previously, casing the place, making sure I chatted up the guards. It often helped being friendly with the people that were often invisible–the ones most people passed by each day without giving much thought to their existence. So when I walked into a building strutting a bold confidence that broadcasted the lie that I had every right to be there, I was most often left alone to do a little "P and E", my code for picking and entering.

Once inside Baron, I had the same challenge all over again. Find my way through the company offices to the place where I needed to do my work. No matter what security procedures were in place, with any company there were lax areas. Some people did not believe espionage happened in real life– certainly not in their corner of the world. This freed me to do whatever I'd been hired to do to wreck a company–especially if it involved electronics or computers.

How did I end up with all this damaging knowledge? College, of course! I'd spent a confining but essential six-year stretch gobbling up lectures, books, articles and papers written by the top electronic wizards–all of which had been preceded by a lifetime of curiosity and nosiness. Before my teen years, I had begun with picking locks and the constant need to tinker. But I wasn't choosy. Give me any device powered by electricity. But my first love was the common household front door lock.

The resort island where I grew up sported plenty of summer homes that stood empty most of the year and not much else for kids to do when they tired of the beach. In a child-like gesture of helpfulness, I left a note inside each part-timer's house suggesting the purchase of better locks and security devices. This was of course, after I picked and entered. But my capers differed from B and E–the breaking and entering of police parlance, in that I never broke anything, except perhaps a stubby nail. I defeated the lock, dropped off a note and left. No stealing, damage, or peeking in cabinets. It was all for the thrill of tinkering with a lock. Therefore, my insistence that I *pick* and enter.

A few locks and years later, I met the processor chip. I quickly learned computer systems inside and out–how to build, hack, repair and enhance them. With the advent of personal computers, effectively knowing how to keep everyone out of *my* systems had groomed me to be an expert on getting into "theirs". And I was damn good at it.

I love the rush of getting into and out of a place without detection! I thrill at using my brains, electronic gear and computer programs to break through a system's barricade–any barricade–whether across telephone lines or a keycard reader attached to a door. Yes, I'm a computer geek, a bit-head, cyber-punk, tweeker. I'd been teased for years and now wore the labels with pride. I loved the work. It was exciting, and getting paid for it made it even more so!

Creating all this electronic destruction and doing it legally kept me all a-twitter and fortuitously employed with California Digital Research and Security. CDRS–the first company of its kind and always ranked in the top five high-tech security firms worldwide–is paid handsomely for its investigative teams to analyze a company's vulnerability for high-tech espionage, theft or destruction of assets by employees or outsiders and the kidnaping of key personnel. The analysis starts at the bottom, so to speak, with screening potential employees and goes on to encompass the entire company with security procedures and equipment. Gazillions of dollars and a firm's survival are at stake. I sounded like the company's advertising brochure. But it's true. Some creep is always trying to get around the system, break the rules, or take what doesn't belong to them. That's where I come in. With electronic gadgetry, along with computer hardware and software, I can give you the tools to protect your company. If what you needed doesn't exist I, and others in the CDRS team, could design and build it. But even the Pentagon can't be totally safe without a conscious effort of its employees.

And that's where Baron Industrial was sorely lacking. During the several weeks I'd consulted there, I'd learned that the attitude of management was that all these security bells and whistles were unnecessary, especially the costs. It was a sadly typical response that usually came back to bite like a school of piranhas. Baron's CIO, Chief Information Officer–as in electronic information–wanted to shake the company up a bit. To prove that anything could happen at anytime. My job was to slap them with a bit of reality.

Okay, so Baron Industrial wouldn't vanish beneath a mushroom cloud, my bomb being of a cyber variety. My bomb program, working a bit different than a computer virus, wouldn't erase their data for good. The point was that they would *think* so. I'd make it reappear after the CIO had his fun.

Back at my office at CDRS, I wrote my report, starting with how I snuck onto the property. My relative youth and love of swimming paid off as I scaled the ten-foot wall to get onto Baron property. Well, that and a bit of rope, a claw, and a carabiner or two. It had been easy getting through to the computer room. No one, especially the ground floor Rent-A-Cops, questioned why I had signed out earlier in the week and turned in my badge–the only legitimate entry into the company I'd made. I briefly waved, flashed them a wide grin and was now strolling to the fourth floor. I brazenly "how-died" a few people in the hallways throwing attention onto myself. Only one employee bothered to ask what I was doing as my software performed circuit rewiring to obtain the number combinations necessary to gain access in-to the computer room. The program was sending out all the possible number sequences, astronomically faster and more accurate than I, a mere mortal, would ever hope to do. When it hit, a soft click let me know I had three seconds to turn the lock.

The nosy employee stepped into the all-too-human trap of good manners. Not making waves or risking embarrassment to question whether I had the right to perform surgery on the lock had curbed his suspicions and I took full advantage. He neglected to check my visitor's badge with security down-stairs, or even look at it closely, which would have given me away. I wore a long-collared shirt so the badge ended up hanging down over my boob. As long as it was socially unacceptable to fondle a woman's breast while scrutinizing her ID, the man wouldn't get close enough to discover the fraud. I'd been working on the keypad, bent over when he approached, asking to see my badge. I turned around and thrust my boobs up at him, intentionally standing too close. In his flustered state, he took it on faith my lie that I was running a routine check on the keypad electronics. There were no computer staff to ask, as they were at their end of the week wrap-up meeting–which is why I chose this time for P and E. The rest was too easy. I'd laughed all the way back to my office. Only three of my recommended security procedures were being utilized and then only half-heartedly. I *love* this work!

Report writing I did not. Containing myself in order to detail all the techniques and fun I had, especially if I wasn't caught, took more discipline than I wanted to expend, and so soon after the thrills. It was late Friday evening but I had no urges except dinner. My best friend Dixie wasn't in town, further dampening after-work activities. She was across the country, back home in South Carolina using her police skills to track down a missing cousin. Truth be told, it's not like I had a date for the evening–nor the rest of the month–I reminded myself. Might as well work, wrap it all up and impress the big boss. As soon as he sat at his desk Monday morning, he'd discover that I'd finished my umpteenth assignment *and* the report way ahead of schedule.

I sighed contentedly. Life at this time in my life was basically heavenly. I'd moved to Los Angeles almost two years ago, primed and longing for the career I'd been groomed for by my lifetime of hobbies and studies. I'd been so impatient to get at it. I'd spent months of unfulfilling work in two other companies while I beat out the competition for a job at CDRS. After passing their exhaustive computer systems tests, along with a long and intensive security background check, I'd finally come to roost with a dream job at CDRS.

A short hop south of work was play. The summer before my final year at school, I'd flown here to California, my fourth trip, for a sort of pre-relocation check. As Pacific Coast Highway meandered out of Long Beach, the last southward city in Los Angeles County, I'd driven into Orange County and its first offering, Seal Beach. I knew instantly that this would be my new home as I turned onto First Street and approached the inlet that overlooked the vast Long Beach Marina where my sail boat was now docked. Sharing my new adventures–my sidekick–Dixie Hightower–best friend since diapers. Coming from a large family, she had decided to find her own crib and experience living alone for the first time. So there we were, fresh, unfettered and adventure bound–living smack-dab in the middle of all the wonder that southern California had to offer. And here I was in a windowless office working my Friday night away.

I emailed a copy of my report to my immediate boss's office. He'd redline it, then I'd incorporate his comments before passing it to the CIO. I debated going home but decided to work on debugging my recent invention for the company. I named it BOB, for Bucket of Bolts, a robot that we hoped to sell to police department bomb squads worldwide. Theo, an avid computer geek like me, was in the lab, as he always seemed to be. It assuaged my ego that here was another young, single person without a love life.

We greeted each other and cyber-talked, keeping it brief as we both had computer needs to feed. I could lose myself in the digital world to the point that earthquakes were ignored. If the roof wasn't falling in, then there was no reason to stop. The electronic world was a haven for me. It was where I thrilled, learned and created programming code that made tasks for work and life a little easier. It was a place where I shined, had found self-esteem and the chance to make my mark. Most appealingly, computer systems allowed a measure of control in a chaotic world. I built routines that avoided disasters. A loss of data? No problem–backups were available. The cyber-world is a place so familiar I'm always at ease. It's a world as safe and comfortable for me as is the beach. Yes, it's an artificial world–but I thrive in it. It is my drug.

My drug of choice that Friday night was RNPL–Robotics Natural Programming Language, another of my own proud inventions. I'd get BOB working so he'd dazzle the governments to write big checks for CDRS.

"*Hey*!" I jerked my head up and saw Theo frantically waving the phone. "It's for you, birdbrain."

"What? Um, sorry. I didn't hear it ring."

"You don't have to tell me. I've gotten carpal tunnel just trying to get your attention." I stuck my tongue out at him and crossed my eyes. Theo was a great pal–he laughed anytime I tried to be funny. Gotta love that in a guy! "It's long distance. From the land of grits and fried chicken."

Now *that* wasn't funny. When I'm at work I never get a call from back home in South Carolina unless it was an emergency. I yanked my feet off my desk, flinging the keyboard on top of the scuff marks my shoes had just made. I grabbed the phone. My heart began to pound. *"Por favor deixo-o sem paz!"* I said under my breath in the Portuguese I'd learned from my Brazilian mother–a quick prayer that all would be well with my loved ones, but still wondering who was ill.

"Is this, uh, Polina?" a voice foreign to me asked.

"Paloma. Who is this?"

"I'm calling about Dixie Hightower."

"Not one of her better ones! Tell Dixie I don't need an anonymous caller to remind me to send her nephews the computer games. I know I promised weeks ago. I actually have them here and I'm going to drop them in the mail tonight." I laughed, omitting that I'd carried the games with me for a week, always forgetting to post them. "Which relative am I speaking with?" A genealogy chart was needed to track Dixie's large extended family.

"Hang on, lady! I don't know what you're talking about. Dixie asked me to call 'cause she needs help."

"What's the matter? Where is she? Is she all right?" I bellowed in a rush.

"Whoa, lady! You're machine gunning me here."

"I'm sorry. I'm worried. Please tell me–is she okay?"

"She's all right, but, um, could you call me back? Your buddy there wouldn't accept a collect call. I'm at a pay phone and I, uh..."

"No problem. What's the number?" I jotted it down, rummaged for my cell phone and hurriedly stabbed at the buttons. A pay phone that allowed incoming calls. That was a novel change. I went for manners. "Perhaps you should introduce yourself."

"It don't matter who I am. You need to get down here. Your friend is in a whole lotta trouble."

"What are you talking about?" I froze, stiff with tension. "Where is she? What's going on?" The silence lingered while I willed the man to quickly spit out the answers to my questions. What had happened to my friend?

"Now, hang on, I gotta make this quick. I don't want no more trouble. I've had enough of that. She needs some help." So he keeps saying, but *what* exactly?

"Name it." And he could. Dixie and I have been best friends since forever. She didn't forget about me when my family moved to Brazil and she visited there often. In our mid teens, she was at my grandparents' house, eagerly waiting, the day I returned an orphan to Hilton Head Island, our birthplace. She had gone the distance for me dozens of times and would sign up for hundreds more. You'd expect that from family. They almost *have* to be there for you. I know. It sounds cliché. But how often in life are you lucky enough to have a friend that by saying she's always there for you–that you simply and definitely mean *always*. Better than having a sister!

"Dixie's in jail."

"What?" I gasped and stammered until tongue and brain synchronized. "Didn't she tell them she was a..." Wait! If she had told her jailers she was a cop with the Los Angeles Police Department, surely they would have given her a little courtesy. Like the proverbial one phone call. For some reason she must have kept silent. Curious.

"Where is she–I mean, the town?"

"Rincon." He pronounced it like stinkin', his tone implying he thought it did. "Just north of Savannah, G-A."

Where Dixie's cousin Lemond lives. He was missing and Dixie had gone home to find out what had happened, where he'd gone. "How did you meet her?"

No Name hesitated. "I was *in* there. In the slammer. Look, I got stopped for speeding and next thing I know, I'm beat up, tossed into a southern hell hole with two punk-ugly white cops staring down at me like in that movie. You know, the one with the banjos."

"Huh?" I quickly caught up to where his conversation had wandered. "You mean *Deliverance*? 'Dueling Banjos'?"

"Yeah! That's the one!" He sounded almost delighted as he da-dummed a few bars of the theme song. When will the South live that one down?

I noticed his accent wasn't southern. "Where were you coming from when you got pulled over?"

"Ohio. Was on my way to Disney World to meet my brother. I stopped in Clyo, Georgia to see an old army buddy. I was passing through Rincon on my way to the Magic Kingdom when next thing–badda bing!"

"What else can you tell me?" I asked.

"Nuthin'. She begged me to call you."

"Well, how is she doing?"

"Best as one can be in that place."

"What do they say she did wrong?" It was a mistake, whatever they said. Dixie wouldn't even *think* of doing anything wrong, especially if it jeopardized her job.

"I've been trying to tell you," he said impatiently. "I don't know much. Anyway, it don't seem to matter what anybody does or doesn't do. It's a holding station. A rat hole. Only four cells. I was there. She was there. She found out I was being popped. I didn't want to get involved. She begged me to call her friend."

I mumbled for a second trying to get a grip. Figure out what to ask. I sat on a corner of desk, rear end smashing my purse. I didn't bother moving it. "I'm three thousand miles away," I told him, although that was probably not a news flash to him. "It sounds like she needs something–someone–*now*. I'll sure help out, but what about her family? They're closer."

"She said something about most of the family being on some trip. Like I'm supposed to be," he reminded me tersely. "But she don't want them. She wants *you*."

"Will you tell her that you did reach me?"

"I can't. I ain't anywhere near there. I took off outta Georgia and didn't stop until I read the 'welcome to the sunshine state' sign. Besides, I don't even know you. Her, neither. I told her I'd phone you. I did. I told you what she said–she's in jail. It was important for her that I tell you exactly what she said. She had me repeat it like I'm some kinda idiot."

"Okay, verbatim. What *exactly* did she say?"

"I need my friend–Paloma did you say?" He didn't wait for a reply. "She said–my family can't help, even if they were here. It's gotta be Paloma. Tell her that she needs to come."

"Why me specifically?"

"Because, lady. You're white."

In 1866, just after the Civil War, the Ku Klux Klan was formed to assert the superiority of the southern white man. Ever since, the KKK has, regardless of race, stalked, intimidated and lynched. Supremacists of today stem from these white terrorists.

Chapter Two

The bubble of contentment that had encircled my life since I'd started working at California Digital Research and Security was quickly pricked mere minutes after the call about Dixie. The killjoy was my immediate supervisor, Brett Craine.

"Paloma. Honey," he said wearily into the phone like an exasperated parent to a dim-witted child. "We need you here next week for the robot demonstration."

"I can email the program changes to Theo during the week. He's much better at doing demos than me." I didn't know if that was true but I was desperate for a bit of leverage.

"Are you telling me again, Paloma, honey, how I should be doing my job?" To anyone not so *ego-testicle* as Craine, the answer was an obvious NO. To Craine, every word not uttered by his own mouth was a personal affront. Until now, I'd been fortunate not having much interaction with him.

On the whole, I work better with machines than people, and wished that a few clicks of the mouse would open a computer program telling me what to say next. After a bit of throat clearing and desperate ah-hums to stall for an epiphany, I squeaked out what I hoped sounded like a very apologetic, "Nooo, sir! Absolutely not! I've got an emergency with my family. I wouldn't be asking if it wasn't *extremely* important."

"Who is it?"

Maybe we were getting somewhere. Craine *was* asking for details. But I knew he wouldn't understand deep feelings of friendship, heck, family either, for that matter. He'd recently freed the third unfortunate wife, one who should have walked down the aisle in the opposite direction. How best to persuade him?

"Uh, my grandmother," I stumbled out with the urge to cross my fingers behind my back for lying. "She practically raised me." Okay, so that much was true.

"No can do, hon. You're needed here."

"Sirrrrr!"

"Got deadlines," he snapped out. "You know how it is." I bet he was checking out his manicure—a habit used to ignore employees, which only made everyone, including his superiors, poke fun behind his back. He start-ed with careful scrutiny of the back of his hand, fingers rigid, then with a silly flick of his wrist, he'd turn his hand around, outstretched fingers folded down for a final close-up examination. Rumor had it that his white pompadoured poodle had the same manicurist.

"Mr. Craine, please let me explain..."

"What part of the no concept are you having trouble with, honey?" His voice tweaked up a few notches. I took a deep breath. We went back and forth, he enjoying my situation immensely, me begging and groveling. "That's the problem with having women in the professional workplace. They always want time off. If it's not because little junior has a cold, it's to pop out another rug rat that gives them even more excuses to whine for time off!"

Dear Mr. Craine was in his early thirties but those rare times when he took his head out of the crack of his butt, he stuck it right into the Dark Ages. "Boss, I don't have any kids, you know that. Besides, I've never asked for time off before. From day one I've put in a minimum of sixty hours a week here."

"Yeah, throw *that* in my face. And now you gotta get away," he sing-songed. "I heard it all before. You're tired, you can't hang with the big boys. See, you women think this working for a living is a cakewalk. But once you get out in the real world you find out what men have been putting up with all these years."

"I'm not going on a cruise!" I clamored unintentionally. I turned the volume down, taking the snot out of my voice. "This really is a *real* emergency!"

"Well, Paloma, honey, I could only give you a day or two at the most. I shouldn't even do that. But I'm trying to be accommodating. I mean, hey–you know me. Nice guy. Two days. That's the best I can do, honey."

"But, I have to go to South Carolina! It'll take that long to fly there and back! I'll need time to actually be there!"

He sighed, but without a drop of sympathy. "I don't know what to tell you, honey. Hell, I'm a nice guy. Everybody knows that. Here I am trying to help, give you some time, but hey–that ain't good enough. As a matter of fact, nothing ever is for you women!"

"I'm sorry, but I have no idea where this is coming from! I've *never, ever* felt that way about you or anybody or anything at the company!"

"So you're telling me your deep job satisfaction made you go over my head to my supervisor and get the best project we'd been offered in a year."

For a second I felt very much the dim-witted child. Volunteers. His boss, Cary– our company's Chief Security Officer–had asked for volunteers for the actual breaking into the Baron Industrial building. I'd spoken to Cary after the meeting and when he mentioned the specifics of what needed to be shaken up at BI, I gave him my ideas on how it could be accomplished. He assigned me the project on the spot. Craine had been there, grinning and patting my back, the whole time.

This type of situation was the part of the corporate world I had been struggling with since leaving the halls of academia. The games one had to play in corporate America, the CYA–covering your ass–was proving to be harder to learn than any degree I'd chased after. While I was trying to show I was a valuable member of the team, it got twisted around. What to do now? I was utterly clueless! Meanwhile Brett was nattering on.

"And honey, you being an almost-new hire, don't think we can't figure out how you managed that plumb assignment. We got a handful of very intelligent men, very easy-going I should add, who've been at the company a lot longer than you. But here you waltz in fresh out of school. Thinking you know more than the guys who've been doing the work while you were playing college-girl. And it's not like you came from any *real* school. South Carolina! Give me a break! I'm sure it's very easy being a winner there. Paloma, honey, you'll have to be honest now. I mean–when's the last time you've heard of anything great coming outta that state? Huh-huh. I mean, what your game is, honey, I've been onto from the beginning, honey. I never seen Cary so taken with any one employee before. You may just bat your eyelashes and God knows what else and have him jumping through hoops, but honey, not this little duck."

His smuttiness gave me the sudden urge to take a shower. Then punch out a wall, blubber like a baby.

"Hey, I haven't got all night. I just left that place," he lied. In the evenings, especially Fridays, a mere nano-second after the clock hits five, he tears out of the building so quickly it could be logged as a weather apparition. "It's Friday night and I don't even walk in the door and the phone is ringing. Honey, let me put it to you this way. Two days. That's it. My way or the highway. What's it gonna be, honey?"

My heart was in my throat and my stomach was battling high seas. "Well, Brett, you leave me no choice."

"I thought so, honey. See ya' Monday, then."

"Hey, Brett. Let me put it to you this way. It's tonight. It's the highway. It's–I quit. Honey."

In the 1920's, the Klan, with eight million members, became a powerful force encompassing all forty-eight states. From 1889 to 1941, over 3500 black people were lynched for attempting to register to vote, joining labor unions, being disrespectful to a white man, looking at a white woman, or for no reason at all.

Chapter Three

I dropped the top on my Mustang, punched number two on my CD player for Metallica, one of my favorite heavy metal groups and flicked the volume up loud to blast away whatever it is we want to banish by cranking up the stereo. Out on the freeway, I stewed over the problems of the past few hours amid thrashing guitars and exploding drums.

Fantasizing with the idea of sending Brett Craine's PC a virus, I mused over the tiny nuggets of information I'd been told about Dixie while bouncing around various plans for keeping my job. Nothing worthwhile had popped into my brain by the time I turned onto Ocean Drive. When I reached my bungalow in Seal Beach, exhausted and numbed, I staggered up the walkway like a ballerina dancing in tar. I opened the door. And screamed.

My house looked like someone opened up a can of whoop-ass on all of my possessions. Stereo components were askew. Software, CDs, videos and DVDs were strewn around, most of them smashed. With only seconds to view the carnage, I was yanked inside and felt a whoosh as the front door slammed behind me. A gloved hand muffled my second cry.

"Stop yelling, bitch." The pathetic sound poured uncontrollably into The Voice's hand. He squeezed tighter until I reigned in my terror. As soon as he released pressure, I bucked and came up fighting, but my efforts proved futile as he tossed me around like a salad. The tough girl act ended when he drew a nickel-plated .9 millimeter and aimed the business end at my temple.

He cleared his throat in several small bursts. There wasn't much use in remembering his face. If I got the chance. His Asian features were distorted underneath the stockings–not mine–I refuse to wear them. "Don't. You. Move." He cleared his throat again. "Or your brains are gonna be all over the carpet," he ended nonchalantly. "Now," he huffed, taking several deep breaths and another burst of throat clearing. "This is what we're gonna do. You give me the disks. Then I get outta here."

It was a moment before I realized it was my turn. My voice shook like dice. "I-I-I don't know what you're talking about."

He cleared his throat in his trio habit. "Playing games is just gonna make it worse."

"I-I-I'm not playing games. Y-Y-You think I'm enjoying this?"

"Where are the disks?" he roared.

"I-I don't know what you are talking about!" I was all whine. He picked me up by a handful of shirt, pressing the gun on my nose hard enough to tattoo it. "I-I-I'm telling you the truth!" He shoved me down on the couch straddling me, pinning my arms down. I felt his breath on my face. His penis grew hard against me. I squirmed unsuccessfully to get away.

"There are other ways of getting what I came for." He ripped open my shirt and pulled up my bra. As my breasts sprang free, he grabbed one and twisted brutally. The scream surprised me as much as him. He punched me, grabbed a handful of hair, yanked me upright and hit me again. With one hand over my mouth, his other groped his way around my body. Filthy words, quiet and terse, split from his mouth. His lips were hot and wet as they grazed my ear. I turned my head away from him and saw that his gun was on the coffee table.

"The diskettes," he said and slid his hand out of my pants. "You and me are gonna talk now. If you yell, you'll get more of this!" He raised his hand slightly above my mouth. I mumbled.

"Huh?" I mumbled again. He leaned down closer to my mouth. I slammed my head up, going for the nose while letting out a screech which burned the back of my throat and down into my chest. I felt his body slacken and mine rose to buck him off me. It seemed as soon as he hit the floor he was back on the couch fighting me. He wrapped one wide hand across my throat, his fingers squeezing. I fought one hand free and moved again to smack his nose, wanting to shove it out of the back of his skull with his brain. I heard a sickening snap and crunch, then felt a wetness wash over my palm. The Voice seemed to shrink in upon himself as he cursed and moaned in agony. I wasted a brief second in satisfaction. Then fear propelled me into action. I scooted from underneath my assailant as I pushed him further into the cushions. I'd become a mad woman, slapping, screaming, punching, pulling, my whole body moving against him with a single purpose of survival. He fought back equally possessed. I grabbed at the panty hose and he twisted his head moving out of reach. I popped his nose again.

"Aaaiiiiyyy!" He immediately collapsed, with more cursing and moaning. I managed a slide and roll until I plopped down onto the floor. I reached for his gun. It wasn't there. I jerked my head back around to the couch but The Voice was still gripping his face in his hands.

I ran toward the back door. As I yanked it open, I was jerked backward, The Voice tugging my shirt violently. I managed to twist around still on my feet, my blouse tearing from the strain. I managed to kick him in the knee which pushed him down instead of backward, so I moved with the flow and went after him with a frenzied left foot. He grabbed my shoe, flipping me all too easily and suddenly I was staring at the cobwebs in the ceiling corner, tailbone smarting. The Voice added a few punches. Then he was gone, the back door slamming against the wall as he retreated through it.

I crawled over, slammed the door shut, locked it, then used the doorknob to help pull me up. With a few gingerly steps toward the living room, my bones still intact, I lurched toward the front door and slammed that lock home. I still didn't feel safe. I sat on the couch sucking in air like a vacuum cleaner while my body shook in spasms and tried to vent the adrenaline. "I'm okay," I told myself again and again, mumbling it like a mantra.

The Voice's gun was on the floor in front of what was left of my stereo cabinet. I stared at it, lost somewhere in my mind. When my brain came to, I used a cloth to pick up the weapon. "Woo," I whistled under my breath. It was expensive–a stainless steel, .9 millimeter Browning, one of their anniversary editions, with Pachmeyer grips. The Voice was serious about his toys. Then I suddenly remembered mine.

Rushing to my bedroom, I briefly reflected on the carnage I stumbled over as I moved down the hall to check hiding places. Under the bed, in a specially made cubbyhole, I felt the grip of the Dan Wesson .357. It too, was a special edition weapon. My grandfather had given it to his only child–my father–then it passed to me.

While I thought about today's events, I roamed the house. Through the rubble I determined the only items actually missing, not destroyed, were computer software and the hard drives to the three computers. They left gaping holes in the CPU cases like missing teeth. Those disks The Voice wanted, whatever and wherever they were, obviously were damned important. Why? Moreover, why did he believe I had them?

I ate a handful of aspirin and acknowledging the Polish side of my family, I used Webarowa vodka as a chaser. And to give a nod to my Brazilian half, cursed in Portuguese from the pain caused when I poked my body, noting the sore spots. Further curses because the blouse I was wearing, a favorite, was not repairable *and* I had Chinese Bad Guy blood all over me. I threw the blouse in the trash and scrubbed off the blood.

Denial, I decided was the best way to cope with the most recent events. I was fine, Dixie was not. I was too chicken to go outside to my car and get my computer. My home PCs were unusable. I'd have to do this the low-tech way. I found the three-inch thick Los Angeles area phone book relatively easily and called airlines with my cell phone because The Voice had ripped out every phone line in the house. I made a list of the next two flights each airline had scheduled. Getting to a southeastern airport hub like Atlanta, Charlotte or Jacksonville wouldn't be difficult, but the connecting flight to Savannah–the closest airport to Rincon–had fewer choices and all flights were booked solid. Like Scarlet O'Hara, I'd put off worrying until tomorrow. I'd figure out then how I'd make the last leg of the journey. I was desperate to get moving eastward.

Dismayed that I'd missed the red-eye flights and would have to wait until morning, I made a pitiful attempt at cleaning. I sorted my belongings in piles of beyond help, limp but making an effort, and unscathed. Then I gave up, dragged my now screenless TV out of beyond help, and used a corner of it for a footstool. Now maybe someone would break in and clean the place up.

Daddy's money had paid for my house, pool, and sailboat. My own paycheck covered necessities like my computers, the never-ending stream of the latest add-ons and other electronic gadgets. I grew angrier as I surveyed the mess. They're only things–but they're *my* things! It didn't take much to convince me that they could stay right where they were for now. But I didn't have to keep looking at the devastation.

I soaked in the tub until the noise in my head lessened to a dull roar, emerging with prune-quality skin and a deep need to get horizontal. Paranoia made me fish the pistol out of its hidey-hole. I placed it on my night stand. The Voice's rod was wrapped up in a cloth nestled with the layers of dust under my bed. Armed and exhausted, I succumbed to the numbing powers of sleep.

1940, Georgia–A barber, with a fondness for liquor, was flogged and left to die by Klansmen. Assistant Attorney General Daniel Duke handled the case, blocking the Klan's campaign for clemency for the floggers. They enlisted one of their favorite politicians, governor Eugene Talmadge. According to Life magazine, the governor replied he once helped flog a Negro. "I wasn't in such bad company," he said. When Duke left to fight in World War II, Talmadge granted the floggers clemency.

Chapter Four

The next morning assessing bodily damage in my bathroom mirror was as painful as moving around. I had slept well–for the first ten minutes. Fitful sleep hadn't helped an iota of what I saw looking back at me. Normally I wouldn't have bothered with any of it. I could pass the bruises off as clumsiness, but going out-of-town and into the unknown, I needed every advantage. And a minor make over. Bruises lined my neck and tattooed my cheekbones and a small patch of my light brown hair had been torn out. Merle Norman on my cheeks, and a little creative hair styling would solve that. On my forehead was a slight welt, lightly purpling, where I'd played battering ram the night before. I made a sweep of my bangs down the right side of my forehead and drowned it and the hair covering the bald spot, with the juice from an ancient can of hair spray. To notice, you'd have to stand very close to me. And whoever was that close would get an ache in their toes! The back of my head where The Voice had dribbled it on the floor, was extremely sore to the touch and kept a headache raging. As expected, there were considerable signs of injury along my hands, arms, torso and legs, but what my brown skin didn't mask, I'd make sure my clothes would.

I drove to Artesia, a veritable United Nations including a large portion of Portuguese immigrants, stopping at Portazil. I bought a potion the Brazilian owner and herbalist swore would quickly erase bruising and swelling. I swore it contained unidentifiable items she'd raked up in her yard. At home I brewed a batch of the awful stuff and chugged it quickly while squirming around like a child chased by a mom with an enema bag.

I called various places begging out of commitments and to the more inquisitive, I told the same white lie about the need to check on my aging grandparents. Guilt seeped into my pores. Aunt Lily would grow rabid, if she knew about me telling a lie. But I wasn't–*really.* Papa and Gran lived on Hilton Head Island, about an hour's drive from Savannah–forty minutes if you let me take the wheel. I'd definitely visit them after I helped Dixie. Besides, I rationalized internally, Aunt Lily told me a lot of things during my one year incarceration in her home. I was a fat, ungrateful, stupid, unrefined twit–those being the most grievous. She was nice enough to put some blame on my heathen Brazilian mother and weak-willed father for moving to that South American den of iniquity. The rest was absolutely my doing. Now I ignored her "wisdom" as a general rule, if not out of spite.

My last call was to my aging grandparents. I gave them a brief run down on what I was planning and that I'd come to the island after I had a handle on Dixie's problem. As expected, they were concerned about the girl they considered my twin and were relieved that I would soon be there to help her.

I'm sure some head-shrinker could make something out of the fact that I felt most comfortable when I had all my machines and gadgets with me. But I didn't know exactly what I was heading into and I got a hinky crawl along the back of my neck wondering why Dixie was unable to talk to me herself. And, I believed, she had kept her police job to herself. Why she'd do that worried a couple of knots into my shoulders.

I needed to take along with me all the tricks of the snoops' trade, thankful for the hundredth time, that the equipment had been with me, first at work, then in my car trunk and not in the house last night. Surely, they would have joined the rest of the stolen or destroyed electronics. I was a frequent buyer at a store called Counter-Surveil-lance, Inc., which I'd dubbed Spies R Us. Spook gear available at the local mall! God bless America!

There were four devices I considered as important as my case of lock picks. The ANG-3000–acoustical noise generator could defeat listening de-vices. If I was in a room that was bugged, my conversa-tion would be blocked. I checked the power indicator on the device and placed it in my suitcase. I added a VL-35, which is your basic top-of-the-line bug detector. It locates listening devices–microphones, transmitters, even microwaves. It was developed to uncover the run-of-the-mill basic bugs, but later, to keep up with the bugging-dropping Jones, it could detect sophisticated eavesdropping equipment–and do it from a good distance away, even in a car or building. The SWD-100 made me giggle like a school girl when I first took it for a test drive–that is until other just-as-cool devices came on the market. With it's bowl-shaped attachment, it could pick up any sound waves as they were deflected off a window, then decode them, revealing conversa-tion from inside a room.

One of the very first bugging devices invented was for telephone use. I had a millennium version that I cushioned between the remaining clothes in the suitcase. My detector could also warn me if a phone conversation was being recorded. Lastly, I slipped one of those ultra-cool devices in the side pocket of my luggage. It was a pocket tape recorder which was advertised to be slim enough to fit unseen into a man's inside suit pocket–a bit chauvinistic but there's hope for a female version. So what? I'd bought the thin tape recorder strictly on a whim. While I'd justified the purchase once at work, its functionality is what made it a have-to-have item. Once the player was in the pocket, the attached ink pen sticks up, all looking quite normal. Pull out the pen to soundlessly activate the recorder. I stared down at the dark pile of equipment. Would it be too much to get electronics in any color other than the typical black or gray?

Airport security would surely puzzle over me today as they checked my carry-on luggage, I mused. It's all legal–up to a point–if you used it to en-sure you were not the one being spied upon. What wasn't mentioned was the opportunity the devices gave to snoop on others. As long as you didn't get caught.

Like a good scout—I was prepared. All packed and everything checked and double-checked. I still had time before I left for the airport. I tried resting, but kept snapping awake thinking The Voice was coming for me. The thought of his hands roaming my body was worse than the pain from the beating and I couldn't stop thinking about it. I tried to read. I attempted cleaning. I sat. I paced. Hundreds of creaks and pops in the house unnerved me in a replay of last night. *Droga!* Damn! My own home gave me the willies! I grabbed my suitcase, PC and backpack. Time to get out of Dodge.

1915: Modern genocide began in Turkey as the Ottoman government heinously tried to eliminate the ethnic Armenians living within their borders. By 1917, approximately one million Armenians were killed and almost as many driven out of the country.

Adolf Hitler admired the racist policies of the Turks and borrowed their horrendous torture and murder techniques. Hitler said to his generals on the eve of sending his Death's Heads units into Poland, "Go, kill without mercy! Who today remembers the annihilation of the Armenians?"

Chapter Five

Moonpie nudged Red sleeping beside her. "Wake up. It's time for your wife to be wondering." After a few unintelligible sounds, his eyes were open and trying to focus. Rincon–Moonpie's trailer. Okay, he remembered that much. The heat made rosy circles stand out on his pale, freckled cheeks. Red wiped sweat off his forehead, bringing it around to slick back the hair that had given him the nickname. As he dressed, Moonpie lay in the bed trying a few poses she'd seen in her dirty magazine. Red turned around as he heard her attempt a seductive moan.

"What the heck is wrong with you? You look like a frog doing the backstroke." She hid her hurt by rolling over, her back to Red and chugged a hefty finger of Jim Beam.

"When are you coming back to party, Red?"

"When I can." The back door slammed behind him.

"One of these days, a man's gonna kiss me goodbye when he leaves," she lamented into the hot, stale air. She knocked back enough booze to blot out her life, not bothering to wipe off what had dribbled down her chin. Out of habit, she quickly touched the key she wore like a necklace and would never take off. All she wanted at this moment was more sleep.

The phone rang. It took leaving the bed and several sorties under trash and clothes to find it. "Howdy," she drawled between breathless panting and put a hand against the wall to steady herself.

"Moonpie, it's Sandra Brice. Shake out the cobwebs."

"Howdy, Brice," she replied, using her friend's last name as ordered. "Hang on a sec." She stumbled back into the bed dragging the phone cord behind her. "How ya doing? When are you..."

"I'm at Logan Airport," Brice cut in gruffly. "I want you to reserve a car."

"You're coming to Rincon?"

"Of, course. We have the meeting. Or did you forget?"

"No. I got it all set."

"Remind the Auxiliary not to talk. This is a surprise for their men."

"You already told me a million times, Brice." Moonpie said wearily. "Did you remember to bring the co..." Brice had already hung up.

Moonpie placed the phone down irritated. She'd never figure out Yankees as long as she lived. Always gruff, rushing around like ants. Moonpie looked at the clock and cursed. Only two hours of sleep and after her night of boozing and sex, she would feel woozy most of the day. She wanted to go back to snooze-land, but if everything wasn't perfect for Brice, there'd be hell to pay. She forced herself out of bed, picked a dress up off the floor, fought to find the sleeve holes while it was over her head, and tugged it down over her naked body. She was dressed for the day.

She opened the refrigerator, searched in the far corners to discover the only meat inside was her own head. Just the thought of going shopping in the morning heat required too much energy at the moment. Opening cabinets to check supplies, she made a mental list. No fancy liquor for Brice. That would require an even longer hot trip over the county line. Moonpie definitely needed an energy boost. She headed back to her bedroom.

She needn't horde her secret supply since Brice was coming to town. Nor worry about the heat much longer because Brice promised a window air conditioner if she got five more women to attend the meetings. She did better, she got six. Well, almost. One was still thinking about it. That Bertrice could *never* make up her mind. She'd have to remember to call her this afternoon.

Kneeling on the dirty floor, Moonpie reached under her bed and pulled out the locked box and a handful of dust. She slid her hand inside the tight dress, fingered her breasts for the chain that hung around her neck. The key was hot and sweaty like her line of cleavage. Opening the box, she shook out the vial of white powder hidden in the Crown Royal bag. With a razor, she divided the coke into two lines like Brice had shown her. She tapped the razor onto the tiny mirror, watching the white powder fall, proud she remembered each step. Putting the tube to her nose she sniffed. Drugs were still new to her and each time she did this she felt giddy, and wickedly horny. And speaking of sex, which was Moonpie's specialty, the coke sure made her go all night. Usually, she drank and romped in the bed with a man or two for a few hours then passed out for twelve. With the coke, she'd reversed. And word quickly got around to all her boys–Moonpie was stuck in turbo.

That kept a steady line to her door, all of 'em panting like dogs in heat. And paying the trailer mortgage, what items food stamps and welfare didn't cover, and all the booze her large gut could hold.

She flipped open one of the magazines she'd bought on her secret trip to Boston. What a wonderful city! Beat hell out of Rincon–the whole South. She flopped down on the bed and practiced a new pose from the magazine–as she did every day. A few minutes later, satisfied she was proficient in position number twenty-four, she lay still, smiling, waiting for the buzz.

In the early 1950s, Asa "Ace" Carter, an Alabama Klan leader, ordered his men to assault Nat "King" Cole during a concert in Birmingham. Later, four of Ace's men received twenty-year prison sentences for kidnaping and assaulting a black. When black coed Autherine Lucy was allowed to attend the University of Alabama, Ace's Klavern was part of the mob that tried to stop her from entering the school's buildings. A hothead who used the group finances for personal gain, Ace, at a Klavern meeting, shot two men with the revolver he always carried when they questioned the groups' finances. They recovered and Ace was tried for attempted murder.

Chapter Six

The slim, muscular man hurried toward the car to answer his cellular phone. He flung the door of the sporty red BMW open, swept the area under the seat, retrieving the phone. "Leprechaun here," he spoke, using his code name.

"This is Base," came the reply.

Ah, the ex-Army, ex-boxer, ex-God-knows-what Karl Swartzman. "Go ahead, Base." He got in the car to shut out the endless Los Angeles airport noise. Leprechaun pictured Swartzman's unwieldy bulk which reminded him of a square with appendages. It didn't help that the man thought he could get by on size instead of brains. As Swartzman aged, hair had stopped growing on his head, but now protruded from his nose. Leprechaun had privately nicknamed him No-Neck when he'd met the man a couple of years ago. It was a wonder his head stayed on his shoulders. Swartzman was wasting time trying to build an empire to save the white race. He deluded himself that he had a mansion when his keys only fit the lock to an out-house.

"This'll be quick," Swartzman said. "Got the Rincon town council coming over to inspect the plant in a half-hour. Like they got a say-so in all a' this." Leprechaun didn't respond so the man would indeed make it quick. "We need equipment *bad*. Most of the last shipment you sent got confiscated by the interfering government–ATF, FBI, DEA. If it had three alphabets, we had it crawling around with the 'gators in that godforsaken Florida swamp."

"Whaddaya need exactly?"

"Some more firepower, definitely. Never can have enough of that." "What kind?"

"Same as before. Pistols, automatics and rockets. Any chance of some night peepers?"

"How many?"

"One hundred to start. I've got some fresh cash on hand but I gotta get the rest outta Boston. It'll take time, so let me know ASAP."

"Give me' til Wednesday, say 0900 hours. Base, what happened in the Sunshine state?"

Swartzman's words sounded heavy, like a manhole cover being dragged uphill. "My sergeant got tanked up on some homemade hooch, decided he could run things on his own." His story wasn't exactly correct, but when your balls are in a vise-grip, you had a right to cover your tracks.

"Gotta fly, my man. Base over and out."

"Leprechaun out." There was a lot of work to do by Wednesday. He leaned back sighing, the jet lag wearing him down. He hated flying East, especially in the summer. But this last trip had been worth it. Leprechaun had stolen the equipment he'd sold to Swartzman and pinned the blame on Henry, a country hick who couldn't hold his liquor. Now he was going to sell the same equipment back, plus the additional Swartzman had asked for. His bankroll was growing and this job would just about put him on the top.

Leprechaun would have loved to have been there to see Swartzman's face when he realized that the Florida camp had been compromised! But he'd been on a fishing trip with Henry. The hick had demonstrated setting up the rods in the ground–no big deal, Leprechaun mused–just shove the correct end into the dirt. That left their hands free for other activities–Henry knocked back a jar of moonshine, while Leprechaun fed Henry to the 'gators. Just so there would be no mistaking who'd become the reptiles' breakfast, Henry's head crowned the top of his favorite fishing pole.

On Sunday, September 15, 1963, the Sixteenth Street Baptist Church in Birmingham, Alabama was bombed, killing and burying four girls–one eleven, the others fourteen–in a sea of debris. The bombing was the fourth in a month, the fiftieth in twenty years, earning Birmingham the nickname, "Bombing-ham". Governor George Wallace, a segregationist, was put under court order to stop the violence stemming from the desegregation of schools ruling.

Chapter Seven

When Randy Beamon wasn't busy terrorizing the townsfolk of Rincon, Georgia, he could be found in one of two places–the Last Chance bar or spying on his sister through the bedroom window. Today, grimy and unkempt as usual, he stood on a cinder block looking at his sister's fat, naked butt.

He'd known she'd be busy at this moment, compliments of Swartzman. Her job for The Cause was to service the men. In exchange, Swartzman demanded the guys make her trailer payments. Randy had watched his sister since he was ten and she, thirteen. He figured she knew, but it must not bother her. Moonpie kept the curtain pulled back and in the summer, the window wide open. It was better than any dirty movie he'd seen at the Savannah drive-in.

And she was there, working hard—if you could call it that. Her skin was the color of cotton, the paleness marred by a never-ending maze of stretch marks. She was on her knees, flesh bouncing and jiggling as Willie, one of his brothers in The Cause, whammed it into her. Randy watched, knowing what would be next. He stuck his hands inside his coveralls, cupping himself.

She silenced Willie's startled yelp by stuffing a breast in his face as she clambered on top. Randy knew each line, but still leaned closer to the sill, sure to catch every nuance. "I jus' love to please my man," she cooed between puffs of air. The bed shook beneath them. "What you want me to do to you, Willie darlin'? You jus' tell your ol' love-muffin Moonpie." She looked down into his eyes and licked her lips slowly. "Ooooo, baby! You are such a hot, big ol' boy, Willie! Ah, yeah! Work it, work it, honey!" She grinned and lowered her face until it was inches from his. "I cain't hear you. Is my little Willie sweetie-pie per-tending to be shy?" He grunted as a response. "Okay, you can jus' lay there and let little ole' Moonie-pie do all the work."

That was the only work she did. At least she was good at it. He'd learned a few things through the years watching Moonpie. Randy placed his free hand against the side of the trailer to steady himself as

his other hand slid up and down his slick penis. Oh, how he wanted
a woman. But he couldn't find any one desperate enough to hang
around.

He moved his hand faster as he watched his sister's breasts sway.
He liked the way the sides of them dented then filled out in round
circles when she let them dangle. Beautiful raindrop pendulums. Her
nipples reminded Randy of Hershey Kisses, swaying, taunting. Willie
lifted his head and popped one into his mouth. Randy's lips made the
same motion. He closed his eyes but it didn't shut out the sight. He
moved his head back, tortured by the forbidden fruit. His hand
worked faster, the image of her seared into his eyelids, his mind, all
over him.

She was talking dirty, loud. It brought Randy's head up and eyes
open. Willie used her hair for leverage as he thrust upward. Randy
thought that shoulda hurt, but it made her go harder–actually mobiliz-
ing the bed. It thumped into the wall and the box springs groaned
under their weight. The noise intensified the couple's movements.
She lowered her breasts, using them to smack his face a few times.
Willie loved it! They flayed around, hollering like a buncha 'coon
dogs. Her big butt went up and down, up and down. Her wide rear,
spread from hip to hip in its circular paleness, ripe with cellulite–was
the reason she was called Moonpie.

*   *   *

Swartzman, feeling grateful that the plant tour was over, shook the
hands of the Rincon Counsel members. After the last taillight
disappeared into the dark night, he headed back to his office. At the
bar he poured himself a tall Crown Royal. With his short neck, ties
were a contestable piece of apparel and the first item off at the end of
the day. Pulling the WRF–White Rebel Force–plans from the safe, he
sat on the couch to skim over them while he untied the noose from
around his neck.

He'd just landed a coup by forming a team in Portland, Oregon, a
group of WRF men concerned with what was happening to their
country. Maybe this would make up for the Florida screw-up. The
plan was to form pockets of dedicated Americans across the nation,
each part of the whole group, but with several independent agendas.
That ensured the WRF would always be standing if the stinking
government sent the Feebies–a group he considered worthless after
Hoover's administration ended–to stop them. If one cell was closed,
the rest could quickly absorb the loss and continue their important
mission.

He'd sent orders to his men in Portland to immediately seek out the local Skinheads, a strong and bloody presence there, and form an alliance. He had something to offer those good soldiers who fought back the tide of MUD—niggers, Jews and gooks–entering their city with their violence, disease and un-Americanisms. For the past decade he had been stockpiling the best equipment available to use for The Cause. He would be willing to share part of his cache with the Skins. Yes, things were steadily moving upwards. Swartzman grinned and sipped his drink.

In 1963, Robert Chambliss, J.B. Stoner, and another man were arrested for the September Birmingham church bombing. They were found guilty of a lesser offense–illegal possession of dynamite–which was later dismissed on reversal. The case remained closed until 1970, when Attorney General Bill Baxley reopened it, bringing protests from many, including a threatening letter from Edward Fields of the neo-Nazi National States Rights Party. On official letterhead, Baxley replied to Fields, "My response to your letter of February 19, 1976, is–kiss my ass."

Chapter Eight

I greeted the South feeling like I'd just survived a two week bender. I felt freaked out, worn out, burned out. The Savannah, Georgia, airport wasn't crowded, so I had my luggage and car rental keys in good time. As the automatic doors split open, I was engulfed in the hot breath of Satan. The dry Los Angeles desert air had weakened me to native weather conditions.

The kid who delivered the Escort smiled and cleared his throat. I shivered in spite of the heat. I'd never hear that sound again without seeing The Voice. And feeling his hands on me.

The small car had been baking in the sun. I draped myself over the steering wheel like one of Dali's wet watches until the air conditioner cooled the inside. As I drove away from the airport heading north, I was immediately confused as to where I was. The roads were laid out differently from my last time here. Or was my memory flawed? I slowed while I dug into my computer carrying case for the maps I had downloaded from the Internet, then printed, while I was waiting for my flight.

In my youth, islanders flew out of the Savannah airport, which was the closest, as our tiny island airport could only support private planes. As Hilton Head Island grew, so did the runways. We could now jet onto the island and be home in under fifteen minutes. So it had been awhile since I'd landed in Savannah. I didn't recognize the facility when I'd deplaned. Like the area around me on this street, the airport had changed, been remolded, built up.

I found the airport on the map and held a finger on the spot while I looked for road signs. I goosed the engine along and shortly spied some ahead. More confusion. I checked for traffic in the rearview mirror and stopped the car. I compared the signs with my printouts, reformed a mental map and got back on track. It wasn't just that the airport had expanded. The darn place was located in a whole new area. I didn't like starting my "case" so discombobulated.

I was excited about coming here, taking charge, helping my best buddy. I had wanted to expand my investigatory career into areas outside of Information Services Departments. Now was my chance, at Dixie's expense. I was very happy I'd be seeing my grandparents–surely by the end of the week. And swim the warm Gulf Stream of the Atlantic Ocean again instead of the freezing Pacific. I'd go shrimping with Papa on the *Katie*. I pictured Hilton Head Island in my mind. The salt from the Broad River permeates everything–the air, the nets, the food and water. My grandfather stands aft surveying the swells. The waves spill over the rails, the spray washing him. On the dock as everything dries, I can follow the salt crust on his wrinkled cheeks like a navigation chart. *Later, girl,* I thought.

I neared Highway 21and slowed. As I turned left onto it, I glanced at the instructions under the map. Rincon was seventeen miles north. I mused about the origins of the town name, wondering if it was Spanish, meaning corner or nook and pronounced–Rin-*kahn*–which had altered over time to how Telephone Guy and the car rental agents spoke it–*Ree*-kin. Being back in the South, it was a must to slide a Jimmy Buffet CD in the player. I fished in my backpack for Bazooka Joe and Jordan almonds and donned the LAPD cap I'd brought for my grandfather. I stuffed two almonds in my mouth and wasted away in "Margaritaville". Singing along to five more beach-bum stories indicative of Buffet tunes passed the time quickly and soon I was approaching the hint of a town. The first sight greeting travelers to Rincon was typical of towns and villages along the Bible Belt. The Grace Community Church, an older white clapboard building with a tin roof had been greeting sinners and the saved for decades. Those gone on to meet their glory were buried in the church yard beside the place where the living continued to get baptized, sing in the choir, marry, then watch their own children do the same.

As I straightened out of a curve, a wooden billboard, looking handcrafted from leftover lumber, brightly announced that the Jaycees, Elks and VFW welcomed me to Rincon, as did the many local churches, details in print too small to take in as I drove by. I knew it would inevitably be followed by a speed-limit sign. Sometimes that notice was tucked away where it wasn't as obvious as the billboards–as were the local cops hiding in the trees nearby. N o t wanting to feed the local city finances, I tapped the brake and did a slow crawl into town thinking it awful everyone outside of Los Angeles was forced to drive so slowly. After a minute at thirty-five, I was itching to get out of the car. I felt I could run faster.

Spying a gas station with a mini-mart, I turned in and left the car running to keep it cool. I headed straight for the soda cooler that

Bubba, the owner of this establishment, had lined up in the back of the store. The clerk didn't look busy and I was the only customer. I scanned the candy aisle.

"Do you have any Jordan almonds?"

"Them those in the can?"

"No." She didn't say anything else enlightening so I opted for substitutes. I grabbed a handful of Charleston Chews. Wow! Squirrel Nut Zippers–an old favorite not available in the West. Two handfuls and one in my mouth now to tide me over until I paid. I waved the candy in the air and pointed to my mouth to show the clerk I was inhaling one immediately. I scanned the remaining shelf. Ex-prez Carter's caricatured face looked up at me with a wide grin from a bag of roasted peanuts. Looking good, Jimmy boy! I added his face to the loot.

The clerk's long hair was in various stages of blondness, parted down the middle with bangs she was either trying to grow out or had trimmed with a weed-whacker. She was skinny enough to hate. When she smiled, I witnessed a set of buck teeth so big she could chew an ear of corn through a picket fence. I felt a brief sympathy for her as the world was often cruel to those of us without model perfection.

"What's life in Rincon like?" I asked.

She grinned again and shook her finger at me. "I known you wuzn't frum around here! I know all my customers, and I ain't seen ya ba-fore. Where ya frum?"

"Los, ah, South Carolina." With little prodding, as any self-respecting southerner would, the clerk amicably went beyond initial introductions and filled me in on some of the local gossip and other tidbits about the town. I was very proud of my skill at getting my first inquisition going so easily.

At first I had to strain, listening, trying to adjust to the clerk's drawl. Each time I return to the South I'm amazed at how I have to adapt. Not just to Southernese, but to the pace, attitudes, the weather. I arrive feeling expatriated–a Sherman in Atlanta.

Lulene, the patch on her smock read, began with a short geography lesson. The town was split by what locals referred to simply as 21, the highway I'd just driven. The population had exceeded four thousand and the town along with the county, Effingham, was one of the fastest growing areas in the state. Not everyone was happy about that. One factor of growth was due to a new computer components plant "down the road a piece", while providing the majority of Effinghamians their income. Not everyone was happy about that, either. The plant spurned further amenities, like the WalMart and their first fast food franchises. Lulene had been a biscuit maker at Hardee's when it first opened, but getting up before the roosters crowed wasn't conducive to a single woman's need to go honky-tonking the night before.

The single traffic light was installed after three teenagers had been "kilt" there last summer. If there had been only two kids in the car, the town would still be minus the equipment, as county laws dictated at least three deaths before a signal would swing at an intersection. My mind began to wander.

"And we got one tiny jail." I perked up.

"A town this small has a jail?" I asked, even though I knew the answer.

"Yep, it's a tee-tiny one. Down Ebeneezer road outside of town. Just where the river splits."

"Which river is that?"

"Savannah," she said as if everyone in the U.S. knew that beside yours truly. "Although it's mostly marsh at the jail. But it's great for keeping criminals locked up where they belong. No convict would think 'bout escapin', what with the weapons the sheriffs carry." She was winding up. Her hands flapped at her side, a flamingo readying for flight. "And then you got them 'gators. They's always findin' thangs inside 'gators. Once my brother gigged one and when he wuz guttin' him wide open, ya know, he found a whole dang dawg collar inside. I mean an *en-tire* collar! Somebudy's missin' them a right nice huntin' dawg, you just better ba-lieve you me. And then one time he found a shoe..."

"Lulene? How are the police?"

"Hmm," she drawled out long and thoughtful. "You just be real careful drivin' 'round this here town. We got some mean *po*-lice an' they don't think nuthin' 'bout givn' you a ticket." She was leaning over the counter talking low. Two buddies sharing a conspiracy. I looked grave and thankful.

"When you say *mean*–exactly whadda-ya mean?" I asked, my grammar apparently heading south when I did.

Lulene stammered. "A-a-a. Oh, jus' thangs I hear. I mean, what *po*-lice don't like people not mindin' 'em? You just be careful an' don't give 'em any mind to pull ya over. If they do, don't be givin' 'em no sass neither!" She wiped up the spotlessly clean counter looking outside furtively as if she expected someone to rush inside and contradict her.

With Lulene's loquacity exhausted, I took my leave and perused the Bubba Buck she'd given me. It was about the size of a real bill, was green, but sported a head shot of the owner, the caption under his chin displayed his name, Bubba. If I collected enough Bubba Bucks, one with each fill-up, I'd get a small discount. No doubt I'd gotten one because Lulene thought I was special. I slipped it in my pocket, a cute memento that back in California, I'd stick up on my office wall–whenever I found a new one.

I dug out my cell phone to call the jail. Before I'd finished punching in 411, I spied a pay phone against the mart's wall that actually had a phone book attached. I decided to use it for the sheer novelty. The government blue page listings weren't long, so in quick time I was dialing the jail. A bored man, who identified himself as Shearhouse, informed me that visiting privileges were weekends only and abruptly disconnected.

"Droga!" I said aloud at the guy's rudeness and because I'd just missed the visiting opportunity. I needed a bit more information. I redialed.

"But, I've just driven in from..."

"That's too bad. Only lawyers can see prisoners outside of visitin' hours." *Ding* went a bell in my head. I thanked the unaccommodating sheriff and hung up. *Bosta! Aqueles desgraçados! Babacas e bundões!* And other naughty words. Feeling better now that I'd gotten that off my chest, I dug out a leather portfolio I used in the B.C. years (before computers). I'd brought it along because of the tons of business cards in the back pockets. Yes, it was a trick I'd seen on TV, but if Jim Rockford could get away with flashing everyone else's cards to get answers, then perhaps so could I.

Ah, Cheryl, my pal the attorney. Luck was on my side. Her card listed only a phone number for security reasons and not her California office address. Preparing for any situation at the jail, I stuck my tiny digital recorder inside the binder. I tried to squeeze both anti-listening devices into my computer carrying case. Heathcliff would only allow room for one. I'd have to improvise.

Heathcliff is my laptop computer. Well, it's really a notebook computer, one of the ultra-slim and lightest of the personal computers. Yes, it is important to us Bitheads to delineate the two. Dixie had named Heathcliff, saying I spent so much time with him, I must be having a romance. The name stuck because I've had better times with that machine than with many of my dates.

I checked the map for directions to the jail. I spied a road in the general direction Lulene had pointed. I flipped to the page of text that detailed public buildings and other places of import in the town. There were two. I was interested in the Ebeneezer Historic Site as it was on the same street as the jail and one of the few places indicated on the map. The history blurb stated the site was the location of the second colony in Georgia, established in 1736. It had been the home of a group of Salzburgers, who were expelled from what is now Austria, because they followed the teachings of Martin Luther. Hmm. The place where people fled from persecution was close to the jail, a building created for that purpose. Only a few turns to make, so I easily memorized the remaining directions.

I drove slowly through town heading toward Ebeneezer Road. *Here I come to save the day!* Traffic was almost non-existent so I did a little sightseeing as I crawled north. As Lulene had prepared me, I passed a Kentucky Fried Chicken, Huddle House restaurant, and a Super WalMart. Next, the turn off to the components plant, Gundersen. This high-tech business was a sharp contrast to the simple life afforded by small town America. Just past the Post Office was the latter half of the small town. Several churches of various denominations were interspersed between a bank, Burns' Service Station, Sloan's Pharmacy, large homes and huge oaks. Tree roots snaked out like arthritic fingers, gnarled and bumpy from disease. The branches arched over the road giving partial strips of shade to the outer lanes, causing a strobe-like effect as I drove through. Moss dripped down, its strands beckoning me as they curled slightly in the gentle, hot breeze. Enormous lots surrounded the houses, making my little square of grass in Seal Beach seem crowded and cramped. But then, I thought smugly, I can cut my grass in minutes then I'm off to the sailboat or beach. I watched a shirtless man push a lawnmower in a straight line. Sweat glistened on his back, darkening the waist of his pants. Heat stroke waiting to happen.

The end of town was punctuated by a Chick 'N' Chat and a water tower that watched the city from above. Lulene had mentioned the tower as a site for teenaged pranks and near-calamities. In spite of a locked gate blocking the ladder, I saw evidence of graffiti on the tank's side. Black spray paint announcing "Seniors Rule!" was about as far away from violent big-city gang tagging–or graffiti–as Los Angeles was to the Rincon city limits. I searched for the sign to the Ebeneezer Historic Site. Right at the tower and a few "country" miles thereafter. These miles were made on a straight and lonely road lined with lush green forest. The pine trees brought back memories of my early teens. The endless hours I'd raked dead straw from Aunt Lily's three-acre yard–a punishment for some infraction of her rules. A horrible sin like eating a snack between meals.

She had forced dieting on me, preparing meager offerings to eat. No seconds and certainly no desserts. And Lily always found out, no matter how ingenious I became at snitching food. I spent most of the fall wrapping bandages on my blistered hands. The summer was spent canning and freezing delicious foods from her garden that I would only get to see on Lily's plate. Eventually I learned she counted and measured every morsel of food in her cupboard.

Droga! Too soon after stepping on Southern soil, the pain floated up with the heat waves forming a sticky layer of dirty blues that engulfed me.

Attorney General Baxley unsuccessfully tried to get information from the fifty FBI agents who investigated the 1963 Birmingham church bombing. Eventually Baxley obtained indictments against Robert Chambliss and J.B. Stoner. A resident of Georgia, Stoner fought extradition, Chambliss went on trial alone. On what would have been victim Denise McNair's twenty-sixth birthday, a jury found Chambliss guilty. In 1980, Justice Department files revealed that then FBI director J. Edgar Hoover had refused to move on the case. The FBI had an eyewitness as early as 1964.

Chapter Nine

Putting the make on Frances Powers, chief purchasing agent of the Los Angeles Police Department, was taking all the finesse Detective Shawn Munson, the Leprechaun, could muster. He wanted her mind elsewhere when she left for the meeting. Five minutes to go. He watched her twitch in the chair, crossing and recrossing her legs. She thought he was cute, he'd heard. The same couldn't be said for this plain woman who lacked any feature that would award her a second look.

"Thanks for the doughnut, Shawn."

"Oh, you're welcome." He sat on the edge of her desk and gave her a good appraisal. He made sure she saw his eyes wandering up and down, lingering on her legs. Her hands went to the hemline of her skirt but stopped. She laid her hands in her lap, looking away nervously.

"Nobody should have to work on a Sunday."

Her smile was almost a straight line of thin lips. "I don't usually. It's budget time, you know."

He touched her lightly on the arm and noted her intake of breath. "You look so nice today, Frances. Did you do something to your hair?"

"No." She touched her coiffure.

"You've lost weight."

"No."

"Come on, don't be shy with me." Her laugh was a little high. *Gotcha.* If you want something from a woman, tell her she's lost weight. Works every time. He took the files from her and laid them on the desk. Frances was about to protest but Shawn had her hands in his, gently rubbing the tops.

"I-I have to go now," she stammered. He stood to let Frances by, but didn't move. Their bodies touched and Francis briefly closed her eyes. She didn't lock up the remaining files–a task she didn't usually forget. "Uh, bye, Shawn."

"Bye," he said smiling with warmth he did not feel. As soon as the door shut behind her, Munson surveyed the room. Most of the clerks were so bored with their job they didn't hassle you as long as you left them alone, especially when Francis, the boss, was away. He searched through the stack of folders on her desk then went to the drawer marked T - U. Travis Industries. He made a copy of the SWAT team's last purchase requisition. As expected, Francis kept detailed notes. He copied those too, before slipping the file back in the drawer and leaving.

In the canteen Munson used the pay phone, dialing toll-free to Travis Industries' customer service claiming he was concerned about the security of his recent equipment order. He listened to the measures the company used to guarantee safe deliveries of weaponry. He hung up satisfied. It was almost going to be *too* easy.

J. B. Stoner eventually was extradited to Alabama, tried for the church bombing and convicted. He fled to Mexico while awaiting sentencing and was a fugitive for five months. In 1983, he was sentenced to ten years in prison, paroled in three years, immediately resuming his racist work. He was one of the Klan leaders who directed the Forsyth County (Georgia) riots in 1987.

Chapter Ten

The sun beat down relentlessly. I maxed the air and rubbed my eyes. Heat waves danced up from the pavement as the car tore into them. More taunted me in the distance.

Ahead, I saw a drab, square brick building, fringed by swamp land. Had to be the jail–it bore the markings of bare, ugly government design. Before driving close enough to be seen, I took off the PD cap and fluffed my hair because it's what everyone did when extracting head from cap. I slipped the digital recorder into my pocket. The leftover secret weapon I'd been unable to hide in my gear could pass as a radio so I slipped on the tiny headphones, and clipped the small box onto my waistband, Walkman style.

At the jail, two uniformed men watched me from the porch. One was tilted back in his chair, feet propped on the top rail. The other embraced a post. They didn't move as I parked beside a white, nondescript car–another government issue. Okay, so there was a huge seal of the Department of Fish and Game on its door. Adjusting the headphones, I moved my body like I was jamming to a tune and assessed what lay before me–a bad imitation of an *Andy Griffith* TV show set. I slipped the headphones down around my neck. Before I slammed the door on blessed coolness, I grabbed the handle of my computer case.

"Howdy. How are y'all?" I drawled in a bonding-with-the-good-ol'-boys effort. "It *sure* is as hot as a Texas chile pepper today." I pinched a piece of my shirt at the shoulder and flapped it to emphasize my weather opinion. "Whew!" I turned to the medium brown-haired bubba who had a toothpick hanging out of his mouth and thrust Cheryl's business card in his face. Smiling my Miss America smile I flicked it over to his partner whose hand was wrapped around a Pepsi bottle. Quaint. I didn't know you could still get them in glass. Officers Toothpick and Pepsi didn't move. Maybe I needed to drop a quarter in each one. I propped the carrying case against Toothpick's post and slipped the business card into its outer pocket. Thrifty. And covering my butt in case they had the urge to check up on the name on the card.

Holding up my business planner like a choir book, I pulled the ink pen out of the hidden recorder being most careful so the Fuzz couldn't see it. "I'm here to meet with my client, a Ms., ah..." I moved the pen down last weeks' grocery list and stopped on sushi. "Here it is, Ms. Dixie Hightower." I remembered to up-talk the last word as was the Southern custom. I looked at the two men who were busy looking blankly back. This audience was as tough as a two dollar steak. I was thinking of doing a tap dance routine for their viewing pleasure when Officer Toothpick finally acknowledged me.

He maneuvered the toothpick to the left side of his mouth by making very funny fish faces, picked a few teeth on the new end, parked the tiny stick between his full lips and stood. He dug his uniform out of his rear with practiced ease. Eeww! The door opened behind them and a small woman with dishwater blonde curls joined us on the porch to watch the show. What I could deduce from where I was standing, she was slightly above middle-aged. She wore an olive green uniform, her hands rounded into fists were planted on her hips. After initial glances at the newcomer, the two men turn-ed their backs in stone dismissal.

"Well, well," Officer Toothpick said then grew silent. He grinned, looked at Pepsi for approval. I counted the seconds silently. "That big ol' nigger bitch you ax-in' 'bout punched Singleton out, down yonder at the plant. Nigger just cold-cocked 'im." His racist words hit me like a sucker punch. "What you doin' seein' to the likes a' her?" Officer Pepsi belched and they both sniggered like third graders. I stuck a fist behind me working it back and forth like an orange half on a manual juicer as a reminder to stay out of trouble. My other paw tightly gripped the business planner. "Huh, you got a' answer, gal?"

"Aw, shucks, fellas. Just a habeas corpus and all that other legal stuff." My forced drawl sounded Hollywoodish.

"Well, gal. I don't think we can let you see her."

"Why not?"

"Well." He paused again, his foot kicking a small pile of dirt. "Sheriff Grainger ain't around and he's t'wun to give the say so. Hey, gal, where did you say you wuz frum?"

"I didn't," I blurted curtly, irritated that he called me gal for the umpteenth time. Reminding myself to stay cool, I tried a smile, but it felt more like a grimace. Remember polite Southern manners. "Carolina, if you must know." I purposely did not mention Hilton Head Island. I'd learned earlier in life the name of the famous resort could spoil the ambience as you were instantly considered rich and

snobbish. "I'll just take a minute and be out of your hair in no time."
I took a step forward.

"Like my buddy said," Officer Pepsi informed, shifting his weight
to the other leg. "Sheriff Grainger'll hafta work on it when he gets
back." The two turned to go inside. The woman still hadn't moved
from her plank of porch.

"When is the Sheriff expected back?"

Pepsi said, "next week or the next," at the same time Toothpick
offered up, "don't rightly recollect him sayin." They headed toward
the doorway.

"Excuse me," I called out gaily. "My client has not had counsel
since her arrest. You wouldn't want problems because of that, now
would you?" They stopped their retreat, both half-turned, looking
irritated. Or was it worry? "Look, boys." I paused to show them I
could, too. Ooo, tough girl. "You both know that what you are doing
is illegal. And there are plenty of places I can go and raise holy hell.
First, I'll petition the courts to drop all charges because her rights were
violated. Piece of cake. She'll be back on your streets in less than
twenty-four hours." Toothpick hitched his pants up by fingering a belt
loop and tugging upwards. I admit I stared at the effort, placing a
mental bet that he'd go hinny-hole digging again. Yep. In front of
God and everybody. I took a breath and went for broke. "Boys, if you
don't think that will work because the judge is your daddy or is in
your pocket I'll turn this over to Ted Turner personally. You know
boys–CNN." I unveiled the tape recorder and rewound it, playing it
for them just past the bitch part. "Now I'm baking like a damn turkey
out here. Let's get moving." Right-o, before I do something else
stupid like impersonate a lawyer and push two daffy cops around.

My female companion was enjoying herself, wearing what my dad
called a shit-eating grin. "It looks like the two of you are actually
going to have to follow the rules! That will be a nice change of pace.
Although it would tickle my gizzard to see you sweatin' under the
camera lights of a dozen or more rabid reporters!" She gave a short
chuckle. "So, what's it gonna be, officers?"

My boys were still hesitating, so I grabbed my case and brushed
past them. It was stifling inside. An ancient Coke machine–the rack
kind–hummed in the far corner. I was thirsty enough to fart dust.
"You got any diet soda?"

"Nope." Officer Pepsi smiled with petty revenge. "You want a
Pepsi?"

"Does the Coke company know?" I asked pointing to the name
emblazoned on the machine. His grin disappeared into a look of
confusion. I didn't bother to explain. Petty revenge, my serve. I sat

in one of the hard wooden chairs, the seat being warm enough to start smoldering. I watched Rincon jail's version of the soda wars. Officer Pepsi wrapped a chubby fist around the neck of a bottle and jerked. Apparently it jerked back. While Pepsi cavorted with the Coke machine, I used the time to look around, taking all of four seconds. Soon the rumbling stopped and Pepsi held the prize out to me. I took the sweet soda out of desperation.

"You gotta pay." I took a dollar out of my wallet and thrust it toward Officer Pepsi. "It's fifty cents and I don't got any change."

"Keep it," I offered. Pepsi shrugged and pocketed the bill.

Officer Toothpick moseyed in to join the party. "I'll have to search your case before you talk to the prisoner," he informed me.

"No problem." I unzipped the case and turned it around but left it on my lap, hoping Toothpick wouldn't want to get close to the enemy. He gave everything a cursory check from four paces away.

"You can't take the computer in with you."

"I have to. Got a hand condition. I use the keyboard to make notes." Toothpick looked dubious. "It's all covered by the Disabilities Act. But you already know that." I stuck a hand out. The desire not to look stupid overrode any concerns that my hand looked perfectly normal. Neither cop protested.

Pepsi mumbled nasty comments about lawyers which didn't hurt my feelings at all. He soon left me and stalked into the office. I scanned the area again in case something had changed from a moment earlier. There were still four desks, two typewriters, and two big oscillating fans that did nothing but nudge the hot air and dust around. The door in the back was composed of bars. The entrance to the jail, I deduced brilliantly. Pepsi returned jiggling a set of keys.

"With the trouble your nigger friend's in, you'd better be a good lawyer," Toothpick warned.

"What are the charges against my client?"

"You'll have to ask the Sheriff." That line came up as often as a bellyful of moonshine. I wanted to shake a different answer out of them both, but Dixie didn't need me as a roommate. I bit down on my tongue and anger.

"Let's go," Pepsi ordered, and I followed him, feeling like I was walking on a water bed as the floorboards sank and rose under his feet. The fleeting thought of being trapped inside with Dixie and no one knowing where I was strained my nerves like a halter top trying to hold up two big ones.

According to a 1959 study, Southern racial incidents that year were: six blacks killed; forty-four persons beaten and five stabbed; eight homes burned, thirty bombed, fifteen struck by gunfire and seven stoned; twenty-nine people (eleven white) were shot and wounded; four schools were bombed, two further attempted bombings and two schools burned; seven churches bombed; four Jewish temples burned and three additional bombing attempts; a YWCA was dynamited.

Chapter Eleven

Deputy Pepsi unlocked a tiny cell that housed a picnic table and two benches inside. I placed the case on the table and waited. Soon I heard a shuffling noise and turned seeing Dixie. I gasped. Her shoulder length hair was dirty and wild. Her face was puffy, the right cheek so battered it was a mushy open wound, reminding me of an overly ripe plum after it had been slammed onto a sidewalk. My eyes trailed down. Her upper lip was swollen almost up to her nose. Where the white of her left eye was supposed to be, it was mostly red and I could see the purpling of a bruise starting from the outer corner. The door swung out and Dixie stumbled in. She wasn't walking right. I looked at her feet.

"Oh, now this is too much. Leg irons? What do you use on the dangerous women, the iron maiden? Handcuffs, too! *Bostas!* All of you." I gave Dixie's six-foot frame a gentle bear hug. We looked at each other, Dixie's face brave while the cop was watching her. When he turned to go, the brave-ry evaporated quickly, silence filling the room. I grabbed her up into another hug.

"Dixie, are you okay? Tell me everything that's happened. Which of these jerks gave you the bruises?" She touched a finger to her lips, her lopsided grin sliding up her face. It looked garish with her right cheek so marred. "Tell me what's going on." I helped her get reasonably comfortable on the bench.

"I'd like to give you the whole story," she whispered, "but the walls have ears. I don't think my Portuguese is up to par either."

"Not to worry, my friend, we'll speak in English and as freely as we want. I came prepared." I touched the case.

"*It is so good to see you,*" she said with a desperation I'd never associated with my easy-going friend. "I had no idea why they were taking me out of the cell. Perhaps a lynching? When I saw that it was you, I was so relieved!" Her smile vanished and the strain took over again.

"Are you in a lot of pain?"

"Not so much now," Dixie said quietly.

"What did the doctor say?"

She looked down. "Didn't see one."

"So you haven't had any x-rays? Pain pills?"

"Nope."

"Aspirin?"

"Uh-uh."

I bit down on my anger. I wanted to rant, but that would only waste time.

"What's wrong with your voice, P?"

"I must have picked up something on the plane," I fibbed. Telling her about my recent adventures would only cause more worry. I walked to the door, stood on my toes peering out the window, looking for voyeurs. When I returned, I opened the case and pried Heathcliff off the Velcro strips I'd put underneath it last night.

"Whatcha got?" She asked still whispering.

"Ms. Dixie," I said in imitation Rhett Butler. "We're gonna find out what these little ol' bubbas are up to." I flipped the switch on the ANG-3000.

"Thank you, Paloma."

"For what?"

"For coming here, getting here so quickly *and*," she waved her cuffed hands over the gadgets, "for all this."

I shrugged. Time to switch to humor, my crutch for emotional moments. "What's the big deal? I'm not leaving these with you. So. What have you been doing in here to keep yourself busy?"

"Brushing up on Negro spirituals. Yessah, massah! No-bi-dy knows da truh-bull I seen," she sang softly in a mock gospel voice. We sniggered as we often do when trying to ease the tension.

"You best hush, child," I admonished, in my grandmother's time-for-discipline-voice. "You're already in a peck a' trouble!" The joking abruptly died off to an uncomfortable silence. We stared at each other trying to read behind the false bravado. Back to business. "We can talk freely while the noise generator is working–it'll block sound to any listening device. But, I'm curious if it was even necessary. So, I brought this." I slipped the headphones on. She shot a fearful glance at the door.

"What if I make a curtain?" I dug for some Bazooka Joe bubble gum, used my back molars to work the hard square into a semi-soft wad and took a sheet of paper out of my computer case. Using the sticky pink goo to hold the paper over the tiny window, I pressed down. "Jailhouse kitsch."

"Lovely. So where's the cake with the metal file inside? Or were you able to pick up a molecular transporter to beam me out?"

"I'll have to work on that next. Where's Gene Roddenberry when you need him? Okay. This is the bug detector," I whispered, back to businesses. Even with the noise generator, I wouldn't put it past the officers to hang around the door, picking up conversation. "We know their intelligence isn't in their brains. Let's see if they have it in equipment." I turned the detector on. I heard the low whine and watched all the diodes turn cherry red.

"Wow." Dixie pinched my cheek. How I hate that. I shoved her hand aside.

"Wow indeed," I agreed. So the room was bugged. I showed her the small tape recorder, played a bit of it, and related the rest of my morning with the sheriffs. "That's the end of my show and tell. Your turn. Start from the very beginning," I ordered her. Although I'd been in on the saga of her missing cousin, Dixie's habit was to hold her cards close to her vest and condense any problems so her loved ones wouldn't worry.

She licked her lips and played loop-de-loop with her fingers. "Well, you know that my cousin Lemond graduated from college."

"From big-city somewhere."

"Chicago."

"Big enough."

"He wanted a change, so he came down to the island for a visit and looked for work. He found a job here in Rincon. A new company that manufactured computer components, circuit boards. Right up your alley."

"Is that the plant at the traffic light?"

"Yep." She took a deep breath and her words began to spew out hurriedly, like she was eager to cleanse herself now that she finally had someone to listen. "Last anyone heard, Lemond was happy with the job. He's renting a small house nearby, got his first new car. He told us it's a great neighborhood, wonderful people living around him. Rincon's limited on activities for a single guy, but Savannah's close and Hilton Head, meaning our family, is an hour away."

"Your ma liked that, huh?"

Dixie nodded. Clarice, her mother, was like most moms wanting the family close to the nest. Early in our friendship, Dixie and I had informally adopted each other's family. Clarice had played a vital role in helping my grandparents with me after I'd returned, a confused orphan, from Brazil. "Between Lemond's visits to the island, Mom's been speaking by phone fairly regularly with him. A few weeks before she left on her trip, he'd become distant. She pressed him and finally showed up at his house after she hadn't heard from him for a while."

"Uh-oh." She smiled and I did, too. We both knew when Mama Hightower had a bee in her bonnet, you might as well sing like the proverbial canary because no one could withstand the scrutiny she would put you under.

"All Lemond said was that he was going through some changes and needed to sort things out."

"Pretty vague."

"Yeah."

"How did he put your mom off with that flimsy excuse?" I asked in wonder.

"I don't know, but he's going to teach me." A look of distress flashed across her face. "If we ever find him."

"Does he keep in touch when he goes walkabout?"

"He's never gone anywhere!" Dixie used her hands as she talked, the handcuffs banging against the table. She glared down at them, gave her head a quick shake, a symbolic casting off of the image of herself bound and chained by metal. "If he did, he would have let someone know. Heck, Aunt Beverly is more strict than ma. She always got a kick out of tearing up our black behinds." She uttered a quick ha, then continued. "When mom and Aunt Bev left for overseas, she asked me to check up on him. You know the rest. Until I left Seal Beach."

That, I did. She'd called Lemond's house and after several days, we formed a team taking turns phoning every hour from work and at home. Finally, we traced down his work number and got the royal runaround. With Dixie's family globetrotting, it was up to her to find what was going on. Both Beverly and Clarice were schoolteachers and after years of raising kids, everyone pitched in to give them a super trip. The women decided on a world cruise, so that they could see a lot, then pick places they wanted to go back to later and spend more time. The kids who were able to, had planned to meet them at different ports of call. Dixie had been trying to worm some time off at the PD for a short vacation herself.

At my house, Dixie had called the Rincon police, but they were treating it like a case of an adult wandering off. Over and over, she'd hang up the phone in frustration, not at all assured from their litany that Lemond "would show up or call soon, they all eventually do". That's when she'd packed her bags and headed home.

"So far, I've just presented myself as a concerned relative, not a..." She stole a quick glance at the door. "Jamming devices or not, I believed it would be worse for me if the locals knew."

"I gotcha," I finished for her, relieving her of the need to say that she was a cop. It could also cause her problems with her commanders back in Los Angeles, especially with the intense scrutiny the PD was undergoing after several recent scandals. "What happened when you got to Rincon?"

"I talked to people at the plant, but nobody had any information. It's as if he vanished into thin air. I got bad vibes there so I decided to case the place. Last Saturday night, I hiked through the woods to snoop, but I had no sooner sat on the ground when two deputies grabbed me and started throwing punches. When I realized they weren't going to stop, I fought back. They held me down, threatened me. Told me I was trespassing." Dixie looked spent as she slumped down using the table to support her torso.

"The two idiots outside?"

"One of them." She described Toothpick. "There's two more just like him."

"Must be something in the water."

"I hope your secret weapons work like you say, otherwise, I'll be ground beef tonight." She pointed to the Pepsi. "You gonna drink that?" I slid it toward her. She drained it in a few gulps.

"What happened next?"

"I kicked one in the balls and took off running. Another one caught up with me and that's where most of these bruises came from."

"Which guy?"

"The one always sucking on a toothpick."

"Shearhouse."

She nodded. "By then I was at the dirt road beside the factory. A car full of teenagers drove by. I yelled something stupid, like 'I'm a victim of police brutality and please call the police'. Ha-ha. Those kids called the local newspaper, the fire department and a few ministers! Grainger, the police Chief, showed up soon after." Dixie's shoulders shook with laughter. "It's funny now, that fire truck tearing down the road! The horn. Wau! Wau! They were so ticked off when they saw it was only a nigger getting the shit beat out of her." Dixie tried stretching her legs but didn't get far because of the leg irons. My cheeks burned with indignation. "I don't think I'll ever cuff anyone again without wincing."

"How have they treated you since that night?"

"They've left me alone. I wasn't able to call anyone. Finally one of the black guys was released and I asked him to call you." Her eyes flooded with tears. She looked away, swallowing repetitively as if that would stem the tide of her emotions. "I'm scared." It came out in a squeak. Me, too, but I kept that to myself. I was struggling with my own ocean of confusion, fear and pain. I hooked my little finger around Dixie's and gave it a quick tug. It was one of those between-friends rituals that started so long ago that we no longer remembered why, but did it each time the chips were down. She tugged back on my finger and we left them intertwined.

"I'm sorry I got you into this. It's too dangerous for you here, Paloma."

I protested, she countered and we volleyed back and forth for a few minutes. "I'm already here," I said sternly. "You know I couldn't have stayed away. I *will* get you help. I *will* get you out of here. *Soon*! And we'll find Lemond. I promise." Her face was wearing the same panic and fear as when she first entered the room. "Dix, do you think there'll be repercussions against you because of my visit?" She shrugged. "I tried to be amicable, but it didn't get me far. I needed to see you, otherwise I wouldn't have known exactly how to help."

"There's no way of knowing until it happens." The silence was uncomfortable, like when two lovers discuss a troubled relationship. There was noise coming from the other side of the door.

"*Bosta!* I wanted to get evidence of your injuries but it sounds like one of the doofus cops is coming."

"Maybe it's better that way."

It took me a second to understand then I went into action. "Go over to the window." The footsteps were getting louder, closer. By the time Pepsi's head was sticking through the outer doorway, I was busy directing a digital photo shoot of pain and torture.

He pointed at my impromptu curtain. "That's not regulation." He snatched the paper, but the gum held fast. He came out of it with a miserably small corner. "I'm gonna have to confiscate the film."

Dixie uttered a small whimper. "Too late," I shot out loudly and snidely. I toned it down a few notches. A bit of lying was in order. "It's all digital and I've already sent the body shots to my law firm's email." Take that! The lies were so easily rolling off my lips. But Doofus cop wasn't all ignorance.

"Uh-uh. There ain't no telephone line in here for you to do that." He propped his hands proudly on his hips.

"Don't need it. Cellular modem." *Nahnie-nahnie, pooh-pooh.*

He mumbled a string of four-letter adjectives that unflatteringly described the female species. "Five minutes," he barked, then disappeared behind the slamming door.

"We better get on record your entire body–whether there are injuries or not. That should ensure that nothing else happens to you. I've set the time and date stamp, also. It's not much, but it's some-thing. We better only see improvement." Tough words, but was it enough to protect her? It wouldn't matter what evidence I had if Dixie was dead. I shook that thought away. I didn't know what else I could do for her until I got legal help. I hoped, I prayed this would be enough. I snapped images of Dixie's face and instructed her to pull her top lip up exposing the through-and-through wound. I zoomed in close, the cut filling the entire frame. "Your arms?"

"I'll need help." I tried pushing up the sleeves but the jail attire wasn't accommodating. Dixie opened her mouth to say something but didn't. When she saw me watching, she attempted a brave smile but quickly looked away. I stared at her hands. They were trembling. "Go ahead, Paloma. Push my shirt down." I unbuttoned the top half and slid it down her thin shoulders. Pockets of broken, bruised and infected skin marred the six inches of her body that we could see. I filmed every indignity. The last area to document was beneath her bra and panties. I worked quickly in case the cops came back. I helped Dixie finish dressing.

We stared at each other. "Damn," was as helpful as I could be. I slid the tiny digital camera back in the computer case then wrapped my arms gently around her.

"I'm soooo sorry, Dixie! I want to go out there and rip some male appendages off! You shouldn't be here. I'd love to bust you out right now."

"We can save that for Plan B."

I stood back at arms' length and scrutinized her face.

"I'm okay, sister." She added, "really," when she saw my skepticism. "I *do* feel so much better knowing that you are here."

"Give me Lemond's address. Then you tell me what you want me to do first–besides getting you a *real* lawyer." Dixie took a sheet of paper and penned a detailed drawing. "They don't have street names and numbers?" I asked.

"What, and spend money on the colored side of town? Sorry, you're going to have to count mailboxes."

"Is there a street sign for the main road into the neighborhood?" I bent over the drawing.

"Blandford Road, but after that you're on your own. Here's Lemond's phone number for what it's worth. If you get lost, everyone knows everybody else so stop at any house." We looked at each other not knowing what to say. "I'll pay you back for your expenses."

"Friendship doesn't come with a price tag," I interrupted. She started to protest. "Hey, you're at my mercy now. End of subject." I packed the remaining equipment into my case. Too soon Officer Toothpick arrived. We hadn't had time to toss around ideas or form a plan of action. As he yanked her out of the visitor's cell, Dixie turned back attempting her lopsided grin, but her fear and desperation was all too apparent. Toothpick jerked her back around. I was on my own. It was all up to me. The clanking of her leg irons echoed in the tiny hall and all the way down into my tattered soul.

Stetson Kennedy, a Southern writer, and a very courageous and resourceful fighter for civil rights, infiltrated one of the most powerful and dangerous Klaverns. Unable to get law enforcement backing, he survived by his own wits as he got the goods on the Columbians–the first important neo-Nazi organization in the U.S. For years Kennedy under-mined the Klan's activities by publishing articles and exposing Klan agendas and members, which included a surprising number of police, judges, and politicians, including Herman Talmadge, Georgia's governor, elected in 1948.

Chapter Twelve

Outside the jail, I jumped into the car without thinking. The fire from the vinyl seat made me jump back out as gracefully as a bull with a thorn shoved in each hoof. I reached in, cranking the car without my foot on the gas petal. I flipped the air on high and shut the door, with me on the outside, and waited. The white rubber soles of my Docksiders were roasting, making my feet sweaty and slippery. How I hate that.

When I looked up, Officer Toothpick was back on the porch doing what he did best–staring. As I climbed back into a cooler vehicle, I saw a white envelope on the console. I picked it up and looked inside. A business card–the Waving Girl Law Office, Alvin Eason, Attorney at Law–it read. Not entertaining for a second that one of the sheriffs passed this tidbit along must mean the lady wearing the green uniform who'd joined us on the porch earlier. Curiouser and curiouser.

I donned the PD cap and drove the lonely road back into town. Turning onto Highway 21, I saw the nondescript federal car from the jail parked at the Chick N' Chat. I whipped mine into the lot. An Arctic chill blasted me as I entered.

The place was spotless, kitchen chrome polished to an eye-squinting shine. The hamburger condiments were covered with plastic wrap. Everything looked fresh. I saw her seated in a booth by the window.

"Excuse me."

She jumped at my voice. "Lawd me! You shore scared my mule!" Her freckled hands were busy making X's on a tightly stretched white cloth. "Name's Aggie Dewitt." She slammed the needle into the fish design impaling the poor thing and stuck her hand out for a shake so quickly, I took a second to get into motion.

"I'm Paloma," I said, noting her firm handshake. "Did you drop this back at the jail?" I waved the card in front of me.

"He's one of the best attorneys going. And I'll admit he's my cousin. Get yourself something to eat, and we'll talk." She turned back to her craft. Apparently I had been given my orders. I sized her up. She was about five-two. Buxom described her perfectly. My earlier guess of fifty-ish stood. Freckles covered every inch of her that the eye could see. On her right hip perched a holstered gun with loops for spare ammo. I guessed it to be a .357. Tough little cookie.

With the smells coming from the kitchen, eating wouldn't be too tough a chore. I approached the counter and stared up at the menu hanging from the ceiling. A man appeared from the back.

"Can I hep' ya?"

"Ice water–a double." The man smiled while pulling up an orange tray from below the counter. He turned and retrieved a plastic pitcher full of exactly that. He placed it and a glass on the tray. "I'll have the two-piece special."

"Mashed potatoes or french fries? Taters are the real thing."

"Yum! Mashed, with lots of gravy. Hold the bread."

"Vegetable?"

"The snap beans, are they canned?"

He was insulted. "Goodness, no! Picked them myself yesterday. You may want to reconsider the bread. It's just coming out the oven."

"There goes my diet."

"You're thin! I'll give you the low-fat margarine. That'll even things out."

"Sold," I said, liking the way this man thought. I rejoined Aggie at the booth. The cold floor melted the heat from my feet, drying the sweat. Good. I was worried I'd have to buy socks, which went against my beach bum principles. I poured a glass of water and risking a brain freeze, drained it and poured another. I used a napkin to mop up puddles of sweat around my neck. I definitely needed to jump into some waves.

"Hot as tarnation out there today."

"Shore is," I replied, mesmerized by the quick pulls of colored thread as her hand swooped down like a pelican.

"Cross-stitch," she explained and quickly showed me the design. I recognized the diamond shape of my home state and a few of the more uniquely shaped islands. "I'm addicted. It's my own drawing of the Carolina coast. Do you do any?"

"All thumbs." I held my hands up as if I expected to see ten of them.

"You aren't from around here, are you?"

"No."

"LA?" I didn't answer.

"The hat," she said indicating my grandfather's gift perched on my head–the letters LAPD emblazoned in gold on the front. I was too stupid to live.

"The general area."

"I'm glad to see the Hightower woman is finally getting legal help."

I hesitated again. "Not quite."

"I had a feeling not." My heart thumped. "Don't worry! You look like a deer caught in the headlights. You were good out there–until you mention-ed *habeas corpus*. It didn't exactly fit. But with that particular audience–no problem." She stopped the X's, grabbed my hand and broke into a broad grin. "Well, lawd me and my hound dog, too! You pulled one over on those good-fer-nothin' rednecks." She resumed her needlework with ferociousness.

I relaxed and let the conversation wander Southern style. She explained about her stitchery which seemed fairly simple, even for me. For most of the design, she was sewing thread X's onto a textile grid. "Are you familiar with the three-dimensional stitchery from Brazil?" I asked.

"I'm not sure."

"It's raised, so the flowers and other elements in the design seem to pop out at you. I'm not that familiar with needlework, but I do know that the stitches and knots are borrowed from all forms of stitchery. You probably know some of them already."

Her eyes hadn't glazed over, so I continued. "My mom and her family used natural items–leaves, dried flowers, seashells and mixed them in with the colored threads."

She stopped her hands for a second to look up at me and grin. "That sounds really neat!"

I tossed out another tidbit I was sure would dazzle her with my smarts. "The threads with the graduated color uh..." I paused, suddenly not so darn bright after all.

"Variegated?"

"Yes, that's it. Thanks. When rayon hit Brazil in the 1800s, everyone loved it because it held up in hot water and nuclear holo-caust. The manufacturers there created the variegated coloring in the thread and it became wildly popular."

"I like it, too. If you use green, the various shades can make a leaf look more realistic," Aggie agreed.

"Right. So when the rest of the world discovered the Brazilian creations, it was called Brazilian-style stitchery. Impressed?"

She smiled like she was suitably so. "I'd love to see some exam-ples. Do you have any?"

"Some. My mom was a junkie, like you." She grinned even wider when I told her I'd send her a few photos and patterns when I returned to Seal Beach. I pulled out my notebook, hit the wake button and typed a reminder in the Notes file with Aggie's business address. Enough small talk. "Ma'am, you mentioned Dixie. What do you know about her?"

"I come over here every now and then on business. It's only twenty minutes down river to the South Carolina line. Some good ol' boys like to shoot animals out of season and think they can sneak back to Georgia without ol' Aggie switchin' their britches." She shook a freckled finger in front of her.

"What I've heard is mainly gossip. It passes for culture in small towns. My curiosity is about as healthy as my appetite. Your friends' name is listed on the jail roster. Don't get many women out there so the name stuck out. After I saw it on the roster, I never saw it on the court schedule. All that's suppose to be public record. If something hadn't happened by this coming Monday, I was going to raise a fuss. Paloma, what happened after you breezed by me at the jail?"

I told her I'd gotten to see Dixie for a few minutes, described her bruises while Aggie winced, then finished with a brief run down on Officers Pepsi's and Toothpick's actions.

"Not much difference from when they were on the porch. I have to won-der what's going on. It's a good thing I was there today. I can help."

"I appreciate it, ma'am. But I have to ask why?"

"I like that. You come out all the way with it. See, I have an ax to grind with Deputy Dawg Grainger." She made a face like someone had rubbed a dirty diaper under her nose. Her head bobbed, hands accentuating her speech when she wasn't attending her needlework. "It's not the first time he's overstepped his bounds. I get my kicks putting him back in his place." She lowered her voice. "When I was at the jail, I heard Shearhouse tell Pitman– the one you call Pepsi–that they were to make life miserable for anyone who came to see the woman prisoner. Ain't nothing wrong with ol' Aggie's hearing." She tapped her ear, coming dangerously close to giving herself a shot with the needle. "I heard 'em from the washroom—out on the porch, those two, like a pair of roosters, bok, bok, bok." She rocked a few times as she laughed, but she never stopped making her X's. "Now you be *real* careful. I don't trust 'em none. Does Dixie have kin in town, Paloma?"

"Yes, a cousin, but I don't know exactly where."

"Don't forget you're in the South. There's only one place, honey. The railroad tracks segregate the town. Mostly, blacks live west of it and the whites on the east." My food arrived and we talked between chews.

"Ms. Dewitt, would you say Rincon's population is around four thousand?"

"Sounds about right. My friends call me Aggie."

I nodded. "Okay, Aggie. Why do they have five police officers? Do they have a lot of problems here? If we had that ratio in L.A. we'd cut our crime rate in half."

Aggie squinted as her smile spread across her face. "I bet so. Grainger is full time. The rest are part timers with other jobs." She threaded the needle with yellow floss and quickly made four X's before I could blink. "I'm sorry, I do have a good wind. You eat."

I've never let much interfere with mastication, especially when the vittles were this lip-smacking delicious, but I didn't contradict my new pal. I dug in and as soon as I pushed my plate away, she was back to talking.

"About you, honey. Where were you born and where do you live now?"

"Hilton Head Island and now Seal Beach."

She didn't hold either location against me. "I'm dying to hear an insider's view of Southern California. Don't think I've met one before. I have a thousand questions to ask you, but I'm gonna call my cousin and tell him we're coming."

I gulped water like a camel preparing for the open desert then paid at the counter. "Excellent food," I told the man.

"Thank you. Come back, have a chat." He held out a white bag for Aggie as she returned announcing we'd meet her cousin at his office.

"Dave, I'm gonna get out of your hair. Tell the Missus hello. What more temptations do you have for me today?"

"Blueberry muffins and a tad of peach cobbler. I threw in a few extra for your friend." Dave winked at us and disappeared into the kitchen before I could take my eyes out of the bag and thank him.

"Aggie, it's Sunday. Is your cousin working today or just doing you a favor?" I asked when we were outside.

"He works all the time! Doesn't have a normal life. Just follow me. When we get to the outskirts of Savannah I'll jump in your car if you don't mind. It'll be easier than tryin' to follow each other in traffic and it's at the crossroads where Al and I go in opposite directions home. Besides, mine's federal and doesn't have a dang drop of cold air in it, the cheap sons of guns. Don't you worry none. I've got it all set." Like a baby chick behind its mother, I followed as ordered to find out exactly what it was she had gotten "all set".

Klan infiltrator, Stetson Kennedy, with an imaginative en-
deavor, contacted the script writers of radio's Superman show,
supplying his Klavern's current agenda and passwords. Super-
man battered the Klan quite accurately by airwaves. Klansmen
were especially infuriated when their own children used current
secret passwords, while playing the Klan bashing super-hero.
Drew Pearson, radio commentator, used Kennedy's information,
broadcasting it as "Minutes of the Klan's Last Meeting".

Chapter Thirteen

Sandra Brice pulled into the driveway of Moonpie's yard and waited before turning off the car and cold air, in order to check her appearance in the visor's vanity mirror. What she saw as authorita-tive, others considered her severe. Her platinum blonde hair, always tightly pulled back, was severely held in place with a simple barrette, and her make-up was minimal. She wore basic suits, expensively cut, flat shoes, and her Bostonian accent was typically nasal and crisp. She liked order, demanded it. She carried no purse. Her briefcase was custom made with compartments for essential office supplies and a few feminine items. Brice flipped open the briefcase that was always close beside her, and slid the car keys into the spot designed for them.

Moonpie's yard was a mine field of knee-high weeds that hid old car parts, yard toys, rusted tools, and occasional vermin. Her trailer, with heat waves wafting heavenward, looked like a squat check-in station at the gates of Hell. Moonpie stuck her round face out the door and waved. "Howdy. How was your trip?"

"Uneventful."

"Are you still in a snit?" Moonpie stepped back as Brice ignored her and climbed the rickety steps. "I'm sorry it's so hot in here. I don't have air conditioning, remember?"

"If you did a good job, you'll get your blasted air."

"I did real good, Brice. I got five women and almost a sixth. They're ready whenever you say."

"I don't want a bunch of snotty-nosed kids shouting and getting on my nerves," she admonished.

"I...I got someone to babysit." She hadn't, but wasn't about to say anything to further upset Brice. Who owed her a favor, she wondered, someone who couldn't say no to babysitting? The scrawny Blackwine kid. Moonpie had lent her and her pimply-faced boyfriend the bed one afternoon so they could hump like rabbits without their parents knowing. Yeah, she'd give her a call as soon as Brice calmed down.

Moonpie clasped her hands together and smiled up at Brice. "I ran out of stuff a few days back. Can I have some?"

"In the car. Go get it. Bring my suitcase. And when you come back, go take a bath. You stink." Moonpie left, head down like a spurned child.

While Brice waited, she stood in front of the fan, reaching for a tissue to blot the perspiration. "I have calls to make while you shower," she said taking the case from Moonpie. "Then we'll talk." Moonpie spun about and marched down the hall, her heavy footsteps vibrating the whole tin can. Brice pulled several papers out of the briefcase and made a quick check of her notes about Gundersen's plant in Rincon and its covert activities. Now she had to ensure that Swartzman was out of the way tonight. She stabbed at the buttons on the phone. "Swartzman? Brice, here." With no preamble, she lied to Swartzman insisting that the orders came directly from the top. All of the partners from the home office were unreachable at a business retreat. Brice had suggested the trip, using each man's weaknesses, stroking each ego. She'd picked the places, paid all the expenses, made sure there would be plenty of young girls, liquor and activities to keep them from sur-facing until the end. She was covered for a week.

"The partners want to move swiftly," she lied easily. "I know it's a lot of reports and action items, but I just got the fax and it reads: Complete by Monday. Understood?" Brice could hear the hostility in Swartzman's grunted yes.

"I'll be in Rincon in the morning," she continued lying. "I'm taking the red-eye out tonight. Questions?" She paused for only two seconds. "Good, tomorrow then." She hung up the phone and smiled. Things were finally taking shape. It'd been a long time coming. *But it would be here soon,* she thought. Brice had created the master plan. *She* would be in charge of saving the white race in America.

*   *   *

Keeping a safe distance, Randy followed Paloma and Aggie out of the Chick N' Chat parking lot. They headed south, toward Savannah, on Highway 21.

Fifteen minutes later, the women turned into the Ride-Share lot at the I-95 intersection. He eased the truck into the gas station and watched. The old woman got in the rental car with the girl. He turned the truck around and waited until they had gone some distance before picking up the tail again. Randy reported their movements to Swartzman and was told to continue his watch. Nearing the heavier traffic of Savannah, he drove closer to the Escort.

*   *   *

After Randy Beamon reported in, Swartzman polished off the agenda for the next White Rebel Force meeting. Freeing the top two buttons on his shirt, he speculated on Brice's impending visit. That bitch didn't miss any-thing and reported nothing. As if Brice wasn't enough, Randy reported that half-breed girl had visited Hightower in jail. Grainger hadn't done his job of keeping the nosy black woman isolated. How was he supposed to run a plant and train men for a race war when every time he put out one fire, another started? Swartzman, fireman of incompetency.

He poured himself a J & B Jett on the rocks, letting the fifteen-year-old scotch flood his tongue with the hint of oak. He sighed as he stretched his neck muscles. More relaxed now, he was ready to work on *his* plans, see Grainger, then come back and get the reports ready for Brice. Swartzman chuckled. He'd been successful so far making the men in his sector believe in him, and he'd kept Brice from finding out his *real* plans. By the time Bos-ton got wind of what he was doing, it would be too late. Screwing everybody was so easy, but the impact would be great. That's what made a strategy good. Keep it simple–but deadly effective.

Swartzman was still amazed by how he'd put it all together. The residents of this town were trusting of everyone and worked hard building computer parts. All to finance *his* dream. And the bubbas out sweating in the woods for him, still clinging to that Yankee-Rebel crap. Swartzman had one big fire to put out–find those diskettes, destroy them and whoever had them. His money was on the half-breed. Brazilian and Polish. Enough to make Hitler turn over in his grave. It was up to him. Again.

Now, to think of a place to hide Paloma out. No place connected with the plant. In the woods. That'd be the best place to force her to talk. And if she didn't? Deep in the woods no one would hear her scream.

Unable to interest state officials in the Klan, Stetson Kennedy turned to the federal government. Even with Joseph McCarthy's fervor over communism, Washington was uninterested in Kennedy's offer to turn over, at his own expense, massive amounts of documented un-American Klan activities. In a desperate move to get someone to listen, he donned his Klan robe and mask and walked into the Capitol unannounced causing quite a stir. The next day, Robert Stripling, chief investigator for the House of Un-American Activities Committee, offered an interview but refused any documentation. Kennedy's efforts with the FBI were also fruitless.

Chapter Fourteen

Shortly after Aggie joined me in my car, I was following her finger as she pointed directions to River Street, a cobblestone lane that ran, appropriately enough, along the Savannah River. The area had definite tourist trappings–the yuppie kind–and I asked my companion about it.

"When you were a youngun' you never came to Savannah?" Aggie asked.

"Only once or twice. We always went to Charleston for our big city trips. My grandparents had friends and relatives there."

"Charleston's a beautiful town! Savannah's a cousin, just a tad smaller."

"I remember a smaller bridge over the river," I nodded my head back and to the left at a newer, taller, modern span behind us. "Wasn't it named after a governor?"

"Yeah, Talmadge. But the truth about him has since been aired. Only the KKK would try and name a public structure after him."

"Hmm. Bet they didn't teach that version of history in the schools," I replied, thinking of several sanitized versions of history in my own home state that later had been debunked. Strom Thurmond came easily to mind. We passed a few small hotels and an ugly power substation, its generators or whatever they were, clashing with the historic scenery we were heading into.

"Oh, lawd me! It was worse when I was in school. We just didn't talk about ugliness. You can't burp these days without someone putting it on TV or in print."

"You have a point. Aggie, tell me about this River Street area."

She nodded, ready to educate. "A while back, the city made these old Civil War garrisons that were forged out of the cliffs into offices, shops, bars, and restaurants. The bricks tearing up the alignment on your rental car were handmade by slaves. Above the shops, on Bay

Street, is the old cotton market." I braved a quick look as I kept my eye out for pedestrians.

On the high bank, huge oaks and rows of hearty azaleas fringed stately Southern-styled buildings and parks. A horn blasted on the river. I slowed, searching for the source, discovering a paddle-wheeled boat painted a patriotic red, white and blue chug by. Further down river a huge tanker was making slow progress, guided by minuscule tugboats slicing a path through the current.

"Beneath the shops are tunnels. I don't know if any are still accessible. A few began at a tavern on the cliff and ended here at the shipping area. In the old days, the tavern owner would generously supply ale to shipmates who unfortunately stopped in for a nip. The poor devils would wake up to discover they'd been shanghaied out to sea!"

"Hmm," I contributed lamely, totally engrossed in the story and the view. In grade school I'd dreamed of being a pirate and I shared this with Aggie. "Dixie and I decided we'd play female pirates, hiding that fact and springing it on unsuspecting evil ones. They of course, being men, would underestimate us because of their perception of women being frail and unable to fight. Then we'd kick butt, take their ill-gotten gains and give them to the poor. Of course, we'd save a handful of the riches for ourselves!"

Aggie possessed great people skills. And when she laughed it was deep and genuine, which would make anyone feel at ease. She was a wonderful listener–giving her complete attention, forming facial expressions at appropriate moments and making one feel extra-special. I hoped I wasn't wrong about her, that she could indeed provide the help that I so desperately needed for Dixie.

Aggie stopped cross-stitching long enough to squeeze my arm, blonde curls dancing as she bobbed her head in excitement. "Paloma! That tavern from the 1700s is now a wonderful restaurant called the Pirate's House. You *must* check it out–especially with your swash-buckling past! You'll find it all really fascinating. And the food beats all!" She tapped my arm and pointed. "Pull over here, honey. I guess we're going to have to park in the pay lot." Aggie leaned in front of me and snipped the ticket from the attendants' hand. "Well, Lawd, me! Every time I come here the price has gone up. Six whole dollars! They're stealing hard-earned money from honest citizens." I couldn't help but laugh. Aggie shot daggers at me with her hazel eyes. "What in tarnation's so funny?"

"Some areas of downtown L.A. charge twenty, twenty-five dollars a day."

"One has to wonder why you live there." I laughed, thoroughly scolded, and parked the car. I grabbed my backpack, stuffing all my gadgets inside to save them from the heat. While walking with Aggie, I took time to check out my surroundings. To my left, a life-sized statue of a woman waving a handkerchief faced the river.

"Wait! The business card you gave me said Waving Girl Law Office. What does the name have to do with the statue?" I slowed my pace on the cobblestone street so Aggie's short legs could keep up with me.

"There are many stories about the Waving Girl. She lived on Elba Island, several miles that way." Aggie pointed down river. "My favorite story is that she was in love with a sea captain. Everyday she went to the river and waved her handkerchief at passing ships as she waited for her lover to return home. He never did. She had an uncanny ability of knowing when a ship was coming, day or night, stormy weather or good, greeting *every* ship, for fifty years. All boats and ships answered her gesture with a blast of their horns. They still do." Aggie sighed, a faraway look in her eyes.

"What a wonderful story! Did she ever marry?"

"No." Aggie tsked twice. "There's more about her and the swashbucklers in local history books. Visit the shops along the river and make sure you get a book or two."

"You bet! Shopping is one of my truly feminine traits. Now, about the Waving Girl Law Office."

Aggie smiled obligingly. "My cousin started it. I'm so dang proud of him! If you don't like what you see, we'll go someplace else. No hard feelings. Deal?" I nodded.

As soon as we entered the office, a thick glass wall confronted me with a metal circular grate in the middle. "Is this bullet proof...?" I felt a jarring and unexpected tug on my pack. Whipping around I expected to see the stocking-marred Oriental features of The Voice but saw instead a Caucasian security guard.

"I need to look in your backpack, ma'am," he said. When my heart finally beat normally, I let him plunder, finding candy, gum, my wallet, an in-flight magazine I'd snitched, CD's, Walkman, and the spy gear. He gave me a quick, scrutinizing once-over before X-raying the pack then holding each device out to me to turn on, showing that it worked and didn't pack C4 or some other explosive. Then he picked up a security toy of his own and moved it over me while Aggie introduced him as Gus.

"Have I stepped into a war zone? Crying out loud! This is Savannah, Georgia!"

"I'm sorry, I forgot to explain." After passing through the grate, an Asian youth confirmed we weren't the enemy and buzzed us through a door as thick as a bank vault's.

"Hello, Mrs. Aggie, it is a pleasure seeing you again," he said politely.

"How are you and your family?" Aggie asked.

"Very well, thank you. I will tell them that you have inquired. I have adopted an American name now, Mrs. Aggie. It's Kevin." He moved from around the desk and took Aggie's hand while she again made introductions.

"I'll stop by their shop next time I'm in town. I'll have a mess of beans and corn for them."

"They will be most pleased to see you. And your generosity is much appreciated." Kevin was slobbering over her. I mean, I was impressed myself, but there are limits. The phone rang and Kevin hurried off to answer it in his more-perfect-than-mine-English. Aggie murmured something about the washroom, and I was left standing in the middle of a no-frills, but nice, waiting room. I busied myself reading the numerous framed newspaper clippings and posters on the walls. The first was a collage of paramilitary-garbed men posturing to show off their guns.

A photo of a Ku Klux Klan rally caught my attention. A red circle with a line drawn through it, indicating no, covered the paper. I moved onto a news story about civil rights attorneys Alvin Eason and William Sherrod who, along with friends and family, aided a group of Korean shop owners in a fight against a white supremacist group. I looked closely at the picture. In the sea of faces, I recognized Kevin. The other Koreans were clearly related to him. In the background stood Aggie Dewitt, hands on hips, looking ready to kick butt. That explained Kevin's devotion.

The other walls were filled with similar stories of hate groups I had never heard of and some I had. Rallies, injuries, deaths, law suits, threats, retaliations, victories for minorities–all were chronicled. Some were local, but the firm was willing to travel. The Waving Girl Law Office got results, but judging from the garrison they worked in, they were paying a heavy price.

"May I help you, miss?" He had the kind of eyes that could get me in trouble–if I was lucky. Sparkling ice-blue strands amid paler blue, the corners crinkled up boyishly when he smiled. His hair was not blonde, not really brown. Brownish. It was darker than Aggie's and sported more wave except for a few ringlets at the tips. He flattened an unruly curl at his temple but it sprang back as soon as his hand left it. The same hand reached out and grasped mine. Expecting the softness of a desk professional, I was surprised to feel calluses. Gardening or farm work, I speculated.

"I'm Al Eason," he said, as I dragged my eyes from his and allowed them to tippy-toe down the rest of him. His arms were buff and tanned, but his torso had an odd shape, like the tin man in the Wizard of Oz. Theory number two, he wore a Kevlar vest. "And you are?" I snapped back to attention.

"Paloma."

"That's a lovely name." His was a pleasant, easy drawl. *Droga, you're fawning, you horny Medina!* "What can I do for you?"

"I, ah, Aggie..."

"Speak of the devil," he said quietly and put a finger to his lips. I turned and watched Aggie's back as she talked with Kevin. Al sneaked up behind her and scooped her up in his arms. As he pressed his mouth to the back of her neck, he made sounds I giggled about as a kid. Aggie's look was price-less. Her attempts at chastising this man who stood heads taller just added to the comedy.

"Isn't she a darlin'? She's always giving me the devil, but I like 'em sassy." He mussed her hair as Aggie tried to slap his arm away.

"Lawd me, Al! Are you having a spell?" she asked sternly and turned her gaze toward me as I cackled and bravely dismissed her consternation. I felt tension leaving my shoulders and neck.

"What brings you to the Waving Girl?" he asked when the joking ended.

"Grainger," she said succinctly. "He's put a black girl in jail in Rincon. Her friend," she added, pointing to me. "She's been there about a week now, hasn't been charged with anything, or arraigned. What are you going to do about it?"

"Good golly, woman, you don't mess around," Al stated.

"Time's awaiting. Dixie Hightower has been in the hands of Deputy Dawg long enough." Aggie's face was flushed, her body rigid. I wondered what this Grainger did that got under her craw. "Come on, Al. Are we going to stand out here all day with the barn animals? My dogs are barking." She pointed to her feet.

Al blew out a flustered sigh and ushered us past another bodyguard keeping watch outside his door. His office was papered with cool, dark masculine designs. The window, thick glass with bars on the outside, over-looked the river. Square indentations marred the carpet where the desk once had been positioned for a lovely view. It was an exquisite mahogany antique now placed at an angle far away from the window. There weren't this many precautions at the mayor's office in Los Angeles. Al pointed to two leather chairs in front of his desk for Aggie and me.

"Al, there aren't any hotels in Rincon."

"I know."

"Well, get Paloma a good one on the river. And at a decent price. She pays twenty dollars a day for parking in L.A." Al didn't move a muscle. "Please," she added. He looked at me while Aggie flopped into the chair and set up her cross-stitch.

I nodded. "Thank you."

"My pleasure." He punched a button on the phone, grinning down at his cousin. "Kevin, please get a room for Paloma at the Riverfront Hotel starting this afternoon. At a good price. She pays twenty dollars a day for parking in L.A." Aggie mumbled disparaging remarks barely under her breath while I again hee-hawed merrily. He leaned back in his swivel chair grinning broadly and aimed a small clip-on fan at himself. His phone buzzed and he excused himself to answer it. Aggie stitched while I counted designs on the wallpaper. Nine across per panel, and how many down? Quickly bored, my eyes strayed to the counselor.

Spouting legalese, he turned sideways holding the phone between his shoulder and head as he dug into a box of files on the floor. Comfortable in his element, he was professionally commanding. Then with business completed, his tone changed into friendly banter.

Suddenly he sat upright and faced forward. *Droga*! He caught me staring. He winked and I felt my cheeks flame. My face cracked into a gargantuan smile. His gaze held mine but I weakened and turned toward Aggie trying desperately to think of something to say.

"You two are cousins." Really clever, Paloma.

"Yep." I watched her sewing X's. "Although sometimes I regret that fact," she said as Al hung up the phone.

"What'd you say, cousin?" Al asked.

"I said it was good to see you. Al, do you need to turn up the air? You're perspiring somethin' awful."

"Thanks for pointing that out in front of company. It's this police vest." I sat back, smugly admiring my powers of deduction. "I haven't had a chance to take it off. I bet I'll sweat off twenty pounds this summer. Then I can stop that silly jogging around the farm. I'll be right back." He returned with the bulletproof vest in hand and some shape to his figure that accentuated his derriere. "Okay, Paloma. Start from the beginning."

What was the beginning? I felt like I had come in the middle of a story and couldn't get anyone to tell me either end. I began with Lemond's disappearance, the problems with getting information from the plant where he worked and Dixie's dustup with the cops. I pulled the tiny recorder out of my pocket, released the disc and laid it on Al's desk. "I also took images of Dixie's injuries with my camera. Well, actually her entire body–for proof of what is and is not injured. I was hoping that would buy a bit of insurance for the cops to keep their hands off of her."

"Excellent idea," Al exclaimed and flashed that sensuous smile.

"I can burn a CD and give you a copy. Ah, listen. The bit at the end, just after I did a brief shot of her leg irons is very personal. I'm hoping you won't need, ah..."

"Don't worry." Al rolled out from behind his desk to perch catty-cornered from me. He stationed his pair of cute cheeks–no, the other ones–on the desk. All this to pat my hand in reassurance. Like Aggie, Al too, had people skills. His demeanor exuded strength and assurance with a dash of laid-back thrown in. With Al's easy-going manner, a person could confess all. Well, almost all. I skipped the part of me finding bugging equipment. Al would probably think me a rank amateur playing games. And wouldn't like me impersonating an attorney. Once he got to know me better, I could always confess my sins. Internally I was wondering how long it would take to free Dixie and just what would happen to her between now and then. Would she have a job to go back to or did all her law enforcement work and training go down with her that night outside the plant when she fought the sheriff's men?

"Al, it's all Grainger's doing." Aggie's hand stabbed the needle at the cloth. It came out a short distance away and sailed toward me. I prepared to duck but her hand headed west and dipped back down. She told him about the jail log and lack of a hearing for Dixie.

"The cops said they have quite a few violations to pin on Dixie," I told them.

Aggie fluttered her free fingers as a sign of dismissal then plunged the needle down again. "Those boys couldn't find their butts if they each had six hands. Bless their hearts."

Al rolled his eyes and shared my laughter. I'd missed hearing that phrase. In the South, you can say the most despicable, low-down, vile things about anyone and still be socially acceptable–every single time. As long as you ended your tirade with "bless his heart". I felt more tension drain away.

"How do we proceed?" I asked.

"It depends on what and who's behind it. What's going on down there is new. I mean new in the sense that the Klan hasn't been very big or all that busy over in Rincon in a long while."

"*Droga*! It's not just a few redneck cops?" I blurted out. "The damn Klukkers are involved?"

A hit squad was formed to flush out Stetson Kennedy whose Klan spying caused such a rage among its members. Kennedy immediately asked to join the group of "ass-tearers" looking for him.

Chapter Fifteen

The sewing machine at Mary and Red Chandler's trailer hummed while her quick fingers made the material fly. Mary could sew Klan robes even if she were blind. It had been fun at first. But she longed for something to break up the monotony of the day. And now with the interminable summer heat, she was growing testy. She hated it all–the trailer, being stuck out in the boondocks several miles north of Rincon with no neighbors, no car, no friends. Total isolation. The one saving grace was the telephone. But only when Red wasn't calling, bugging her, wanting her to do yet another chore for him. As if it could read her thoughts, the phone rang, startling her. In case it was Red calling, she raced to the TV to turn off the sound. *Oprah* cut to a commercial. Good, she wouldn't miss much of the show. "Hello," she said tentatively, hoping it wasn't her husband telephoning, but knowing it was.

"Do you always have to sound so bored?" He snarled.

"What do you want, Red? I have to get these robes done for tomorrow night."

"How are the boys?" he asked, butting in.

She sighed lightly. "Not as bad as yesterday." He never asked about her, but she always wished for it. Stupid!

"I got to work a double."

"Oh, I'm sorry," she replied with fake pity. "We'll miss you." What a bold-faced lie! Mary didn't mind Red working double shifts. With three kids and another on the way, they desperately needed the money. Having him underfoot constantly is what got her into this mess anyway. Thank goodness he'd finally found another job.

"How many robe orders did you get?"

"Four," she lied, cutting two off the figure. "Why?" She had learned to be forever alert, always on guard. With Red, there was always something simmering just under the surface.

"No reason. Just trying to show my wife some appreciation. What's your problem?" His voice was getting that sharpness that had become all too familiar.

"I'm sorry." Must she always apologize for everything she did in life? "It's the heat. Coming up on the hottest part of the day. Jerrod kept me up most of the night with his fever."

"Well, that *is* wimmin's work. You complaining 'bout that now?"

"No! No! Just explaining. That's all."

"Hmm. Okay. Well, goodbye."

She hung up the phone more despondent than when she'd answered. This was the sum total of her life after a bright high school term? So far, she'd accomplished having babies and sewing uniforms for the Klan. There was no set fee for the work. People paid what they could, the Klavern subsidized the rest. But more important to her, Red hadn't thought to put the two fees together, so he didn't question the small amounts when he demanded that she turn over her earnings. She'd asked Red to get a vasectomy after the second child, but his face turned a dark shade to suit his nickname and he'd indignantly lectured her about not having *his* body parts interfered with. She then volunteered to have her tubes tied but he wouldn't have it. Did he stick around to help take care of his offspring? Red only liked her when she was pregnant. Said it was her duty for the Cause.

Before Mary sewed the Klan patch on the sleeve she turned up the TV volume feeling like she was doing something illegal. Her husband demand-ed that she not watch Oprah because she was "colored". He'd caught her once, several years ago, and punched her in the face. When she arrived at her parents, crying and bruised, her father scolded her for disobeying Red and for fleeing the beating. Then her mom started in on her. The "good provider" song and dance. Mary should be content with a man like Red. She even believed it for a while.

Then she realized she had to do something or she'd drown. The despair in her life weighed down on her like a cement shroud. Now Mary walked a dangerous path and had to be careful that her husband didn't, nor anyone else, find out. But it was time something good happened to her, no matter how small. She yearned to be able to think about herself instead of Red. Always Red and the boys.

Her youngest son, Timmy, came racing into the room, his toy gun firing away at an imaginary target. She looked at him–red curls, fair skin and freckles–a mirror image of her husband. Timmy aimed the gun toward the TV screen, sighting the barrel on Oprah's face. He cocked it, just like his daddy taught him. Mary watched him squeeze the trigger. "Bang, bang. You dead, nigger."

Stetson Kennedy's work helped Georgia revoke the Klan's national charter. He then attempted to establish it outside the state, appointing himself as Imperial Wizard. He appointed a Catholic, a Jew, an African-American, a Native American, and a Japanese-American as charter members. Had his attempt been successful he would have had control of the Klan's name and uniform, prohibiting any racist group from calling themselves the Ku Klux Klan. Kennedy, over forty years later, is still fighting racism while the Klan continues to retaliate against him for his efforts.

Chapter Sixteen

Al visibly blanched as soon as he heard me utter damn. So, he had a bit of the "good ol' boy" in him–females are ladies and should conduct them-selves appropriately. I filed that away in my mental data bank.

"There's been one or two hate incidents in Rincon during the last few months. But nothing that unusual." Al rushed on. "I'm not downplaying any of it. Any place where there are a few Klansmen, you'll always have something hateful going on. Our information is that it's a very small group. Rincon doesn't have a problem that's any more or less than other small towns. Bias crimes last year for the town were three or four. Mostly gutless acts–when no one is around to witness it. Racists flyers in public places, bricks thrown through an AME church window. There's always name calling and the occasional truck load of rednecks driving down the middle of Rincon waving the rebel flag. Note that a minute ago I said the *reported* hate crimes. Our intelligence always uncovers some that were not reported.

"Law enforcement is now tasked to track hate crimes, but there are problems. This type of incident is hard to prove or solve and often is considered the least of a police department's worries. They feel they have bigger issues. Some states don't have any hate crime statutes, so what can you track? Also, victims are afraid to report the event. Some are afraid of repercussions." Al paused and looked at me with those intense eyes. "To make it even more complicated, the acts aren't always perpetrated by the same people or groups. Harder to trace, get a handle on it."

"Great," was all I could come up with.

"I haven't heard any rumblings along the grapevine about anything heating up in Rincon. And I haven't heard about any specific group or person targeted for harm."

"Until now," I said. Aggie agreed with me, her head bobbing like a fishing float on water. "Al, if the Rincon hate scene is like you've just described–then what the heck is going on?" I meant with Dixie, but Al didn't need clarification.

"I don't know, sugah, but I've got contacts all over creation. My group is spread thin right now. We got several big cases coming up, but I'll get one of them to start gathering intelligence."

"That sounds like a contradiction in terms–hate groups and intelligence." They thought that was cute. So did I.

Al adopted a serious demeanor. "It could be that Dixie or someone in her family ticked off the wrong person."

I stood up, zooming in on a need to pace–as if that itself would set in motion getting Dixie out of harms way. "Okay. But who, then? No one has done or said anything indicating that–except the doofus cops. And I don't think they are smart enough to be acting alone. Finding Dixie sitting in the bushes at night–okay, it may be strange except at a nature reserve–but it isn't illegal. What could she have done, or appeared to, that made the cops go after her like they did?"

"Honey, it could be because they were bored, had too much arrogance that night, and happened upon the type of person they focus their hatred on–a black person. And Dixie was the one." Aggie spoke gently and I noticed that her hands pulled the thread with more ease. But it didn't last long. She was soon fulminating about hate mongers, Grainger mostly, and yanking hard on the thread after completing each half of an X.

Al walked to a small corner table and poured three glasses of water over lots of ice. "She's right, Paloma. That just might be the reason."

"Merda, porcaria, aqueles desgraçados." I threw my hands up in defeat and plopped back down into the chair amid a whoosh of air.

"Spanish?" Aggie and Al asked in unison while Al passed around the water.

"Portuguese." I gulped my water down. Umm. The cold liquid was as refreshing as a plunge into a cool ocean. When I saw their questioning gazes I continued. "My Polish father traveled to Brazil, met and married my Brazilian mother."

"What, exactly, did you say?" He had to ask.

"Ah, it's a bit hard to translate," I fibbed to save a bit of face and virtue. I had a problem holding my tongue, but at least most people were clueless to my obscene name calling when it was done in another language. "It's like an expression of–oh, my goodness, what's the world coming to," I supplied hoping my face didn't broadcast the true meaning of your basic four-letter blasphemies.

Aggie scrutinized me thoroughly which caused my cheeks to flame an embarrassing scarlet. She saw right through me! "Paloma's a different one, cousin Alvin!" Aggie leered across the desk at him. He seemed flustered, taking his turn flattening the carpet with his shoe. I missed something between the two of them, but they didn't enlighten me.

"What were we talking about before my cousin so rudely inter-rupted us?" Al asked while Aggie let that one pass without vocal or facial comment.

"Paloma doesn't seem to be warming to the idea that what has happened to Dixie could just, ah, happen, no reason other than another person's ignorance and hatred."

"Ma'am, it's not that I don't believe it. I–I guess I'm just so far removed from that type of mindset."

"We understand."

"Dixie and I both have had a little experience with racism. Some people consider me white, others don't. And of course, Dixie is black. She doesn't go for the African-American label. What was shocking to us, at least at our ages when this occurred, was that we each were hassled by our own race. About hanging around with each other. Dixie and her family received more flack. They were called oreos, chastised for being educated, or by sounding white or acting "too white". What does that mean? I remember being surprised that minorities, who should be sensitive to discrimination and happy that we were color blind, expected us to hang with our own kind. But fortunately it didn't happen a lot on the island. Before the tourism boom, we were a small group trying to survive, especially during the off-season. It was also unique from mainland living because there was a greater influence from other people and cultures from all over the country and world. Once when I was in Florida, this guy got in my face and screamed that I was a "damn Cuban who comes up from Miami to steal crop picking jobs from decent true Americans"."

"What did you say to that?" Aggie asked, looking up at me.

"I replied with sign language." Al kept a poker face and offered no comment. Aggie chortled, satisfied with my answer. I continued. "As for how racism affects our country or any facts or impact studies, I'm clueless. I can surf the web this afternoon. If it *is* true that Dixie is solely a victim of hate, I'd feel more comfortable if I had a better grasp of the subject."

Al seemed pleased with my plan. "For years the Center here has been gathering intelligence and sharing it with anybody who is interested. We've researched the data extensively and have professionals analyze it from nine ways to Sunday. If you like, you can take some with you."

"Please, sir."

"Enough of polite Southern manners. That 'sir' business is making me feel old."

I resisted the urge to reply "yes, sir". It was an expected quip, but I often do the unexpected. "Al, do you think Grainger could be up to something? Maybe Lemond, then Dixie, got in the way?" I asked.

Al took his time before answering. I'd noticed that habit previously and liked that he gave my questions serious thought. "Grainger's racism is no secret, but in the past he's always needed an audience or an agenda. With what you witnessed this morning, Paloma–blatantly disregarding the law when it would be so easy to expose his actions, not to mention brutality..." He threw up his hands in supplication.

Aggie butted in with, "I don't believe he's doing this just because he got up on the wrong side of the bed."

"As I've said before, there hasn't been a major presence of Klan in Rincon in many years," Al reiterated, leaning back in his chair. "But when there is a recession, the disenfranchised and uneducated want something or someone to blame their situation on. There has been an increase in minorities–Asian and Hispanic–moving into areas that have for decades, maybe even the past century, been all white or all black. Minority migration gets those that believe they are alienated all riled up." Al rustled through the papers on his desk. "I have some of the latest data we've compiled–if I can find the right pile." Although the stacks were neat, his desk was completely hidden. This could take time.

The seconds ticked by slowly. I sat thumping my foot. "If the Klan is almost a non-presence there, who's bankrolling the eavesdropping equipment in the jail? Certainly not a small town police department."

He stopped mid-movement and gawked at me. "Sugah, you are full of surprises! Pray tell, how you found out about bugs in little ol' Rincon jail."

Big, fat mouth, Paloma. Al didn't seem upset about it so I sat tall, eager to brag about my gadgets. "I came equipped with an acoustic noise generator and bug detector." Al walked to his bookcase and opened the cabinet.

"You mean like this?" He pulled out earlier generations of the same equipment and gave them to me. "You are interested in this kind of electronics?"

"Very much. Tools of my trade." I explained my work in detail, expanding on my earlier explanation of being a computer security analyst while I grabbed my pack and pulled out gear. I left out my recently unemployed status. Like two proud men comparing their new sports cars, we showed off the prowess of our devices while Aggie showed her disinterest with an occasional head shake and tsk, tsk. But she never stopped stitching.

"So, Al, you have a problem with eavesdropping?"

"At the office initially–until we got smart. A law enforcement friend turned me onto these gadgets. After we sued the Cobb County Klan and won–which shut them down by the way–it all went crazy. When the GBI–Georgia Bureau of Investigations–stepped in to help, they found bugs everywhere, even the bathroom."

"Maybe the john looked like a Klan think tank." They both laughed, Aggie less reserved than Al. I chatted about his equipment and the new models available, taking over briefly until I realized I had commandeered the conversation. "Sorry. I didn't mean to prattle on. I'm obsessed with techno-logy."

Al touched my arm with two warm fingers. "Don't worry, sugah. It's refreshing to meet a woman so interested in these things! And such a pretty one at that."

Aggie seemed surprised by his remarks. She had one hand against her cheek perfectly imitating Jack Benny's dumbfounded look. I blushed and grinned like a Cheshire cat–or "Chessie cat" in Southern-ese. So much for subtlety! Drooling and heavy breathing surely must be just around the corner. "Thank you," I replied and felt myself blush. Aggie went back to her stitchery, keeping an eye on Al every now and then like a mother with her child in a china shop.

"Which hate group is the most destructive?" I asked to get us away from more personal conversation.

"The scariest, most violent are the Skinheads. Many are teenagers. Gary, one of my operatives, followed a recruiter for the Skins several years ago. The guy hung out in parks and other areas where youth go. When he found someone who seemed lost or didn't fit in, he'd talk to them. Some kids have bad home lives, others live on the streets. Along comes a guy who seems friendly, concerned and offers them a place to live. Kids are very impressionable."

"The recruiters are pimps," I said. "They peddle hate."

"That's a good way of putting it." Al nodded as he played a good host by refilling our water glasses. "Our material will give you a good synopsis of what we're dealing with. It's surprising how some people think it's mainly a Southern problem."

I heard a ship's horn out on the river. It was a comforting sound to the water rat in me, in sharp contrast to our discussion. "Tennes-see–wasn't that the birthplace of the Klan?"

Al nodded. "Lately Tennessee's actually reduced the number of active organizations. You have to look at the nation entirely. It's certainly not just a 'Southern thing'. For years Idaho has been a hot spot for hate groups, even before all the recent news about militia groups. Mind if I give you a bit of background?"

"Please."

"The Christian Identity was started by Wesley Swift in the late 1950's believing white Christians in Northern Europe and America are the true Israelites. A former aerospace engineer, Richard Girnt Butler, was a member and in 1974, moved from California to the Idaho panhandle and built a compound called Church of Jesus Christ Christian. The Aryan Nations was formed from that group, which spawned a paramilitary group, the Silent Brotherhood, more commonly know as The Order."

"Each time they breed, the offspring is more violent," Aggie added. "The younger hate mongers get into that wild rock music. What's it called, Al? Something like death stuff."

"Death metal. Groups like *Slayer, Seig Heil*," I added, finally able to contribute in the discussion. "You mentioned that newer hate group–The Or-der. I remember them. They were busy, weren't they?" I asked.

"Yes. The Order was into large robberies. They also bombed and attack-ed minorities and federal officers and murdered people brave enough to speak out against them. They were known to stockpile weapons, especially MAC 10's."

"Wow!" I exclaimed. "MACs are automatics, machine guns. And illegal. They were created for one purpose. To kill. They fire so many bullets in a few seconds that you can't use them for anything else. Not hunting. You'd decimate a rhino in a blink of an eye. A MAC bullet can go through a cement wall."

"I'm impressed again, sugah!"

While he looked me over, I got back down to business quickly. "What group was Timothy McVeigh affiliated with? He was into some book–like a Bible for far-right extremists, right?"

"Yes. The *Turner Diaries*. McVeigh's actions in Oklahoma City were almost verbatim from a section of the book–from renting the truck, the type of materials and how to mix them into a bomb."

"Who wrote it? Some yahoo who took ten years graduating from elementary school?" I asked, feeling clever.

Al smiled briefly. "Unfortunately, no. If it had been, perhaps it wouldn't have made such an impact. William Pierce wrote the *Turner Diaries*, in 1978. Pierce has a doctorate in physics, taught at Oregon State and is the leader of the National Alliance, another neo-Nazi group. All of these groups have affiliations with each other. His book portrays the violent overthrow of the federal government, and systematic killing of Jews and non-whites in order to establish an Aryan world. Like McVeigh, the *Turner Diaries* was the inspiration for The Order. They committed murders, robberies, counterfeiting, and bombings. Their leader, Robert Mathews, said the bank robberies they committed were the beginning of the American Nazi revolution depicted in the *Turner Diaries,* and from that, an independent Aryan nation would be created in the Pacific Northwest after their huge race war. Mathews was killed in a shootout with the FBI in 1984. Most of the other leaders are serving long prison terms." Al knew his stuff. He didn't need any cheat sheets to recall the data.

"If you bear with me another moment. You'll see something taking shape." I nodded for him to continue. "The Order's leader is dead but not the revolutionary movement. The next one to hit the news was Tom Metzger of WAR–White Aryan Resistance. He was significant because he embraced technology like David Duke did a three-piece suit. In the early 1980's, his group had a cable TV show *Race and Reason*, a computer bulletin board, a newspaper *and* a hate line. As in toll-free." Al handed me pamphlets he'd dug out of the stack he'd been rifling through. "Nowadays, William Pierce and other groups who've kept their agendas hidden somewhat, are embracing the media and going beyond what Metzger did. Pierce created a publishing business which pushes such notorious titles as *Mein Kampf, The International Jew*, and of course, his own tomes. They even had tax exempt status for a while, until the IRS stripped it away. Pierce appealed. The Anti-Defamation League and other similar groups submitted a brief about Pierce and his agenda to the U.S. Court of Appeals. The Court upheld the IRS ruling. Pierce edits hate bulletins for the National Alliance. They create a racist comics series and have web sites. You name it, they'll utilize it."

"Al, I read in one of my computer magazines a few months ago that there are now ethnic cleansing computer games! *Droga!* These web sites and comic books zero directly into our country's youth. It's more effective and reaches a wider audience than going around parks and places where kids hang out. So," I continued as my brain raced to sort out and comprehend all this new information. "Now these groups are embracing the technology of today via public media. That takes lots of money. If they are not wealthy then they have to get it from somewhere."

"Exactly," Al picked up, smiling broadly at me. "You catch on quickly. They are like organized crime units that do what they can, mostly illegal, to get funds. Or you have groups like Osama bin

Laden's. In his case, he had tons of his own money from the very beginning."

"Al, what about women, girls? Dixie has told me often that they're be-coming more involved in gangs, violent crimes and such. Do they have any kind of presence in hate or militia groups?"

Al glanced at his watch before answering. "Certainly." He paused. "You'd like Tom Metzger's daughter." He grinned suddenly and kept his eyes on me.

"And this would be because...?"

"*Miss* Metzger has stated that a Jewish woman started the feminist movement to get other women into man-bashing and to lower the white birth rate by getting women out of the home. She and her followers believe that the primary function of women is to give support to their men and have babies."

"I can see how that would be an irritant to most *normal* women," I said sardonically.

"The men in the hate groups are known to disappear on 'secret missions,' which usually means they are out cheating on their wives. But that kind of behavior is taboo for the women. But their roles are changing somewhat in these groups. There is an excellent study on women racists that I've included with the information I have for you." Al checked his watch again. I took it as a signal to be on my way and crossed the floor to stand beside Aggie.

"I'd better leave so you can start on this situation with Dixie. May I ask what you have in mind?"

"You may. Didn't Aggie tell you I was a snake charmer? I've had a few run-ins with Sheriff Grainger. I know what makes him tick." Aggie and Al exchanged another meaningful glance.

"*Legal!*" As in *lee-gál*, the Portuguese equivalent for "that's cool"! "*Maravilhoso!*" Wonderful!

"I'm glad you're pleased, sugah." Al's voice was deeper, sexier and I could feel myself blushing again. This was a strange reaction to a man I'd just met and I wondered if I'd suffered brain damage during my Seal Beach attack.

"Thank you for such quick action," I told him.

"I need to make a few calls first, take care of some items. Cousin dear, are you going to be around this evening? Then why don't we take Paloma out to dinner."

"Pirate's House?" Aggie asked excitedly then looked to me. I nodded.

Al smiled. "Of course. I need to speak to Paloma a moment." With no sass Aggie packed up and left. Al took over the chair she'd vacated and motioned for me to sit beside him.

"Is this about a retainer?"

He shook his head. "That's not why I asked you to stay behind. I wanted to make sure you are satisfied with me as Dixie's attorney. Aggie is a bit overwhelming at times, but she means well."

"She certainly does. I did come south prepared to hire an attorney. But Dixie should have the final say-so."

"Absolutely. The Law Center works *pro bono*, so don't worry about a fee. Although donations are accepted." He smiled companionably. "Paloma, Grainger and his cronies usually aren't accommodating. How did you get in to see your friend today?"

"*Mandinga*." Puzzled, Al squinted at me. "Brazilian witchcraft."

He chuckled. "Sugah, I better keep my eye on you." I feigned innocence. His smile was replaced by seriousness. "If Dixie agrees, I think it's best right now to find out what they're charging her with, then get her out of jail. I think *that* is top priority. Then we can go after the ones who hurt her."

"Sounds okay to me. Clear it with Dixie. What about Lemond?"

"Who? Oh, yes, sorry. I get tunnel vision. The truth is," he admitted, shrugging his shoulders. "His disappearance is out of my league. I know a GBI agent who might be interested, but unless we find out more, there isn't clear-cut, tangible evidence to prove Lemond didn't just take off."

"What about Klan involvement? Wouldn't that get the feds into it?"

He shook his head. "Not on rumors only. Don't get me wrong. That'll make them, uh, perk up. But..."

"They'd need something tangible," I finished for him.

"I'm sorry, Paloma. We can keep on Grainger, ask for progress reports on what he's doing to find Lemond. He'll have to do something then. Once Grainger knows I'm looking out for Dixie, he'll be more compliant. Even if the Klan is involved. He's smart enough to know it can blow up in his face–big time." He smiled reassuringly. I stood and he escorted me to the door, hand on my elbow like the Southern gentleman he was.

"Thanks again for everything, Al. I was thinking of shopping for Dixie. She doesn't have anything with her. And I want to get something to cheer her up and to pass the time."

"No glass is allowed inside the cells. Make anything you buy non-threatening, easy to search." He gave me the run-down on River Street shopping. I asked about Jordan almonds. "A vice of mine."

"There's several candy stores. I'll have reservations for dinner at seven."

"I'll check in now, then drop off a copy of the CD of Dixie's injuries. I'll leave it with Kevin."

"Perfect. Enjoy your afternoon, sugah." He retreated into his office with a smile of straight, white teeth a dental hygienist would love and closed the door behind him. I left with Aggie, lost in thoughts about Al. Wondered, supposed, assumed. One thing was certain. He *was* a charmer! Then I wondered about me. I'm not easily captivated. And I hadn't even minded the "sugah" part.

President Warren G. Harding was inducted into the Klan in a robed and masked ceremony conducted in the Green Room of the White House. He took the oath while using the White House Bible. To obey the edicts of the Imperial Wizard, Harding presented William Simmons with a War Department license plate for his limousine as a token of esteem. The license plate exempted the driver from traffic citations.

Chapter Seventeen

Now that Swartzman had nearly completed the three-mile drive to Rincon's jail, the temperature inside his Lexus was finally comfortable. He slowed as the car ahead turned into Moonpie's driveway. He stepped on his brakes, jaw dropping in surprise. "Sandra Brice? Can't be. Not at Moon-pie's. Besides, she said tomorrow." Swartzman memorized the tag number as a precaution, noting the rental bumper sticker. He wanted to wait, verify who got out of the car. But in these boonies, he was as noticeable as a naked man at a church social. Speeding away, he called the plant ordering Red off the loading dock and to get near Moonpie's to tail her visitor. A little paranoia is healthy.

He drove into the dirt lot of the jail and slammed on the brakes making dust fly. He watched the two worthless deputies fan the air and cough. Once it'd settled, he climbed out very amused with himself. Grainger greeted him at the door. Swartzman, ignoring the humorless man's protestations about errands to run, walked into his private office.

"What you got to drink?"

"Yukon Jack, Pepsi."

"I'll take a Pepsi. You need to get something decent to entertain your guests." Grainger's handkerchief was on his desk. Swartzman used it to wipe his face and neck while the sheriff begrudgingly left to wrestle the soda machine.

"Grainger," Swartzman said when the sheriff had returned. "You can't think of something useful for those two deputies to do other than stake out the porch?" He sipped the soda.

"It's a slow day."

"But you don't think ahead. You have to be proactive, not reactive. That's why you'll never get very far. They should be out training for our mission, finding recruits. We need more young blood in the White Rebel Force."

"They're so dim-witted, I'm not sure they could find their way out of a Croaker sack," Grainger admitted.

"Send 'em to me. I'll whip 'em into shape." He remained standing, forcing Grainger to look up at him. "I got something for you." He tossed a large manilla envelope on Grainger's desk.

"What about her?" Grainger asked, holding the photos of Paloma. "She's already been here. My boys told me they sent her packing sand. I figured you already knew it."

"Yeah. I got a tail on her."

"What the hell are you doing then? Checking up on me?"

"Smart man. Good thing you passed the test. Any questions?" Grainger shook his head. "I have a rental car for you to trace." He scribbled the tag number on a letter Grainger had just spent one hour typing with his two index fingers. "I need it ASAP. Call me." Swartzman strutted out of the building.

"You jerk," Grainger yelled into the empty office. "You parade your Yankee butt in here like you own the place. You can't push me around! *I'm* the sheriff." He crumpled the letter and tossed it at the door. "Shearhouse! Pitman!" When he got no answer he headed swiftly out of his office. "You piss-poor officers want to come in here?" The two men moved quickly inside.

"Find out who rented this car." He motioned for one of them to pick up the piece of paper. "When you have the information, radio me," he said crisply. "And I need this yesterday." Grainger shut the door behind him, stalked outside to his car and drove off.

* * *

It was time. For months Brice had worked and reworked the WRF Women's Auxiliary plans and speeches anticipating this moment. Finally the chance to stomp all the patronizing company men into the ground. And then take charge. In the growing dusk she watched the women motor across the river to the island dock. Only she and Swartzman had keys to this property and he was in Savannah now, busy doing the bunch of nothing she'd ordered. Brice walked the short, narrow path through the woods to the cabin and waited, her heart thumping in excitement.

While the women filed in, Brice consulted the notepad of information Moonpie had collected on each of them. None of it was earth shattering, but the more you knew of a person, the easier to manipulate. The women all had two things in common–their husband's membership in the WRF and low-to middle-class social stature. Only a few worked outside the home–something that needed to stop. All had at least one child. They would need more. Moonpie counted heads and signaled that everyone had arrived. Brice ordered her outside to the boat dock as a lookout for anyone plagued with unwanted curiosity. She did so grudgingly, bottom lip poking out.

"Moonpie!" Brice put an arm around her shoulders. "Don't be upset. You're doing a wonderful job helping me."

"Really?" Moonpie reacted to affection like a slobbering puppy.

"Yes, you know I don't compliment unless I mean it. You gathered great information on the women."

"That's stuff everybody knows."

"But that's what I asked for. Now I need you to be our security watch for tonight. You are the only person I trust to make sure no outsider discovers us." Her words, the lies, worked easily on ears not used to hearing compliments. "Go down to the dock. Watch for any boats. Anyone who isn't suppose to be here."

"What if I see sumpthin'?"

"Stop them."

"How?"

Brice sighed heavily. "Send them away."

"How?"

"Can't you figure anything out for yourself?" Brice barked loudly. Oh, no. The girl was going to cry. Her chin quivered like her thighs. "Look," the Bostonian spoke with conciliation. "Just go out there. If someone comes along, keep them busy. Any way you can," she added hastily to avoid more of Moonpie's single-worded questions. "Go. You can do it."

"You bet, Brice. I'd do anything for you." Moonpie left the small building with a businesslike gait. She was on a mission. Not that she had a clue what, exactly, that mission was supposed to be.

Brice stared at the large woman's retreating figure. Moonpie could not grasp the concept of control or being controlled. And Brice instantly spotted that weakness in the woman. She had learned very early in life which side of power to be on. And men, white men, most often held that power. So she pushed, twisted and cajoled every situation with a man, steadily working toward her goal. To steal their power. To be the one in control. Brice had learned that with many, it was simple. Pretend to be the woman that their insipid egos lusted for. And men became very stupid around the three B's—bed, broads and booze. They'd tell their mistresses *everything*.

Secrets held for years, kept from spouses, would be unleashed to meld together with the restrained desires and frayed ambitions of married men. These men squander away the vitality of passion and living. They keep their secrets and desires from the *one* person they should be sharing them with. But inevitably the relationship, the women and any and all possibilities of an exciting, wondrous life would be tossed aside. Only to lay dormant in the ruts, worn-out and weary, in the complacency that marriage propagates.

*　　*　　*

"I take at least two showers a day in the summer. Lawd me, that sure felt good!" Aggie emerged from the hotel bathroom wearing a pink flowered sleeveless dress–a vast difference from her olive uniform.

I showered next, beads of sweat forming on my forehead before I'd finished drying myself. Lawd me, I hate humidity. "You seem prepared for anything," I said, indicating the small case from which she, like a magician pulling an unending succession of rabbits out of a hat, removed toiletries, a stack of reports, her cross-stitch, and a paperback novel.

"I never know what I'm going to stick my nose into next! My car is mainly an extension of my closet."

"Speaking of cars."

She finished for me. "I've got an appointment near River Street and I'll walk. If there is time afterward, I have a ton of paperwork to do, which I'll work on this afternoon. Al will collect me for dinner. You go on and do whatever you need."

Last chance to be nosy. "Aggie, what is it with this Grainger guy?"

"Are you asking why do Al and I detest him?" I nodded. "He's an asshole bigot." She spoke so vehemently I didn't dare smile at her bluntness. "When Al first moved here to start the Center, he practically camped out at the jail–there were so many black people needing his help."

"I see."

"Not completely." She took a deep breath before answering. "Grainger is Al's step-brother." With that zinger, Aggie left for her appointment.

Oklahoma: 1953–A state court deprived Jean Field of custody of her two daughters due to letters she had sent them while they were visiting their grandparents, counseling them against racial prejudice. The children were placed in their father's custody although he had deserted the family for ten years and admitted in court he was an alcoholic, a forger and had committed incest.

Chapter Eighteen

Across the river where the women embarked on their boat ride, four of Swartzman's WRF men argued over who would be the babysitter for the night.

"As I recollect, it was me last time." Andy, a forklift operator, stated firm-ly and turned away to dig another beer out of the cooler.

"You did not, you lyin' sumbitch." Willie, whose mouth often got him in trouble, his brain never quite figuring out why, challenged Andy while adjusting himself in the crotch. A cap of some sort was always perched on Willie's head, hiding a receding hairline. Even when making love, the WRF men speculated. He had a special rack to wash his ever-expanding collection and in the dishwasher, of all places! When the gadget had arrived in the mail, he'd carried it around for a week, showing everyone, slipping the cap over it and repeating often, "ain't this the dangdest thang you ever seen?" When not in use, the rack was hung with honor among caps, stuffed fish, and mounted deer heads, all which wrapped around his garage walls four times. "Red had 'er last," Willie blabbered. "I seen his car at her trailer." The men sniggered.

Red swung around and shoved his fist into Willie's stomach, doubling him over with a groan. Willie sacrificed the beer to keep his hat in place. The men stood dumbfounded as the can rolled down the concrete slope, the river swallowing it up.

"Hey, Red whatcha hidin', actin' dat way wid Willie?" Andy dared to ask. The guys cackled, empowering him to push a little further. "Stop wasting good beer." Red stood with his fists clenched, challenging. He stepped toward them.

"You dumb country bumpkins. I can't leave you for a minute." They all jumped at Swartzman's voice. They parted the circle to allow the newcomer to move into the middle. "Have you decided?"

"We wuz fixin' to," Andy replied.

Swartzman placed the night vision goggles in his nylon bag and picked up pine straw from the ground. "Everybody take a piece. Shortest straw wins."

"You mean loses," Andy snorted.

"Oh, man!" Willie stomped as he compared his short straw to the others. "This just ain't my night!" Andy imitated Moonpie dancing at the Last Chance, pretending to knock over tables and people as his hips swayed from side to side.

"Cut the crap. Let's get to work." Swartzman ordered. "Andy, you're lookout here. Red, after you drop me off, take the boat and anchor it half way. I'll signal when I'm through."

"What am I suppose to do?" Willie asked his boss.

"I need thirty minutes. Keep that cow Moonpie occupied. How you do it is up to you."

* * *

Brice passed out leaflets warning of the trouble ahead with inferior races and the rise of feminism. "Ladies! Let's get down to business." Their voices fell away. "When I started, I hoped for a group of the best women in town. With all the work you've been doing, I see that I got what I wanted." Brice paused, letting the praise sink in. "You are all aware of the struggle your men have been enduring in the fight for their families. Now's the time for you to help them! We need good, Christian women like you." Brice pointed and swept the crowd. "You can help save this country from the Jewish-Communist government and from the feminist dykes. We must stem the tide of MUD that comes into this country to get a free ride off our tax dollars."

In the darkness, Moonpie could hear Brice's charismatic voice and found it comforting during her lonely sentry. Brice would definitely come out on top. She listened as her friend named great leaders who had fought for white power–Hitler, then through a list of men she'd never heard of. Moonpie realized the local Imperial Wizard, Wyman Hughes' name wasn't mentioned. He was a has-been. Everybody knew that.

She turned to scan the river wondering what she'd do if someone came along. Shrugging her shoulders, she walked the path by the river as Brice instructed. At the north side she paused. Her breath was knocked out of her with a deep thump and she fell to the ground.

"Hey, Moonie, Moonie." It took a moment for her to realize the person busy rolling her over and climbing on top was Willie.

"Willie, you moron. That hurt!" Willie grinned and sucked on her neck. The salty taste of sweat and the flowery smell of cheap perfume fused on his tongue. He pulled harder on her skin. "You animal," she said playfully.

"Yee-hi!"

"Shhh!" she said putting a finger to her lips.

"Why?" He nibbled the spot he'd just sucked on.

"Someone might hear!"

"And just who might that be?"

"I can't tell you," she whispered. Willie thrust his leg between hers and made jerky upward motions.

"Not even if I make you happy?"

She squirmed until he was off her. "I thought you didn't want to be with me anymore. You haven't called or come by." He put his hand on her stomach and jiggled it, feeling the fat quiver. "Willie, you know I don't like that."

"And you know I like my women big." He made pig sounds as he rooted around her bosom.

"Be quiet!"

"Who's gonna know?" He stood.

"Your wife, for one."

"Then let's get in the boat."

"You don't care she's here?"

"She's doing her share for the white cause. As long as she goes straight home to fix my supper, I don't care. Let's go, Moonie."

"I can't. I have to stay and keep an eye on things."

"Good job you're doing," he said getting up. "I snuck right up on you." He grasped Moonpie's arms, helping her back on her feet. "We can keep watch from the boat. That'll be better anyhow." Moonpie agreed.

Willie eased them into the current without starting the engine. Moonpie searched the boat. "Willie, you forgot to bring something to drink." She turned away annoyed. "Hey, there's somebody outside the cabin. Look!" She pointed, making jabs in the air toward Swartzman silhouetted in the cabin light. "Turn the boat around, Willie." Her voice grew louder with each syllable. Willie's hands felt clammy.

"Lord, get me outta here," he mumbled.

"What are you going on about, Willie?" Last time, she'd gotten so wild he'd gotten a little scared. Thought she was going to rip it right off him. Now her loud mouth was going to let everyone know clear to damnation what was going on. He quickly anchored the boat urging her in desperation to keep quiet.

Her back was still turned as she hollered again about the interloper. With absolutely no finesse, Willie thrust his hand as far up the dress she'd outgrown thirty pounds back allowed. The sounds coming out her mouth now were more of a purr. "Good golly, you ain't got a stitch a' underdrawers on, Moonpie."

"You know I like to be ready." That's what he was afraid of. She turned quickly, pulling him into her body and locked her lips onto his, making smacking sounds when Willie pulled back startled. She slid the dress over her head and sat down on the bottom of the small boat, hips squeaking against the fiberglass as she wedged herself between the seats. Moonpie closed her eyes and moaned loudly. He watched her hand slide down across her large stomach and head directly to her crotch. Willie gaped, astounded at her brazenness. She was actually going to touch it! With two fingers, Moonpie spread herself apart. She looked at him and licked her lips clock-wise, just as her book instructed. Willie tried swallowing the lump in his throat and checked the time by pressing the light button on his watch. Swartzman had said half an hour. He hadn't spent this much time a' lustin' on his honeymoon. *Oh, Lordy. Why me?* A long twenty minutes to go.

* * *

They needed a race war, Brice believed, and women were natural leaders. They were most fanatical when their mother-instinct was heightened. "And the women in this room will be at the head of the white parade marching to victory! Imagine a state with only the *chosen* people! No inferior races raping our daughters, murdering our sons, stealing our property for drugs!" The women clapped and cheering heartily. "But most importantly, women will have stepped in to show our battle weary men the way!"

* * *

Swartzman risked looking in the window although he recognized Brice's voice. That idiot Grainger had come through on the tag and car rental trace– hers. Red had tailed Brice to a hotel and was searching the room minutes after Brice left for her not-so-secret meeting.

"Yes!" the women thundered. He moved into the sheltering darkness.

"Good!" Brice told them. "You are a vital force to the cause! We must do what God put women on the earth to do. Deny the feminists who go out of the home and leave their children to raise themselves! If they didn't act like men they'd still have one living in their home! Just the way it should be!" More applause came from the group.

Swartzman had heard enough. He couldn't fault Brice on her delivery. She always could get the troops fired up. It was her backstabbing that tripped her up. And Brice–a mere girl–was trying to take his command out from under him! It was laughable! But any transgression toward him was a move against the Cause and vice versa. He knew how to handle people who crossed him, and Brice, a female, would be easy. Until then he'd have to watch his step. No telling who was in with the bitch. He felt the urge to burst in on the group and teach Brice a lesson in front of everyone. He rein-ed in his emotions and tamped then into a hard ball inside his gut. He left for the dock to signal the boys.

*　　*　　*

"You can't support your men and bear children to help save the white race if you are at an office or going to school! Our strong white men *need* the jobs. They deserve them! Don't you take their reward from them!" Mary Chandler, whose thoughts had drifted, snapped to attention and glanced around furtively. Did someone know she went to school on Tuesday nights? Everyone was looking forward, eyes glued on Brice. She sighed in relief but remained alerted.

"It's the men who need the schooling so they can get good jobs and keep the niggers and greasers from stealing them and ruining American businesses! God only intends for the white man to run this town, this state, this country. We must rally around our men! We have our own branch of the White Rebel Force and we will join with women across the U.S. and Canada. It's what the Good Book tells us," Brice added, remembering she was in the Bible belt. Next time she'd have one for show and tell. *She should have brought the one in her hotel room* she thought. She sipped water and got ready for the next round.

"You must keep a spotless house for your man to come home to after his fight for justice. Keep your family fed with three good meals. No cereal in the morning. Get your tails out of bed and feed them *real* food! The only thing women need to feel loved and honored is to do your man proud–the man God has given to rule over you and guide you. *Submission is joy!*" The women were shifting, energized. The meeting took on a frenzied air. Assignments were given and section leaders chosen to help guide new recruits. Once completed, the women looked expectantly at Brice. Now it was time to seal their allegiance. *Allegiance to me,* Brice thought!

"Ladies, although we have taken major strides in the past few months, I have some sad news about someone here tonight. Someone who has been undermining the cause." Brice's voice seemed to thunder in Mary's ears. Everyone looked around accusingly. Mary was frozen in her chair, her heart pounding furiously.

"Who's the traitor?" Enid shouted, fists clenched with rage.

"Why don't we let her tell us? Confess and ask forgiveness! Now, or it'll be too late!" Brice paused. No one was blameless and this tactic usually worked to root out any troublemakers, therefore she rarely needed to spy on the female members. The conscience did the work for her. "Come, ladies. Don't we want to help our wayward sister?" The group searched through the audience again. Mary forced herself to look around. Veronica, a fervent follower of the cause, could contain herself no longer. She jumped to her feet, red-faced and shrieked, "I know who it is!"

"Who?" the women roared.

"It's my own sister!" Mary's relief was almost audible. She was safe for a little while longer. However, Veronica's sister, Missy, paled. The two women on either side grabbed her arms pulling her to her feet. Missy tugged and twisted uselessly.

"I ain't done nothing! She's lying!" Her blue eyes opened wide in fright.

"My sister has been taking birth control pills!" Veronica shrieked, standing to face her sister.

"Veronica, how could you do this? You're my sister!"

"Missy." Brice spoke controlled and even. "You know that's against the cause. You have secretly undermined it by making yourself barren. She," Brice's voice rose, "has willingly lied to us!"

"What I do to my own body is no business of yours!" Missy shrilled. The women converged around her, pushing and pulling her toward the front.

"Repent!" Veronica commanded. "Repent, you conniving whore!"

"Go to hell," her sister shot back. The women hissed at her impudence, spitting and slapping Missy's face.

"What's the punishment for our fallen sister?" Enid yelled. Brice pulled over a large cardboard box. Enid flipped the top and passed out the contents. "This is great, Brice," Veronica said, grabbing a wooden rolling pin and wielding it like a knife.

"My husband's gonna get all of you if you hurt me!"

"If that's so, then why was he so angry when I told him what you'd been doin'?" Veronica's nose was almost touching her sister's. Missy's mouth opened, spittle sliding down her chin. Her eyelids fluttered as she fainted, but the women held her limp body up. Brice gave a sharp slap on each cheek that brought Missy around. "Let's beat some sense into the heathen!"

"Remember how I taught you–injure, not maim."

"White power!" Veronica yelled striking first. *Whack*!

"White power!" the women chorused. *Whack! Whack*! "White power!" *Whack*! "White power!"

Georgia: 1964–Lieutenant Colonel Lemuel A. Penn, World War II veteran and Army Reservist from Washington, D.C. spent his active duty training at Fort Benning with two other black officers. Penn was driving outside of Athens and heading for home, when his car was overtaken by members of Robert Shelton's United Klans of America (UKA). The Colonel was killed instantly by a shotgun blast in the jaw. The other men were asleep and slumped down in the car, escaping injury. Penn had not been safe in the country he'd fought to defend. James Lakey, UKA member, confessed he was driving; Howard Sims and Cecil Myers fired the shots. Sims and Myers were acquitted of murder. The federal government brought civil rights violation charges against the two. They received ten-year prison sentences.

Chapter Nineteen

Aggie and Al were getting out of his car as I turned into the Pirate's House restaurant parking lot in downtown Savannah. I tooted the horn and they waited. I gave the building a dubious once-over. It looked weathered and unimpressive.

"This is a great place, I promise." Al urged, reading my mind. "It's Aggie's favorite."

"Well, lawd me, Paloma! If you like really good sweets, this is the place. They have a separate dessert menu. It's *real* thick, like their slices. Some of them have won prestigious awards." Aggie's eyes rolled toward heaven. As I entered the restaurant, I instantly fell in love. It was richly decorated in antique nautical themes. "I'm proud to say, I've tasted most of them and they..."

I followed her gaze to Al's face. "I'm hungry and the hostess is waiting. Can we discuss dessert *after* we order dinner?"

Aggie winked. "He just doesn't understand, Paloma. We'll disregard his ignorance." She smiled coyly at Al and swept me along with her.

"Geez, where are we going?" I asked as we wove our way through a maze of rooms. "This place must go into the next county."

"Twenty-three dining rooms," Aggie said, handing me a brochure from a bin hanging on the wall.

"Is that all? The builder musta drunk on the job," I said, looking at a sketch of rambling rooms.

"The owners kept buying up adjoining properties and just merged them together just as they were."

I could believe it. I lost my bearings as we went through and around, fearing we would fall victim to the tavern owner and wake up on a ship headed for some exotic South Pacific port. In the Captain's

Room I stopped to look around and discovered that the ceiling beams were hand-hewn with wooden peg joinings.

"*Maravilhoso*! It's lovely," I spoke dreamily.

"Lawd me! Isn't it! Come over here. I want you to see this. Remember me telling you about the shorthanded ship's masters?" I nodded, wondering how she kept talking about what I was thinking. "This large hole goes down to the tunnel. This is where they smuggled them out!"

The space was about the width of a well and was chained off for safety. "The tunnel ran from a rum cellar beneath the Captain's Room to the river," Aggie went on. A plaque hanging above the guard railing told of how a Savannah policeman, who'd stopped by the Pirates' House in 1891 for a drink, awoke on a schooner sailing to China. It took him two years to get home. I felt jealous of his adventures as we left for the Treasure Room where framed pages from a rare edition of *Treasure Island* hung on the wall.

"That's right! Robert Louis Stevenson wrote about Savannah! I read that book many times. Sometimes Dixie and I took turns playing Flint and Billy Bones." I gave an evil pirate laugh.

The restaurant hostess joined in the history lesson, "Old Flint, who buried the riches on Treasure Island, is said to have died here in an upstairs room, Billy Bones by his side." She leaned toward me with a secretive smile. "His ghost still haunts the restaurant on moonless nights."

"Is there a moon tonight? I hope not! I've always wanted to see a ghost." In the dim room with authentic decor, it took little bidding for my imagination to turn diners into blood-thirsty buccaneers. Above the din, I swear I heard Cap'n Flint's reported last words "bring aft the rum!" *Billy Bones, you old salty, you had all the fun.*

We finally reached our table, and quickly ordered. Al chose an appropriate wine which we drank while waiting for our meal. A water fountain's soft patter on tile refreshed the room while we chit-chatted. "I'm starved," Aggie commented.

"We could tell. You ordered half the menu," Al commented.

"I ordered the other half," I spoke up. "I'm starving, too."

"Al, I've waited long enough. Spill it. Did you make any headway with helping Dixie?" Al filled us in. With excruciating detail. But he was holding out, saving the best news for last.

"Dixie will be arraigned day after tomorrow–Tuesday."

"Not tomorrow?" I bellowed, then instantly regretted it. "I'm sorry. I'm impatient and very worried." Al patted my hand sympathetically.

"It's the best I can do. The judge isn't available until then." I was saved from further comment as a plate was shoved under my nose.

The briny smell of raw oysters assaulted me. Aggie and I quickly slurped down a naked dozen each. Al made a ceremony of adding lemon, sauce and carefully pulling each oyster off its shell with a baby fork. Soon after, the main course arrived.

Talk was minimal as we stuffed ourselves with flounder, trout, and catfish that rivaled any I'd feasted on before. Afterwards, I studied the multi-paged dessert menu, all touted to be calorie free! I chose a silky trifle, loaded with fresh fruit and cream. I thought of Dixie, wondering what minimal fare she was sustaining on and I said so. In unison, Al and Aggie reached out to pat my hands in understanding.

"Hand patting runs in the family," I commented and tried to keep a pleasant look on my face. They'd both been so helpful and I didn't want them to think me ungrateful. I knew Dixie would soon be free.

Aggie had selected the Black Bottom Pie and ate with the same abandon she'd shown throughout dinner. We traded spoonfuls and I decided I wanted to live at the table. I could go down the dessert menu each day and die happy, clogged heart valves and all. Conservative Al chose coffee.

"Cousin, have you taken leave of your senses? Coffee only, hurmpf."

"If you two can stop feeding your faces, I'd like to ask a few questions."

"I'm perfectly able to feed my face, as you stated so lovely, while you flap your gums." Aggie stuffed another piece of pie in her mouth. "I'm all ears."

"That's about the only place left where you haven't stuffed some catfish."

"I need the energy to put up with you."

Al took another sip of coffee. "Paloma, tell us about Dixie. How did you meet?"

"We've always known each other, but my most vivid memory was the first day of kindergarten. Our mothers had dressed us in pretty little frilly dresses. I walked onto the playground and saw Dixie flipping over the monkey bars, dress wrapped around her neck. When her mother caught her and scolded her, she looked over at me with this silly lopsided grin. We've been salt and pepper ever since."

"I'm surprised you left Hilton Head Island. It's lovely there," Aggie commented.

"Dixie and I wanted a new adventure. We live in a small, quiet, coastal town, an arm's reach from the bustle of LA."

"Why that particular spot?" Aggie asked.

"Weather, beach, attitudes, and to experience a big city for a while. Just something unlike South Carolina. The desert, the western states are certainly different. My choice of a city is a beach town, but not with people jammed together in the sand like some of them up North. There's plenty of open beach no matter where you go in California. Seal Beach's Main Street is a walking area, and the town is full of surfers, sailors, artists. People stop and talk to you whether they know you or not. But I don't want to let anyone know such a place exists that close to L.A. It's mine and I don't want anyone to ruin it." I smiled at Aggie.

"You're secret's safe with me. I promise, I'll come to visit, not to stay.

Al knew how to draw more out of me without me realizing it. I talked about myself more than I had with people I'd known a lot longer. Each time I cautioned myself that it was time to zip it up, I found myself ending another tale.

"There's a bit of you that's Southern but I'm surprised there isn't more." I told them about living in Brazil, avoiding talk of my parents' death. I sensed Al wanted to ask more questions but the waitress thankfully arrived with more coffee. We busied ourselves adding cream and sugar to our liking. Al steered the conversation to Dixie and her family.

I regaled the pair with a few funny stories and wrapped up our youth roaming the island by trying to explain why Dixie's family meant so much to me. "If it hadn't been for Dixie and her mom, I'd still be introverted and shy."

Al almost choked on his coffee. Before speaking, he wiped his mouth on the cloth napkin. "I'd say outgoing. Daring. But you definitely aren't shy."

"Which would you prefer?" I asked, while Al blushed and Aggie snickered. My question hung in the air.

"Isn't this nicer than all the talk about the Klan and other hate groups?" Aggie asked, coming to his rescue. Our plates and cups were empty and no one seemed able to pack any thing more into our stomachs. I knew the evening would be winding up soon. "Sorry, Aggie, but before we call it quits, I'd like to ask Al something about the Klan." She nodded and we both focused on Al. "The booklets I've read so far don't mention how the Klan started. We certainly didn't learn about it in school."

He cleared his throat. "It was soon after the Civil War in Pulaski, Tennessee. Supposedly, started by men who thought that life on the farm after being in war was anti-climatic. They decided to play harmless pranks on the townsfolk. They formed the KKK."

"Did it just evolve into evil?"

"I believe it was that way from the start. I said a moment ago, it was *supposedly* men playing harmless pranks. It is documented that the Klan formed as a response to the changes in the South after their side lost. What did losing cost them? Slaves. Historical data also shows that the first Klansmen covered themselves and their horses in sheets." He stopped, as if that explained everything. I pursed my lips in puzzlement. "Back then," he continued. "Horses were like cars–recognizable just like your neighbor's vehicle. If they were only having fun..."

"Why all the secrecy, hiding it all behind sheets." I finished, impressed with his analysis. Aggie stifled a yawn which started a chain reaction.

"So, cousin. Are you still with us?" Al asked.

"I think we need to call it a night," Aggie answered. "I'm beat."

Al checked his watch. "Later than I thought. If there's any news on Dixie's case tomorrow, I'll call you at the hotel. Otherwise, I'll come by and pick you up for the arraignment on Tuesday."

"What time?"

"Seven." I'm sure he meant A.M. I'm not fond of early mornings. "Cousin Aggie, are you staying with me tonight?"

"No. Just drop me off at the Reducer for my jalopy. If I can make it Tuesday, I'll be there to see Grainger lose again. I've explained Grainger to Paloma, by the way." Al's face made comment as it hardened and his eyes tightened briefly.

I thanked the pair for a lovely evening, turning down Al's request to see me safely to my hotel room door. He looked relieved and way past his bedtime.

Fortunately, I'd left the air conditioner running full blast and it was deliciously cold inside my room. I quickly brushed my teeth, pulled on a T-shirt and crawled between the cool sheets. The bed was just hard enough, the pillows firm. Perfect. Until a scratching noise and heavy whispers brought me out of a deep sleep.

South Carolina Senior Senator Strom Thurmond, led a walk-out from the Democratic Convention in the 1948 presidential election to protest the civil rights platform. Thurmond became the leader of the States Rights Party, and a candidate for president. Dubbed the Dixiecrats, *Thurmond carried South Carolina, Louisiana, Alabama and Mississippi in his upset over Thomas Dewey. Thurmond campaign rhetoric: "the progress of the Negro race has not been due to these so-called emancipators...but to the kindness of the good Southern people...there's not enough troops in the army to force the Southern people to break down segregation and admit the Negro race into our theaters, into our swimming pools, into our homes and into our churches."*–Strom Thurmond and the Politics of Southern Change, *by Nadine Cohodas.*

Chapter Twenty

I quickly looked at the digital clock on the dresser. 3:42. My heart revved. A few seconds later, sound came from the sliding doors that opened to the garden and pool area. I didn't need anymore convincing.

Having no other weapon, I pulled a chair out from the small corner table and waited. The door slid open slowly. I lifted the chair over my head. A shadow stepped into my room, arm extended, pushing the curtains back. I crept a few steps closer and brought the unwieldy chair down, banging the glass more than the interloper.

"Owww! Haul ass, Randy!" A male voice exclaimed in excitement, and after a bit of shuffling, took his own advice and hightailed back from where he came. I took off after them. When I could focus in the security-lighted patio, the two crooks were almost at the other side of the courtyard. They scaled a kudzu-smothered brick wall as I reached them. I hurled myself into it as the last guy went over the top. I grabbed his shirt collar and held on tight, impeding further escape. So I thought. As his shirt tore, he pushed me with enough force to knock over the entire 49er starting lineup. I immediately re-heaved, this time onto his leg and played tug-of-war with his partner on the other side. "Randy, leggo! You gonna rip my leg in two!"

"Don't say my dang name, you idjit!"

I looked up and saw the other yahoo, hair so grimy it was almost into the dreadlock stage, throwing good-sized sticks and debris down. When he plunked a small wrench on me bulls-eye, I slipped down, releasing my prisoner.

Great, head injury. I hate that. The pain quickly found whatever part of my brain that signals a headache is coming and it was going to be a doozie. A wave of dizziness swept over me and I lowered my head and closed my eyes. I heard a vehicle on the other side of the wall rev up and speed away.

As Inn security escorted me back to my room, I discovered I was flashing my fellow hoteliers a nice view of underwear and thigh. Well, one of life's mysteries solved. I'd always wondered why my grandmother warned me to always have good underwear on. I slipped on a pair of shorts and moved to an upstairs room.

The Savannah police admonished me for giving chase. I pointed out I wouldn't have learned that one thief was named Randy. Like that was a big clue. The cute cop pointed out I wouldn't have an egg-sized lump on my head if I'd stayed put. *Touché*. I had enough presence of mind to ask for their names and work number–just in case. I got a business card. But not from the cute one. I never do.

I got back into bed, jumping at the sound of noisy crickets and a host of other sounds, while my head punished me for a lifetime of sin, real or imagined. Sometime between napping and morning I remembered the cap worn by the tool thrower advertised Rincon Funeral Home. Was business so slow they needed volunteers? In spite of the silliness of the joke, I cracked up, releasing tension but smacked my head against the homemade ice pack, banging into the knot the ice was there to help. It was a toss up between which hurt most–the growing lump or the ice freezing a patch of nerve endings on my scalp. Hurry up sunrise.

*   *   *

"Dang, Randy. We almost had it! But she was awake!" Randy slammed on the brakes, drove over the median and abruptly stopped the truck in the Savannah Civic Center parking lot.

"But we don't 'cause you cain't do nuttun' right!" He whacked his head a few times into the gun rack for emphasis. Billy Ray tensed and prepared to run if necessary. When Randy was pumped he was a paroxysm of chaos. "You sumbitch! You choked!" Randy was out of the truck kicking a street light pole then pounding it with his fists. When he tired of metal, he moved to his shadow. Billy Ray watched every move, his senses on full alert. Suddenly, Randy darted toward a tree, running up the trunk a few steps before gravity pulled him down, feet smacking down onto the pavement. Seconds later he was back in the truck, winded but sedate, knuckles bloody and raw. He stuck his head out the window, put a finger on one nostril and blew. He thumped a persistent string with his finger, shook his hand then wiped it on his pants.

"B-Ray, my bo-ah! Give me the Beam." Billy Ray fished under the seat as if his life depended on it, thrusting the bottle toward his deranged friend. Randy chugged down a good three fingers. "I think it's time to have a party." He shifted into drive, gave a few hearty rebel yells and headed toward Rincon.

*　　*　　*

The Leprechaun waited patiently in the 108-degree California desert night. His digital watch read 2:33 A.M. Twenty minutes to go, give or take a few. Leaving Los Angeles earlier had been easier than usual so he arrived in plenty of time. He squatted down behind the service station Dumpster as a car headed near him. Hiding so close to it, Leprechaun could smell the coffee the driver brought out of the store before the door was closed and the car backed away. The expanse of desert surrounding him was filled with sounds of insects and other invisible night creatures. He passed the time remembering when his truck driver father took him along on the big hauls from Boston to Miami. As a boy, he'd been thrilled.

After money–and lots of it–that's what he lived for–the thrill. This was just one more risky plan coming to fruition. Another load of equipment to steal and sell to Swartzman or anyone else. The adrenaline was pumping now. He loved the feel of it. Almost as good as a woman.

At 2:54 Travis Industry's big rig pulled into the station, as Leprechaun knew it would. This was the only service stop in the desert for nearly seventy miles.

The driver pointed the rear of the truck at the Dumpster and once perfectly aligned beside the other three rigs, he hissed the breaks to a stop. The countdown to destruction began.

The driver climbed out of the rig, engine still grinding, and headed for the restroom in the back of the station. Leprechaun swept the area–no one looking–and crept to the cab. He stepped up to peek inside. The window was partially open and snoring sounds drifted faintly from the sleeper compartment. *To hear sounds above the engine noise, that driver was sawing serious logs,* Leprechaun thought. He opened the door and slid noiselessly over the seat pulling back the curtain. Covering the man's mouth with his right hand, Leprechaun shoved a blade in the stomach and lifted up. The man awoke and uselessly tried to knock away his opponent's strong arms. Leprechaun kept the upward pressure on the handle until the man stopped fighting and died. So quick. So easy.

He rolled the guy onto his side to allow room for him to hide in the sleeper. Soon the Travis employee emerged from the restroom and headed into the store. He returned with the inevitable large coffee truckers survived on, and some junk food supplies. Leprechaun closed the curtains, leaving only a sliver of space. He fabricated snoring sounds.

The door creaked open, the driver belched as he sat down. He made wet slurping sounds drinking the coffee and flicked on the inside light. He sorted through a stack of tapes, chose one and slid it into the deck. Leprechaun was a patient man. Let the guy live a few minutes longer. The trucker opened the chips, shoving a handful into his mouth. He stopped in mid crunch, sniffed as he looked around. "Oh, gross, Sammy," he said softly with a light chuckle. "You cuttin' the cheese again in your sleep? Told you to lay off the chili beans." Not waiting for an answer, he completed a series of shoulder and neck rolls, popping a few joints. The light went out. He revved the engine and reached for the gearshift.

Leprechaun came from behind the curtains and pierced the man in the side, lifting upward in the same manner as before. In an attempt to save himself, the driver reached out. Leprechaun quickly brought the knife around, flicking it across the outstretched arm. The man leaned forward gripping his wound, groaning as Leprechaun thrust the knife back deeply into his side. The trucker shuddered then quietly died.

Leprechaun pulled him out from behind the steering wheel and shoved him half onto the floor and passenger seat. He climbed in to take the wheel and after a shaky start, eased the truck onto I-10 West. The highway was still nearly deserted. Only three miles to the hideout.

At the Revas Road turnoff, laid out north and south into even more desolate desert, he drove to a small abandoned warehouse built near a mine that had promised more than it delivered. Tonight it would keep the Leprechaun and the rig out of sight while the equipment was transferred from the Travis Industries' truck to a nondescript rented one.

*   *   *

The leader spoke. "Klansmen, face the cross." With a swish of robes, the bodies snapped to attention, turned and bowed, their fiery torches bobbing down with them.

In a chorus they replied, "for my God, for my country, for my family, for my Klan."

"Klansmen, approach the cross," ordered the Grand Dragon from the circle middle.

The men came forward in unison and tossed their sticks at the bottom of the cross. The fire shot up the timber. Soon the crackling noises from the fire could be heard throughout the Southern night.

Mississippi: 1964–The car carrying three civil rights youths–Michael Schwerner, James Chaney, and Andrew Goodman–was stopped by Deputy Sheriff Cecil Price. Later, the three men disappeared. Fellow activists raised an alarm and Attorney General Kennedy ordered the FBI to investigate the case as a kidnaping–a federal offense. When Schwerner's station wagon was discovered, burned, in an isolated area, President Johnson ordered FBI Director Hoover to go to Mississippi to hunt for the murderers.

Chapter Twenty-One

"Hey, baby."

"Whoze this?" A deep throaty voice answered.

"A little Leprechaun."

"Sorry, I can't tonight." She coughed. He could hear clanking glasses and music in the background.

"You're spreading them for someone else tonight!" he accused angrily.

Her response was blasé. "You know how I make my living."

"But you knew I was going on a job." It was getting hot in the car. He cranked it to turn on the air. "You knew how much I'd need it afterward."

"Need *it*–not me. Leppie, baby, you think I can just lie around waiting? I got two kids and rent."

"But I got to have *you*." It was the first time he'd said that, a slip his steely and reclusive psyche rarely allowed.

"There's plenty of beaver on the stroll on Sunset. Or why don't you call Janice? She's clean."

He spit into the phone. "She's a worthless lay. I have to hold back. You know I can't do that!" He loosened the tightness in his voice. "I've got piles of money."

"You always do. I can't. I'll be done at six. Come by then."

"I can't wait," he nearly choked on his growing desperation.

"Jean's good. You roughed her up last time. But I explained it. She's new to the game. Call her. She'll be okay this time."

"You didn't tell her about me, did you?"

"Only about what's between your legs. Baby, I got work to do." The click echoed in his ear. He threw the phone at the passenger door.

"Bitch! Why is she doing this to me?" He sat in the darkness, breathing deeply, pulling another beer from the bag, throwing the empty out the window. Thinking. Cigarette. Beer. Thinking. He had to be careful what type of girl he paid. He didn't want anyone to mess up what he had going. His need was too urgent to go bar-crawling. All you got was some air-head too drunk and doped up. That left the hard-up ones. He found the phone and while making another call he quickly changed personas. Now he was soft, comfortable. Everybody's good-guy.

"Hello?" Frances' sleepy voice answered. He could hear her fumbling for something.

"Frances?"

"Yes, who is this?"

"Guess."

"I don't have any idea."

"It's your little Leprechaun."

"What? If this is your idea..."

"Frances, calm down. It's Shawn. Shawn Munson."

"Shawn, what are you doing calling me? I mean I'm glad, but I...I'm surprised."

"I can't stop thinking about you. I woke up and couldn't get back to sleep. You're in my every thought. And I'm..." He lowered his voice sighing. "I'm so lonely." He pretended to laugh self-consciously. "I know this is crazy, but can I come over? I'd like to see you."

"I don't know."

"Why not? Oh, I'm sorry. Maybe you aren't alone." He stammered to the woman that he knew was alone. "I understand, I'll just..."

"It's not that. I worked late tonight. I had a stack of purchasing requests for the Chief. You know we all have to look good for the new guy." She paused. "I'm alone."

"That makes two of us. We can drink coffee and talk. I just want to talk to you. *Please.*"

"I'm not dressed and my place is not cleaned..."

"I'm a bachelor, remember? I'm sure everything's fine. You just slip on something and don't make a fuss. Okay?"

"Okay. I'd like to see you, too." He drained his beer, grimacing at the image of Frances' face looking up at his. But everybody looks the same when your eyes are closed. Giving himself one more check for blood or any other telltale signs from tonight's excursion, he pointed the car toward Redondo Beach.

* * *

Sunrise reared its ugly head and brought my friend Mr. Humidity. I'd given up on sleep not long after I hit the sheets the second time after the aborted robbery. Reading the racist material Al had given me hadn't made me sleepy. The horrible stories only got my blood pumping.

I braved a look in the mirror. The herbal remedy was lessening the signs of bruising remarkably but the knot from the wrench seemed large enough that I could pass myself off as a conehead. After dressing, I walked to the scene of the crime, but only saw lovely flowers and a few spots where the kudzu was damaged by our free-for-all.

Not knowing what to do with myself, I checked out the other side of the wall where they'd stashed their vehicle. Perhaps the guy had been nice enough to leave his wallet or vehicle registration. Nope. Nothing to indicate who my assailants were. Perspiration had already soaked my blouse half way down my back and underarms and it wasn't yet 6:00 A.M.

I turned to go and stumbled on a root from a nearby oak. I lay face down in the dirt telling myself that the day was still young. As I stood, I saw a shiny object beside the errant root and picked it up.

It was a pin, warmed by the sun, attached to a piece of red cloth. The guy's shirt I ripped last night was red! I tossed the pin back and forth in my hands examining it. Green enamel letters, A-Y-A-K, against a white background. Ayak? I shrugged, stuffed it in my pocket.

It took six cups of coffee before I believed my eyes would stay open for a few hours. I ordered breakfast, but did nothing more than push it around on my plate. I killed time until 8:00 and tried Al's office. He said he'd be right over, that he had an hour free before meetings. I told him it wasn't necessary. So we met in the hotel restaurant.

"Did you spend the night in a juke joint?"

"Everyone's a comedian," I grumbled. I filled him in on last night's jog around the courtyard. "Do you think it's connected?"

"I don't know, but we shouldn't rule it out. What do you think?"

"I have this feeling–like my skin's crawling. One yahoo wore a gimme cap advertising a funeral home, of all things. In Rincon. I know advertising tries to hit people over the head with their messages, but these goobers went too far." Al smiled and patted my hand. "If I were going to break in, know what I'd do? I'd pick the Hyatt down the street. Richer clientele."

"I'm sorry you don't like the accommodations my staff picked out for you."

Moaning inside, I hung my head defeated. Foot in mouth again. "It's not that, I meant..."

"Paloma, look here." I did. Al was grinning.

"I hate lawyers."

He winked at me. "Maybe they picked this hotel for logistics. Less security, easier locks."

"There are rooms here that are less obvious than mine."

"I hope you moved into one of those." We spent a few more minutes tossing around theories, but quickly depleted ideas. I felt a sharp poke in my thigh.

"I almost forgot," I said digging out the pin. "I found this around the place that I heard their car take off. It says AYAK." I held it up for him to see.

Al jerked back like he'd been shocked. "Hot food!"the waitress yelled, doing her best to keep the tray balanced and her eye on Al's shoulder.

"What?" I asked excitedly. He made a wait-until-we're-alone face. So I did.

"It stands for–are you a Klansman," he whispered. "Anyone can be approached safely to find out if they are Klan."

I dropped the pin like it could poison me. We stared at each other until the waitress asked if something was wrong with Al's order. We knocked our-selves out like good Southerners convincing her everything was great.

"Want more coffee?" She asked. It would be the tenth for me. What the heck, I'm young still.

"I don't like it," Al finally said and attacked his breakfast of eggs, grits, bacon, biscuit and sausage gravy.

"I'm not feeling warm and cozy either. Do you happen to have any aspirin?"

"There's some at the cash register."

Don't ask me how I missed it the first time. I slid out of the booth, sweaty thighs making an unladylike sound. The tablets were in those little metal containers and I played hell trying to open it. "Stupid thing is adult proof," I mumbled.

"Paloma, last night could have been a little intimidation–leave a gift for the morning but you woke up. Or they were going to give you a warning."

"What kind of warning–second-hand smoke kills?"

"More like the fist kind." On that cheerful note we exhausted last night. Time to poke into Al's personal life.

"I want the untold story of Al Eason, Freedom Fighter. Why civil rights law?"

With only a brief bout of hemming and hawing, he began his story. "It wasn't planned. I was raised on a small farm. My daddy was poor. He leased an acre or two outside of Baxley–that's a couple of hours west–from the town's main rich guy. The folks hired to help pick the crops were all black. That's the only kind of work they could get. I played with their kids and didn't think anything of it. When I started school, I didn't understand why my friends couldn't go with me.

"My father taught me to respect anyone, regardless of color. Being poor, we hardly left the farm, much less the town we lived outside of, so I grew up isolated like you. When I got out in the world, I got that good ol' hard knocks education." He stopped and filled up on more pancakes. "I worked myself silly to go to college. In church, I grew tired of the people who lived a double standard–love your brother, do unto others–as long as they were white. The KKK was rampant in my town once the civil rights movement was in full swing. They marched, burned crosses, destroyed property, threat-ened and beat up people. I recognized some deacons from the church I'd grown up attending. One summer when I was home, they burned a few crosses in my daddy's yard."

"Why?"

"Because he was helping the farm staff learn to read and write. They intimidated my mother whenever she went into town." I shook my head saddened by his narrative. "My dad told me that summer his time had passed. It was up to me to see that things changed. I forgot those words until I was a fat-cat lawyer up in Atlanta, raking in the dough. I was watch-ing the news one evening–some racial stuff on TV. I was married but wasn't happy in the big firm–all facade. I couldn't take anything or anyone at face value. Especially my plastic wife." He paused. "So I quit. Liquidated my assets–the partnership, stocks, property and then my liabilities–mostly wife. My daddy died during that time. That's when I started the Center, to help out people who have no voice. Just as my father did in his own small way. It's a living testament to his life."

"Wow!" was about as wordy as I got. What *could* I say to some-thing like that? I let Al concentrate on his food.

"You know, sugah," he said when he came up for air. "I think I'm going to like you." I looked over, lips pursed waiting for the explana-tion. "I can't count how many times I've had to do business over meals instead of enjoying my food. Or make polite conversation while making sure nothing falls out my mouth. I've actually tasted what I ate today." He scooped up the remaining gravy with a piece of biscuit and sat back looking satisfied. "Aggie has adopted you already."

"She's wonderful. I hope I'm as spunky when I'm her age."

"I've no doubt. But don't let her hear you mention her age. Are you sure you don't want anything?"

"Positive."

"You're not one of those women who is constantly dieting?"

"Isn't that what men are after-thin, blonde, submissive?"

"Personally, I've had it with women skinny as rails. You take them to a wonderful steak and seafood place and they order a salad and water. When you hold them, they feel hard as a sack of potatoes."

I laughed out loud. "I pay dearly for what I consume. I have to swim miles and miles." I checked the time. "Have you remarried?" The direct ap-proach. I'm famous for it.

"No. Not many women will put up with the constant threats I get." The waitress came to our table with the check and we left shortly thereafter. At the lobby door, Al was futzing with his wallet trying to shove it into a pocket. I was baking, my head banging, so I threw open the door myself. "Why can't a man open a door now and then for a lady?" He asked.

"You can. You just have to do it more quickly." I opened his fingers and dropped my hotel key in. "If you must."

"You sly she-devil."

I defended myself in my best Scarlet impersonation, batting eyes and fanning my face with a hand. "Why on earth would you say such a thing?"

"You kept me talking the whole time. Last night, Aggie and I had to pry information out of you."

"I don't remember it that way. I'm embarrassed at how I dominated the conversation."

"Nah, sugah. If Aggie hadn't been there, I'd never have heard one personal word out of you. Next time you won't get away without telling me about yourself."

"Are you waging a bet, Mr. Eason?" I winked as he opened the room door and allowed me to pass.

He politely stayed on his side of the metal threshold. "How does your boyfriend handle you?" Ah, the indirect approach.

"Who said I only had one?" I shut the door.

An FBI task force paid White Knights of Mississippi Klansmen for information about the deaths of Schwerner, Chaney, and Goodman. In August 1964, an informant tip led the FBI to the missing youths, now entombed in an earthen dam. As murder is not a federal offense, Mississippi officials refused to acknowledge it ever happened. This would mean that the three activists shot, then buried themselves in the dam. Civil Rights violation charges were filed against the major figures– law enforcement officers, a reverend and a top Klan official.

Chapter Twenty-Two

Generally, my bones carry more weight than, thankfully, shows. Except for when I heave swimming attire over them. I self-consciously walked to the pool and dove in. The water wasn't cool as I'd expected. The relentless southern heat didn't stop at sundown, as it did in Los Angeles. So there was no nightly cooling of the pool water. I swam laps for thirty minutes then soaked up some rays and pondered life.

Dixie. Why did I think I could help her? All I could do now is wait until her arraignment. But what about after that? She will still have whatever charges the idiot Grainger dreams up. What if she doesn't get out on bail? They could fix that like they did arresting her. *Stop it*, I told myself. *Think.*

My mind wandered, as it so often does, to computers. In my work, gathering information is crucial for an accurate analysis–and for success. And with the always-changing computer industry, staying on top of the latest technology and information is just as important. With security my bailiwick, I'd become addicted to data. Gathering and analyzing it was how I function-ed. At the moment it was all I knew to do to help Dixie.

I had taken my notebook computer and Al's information to the pool with me. In his office, he'd given me a short history of the main hate groups in America. So this afternoon I'd focus on specifics to get a handle on racism. Percentages. There's always statistics for any topic. I'd also need to educate myself on the Klan since Al told me that was the only known hate group in Rincon, even though it hadn't been very active. He'd given me a thick stack of materials to read. Comparing that pile to what little I knew currently of hate groups was tantamount to having my head buried in the sand. Well, ignorant no longer. I thumbed through the papers until I spotted a title heading–The Klan.

Page one was a Klan version of an organizational chart. Imperial Wizard was the head of a particular group, like a CEO of a nationwide business. Each office was called a Klavern, governed by a Grand Dragon, the top manager. In Klandom, the line managers were hydras and there were nine of them. A province was vested with a Grand Titan, assisted by his twelve Furies. Geez, I getting lost already.

An Exalted Cyclops had twelve Terrors helping him as he led local chapters. The rites of the Klan was contained in the Kloran which, the information read, detailed "*karacter*, honor and duty". Enough of that *klaptrap*, I thought and *kleverly* so!

I flipped to the next page which contained a list of sources for the reports and ended with references for further study. My eyes zoomed onto an Internet address. Right up my alley! I booted up Heathcliff, moved under a picnic table umbrella and draped a towel over us so I could read the screen. Southern Poverty Law Center. I'd heard about the SPLC. Created by attorney Morris Dees, he'd gained notoriety, and national attention, by suing different hate groups for civil rights crimes, resulting in bankruptcy and forfeiture of the organization's properties. Al had told me that he'd modeled his own center after Dees'. I typed in the web address and scanned their home page. Soon I was clicking my way through their data, noting sadly, there was a wealth of it.

I clicked onto a button called *Intelligence Project*. One could never have enough of that! The SPLC divided the various hate groups into seven categories–Klan, neo-Nazi, racist Skinheads, black separatists, Christian Identity, neo-Confederate, and lastly, the ubiquitous Other. Each category was assigned a symbol–little white pointy heads for Klan, swastikas for Skinheads. A national map bore these symbols for each state, wherever a hate group was located. Some states were practically filled up with groups, others only a few. No state was empty of symbols, meaning none were hate-group free.

I clicked on Georgia and the screen filled with a detailed map, the hate group symbols popping up in various cities and towns. For 2001, the state was recorded as having thirty-one known groups, hate incidents–one hundred fourteen. A hyperlink jumped to a section that detailed each racist incident, grouping the crimes committed into categories like vandalism, threat, murder and assault. Each individual incident was then detailed with the date, city and a synopsis of the crime. The listing included, but infrequently, any legal action taken against a person or hate group. Another hyperlink brought me to a listing of human rights groups in the state. Good versus evil.

I left the Georgia area to check out other state statistics. South Carolina listed thirty-five groups and one hundred thirteen reported incidents; Califor-nia had forty-two known groups, 1,372 incidents reported; New Jersey came in with nineteen groups, three hundred sixty-eight reported incidents. That state hosted a larger number of Skinhead groups than the other states I'd read about. I reined myself in, not needing to get too bogged down in details. Refocused, I returned to the home page wondering about national totals, found a button for that and clicked on it.

The *Intelligence Project* tracked close to seven hundred hate groups during 2001. Scanning the national data, I suddenly stopped, hitting upon a startling statement. The SPLC estimates that approximately 50,000 hate crimes occur each year in the United States alone.

Equally surprising, was learning that the vast majority were committed by people *not* affiliated with extremist organizations, but by the average Joe. I chewed on that.

With only a fraction of racist crimes being reported, what I was seeing was only a small glimpse into the vast problem of hate and extremism in America. I ended my web crawl reading that experts considered 2001 a year of solidification of America's hate movement. It confirmed what Al had told me in his office. Secret groups were now going public with their agenda and they were joining with other extremist groups–unity clearly the goal, it was "a hardening–a Nazification–of the ideology of right-wing revolutionary groups". A chill engulfed me. I shuddered in spite of the insipid heat. And now a dear friend had become a victim. The chill burned into anger. I pushed aside the notebook and hit the pool again, to swim out my indignation.

Fatigued, I climbed out of the pool and flopped down onto a lounger. I dozed off, but quickly snapped awake moments later to find Al's papers flying around in the breeze. Moaning curses, I raced around barefoot on the hot cement gathering them up, glad the pool area was fenced in to block further escape. Plopping back down onto the chaise lounge, I checked the papers for damage. Several of them had taken a wade into the kiddie pool. I sopped up the water with a hotel towel. Blotting off the last wet paper, I focused on the text. It was a list of known Klansmen in Effingham County, divided by towns. Fourth under the Rincon heading was a name. Randy Beamon.

"I remember!" I hollered, jumping up in enthusiasm and ignoring the cautious looks I was getting from passing guests. The buddy of the cap-wearing thief from last night had called his partner Randy! "*Isso é tão legal!*" I exclaimed, switching from my usual Portuguese curses to "this is so cool". I dashed inside my room, showered quickly and sat in front of the air conditioner. My thoughts churned like stormy seas, tossing around to and fro. To sort them out I pounded on the keyboard, putting all events into Heathcliff that had happened since my arrival. Then I listed theories, suppositions, and lastly, questions. There were many.

Where is Lemond? Who is responsible for his disappearance? What in-formation did he have? What diskettes did The Voice want? Why does he think I have them? Are the events in California connected with Dixie? If so, why? What is going on at the Gundersen plant? Why were Randy and a goober buddy breaking into my room? Is the Randy who broke in named Randy Beamon? Is Dixies' treatment by the police part of a bigger conspir-acy? If so, what? When I finished, I read and reread the pages. I had one answer so far, and it was only a partial–a Randy broke into my hotel. Now what? I was itchy. It was time to go back to Rincon and find the would-be thief named Randy.

*   *   *

In Rincon, the temperature from the C&S bank sign registered 9]
degrees, a few of the LED lights another victim of the withering heat.
Alice in Chains' *Dirt* CD blared from the cheap car speakers. I sang
along to "Hate to Feel". Weather wimp that Al labeled me, I pulled
through the drive-in window and asked a teller for directions to the
funeral home. It was a short ride and I parked under a tiny bit of
shade from a pine tree.

It was just as still inside as such places are expected to be. I
thought of the corny jokes of my youth–business is dead, you stab
'em, we slab 'em. A new one popped into my head to fit the
occasion–you burn 'em, we urn 'em. A buzzer sounded behind me as
the front door closed. Time to act like a grown-up. I waited in the
empty foyer wondering if business was, indeed, dead. Momentarily
a woman, in her late forties, auburn hair, came out of a back door.

"May I help you?"

"I'm not sure," I stammered. Some sleuth I was. I hadn't made up
a cover story before tearing after this slim lead! So I smiled. "My
name is Kate," I lied for some reason, using my grandmother's name.
We shook hands.

"Wanda."

"I'm from out of town and I'm looking for my brother."

"We have no one here at the moment."

I gave a quick "ha" at her mistake. "I don't mean he's here, dead.
But here in town." She looked puzzled.

"He came to see friends here, but he never returned home. He was
hanging around a guy named Randy who wore a cap advertising this
funeral home. I know it's a long shot, but I thought I should check
here." I wrung my hands. "I don't know what else to do."

"Sweetie, the caps aren't going to be much help to you. Mr.
Harrison had a bunch made and he passes them out like candy. He's
not here at the moment, but I'll check with him when he returns.
Where can I reach you?"

"I'm staying at...I-I'm hard to reach. Is it okay if I check with you
tomorrow?"

"Sure. I'm sorry I can't help more. The name Randy is plentiful
'round here. Where are my manners? Please come sit down. Would
you like a glass of ice tea?"

"Thank you kindly, but I best be gettin'," I drawled and did so. I
hadn't thought I'd get much information here, but I felt disappointed
nonetheless. I had the urge to grab someone by the collar and blurt
out that I had a friend in jail for no reason and weren't they concerned
about what was happening in their town? The blues. I cranked up the
volume after sliding in a Stevie Ray Vaughan CD. That guy could
bend a guitar note and have it cry for mercy. Yeah, Stevie, I had me
some Texas-sized blues. Sho' 'nuf.

Now what? I saw a pay phone outside Sloan's Pharmacy. On the
far side of the parking lot, a scorched oak tree gave the Escort a small

respite from the sun. To prove to myself I could function without lugging my electronic equipment everywhere, I left it all in the car, remembering to keep the windows rolled down.

I'm most familiar with pay phones that have no directory attached to the wire and the phonebook thieves didn't disappoint me this time. How anyone could get through all the metal tie-downs to steal one always amazed me. I confess, I'd tried snitching one before and gave up, claiming exhaustion and frustration. A few pieces of wire had defeated Paloma, hacker of the cyber world. I've even kept that defeat from Dixie.

I went inside the pharmacy to borrow theirs. No listing for any Randy/Randall/R Beamon. I went back outside deciding to check with directory assistance. The phone, hanging on the outside wall, had been cooking all day in the blazing sun. My fingers danced like a line of Rockettes along the handset to avoid burnt flesh. You'd think that would have been enough of a warning, but out of habit I plopped it against my ear. The sudden heat caused me to drop the handset, bang my hand a few times trying to grab it, drop my change, waste more time, whine about it and start all over again. No luck with 411. Next, I phoned the Gundersen plant and asked for their Personnel Department.

"Yes, this is Midge from the C&S bank," I said, pinching my nose in that high-tech method of voice disguisement. Why did I bother? No one knew me. Too much bad TV watching. "I need to verify employment for a Randy Beamon." I heard keys clicking in the background.

"I'm sorry we don't have anyone who works here by that name," a sweet voice informed me. Hmm.

"Could he be new?"

"Not unless he was hired today. We're very computerized."

"How far back do your records go."

"To the beginning since we haven't been open that long. Randy Beamon has never worked here. Sorry."

"Somebody here's gonna get it! I'm glad it wasn't my mistake. Thank ya' kindly." Dead end number two. Now what?

I needed information, so what better place to get it than the local bar? In a town this size, it must be on the main drag through town. I climbed back in the Escort and did a slow crawl down Highway 21. I didn't see anything resembling a drinking establishment, so I turned off to hunt one block over on each side of the highway. Churches and homes aplenty. At Bubba's Pump N Save I turned in. Lulene was behind the counter again, so after I pumped gas, I pumped her.

"What about that plant down the road? It looks fairly new." Lulene pulled a box of Marlboro's from the rack, tapped it several times on her wrist and was puffing away in record time. She turned her head and exhaled. The smoke still wafted over to me as I knew it would. I took a step back.

"Yep, only been open 'bout nine months."

"What kind of a plant is it?"

"What I hear is they make pretty high falutin' parts for computers and stuff like that. But most of the people hired from Rincon work the 'sembly line. Guy I used to date works there. I finally dumped him 'cause alls he ever wanted to do was go huntin' and fishin'. Now, I don't mind a bit of fishin', long as someone baits the hook for me. I just ain't gonna mess with no worm, now. You can swear on the Bible 'bout that! Lordy, me, those worms are so slimy..."

"Ah, Lulene, what does your boyfriend do at the plant?"

"Ex-boyfriend." She stared at me to see if I got it.

I did. I urged her to elaborate by nodding my head and widening my eyes. She deciphered my code and explained. "Says he puts weird-looking gad-gets here, 'nuther'n there. I heard tell that the Town Council hoped there'd be more supervisor po-sitions for the townsfolk. The owners promised they'd eventually train the locals but they ain't yet."

"Where are these people from?"

"Don't remember. Some big Yankee city."

Hmm, that narrowed it down. "Lulene, where's the local bar?" She took a long drag off her cigarette and held the smoke while she looked at me. An errant string sneaked out of her nose. She began choking. And she coughed. Then she heaved, doubled over like she'd taken a sucker punch to the gut. Each time she looked up her eyes bugged out at me in desperation, teary and red. I asked if I could get her anything while wondering if I had stomped on the toes of a Pentecostal-evangelical-fundamentalist-biblical-orthodox teeto-taler. "I'm sorry, Lulene. What did I say? I just need to find somebody and I thought a bar would be a good place to start." She was gathering her composure and depleting her second "Co-Cola". After several more hacks she was semi-normal. She took another drag on her cigarette. In spite of my intense distaste of coffin nails, I was impressed at her willingness to get back into the ring so quickly.

"Oh, honey, now don't you go worrying 'bout offendin' little ol' me. I have a nip or two myself, although it goes straight to m'head." She made a silly giggle that convinced me I didn't want to be her drinking companion. "I jes' forget you ain't frum 'round 'ere. Ain't no honky-tonks in Rincon, honey, account a' some law. The closest place in Effingham County you can buy booze is Guyton. No likker though, jus' beer n' wine. Cain't stand beer m'self. Tastes like warm camel piss."

"Geez, thanks for sharing that."

Her laugh sounded more like someone having a seizure. "Woo-hoo! You sure are funny girl!" I shifted my feet waiting for her to get herself together again. "Boy, did that cause an uproar when word got 'round 'bout that!"

"What?"

"Guyton getting booze. People wuz..."

"How far away is it?" She plucked a map off a spin rack and moved back to her spot.

"You have ta look for Springfield on these dang thangs, Rincon ain't never listed." She leaned over and pointed to a spot on the red vein half an inch from Springfield.

"That'd be Guyton, but it don't look right." She dropped some ash on the paper and brushed it away. Charcoal smudges marked a path eastward toward Carolina. She folded up the map. "But, gosh almighty durn, you don't need no map. I can tell ya how ta get there." It wasn't what I'd asked for. I just wanted a brief run down of the area, but I didn't correct her. With lengthy discourse, she gave me directions to Springfield, through it and on to the sinner's paradise.

Her hand movements made her appear to be leading a cheer at the two-minute warning. "Either the second or first light after driving 'bout ten minutes, turn right and follow it down to the stop sign, 'bout two minutes. If you don't see a sign, then go back and look for Stanley Mac's Tire and Tractor Service. It's a tee-tiny ways past there. Then turn right. When you get..."

"Thanks, Lulene, but I'm not good at mazes. I'd end up in some pasture trying to get directions from a cow."

She let out a high ear-piercing laugh and did some kind of jig that included stamping her feet. "I sure hope you're in town for a while! Boy, howdy! You an' me–we need to go out and *par*-tay!" I ignored her social invitation.

"Why are directions in the South done in minutes and buildings, Lulene, not miles and street names? Is it just to confuse the out-of-towners? Do y'all get your kicks watching us drive around in circles?" Lulene let out another bout of seizures. I'd have to admit I was getting a little goofy myself. "Is there any place closer than Guyton?"

"What?"

"A honky-tonk."

"Oh, I thought you only meant in this *county*. Well, right outside Rincon, going to Savannah, is a club. See, it's in Chatham County. I don't go there much 'cause the guys from the plant hang out there and theys always fightin'. Or worse is if I run into my old boyfriend. My last guy is dating my soon-to-be *ex*-best-girlfriend. Can you *buh-lieve* the nerve a' her? All the time I was dating that rotten..."

"Excuse me, I'm sorry about your dude, but are you saying the closest bar is back toward Savannah?"

"Yep." Finally. "Stay on the highway and you can't miss it." I obviously had, as I had driven down that road several times earlier.

"Thank you, Lulene. You are a Godsend. I hope your boss pays you well." That brought on another story, this one about the woes of working for minimum wage and a married boss who couldn't keep his hands in his pockets. "Quit."

"It's the only job I can find."

"Listen honey, that jerk lays one fat finger on you, turn around and give him a foot in the *cojones*." When I explained to her that *cojones* were the "other" jugular vein in a male's anatomy, then explained to her what area that second jugular was located, her hands flew to her mouth, eyes widened in surprise.

Her words came out in a rush. "Golly, bubba! You want me to kick him in the, well, gosh, I couldn't do that! No, I couldn't! It would hurt 'im!"

"Isn't he hurting you?"

"Well," she spoke admittedly. "He don't pinch *real* hard."

I took a deep breath keeping my voice free of impatience. "I meant, doesn't he hurt you on the inside when he gropes you?"

"Well, yes." She looked back at me so forlorn and worn down, like I was the one who degraded her. "What if he fired me?"

"I don't think he would. He has a wife?" She nodded. "Threaten to tell her."

The child got a lollipop. She exposed her buck teeth and a good inch of gums as she smiled. "Thank you, ma'am! I'll have ta think 'bout it. Hey! What's your name?"

"Kate, pleased ta met ya." Might as well stick with the lie I'd told earlier, stay in deep cover. She asked me to show her a few kicks. I'd bet the farm Mr. Roving Hands would be so surprised that she'd made even a tiny assertive tactic that she wouldn't need to worry about a proper stance. That is, as long as she kept her balance.

"Thanks again for your hep. You sure are one tough ol' broad, Kate."

"Well, geez. You're welcome, Lulene. See ya."

When I climbed in my car, I saw Lulene knocking over the coffee cups on the counter as she practiced her moves. They'll be looking for me as an accessory. She was aiming high enough to catch a man in the throat.

Mississippi: 1955, Belzoni–Reverend George Lee was killed for leading a voter registration drive. 1955, Money–Emmett Louis Till, a black youth from Chicago, was murdered for speaking to a white woman while visiting relatives. 1959, Poplarville–Mack Parker was taken from a jail and lynched. 1964, Liberty–Louis Allen witnessed the murder of a civil rights worker. He was later assassinated. 1967, Natchez–After a promotion to a "white job", civil rights worker Wharlest Jackson was killed.

Chapter Twenty-Three

Concentrating on her walking, Frances returned to her living room with glasses of Irish whiskey. Hardly an imbiber, she'd needed something to squelch the panic from being alone with Shawn Munson in the house. She was so lucky. Shawn was very good-looking. And actually in *her* house! When he'd waved the whiskey bottle up in greeting at her front door, she had been more relieved than surprised. Then alone in her kitchen, she'd anxious-ly gulped two mouthfuls, grimacing at the foreign taste. She would have preferred ending it there, but she'd succumbed to Shawn's insistence to join him in a second drink. From now on, she knew she'd have to take it much slower.

In the living room, Shawn stood at the small stereo looking at her pitifully short stack of CDs. As she seemed to float into the room, he turned and went toward her, taking the glasses and placing them on the table. Then he took her hands and gave them soft, gentle kisses. She tried to pull away, by reflex and anxiety. Shawn tightened his grip and came closer, like Cary Grant did in the movie she'd watched the night before. Shawn's lips followed as he slid her sleeve up. He raised his head and smiled. She sighed at the sheer romance of the moment. He kissed her neck, lingering.

"Oh, Shawn. I've been so lonely."

"I know." He nibbled the left side of her neck and moved to the other. Her desire overwhelmed her, made her feel wicked.

"Ohmygod," she moaned when his hand rubbed the blouse over her breast. Then her body stiffened, alert.

"What's the matter?"

"It's too soon. I don't know you that well. Isn't this wrong?"

"What does your heart say, Frances?" Shawn implored. She grabbed his head and jerked it toward her, smothering him first in her bosom then with her lips. He forced his tongue into her mouth. She greedily sucked it as if that would bring him closer into her heart.

"Ouch, not so hard."

"I'm sorry." she stammered, embarrassed, and backed away.

"Where do you think you're going?" He smiled sweetly. "Not when you just got me all hot." He wrapped his hands around her, pushing his pelvis into her body.

"Ohhh. I don't know what to do!" she whimpered.

"Nothing," he said softly. "Just follow me." His tongue made soft circles in her ear. Her knees buckled. Shawn grabbed her rear and pressed her harder into him. As she wrapped her arms around his neck, they almost toppled to the floor. She needed him to touch her–wanted it. Shawn lifted her up and carried her to the couch. They tumbled down onto it.

His foreplay was tentative, searching. Frances concentrated on what he was doing, learning for their next time. She lay there watching Shawn, trying to block out her father's maniacal fire and brimstone lectures. Touching a man, kissing one was evil. Frances let down her guard, relaxing as the warmth from Shawn's hands penetrated her clothing.

He tore at Frances's blouse, ignoring buttons, yanking down her bra, popping a strap. His mouth was confident, his hands now familiar with her body. Shawn's speech was garbled and strange. His hands moved faster from one area of her body to another. Frances sensed a change and couldn't remember when he'd gotten her skirt up and panties down. She couldn't keep up, he was everywhere all at once.

"Shawn, wait," she panted. "Slow down, it doesn't feel nice any more." He moaned, but it was tortured, not passionate. He put her arms above her head, gripping her wrists tight with one hand. The other penetrated her roughly, fingers in places no man had ever explored. His hands were hurting now, his lips equally wounding. She gasped and tried to slide from under him. "Not so rough." Her pleas intensified his movements. "Shawn." His eyes were closed tight, blocking her from getting through to him. "Shawn!" she yelled, her heart beating wildly.

He looked down and seemed surprised to see her.

"You're hurting me."

"You're just like that slut, aren't you?"

Frances' mouth opened in shock. "Wha-a?"

"You get me wound up and now you want to stop! Or you hold it away, dangling your need in my face. You want me to stop?"

"No, I don't want to stop! You were going so fast. I was scared, ah. I was scared how you'd be when you, um, got on top." He laughed deep, the sound booming in her ear.

"You can't even say it. You're old enough now–way old enough. Don't you know that, Frances?"

"Don't make fun of me, Shawn. Please." She looked hurtful at him. He looked back, cold and brooding. "What's wrong?"

"I thought you were different. You tease! You use what's between your legs to make men suffer. You're like all the rest–wicked and cheap. I'm leaving."

"No, don't!" Shawn had said the same things as her father, night after night as she and her sisters grew older. He'd warned her about the thing between her legs. Daddy was right! She had put herself–her desires–above Shawn's. Her daddy said that was wrong, too.

Shawn stood up quickly, brutally. She was flung down by the abrupt dismissal. "Are you going to help me?" She nodded frantically. "Or did your preacher daddy tell you to never put out to the desires of men?" He raised his voice, imitating the fervor of evangelists he'd seen on TV. "Did he tell you that fornicating was evil? How do you think you got on this earth? Can you say it, Frances? What is it we're doing here? What's it called?" Frances put her hands over her ears blocking the hurtful words, shutting out the image of her father standing over her shouting out scriptures, the endless warnings about the evil desires of women that cause men to stray. Shawn grabbed her shoulders and shook her. "Are you able to please me and stop your whining?"

"Yes!" Anything to stop his shouting! Stop her deep loneliness. She burst into tears and hurried after him. "I'm sorry! Please don't leave. Give me another chance. Please!"

Shawn yanked Frances down onto the floor. "Can you please me, wo-man?" He spoke in her ear. "Or do I have to leave and find someone who can?"

"D-d-don't leave me, Shawn. Whatever you want, my darling."

His temples finally softened. He smiled down at her, his hand rubbing her cheek. "I knew you were the one." He pulled her over, sliding her blouse halfway down her arms, binding her reach. Shawn started again like before. Slowly, then rising. But soon the shift inside him materialized again. His intensity and movements were building along with the grief he inflicted. He tore her skirt to get it out of his way. He never lingered in any area for long. His movements were frenzied—searching, never finding.

This time Frances succumbed to the carnal ritual, to the evil she had become. He probed her entire body while she watched him move, tormented, and listened to his pleas. Felt his body turning, straining. Watched his hands twisting her, molding her body into the ways he wanted, ways she'd never imagined. Frances tried desperately to be what he needed, do as he commanded. She grew fearful. Immobile. Afraid of the storm of emo-tions this man evoked. But as sweat rolled down his face and mingled with hers, she heard herself moaning, begging, wantonly calling out her love for this strange, brutal man. As they soared together, they felt the unleashing of their separate demons that drove them both.

Alabama: 1965, Selma–Reverend James Reeb, civil rights march volunteer, was beaten to death; outside Selma–Viola Gregg Liuzzo, a white housewife and mother who wanted to help with the Selma march, was killed by the Klan while transporting participants; Marion–Jimmie Lee Jackson, another marcher, was killed by a state trooper.
South Carolina: 1968, Orangeburg–Highway patrolmen killed student protesters Henry Smith, Samuel Hammond, Jr. and Delano Middleton and wounded twenty-seven others.

Chapter Twenty-Four

It was there. At a bend in the highway. The Last Chance. Appropriately named as the sign denoting Effingham County was closely shaved by the parking lot of the bar. One step north, you were in dry county. One step back, have a beer on me.

Minus the porch, the nightclub was built like the jail–square, nondescript cinder blocks, barred windows. The color scheme was exceptional– flophouse blue with a stripe of black at the top and bottom. On the roof, two wide metal pipes stuck up making the Last Chance look like a giant piece of Leggo.

Parking habits were similar to those in Brazil—pile 'em in, sort 'em out later. Pickup trucks dominated the lot. Not your tiny Japanese models, no! These were *real* trucks for *real* American boys! Rebel flags hung in the back windows behind gun racks. Dog cages lined the beds of the hunter's trucks while white metal tool boxes stretched from side to side of laborers' vehicles. A few cars hid among the trucks' shadows.

I entered the Last Chance to a blare of country music with pool balls clacking amid talk and laughter. Smoke wafted around me like a three-alarm fire. The majority of the male population gawked as I wove around tables to the bar. It wasn't that I was anything special, just the new boobs in town. I could feel eyes boring holes in my back and an occasional hand on my rear. I needed to endear myself to these folks, so I resisted the urge to break every male finger in the joint. Climbing up on a ripped vinyl barstool, I looked into the dirty mirror that lined the wall and saw a pair of eyes looking back.

He wasn't my type. But if you listened to my friends, there isn't one. The gazer nudged his buddy. They had a short consultation, then looked my way. I got a little Groucho move from the guy's eyebrows, which I interpreted as–*come on, toots, let's have some fun!*

The three guys on my right, lined up at the bar like seagulls on a fishing pier, were sneakier in determining my merit. One pretended to check the time on the unplugged clock on the opposite wall. The other two used a series of eye-ogling techniques: the cough and lookie-lookie; sip of a drink while roaming the eyes; the racquet-ball–eyes dodging around the room between stolen glances.

Four pool tables jammed the back. The cash register was keeping company with a double-barrel shotgun. A large red diamond-shaped sign, imitating our metal road signs, warned "No Assholes". The Last Chance was drenched in *Eau de Stale Urinal* with a hint of tobacco smoke.

"Can I hep ya?" The waitress sailed over popping her gum, getting about three per chomp. I was jealous. I could only manage one.

"What kind of beer you got, bottle?" She flung a thumb behind her to a cooler crammed in the corner. I peered in the part I could see, sorry I wasted the eye-strain. "Do you have any imported beer?"

"Sure, honey." Pop, pop, pop. She slid back a cooler door hidden under the counter. "We got Coors!"

"I'll take it." I laid a twenty on the bar and debated my next move. The door opened, evening sun filtering in, creating a haziness reminding me of L.A.'s smoggy days. A man stepped in wearing jeans so tight you could tell his religion. After him, three women sashayed inside to a chorus of catcalls. Male eyes followed, hypnotized by the women's rears. Their joy at the attention showed in their peppy walk. A yelp behind the counter broke the spell. For some of us.

An overzealous customer accosted the waitress. Her movements were choreographed and efficient. She gave the drunk a push to remind him who was in charge, slammed the register, swirled around, counted change, plopped it on the counter, spun the other way to the cooler retrieving six long-necked Buds, wove them through her fingers as she flew past and served them with a sliding maneuver that would be coveted by any hockey player. Whew! *This* was a woman of the new millennium!

"Boy, howdy," I said having learned that opener from Lulene. "You sure know how to handle yourself! How many guys can you take on at a time? Hi, I'm Kate," I lied when she returned behind the bar.

"Nancy," she replied, saying her name in three syllables, shaking my palm in one.

"Do you work this place by yourself?"

"Yep, and now I own it. My old man ran it in the ground, played around on me, got hisself in trouble. I decided to stay on. I like it here, 'specially now he's gone." The guys at the bar laughed. I did too. "After what I went through with him, these guys are a picnic." Nancy's face was worn with deep trench-like lines, earned by someone who'd been to hell but had kicked enough ass to find her way back. I tried my lost brother story on her.

"Sounds like Randy Beamon, but he ain't in no position to hep anyone."

"Why's that?"

"He's about as pitiful as eggs without grits. Always in trouble."

"What kind of trouble?"

"It's never big stuff." She leaned closer. "He's too stupid." I liked her frankness. She tapped my arm. "Now, he talks big. That he does. Says he's helpin' build some kind of empire. I stopped listening to his mouth a few seconds after I first met 'im." She cackled, but it was a nice, deep sound. "I'm usually too busy watching his hands, making sure they ain't on me."

"Sounds like a real prize."

"Hey, guys, this girl's looking for her brother," Nancy said to the men at the bar. "He's been hangin' out with Randy Beamon." They all sniggered.

"Check the jail," the gull on my far right said. The middle gull slapped him on the back laughing.

"Randy's been working." That produced a gaggle of giggles. "At the plant!" Har-har.

"If he ain't been fired yet." The middle gull was shaking his head. "That ol' boy's been sucking up to the plant boss ever since that Yankee put a toe in southern soil. Brags all the time, he does, about this high po-sition he's supposed to have there."

"Yeah, and all the money he's raking in." More giggles. "Only problem is nobody's ever seen him do a lick a' work!" The gull closest to me had to accentuate his laughter by drumming on the bar with his palm.

"Yep, his head lives in Fantasyland."

Nancy had been fishing in the cooler for more beer. She straightened and rapidly began popping off the bottle caps. "He'll be here Friday night. It'll be payday. That is, if that ol' blue junk of a truck can get him here."

I wondered whose information was incorrect–the gulls here at the bar or the woman at the plant when I'd phoned about Randy. "Do you know where Randy lives?"

"Depends on who he is seeing at the time," volunteered someone else.

I drained my beer. "What does Randy look like?" Nancy described him as about her height, 5'6", dirty blond hair, shoulder length.

She leaned toward me again and spoke quietly. "Let's just sum it up like this–he's ugly enough to vomit a buzzard. Greasy. Never bathes. Oh, yeah. He's got a tattoo, right forearm. Crescent moon with the name Moonpie across it."

"That his wife or girlfriend?"

"Sister." I froze not knowing a socially acceptable response.

"Yep. Makes you stop and wonder, don't it?" Behind me I heard a commotion.

A customer yelled as he twirled his partner twice. "It's time for some *daint-sin*, Nancy!" Daint-*sin*? So that's why the Pentecostals shun it. The dance floor was a small circle made from sliding the tables into a corner. Three couples stomped around looking like they were smashing bugs. Then they'd spin around, leap in the air, smash more bugs. Stump-jumping, my grandmother calls it.

"I guess I'll be going now. Thanks for all your help, Nancy."

"Will we be seeing you on Friday?"

I nodded. "What's a good time to be here?"

"Oh, about dark-thirty."

"See ya, and don't hurt anybody when I leave." Nancy smiled and gave me a triple-pop gum salute. Before I could pry my sweating butt off the stool she was out on the floor sweeping beer bottles onto her tray. I left the ten and change she'd put on the bar but took the ones. I wanted Nancy on my side.

Outside, I inhaled the fresh night air with gratitude. I twisted through the vehicles heading toward the Escort. "Kate! Wait a minute." I reached the car and dug in my shorts for the keys. "Kate! Have you forgotten your name?"

"Basically," I mumbled to myself. *Idiota*, I mentally chided myself. Some undercover work I'm doing. As the figure jogged closer, the street-light illuminated him. The middle gull. The guy had only-in-the-stomach pudginess, and looked pregnant if you ignored the chest hairs peeking over the T-shirt neck. He wore a Garth Brooks hat making him look as goofy in it as the country singer.

"What do you want?"

"You were asking about Randy Beamon."

"Yeah?"

"Well, I happen to know something about him."

Internal warning systems went on red alert. I reached in my pocket and interlaced the keys between my fingers. Something about him said, "RUN!"

"Hey, I know where he's staying."

"Where?" I asked.

"I can take you there."

"I don't have a lot of time. Just give me directions, please."

"It's out in the country. You'll never find it. I'll take you." He stepped toward me. I stepped back.

"Sorry, but my mommy told me to never ride with strangers." I put my hand out, traffic cop stop style.

"What's the matter with you, gal?"

"Nothing." My short reply seemed to stump him. Then he slapped him-self lightly on the cheek.

"Dang 'skeeters. They bitin' harder this year."

I had nothing to contribute to this detour in the conversation. I could almost see the gears turning between his ears. His eyes cleared and he switched back to the original subject. "You ain't a very friendly gal. Here I am tryin' to help you and you acting all stuck-up. You ain't one of those funny gals are you? They be everywhere these days." He sneered and advanced again.

"What are you talking about?"

"You know. Queer."

"Filho da puta. Idiota!" I cursed. "Get out of my way! I'm leaving! Alone!"

"I'm taking you *now*. Let's go." Suddenly he was in my face, arms bear-hugged around me. I panicked momentarily, but realized I had freedom from the elbows down. The smell of beer was strong. As he stumbled, I shifted my weight forward.

"Get off me!" I yelled loudly while I reached up and raked his back with the car keys. His hold slackened. I pushed him off and went for his face while I kicked him in the knee, sending him staggering backward.

"You dang ugly bitch!" He bent over, a hand on his cheek. "Why'd you use the keys on my face?"

"Because I don't have any fingernails!" The door to the bar flew open. Nancy glided up as if she were taking curb service, double-barreled shotgun pointed in our general direction. She pumped it, the clicking sound putting the fear of God in us. We froze in our tracks.

"Jerry, get your tail in your truck and go on home." Jerry stumbled to his truck staying in the sights of her weapon until he sped away.

"Thanks, Nancy, how did you know..."

"Honey, I don't know what you got going here, but people are acting stranger than a lunatic under a full moon. There was a lot of whisperin' soon as you left."

"Why? What about?" Finally a little information!

"The only tip I get around here jingles in my pocket. Now get on away from here. I won't have no trouble in my place!"

I'm sure I levitated to the car, taking only seconds to be headed back toward Rincon. This time I'd look for Lemond's house. My eyes burned from the smoky bar. The smell of exhaled tobacco permeated the car. I dug into my backpack. No Bazooka Joe, no Jordan almonds. Suffering from vice deprivation, I sped into the impending darkness.

*   *   *

Back on the outskirts of Rincon, I saw the volunteer fire department, surmised it was Blandford Road and turned left. It was nearly dark as I crossed the railroad tracks. My headlights briefly illuminated tidy yards, an occasional trailer, open fields and rows of tall corn. It was a bit tricky and once I stopped for directions. Counting mailboxes, I pulled into the yard of the thirty-seventh one. Something moved out of the corner of my eye.

My heart thwacked suddenly. I inched the car forward, keeping my attention on the darker corner of the yard. The car dipped into a crater. My head pitched forward and cracked against the steering wheel. *"Puta que o pariu!"* Cursing in a romance language was a bit more flowery than Eng-lish. Go back to the bitch you came from—well, it just said a little more than a simple damn or hell.

The pain in my head smarted enough to make even a hard-shelled Baptist happy at the retribution. I rubbed the sore spot only to increase the agony. Moving slowly, I saw something again by the tree. Distracted, I rolled into another pothole.

"Enough!" Yanking the gear into park, I slammed the door behind me and marched toward the tree. As I whipped around it, I found myself tap-dancing with tree roots and smacked down on my butt. I looked up, mouth frozen open in horror. "Ahhh!"

Involuntary whimpers filled the quiet as I crawled backward. My throat needed another three inches of space, the muscles spasmed tightly. I rolled over, hanging my head, and got up on all fours. Vomit spewed on the grass splattering onto my hands. My promise to Dixie was now fulfilled. I had found Lemond. He was swinging by his neck from the tree.

"Rick"–Skinhead in the Army: "All those greasy Mexicans used to come around and stick needles in their arms. We'd get pumped on Skrewdriver *[Skinhead rock group] and throw them out the window. We'd call it a fire drill." Rick, like many other Skinheads, takes an anti-drug stance while smoking cigarettes incessantly. A Skinhead girl: "I don't like Hitler at all. He killed Anne Frank and that was a good book."*–Boston Globe 2/12/89.

Twenty-Five

No telling how long I sat there staring, my mind reeling. The glow from the headlights cut into the darkness illuminating the agony Lemond had suffered. His broken neck made him look like he'd just nodded off. His lip was cut deep enough that a flap dangled down exposing teeth and gums. His eyes were swollen shut by bruising. Lemond's feet were bent downward at the middle from whatever device had crippled his arches. There were many small circular burns, rimmed in black, dotting his exposed skin. Orange clay was smeared in patches, making him look like a tragic model for a cubist painting.

"Lemond," I said out loud into the evil night. "I promise that I won't stop until I find out who did this to you!"

The neighborhood was quiet except for a barking dog and occasional noises from the row of neatly kept houses. Lemond's home was dark, but I climbed the three stairs, crossed the tiny porch and knocked anyway.

I waited a few beats, banged on the door again. As expected, nobody was bunking in his crib tonight. I could postpone my role as grim reaper. Now what? I did *not* want to be the one to notify the local police.

"What business you got here?"

I spun around like a dervish and clutched my heart. *"Droga!* Excuse, me, ma'am." The lady walking from the side of Lemond's house was AARP-aged, white hair taking over the black, almost hefty, and trying to hide a bit of snippiness behind a cautious veneer. Her broom was beside her, but I knew it was loaded and ready for bear.

"Uh, I, I'm a friend of Lemond's."

"I ain't seen you here before. And I know most of his friends." *White girl*, hung there unspoken between us. From the corner where she'd appeared, a thin, leggy and beautiful teen-aged girl walked up with a small boy on her hip. Her skin was smooth and brown. I smiled. She smiled back and bent over to let the child roam free.

"Take your nephew and go. I told you to stay out of this," her mother ordered, with more snap than when she'd addressed me. An older man, her husband, I guessed, skirted all of them and came to stand protectively beside Broom Lady.

"What's going on?" He asked quietly. Suddenly the broom jerked, the lady turned rigid, then her body shook. A low-throated wail tore from the bowels of her being. We all froze, staring stupidly at her. I didn't know whether to start CPR or find some holy water. She gasped, covering her mouth and her howls abruptly died off. The silence was equally piercing. Crickets. My next coherent thought was that she'd even scared the bejesus out of the crickets. Then the neighborhood erupted in sound and motion.

Car tires screeched on the road in front of the house. The little boy echoed the Broom Lady's wails. The man shook her. The girl nearly knocked over the baby as she ran toward the tree. She stopped, backed up, stumbling in drunken circles. Porch lights snapped on. Doors opened and shut. And I just stood there cataloging every detail. Once again gathering data for later analysis.

"It's Lemond? He's dead? I knew it. He's been gone too long. *I felt it.*" She pounded the spot over her heart. "Right in here. Oh, my dear lord." She sighed audibly, dolorously. "That poor honey chile! Aaaagggggh!"

The yard filled with neighbors in panic. People gathered in the yard, quickly taking in the scene. I watched them screeching, flailing at the air. They were sucked into the awfulness, pulled unwillingly to the sight of the young man hanging lifelessly from the tree. It was sickening. It was death. Overkill. Unimaginable horror. It was history. Struggle. Abuse. Suffering. It was hatred. It was evil. It was the *rope.*

"They hung him like an animal! How could anybody do such a thing!" A young boy asked me as he collapsed, sobbing at my feet. The sounds of grief and wailing were like a razor tearing at my heart. I stood, still rooted, unable to move while taking it all in.

More people were approaching from the road. Two middle-aged women flanked an old man who held a thick stick for support, white hair framing his head like a shiny halo. When they were close enough to see, the women broke into a run.

"Lord have mercy! They hung Lemond!" The women knelt beside him, embracing each other and rocking, their high female voices rising up from the anguished huddle. The old man stopped near the Escort, staring at Lemond, tears streaming down his face. His lips were moving but I could hear no sound.

"Cut him down!" I flinched at the sound. "Oh God, please cut him down! Animals. They ain't human, who done this!" The teenaged girl broke through the crowd and hands grabbed at her, pulling her back. She reached out, her fingers trying to crawl toward Lemond.

"We need to call the police," I spoke softly.

"Police? What's an all-white police gonna do?" The Broom Lady turned on me as before, her face full of rage. "He's nothing but a dead nigger to them! Good riddance! That's what they'll say. They wouldn't even go look for him. He might have still been alive. The police'll be wanting to take him down to the center of town to show off," she yowled and collapsed back into herself.

"Yep, ain't nobody care about us niggas," another agreed.

I turned away from the crowd to fish my cell phone out of the rental car. I dialed Al's number, waited for various clicks and changeovers as his service transferred me from number to number until I caught up with him. I used the time to flat-line my roiling emotions. I gave him the tragic news. He seemed genuinely concerned, saddened and enraged at the news. It was a small comfort for me. We had a short discussion, tried to form a decent plan.

While waiting for him, I would phone the local cops to report the murder, giving enough details about the crime without leaving my name. He would make a few calls and be on his way here. I gave him directions. "Al, do you think something will happen to Dixie next?"

"I don't know, sugah. I wish I could tell you something definitely. I'll see what I can do." I ended the conversation by telling him that I needed to find a way to get in touch with people on a cruise ship, explaining about Dixie's family on vacation. "I'll get Kevin working on it immediately." I didn't want to hang up. His take-charge manner was reassuring. I held the phone tightly like a lifeline. I had run out of questions. We said goodbye.

I paced behind the car, not wanting to join the others. I didn't want to reconnect with their grief. Didn't want to feel it. I knew all too well how awful it was. Behind me I heard the old man with the stick. I turned to face him. He'd been eavesdropping.

"She was here before."

"Dixie?" He nodded.

"She spent a good long while with me one afternoon. Told me about Lemond, her family. You." He sighed deeply, forlorn, and glanced over to the tree and back. I was busy viewing the local flora and fauna uncomfortable and unsure what to say.

"Do you realize what may happen because of you?" I steeled myself for a lecture and waited for him to continue. "A white woman sticking up for the colored–to help Clarice's Dixie." For some reason I couldn't look at him, finding the toe of my left Docksider holding my gaze. He cleared his throat but didn't say anything. But he wasn't going to let me off that easily.

I finally focused on him. In the growing darkness, I could see the pain on his old, wrinkled face. It tore him open, watching Lemond's crumpled form, but he held it, struggling, so that he could form it into something, to mold it into a workable sadness. "Honey chile, do you realize what could happen to us all? To you?" I hadn't really sat down and pondered it until he mentioned it and I wasn't very thrilled now that he had. But I nodded, keeping my thoughts to myself for a change. "Do you have the strength to finish this out?" I knitted my brow in question.

"This is only the beginning. The devil's come to this neighborhood. Who knows when he's gonna leave? He's after this family something awful. Do you have enough faith to take on Satan?" I wasn't sure about the devil, but I was certain about Dixie and her family. The old man's eyes finally moved and locked on my face as if to read me.

"Yes, sir. That's what I'm here for."

"Well, sister, my church and I, we'll all be praying for you. You're one of God's angels. He'll protect you. This will be remembered as the summer of evil. It must be cut down like the 'cane in the fields. God bless you, honey chile."

"Thank you," sounded stupid, but I had no other words. I left the man standing in the same place he'd stood since he'd arrived, the watchman, one hand gripping his stick, his eyes locked on Lemond's body.

Alan Berg, a popular, outspoken, Jewish radio talk-show host from Denver, urged anyone in his audience who hated Jews or blacks to call in. His belittlement of members of the racist group The Order, garnered their ire and his name on their 'hit list' of people who threaten the existence of the white race (which included Henry Kissinger and Fred Silverman). In June, 1984, Berg was gunned down in front of his home with an illegal Ingram MAC 10 (machine gun). Berg's murderer, David Lane, co-founder of The Order, fired thirteen shots, causing thirty-four wounds as the slugs bounced around his body. Lane calls himself a prisoner of war, stating he is incarcerated for crimes committed while in battle and in the interest of the cause, and Berg was an enemy of that cause.

Chapter Twenty-Six

Al made it from Savannah to Rincon before the local police drove their few miles. There was no need to count mailboxes. A crowd had gathered by then. I'd taken steps to keep them from getting too close to Lemond and spoiling any evidence that could be gleaned by trained eyes. Al approached, concern etched in his handsome face. I resisted the urge to fling myself into his arms. "Sugah, are you all right? You look a little peaked." I lied and told him I was okay. "Did anyone tell Grainger I was on my way?"

"And ruin the surprise?"

He put an arm around my shoulders pulling me in. "Good girl." He glanced at his watch as another car squeezed behind his. Two men, suited and tied in the stereotypical government agent manner, motioned to Al. We all trailed behind him. "This is Bruce Vontana, Georgia Bureau of Investigation," Al told the crowd of neighbors. Vontana gave a crisp smile and waved.

"This is your state buddy?" I asked Al. He nodded. Vontana was baby-faced, naive looking. I didn't believe it–although it was a great persona for an agent.

"I'm Perry Taylor," the black man beside him said and held up a badge. "Until I moved here, I thought Mississippi was the hottest place on earth," he said, relieving a bit of the tension. "I'm Vontana's partner. We're here to investigate this terrible murder. We'd appreciate any help. Anything you can think of, no matter how insignificant it may seem, please let us know. All information will be kept confidential. You don't even have to give us your name. We're from the state, so we don't–and probably won't–have to work with local law enforcement. From what we've been hearing, they aren't interested anyway." Whispers of agreement rose from the crowd.

Vontana took over. "A crime scene investigation team will be here shortly."

"My Nancy Drew here has kept the area surrounding the body off limits," Al told them and smiled at me. "She found the body."

"I doubt we'll find anything useful, but it was good thinking," Vontana said. They split the group of neighbors in half, each agent

taking a section for questioning. I quickly picked the lock to Lemond's front door so the crime scene team could enter without
breaking it and just as speedily explained to the surprised agents and
Al of my part-time job on the island. Only locksmiths and thieves
carried picking tools and my former occupation and a still-current
license made my possession of them legal. I traipsed back and forth
as gopher for Al and his GBI buddies, careful not to look at the tree.
The yard continued to fill as neighbors arrived shocked and grieving.
Others went home to bring back food and drinks. With only two
agents, and Al doing what he could, it would take a long time to
question everyone.

As a basket went around for monetary contributions for Lemond's
family, Grainger arrived. It'd been more than two hours since I called
in the murder. When he realized the GBI was on the scene, he
stomped around, a red-faced Rumpelstiltskin. I relished every second.
He soon left to protect the other side of the railroad tracks.

The group of neighbors who had stayed during the lengthy crime
scene investigation passed the time harmonizing while my mind
worked its habitual jive, head whirling, itching to flee. *Amazing
Grace* filled the dread-ful evening. Everywhere I went, *a cappella*
sadness followed me.

I glanced over at the crowd as their voices lowered, ending the
hymn. The teen-aged girl stepped out from the crowd, her voice as
lovely as she was. But her agony was palpable. She began a tune I'd
recognized as one of Billie Holliday's. "Strange Fruit" had been
recorded decades ago, but sadly it still held truth for today. I closed
my eyes and let her voice surround me.

> *southern trees bare a strange fruit*
> *blood on the leaves and blood at the root*
> *black bodies swinging in the southern breeze*
> *strange fruit hangin' from the poplar trees*
>
> *pastoral scene of the gallant south*
> *the bulging eyes and the twisted mouth*
> *scent of magnolia sweet and fresh*
> *then the sudden smell of burning flesh*
>
> *here is a fruit for the crows to pluck*
> *for the rain to gather*
> *for the wind to suck*
> *for the sun to rot*
> *for the tree to drop*
> *here is a strange and bitter crop*

Upon hearing the haunting words, the agents busied themselves
with shoe checking, heads down, keeping their emotions hidden. I was
relieved when it was finally quiet. The old man took his stick, moved

it left and right, parting the crowd like Moses dividing the Red Sea. He stood just behind the technicians working on Lemond's body. He prayed aloud, his congregation sprinkling amens here and there.

Images of my mother. Dead. Ready for burial. Flashed into my mind. My gut wrenched harder as I remembered the pain and loss that had overwhelmed me and my father. My hands flew to my temples, as if that could stop the horror of both the past and present devastation. Why do I do this? *Keep digging that hole, Paloma, and having to crawl out.* My eyes were pulled again and again to the tree and Lemond's battered body as the past kept creeping into my mind. My father's twisted body after the accident. My mind was a View Master of death as one horrible scene flipped to another, my finger on some imaginary white button unable to stop, always advancing to the same three terrible sights. Mom. Dad. Lemond. Mom. Dad. Lemond. *Stop it!* My panic rose. Feeling the black pit of hell that always threatened to suck me down into its quagmire each time I remembered. I had to make myself not run screaming to the car. As I drove onto Blanford Road, I made sure not to look anywhere but straight ahead.

Later that evening, at the hotel, I had a message from Al. The desk clerk read in a bored voice. "Where the heck did you run off? Would you like to have a late dinner?" The heck was a nice touch.

After leaving Lemond's, I'd come back to the Inn and I immediately went for a swim hoping to calm the madness in my head. It was late and I sighed deeply, weary to the bone. I was hungry but didn't want to eat in the hotel room. Didn't want to be alone with my thoughts. I needed people to watch and occupy me while I ate. I showered and donned one of my nicer shorts set, slipping some bills, driver's license and hotel keycard in the back pocket so I wouldn't need to lug my pack.

I'd missed Al. When I passed the Waving Girl Law Firm the building was dark. At Spanky's, I ate a seafood sampler appetizer and drank a few beers. The place was packed and looked like fun, except when you'd had a day like mine. I yawned long, my mouth straining at the corners. On the way back to the hotel, I stopped at the Savannah Sweet Tooth to stock up on vices, gripping the bag of Jordan almonds like gold.

The pedestrian walkway was relatively empty with couples taking late night strolls with occasional party crowds filling the quiet with boisterous chatter. The trendy stores were closed. I window-shopped, looking at clothes only an anorexic could possibly wear. Taking my larger frame to the Savannah River, I stopped, leaned against a sign post, noticed it was a bronzed historical marker and felt obliged to read it. I squinted in the dim light. It was at this site, in 1733, that James Oglethorpe chose for Georgia's first colony. If I remembered correctly from earlier map reading this week, at this spot I was about twenty miles upriver from the Atlantic Ocean. We'd learned in school that Oglethorpe arrived with a boatload of debtors from the English jails to help build the colony. Class dismissed. Now what? I looked down at the river. The bourbon-colored water looked black in the darkness.

Bits of trash floated quickly by in the swift flow. Big engines revved, filling the docile night. I finally turned and crossed the street, more than ready for bed. Tires pealed and raced out of the parking lot on my right. Back on River Street, a truck turned right, cutting off oncoming traffic. I stepped back as a precaution. The driver gunned his engines and headed straight at me.

Alabama: Tuscaloosa, 1981–The United Klans of America, at that time considered the most violent Klan faction, kidnaped, beat and lynched nineteen-year-old Michael Donald and hung his body from a tree. A group of Klansmen, including Titan Bennie Hays, gathered at a house across the street from where Michael's body dangled. Hays said of the hanging: "A pretty sight. That's gonna look good on the news. Gonna look good for the Klan." Hays then walked over to the body and his look of admiration was caught by television cameras. This action would prove to be a burden in Hays' future.

Twenty-Seven

Swartzman's office was becoming his home. He knew from the beginning that it'd be that way, so as plant manager he made sure he'd gotten a good chunk of space reserved for him when they designed the plant. An extra-large, comfortable and expensive couch on the far wall was used for napping when long hours made him weary. There was a well-stocked bar, a shower in his private bathroom and the best view in the plant, such as it was. His window overlooked a field and part of Highway 21–not exactly the perk that got him to leave Boston and move to the Land of Humidity. He'd complained about summers in Boston most of his life. No more! Before going back to his desk, he turned the thermostat lower. The air conditioner moaned to life.

Slipping his shoes off and propping his feet on his desk, he studied the file on Cleveland "Red" Chandler. He read about the young man's early life– looking for vulnerabilities, crises–anything he could use to his advantage. Red's father had died when he was twelve–heart attack. Wife's name was Mary, had three children and one on the way, and he'd quit an eight-year job with Dixie Crystals sugar refinery because they'd messed things up with affirmative action. When a black became his supervisor, Red Chandler became unemployed.

"Mr. Swartzman?"

"Red, come in. Have a seat." He pointed to a chair at the large meeting table beside Swartzman's desk. Red seemed a little fidgety.

"Drink?" Red didn't answer until Swartzman held up his glass. He passed over the row of good, expensive booze–didn't want to waste it on an uncultured bubba–and poured an inch of cheap bourbon in a short glass. Swartzman poured himself a J & B Jett. "We have ourselves a problem." Red tensed. "Now, son, I need ya to help me out on this one." He could tell Chandler was wondering what he'd done wrong, instead of exuding confidence that if he'd been working hard and honestly, the summons must be about something or someone else. Swartzman jotted down "needs assurance" on a legal pad and turned it over so Red couldn't see. "Can I count on you?"

Red shrugged, worry still crinkling his brow. Swartzman made himself smile briefly. Didn't want the guy too relaxed. "There's a growing problem with a guy I got doing some work for me. You know him. That someone is Randy Beamon."

*   *   *

The truck headed toward me on River Street. It took a second for me to digest reality and act on it. I stepped back onto the sidewalk. The driver compensated. Behind me was a small wall to keep pedestrians from tumbling down into the well-lighted parking lot. At the other end was another wall along the riverbank to keep cars from taking a swim. I chose the parking lot, jumped over its stone barricade and landed onto the asphalt with a foot stinging slap. Curious about my pursuers, I looked behind me.

The truck doors swung open and two guys quickly climbed out of the cab. The passenger I didn't recognize. I looked at the driver. In the dimness I could see his shape and my mind flashed to the hotel courtyard. Randy Beamon? Had to be. It was the only thing that made sense. In the back of the truck a huge blob of a woman sat up. Randy yelled something to her and the mass disappeared again. I ran.

When I got to the end of the parking lot furthest away from them, I climbed the steps, crossed the street, and headed for the restaurants. Randy ran down the cobblestone street to greet me. Horns blared from vehicles stuck behind the driver-less truck. The men split up. Randy was gaining on the left. That's when I noticed he was hiding his right arm slightly behind him. That means trouble. I needed to find cover. And fast. He brought a rifle around in front, shouldered it and fired. I'd already lunged down and was half way under a car. I heard the ping as the bullet struck metal. And the surprised cries of pedestrians who'd been alerted by the sound of gunshot. I braved a look around to plot my escape. Randy's buddy was still advancing on the right. Yahoo with gun on left. Running forward would put me right at his truck with the two of them closing in behind me. I turned back and dashed through the parking lot again. Pppbblltt! Cement splattered in front of me, pieces stinging into my legs. His aim was getting better. Only one place to go. Pausing just briefly, I climbed up the wall and dove into the racing waters of the Savannah River.

*   *   *

Swartzman waited in his office for Red to phone with an update. The young man had seemed eager to be Randy's shadow. To pass the time, he worked on figures to determine how much equipment was needed to make the twenty satellite WRF units fully functional. The computer cursor winked at him unbudgingly.

"When I clicked FILE, I meant I wanted them back!" He slapped the monitor. The cursor continued to blink patiently. After a few more misfires he pulled out the instructions, angry he had to do so. Following the list to the letter and several tries later, he was able to open the second set of records–those of the WRF. In the off chance that someone discovered the files on this secret organization, he'd created an excuse–he was creating his own *Turner Diaries*. The worst he could be accused of at first glance, was being the bigot that he truly was. And while it was still a somewhat free country, that cover would give him time to assess the situation and annihilate any threat. But now the worst had happened. That damn black kid had found the financial records, read the reports and started nosing around. Just a cost of doing business. The phone rang, he snatched it up.

"Hello." He answered irritated.

"It's the Leprechaun."

Swartzman's tension lessened. "Talk. The line's secure."

"Your night's gonna look a little brighter soon."

"How many?"

"I've got ninety-nine rifles, one hundred four goggles, five M-16's, and three grenade launchers."

Swartzman let out a long whistle. "My friend, you are right on time. Okay, the Georgia camp is taking the slack for Florida until I can get it going again. Next will be Idaho. We're very active there. Hold on, I'm logged onto my computer. I'll be able to give you the breakdown for shipping." They discussed delivery arrangements. "You'll get forty percent now and the rest will be transferred within twenty-four hours of delivery. Agreed?"

"Agreed." Swartzman hung up, pleased with the good news. He issued a fake purchase agreement for company supplies that would never be order-ed, then attached a message for Finance to arrange payment to Leprechaun's fake company. Adding in the new figures of equipment, he propped his feet on his desk, keyboard on his lap and watched while the computer performed its number crunching. He paged up and down the screens, marveling at what he saw.

"What the hell..." Swartzman's feet struck the floor. He put on his glasses but the numbers stayed the same. He dug out all the hard copies of inventory and double checked the figures. He flung his glasses on the desk. Three rifles missing, two goggles, four pistols and six cellular phones. He still didn't know where Randy Beamon was, but now he had an idea of what he'd been doing.

Michael Donald's mother Beulah, with help from attorney Morris Dees of the Southern Poverty Law Center, filed a civil suit claiming her son's murderers were carrying out their organization's policy. She asked for compensation damages in the death of her son. Former Klan members testified they'd been directed by Klan leaders to harass and kill blacks. An all-white jury awarded seven million dollars in damages–the first time in history that a jury held the Klan responsible for the actions of its members. Mrs. Donald received the Klan's only significant asset–the deed to their headquarters, later sold for $55,000. Mrs. Donald died soon after.

Twenty-Eight

Randy had been driving like a maniac since leaving River Street and the second blundered attempt to get Paloma. His sister Moonpie was in the back of the pickup, rolling around at her brother's whim.

"Randy, slow down! The cops'll get you," Moonpie implored after she'd stuck her head through the truck's small rear window. "And you're 'bout to throw me out the back." Randy took his hand and covered what he could of Moonpie's face, shoving her head back. He slammed the window shut and made an abrupt lane change. His sister fell over and banged her head on the truck bed. Tears puddled in her eyes. "I'm tired of giving and giving! Helping everyone and getting shitted on for my trouble! It's been this way since I was born," she lamented to the stars. She heard Billy Ray take up for her. Too little, too late.

"You shouldn't treat your sister so bad," Billy Ray said and immediately regretted it. He whipped his head back as Randy's fist grazed his nose. He gripped a wad of Billy Ray's shirt. "Stop, Randy, damn you."

Spit flew from Randy's mouth as he spoke his terse words. "Don't. You. *Ever*. Tell. Me. What. Ta. Do. You asshole! You wouldn't be where you iz today 'ceptin' fer me. You got that, you dipstick?" Billy Ray had heard this before and found it as interesting as watching a test pattern on TV. "I'll treat dat whorin' pig da way she deserves. She ain't nothin' but a lazy, fat-ass screwin' machine. Besides. *She's only a girl*. What'm I s'pose ta do, B-Ray, treat her like one a' us? Man, you never wanted nothin' to do with her bafore anyhow." He laughed depravedly. "You finally got a stiff willie? Dat why you a'worryin'?" He leered, baring teeth so covered in brown fuzz he'd have to use a surgical blade if he ever decided to clean them. He played chicken with an oncoming car, nearly clipping them. As the other driver blared his horn in panic, Randy threw him the finger as he passed.

"Idjit! I wuddn't even close." He dug a finger in his right nostril. Billy Ray wished he'd puncture his brain. Randy pulled his finger out of his nose and rubbed it on the underside of the dash. He then inspected his finger and wiped it on his pant leg. Billy Ray sighed. He knew Randy's moods, and his friend wasn't about to shut up anytime soon. Especially with that fifth of Jim Beam so empty and most of it in Randy's belly.

"Why you bein' so upstandin' for dat ol' fat pig back dere? Dumb ol' hawg." He jabbed Billy Ray roughly in the ribs.

Although it hurt like the dickens, he let the poking slide. "She does anything you ask," Billy Ray replied. "I think you ought to give her a little bit that's due her. That's all I'm sayin'." Randy unexpectedly slammed on the brakes. Two thuds sounded as Billy Ray and Moonpie slammed forward. Billy Ray snapped. He'd held his temper as long as he could–about a whole da' gum year. He pushed Randy into the door.

"Would you stop actin' like a jerk, Randy? That hurt! You've done nothing but screw up all night. You told me that Dad ordered you to shake that half-breed up, not hunt her down and shoot her." Randy lit a cigarette with his Zippo lighter. In its glow Billy Ray saw the rage come to a full boil. He froze, expecting a fight. Randy was breathing hard, one hand squeezing the steering wheel, the other ripping the gears as he shifted violently. The truck was flying down the highway now. Billy Ray relaxed a little. Randy revving up the truck was a sign that he was calming down. Randy slammed a tape in and cranked the volume up until his speakers were distorting "Free Bird", that old Southern anthem of rebelliousness.

Just north of the Rincon city limits they turned down Willow Pea Lane, a dirt road that led to a new branch of the Savannah River. Recent dredging had exposed loose soil. The river had quickly carried it away but created a small inlet. Mother Nature then developed a very popular fishing hole, if you knew of its existence. At night it was a frequent necking place for teens.

"Why'd you turn here?"

"Shut the hell up!" Randy banged on the steering wheel then punched the dash. Blood trickled from the torn skin. Billy Ray was stunned. Watching from the rear window, Moonpie felt her throat tighten. She'd seen Randy like this before and it meant trouble. He pumped the gas pedal like he was stomping roaches. The truck spun on the dirt surface then lurched forward. Moonpie coughed as the dust engulfed her. Minutes later Randy slammed on the brakes.

Billy Ray's head snapped to the right as Randy's fist slammed into his cheek. Moonpie took her cue and jumped out of the truck. Randy was after her before she got more than a few steps away. She fell to the ground as he jumped on her back. He gripped her hair, pounding her head as Billy Ray grabbed his shoulders. The three of them rolled in the dirt and eventually Randy was pulled off his sister. Billy Ray punched hard, knocking the wind out of Randy.

"Now, Randy," Billy Ray said panting. "You go cool off. You ain't got no right doin' this." The two men stood facing each other as Moonpie rolled to her side, sobbing.

"Randy, you done broke my nose," she lamented. Her brother took a few steps backward and adjusted himself several times in the crotch with the same gestures he used to changed his truck's gears.

"You okay, honey?" Billy Ray tried to turn Moonpie toward him. He heard the sound of the truck door opening. "Randy don't you leave us here! Your sister needs to get her nose checked out."

"Leave me alone! You don't give a shit about me, Billy Ray," Moonpie choked out between sobs. "And you ain't never did! Why don't y'all just leave me here to die? Isn't that what y'all want?" Moonpie's body shook as her shrieks filled the night. It was spooky out here with only the truck's headlights to illuminate the darkness. Finally he got a look at Moonpie's face. Billy Ray no longer wondered why she was hollering so loudly. If it wasn't broken, then it darn sure was close to it. He didn't like to see anybody suffering. He felt pressure on his back and froze.

"You bastard. I told you not to boss me around," Randy said.

"Randy, get the gun out of my back. I wasn't tryin' to boss you around. Let's get her to the hospital. Okay, Randy? Take it easy now." Billy Ray's last statement ended on a high, skittish note.

"I don't give a shit about her or you. I'm gonna teach you both a lesson! You sayin' she always does what I tell her. So let's see it. Huh-huh." He wiped his face with his sleeve and waved the gun in front of Billy Ray.

"See what?" Billy Ray asked, his fear rising so high he could almost taste it on his dry tongue. Randy shoved him forward and he toppled over Moonpie.

"Leave me alone, both of you!" She got up on her hands and knees crawling away. With his Doc Marten's, Randy kicked Billy Ray's ribs twice and moved around to his sister. He paused to take a drink of whiskey.

"Where the hell you think you're goin', my sister, the town whore?" Randy grabbed the back of her shirt and pulled.

"Randy, leave me alone! Fool!"

"We'll see who's the fool here." With some effort he turned Moonpie onto her back. "You fat slob. You go after every one o' my friends. Turn them against me. You're just a girl, a slutty whore." He stabbed a finger at himself. "You wouldn't have nuttin'if it weren't for me." He held his face inches from Moonpie's injured one. He watched the fear heighten in her face and enjoyed it. "But you could never get that through that fat dumb head of yours." He shook Moonpie as he spoke. "I'm gonna teach you a lesson." As Randy released Moonpie, she coughed and gagged on air and blood. She turned, putting her head down around her knees.

"Get up, you chicken shit, Billy Ray!" He emphasized his words with another kick aimed at his friends' backside. "I said *get up!*"

Billy Ray stood, arms hugging his wounded ribs. "Randy, we didn't mean nothin'. We know you're the boss. You always was smarter than both of us." Randy laughed at the hope in Billy Ray's voice.

Randy stepped toward Moonpie. She sensed his movements and crawled away uselessly. He straddled her back and stuck the gun to her head. "Your lover boy here says you always do what I say. An' I don't appreciate it 'nuff." He waved the gun in Billy Ray's direction. "An' Ray, he ain't got no guts to do nutin' 'bout him wantin' you, Moonpie. So, I'm a'gonna do you boff a favor. See, Billy Ray don't never get none with his needle dick. He needs a woman dat knows what she's doin'. Dat's where you come in, girlie. You be showin' him da ropes, what he's been a'missin'." His head rolled back, wicked laughter exploded from his lips. He swayed, giddy and drunk on hate. "An' fer you, my sweet little sister. You been wantin' to add 'im to your long list of victims, so tonight I'm a'gonna let you have 'im." He fired the gun several times in the air. "Wooee!"

"No, bubba. Please! I'm really hurtin' *bad*. We can do this some other night. Okay? I just want to go home. Please, bubba, please!"

"Get 'im, Moonpie." He looked down and jerked back suddenly. "You filthy pig!" Randy got up and stumbled away from his sister. "She's so excited to get you Billy Ray, she done gone an' peed in her drawers." Moonpie cried, face down in the dirt humiliated. Randy stepped back into the light. Billy Ray was horrified at what he saw on Randy's face. The guy was having *fun*!

"Look at 'er gruntin' in the dirt like a fat ol' pig! He-he!" He shoved the gun down his terrified friends' pants. "I'm gonna play a little target practice, unless you tell Moonpie what you want. Drop your drawers and show her what you got!"

Billy Ray didn't move. Randy cocked the gun. "Randy, cut it out! This ain't funny no more!" Billy Ray wailed now.

"One, two..." Billy Ray unzipped his pants looking at Randy for word to stop.

"Put 'em to your ankles." He shook his friend's waist then roared as he watched Billy Ray's organ swing. Randy ordered him to walk. Hindered by the clothes around his ankles, he awkwardly circled and stumbled around Moonpie, again and again as Randy shouted instructions. Billy Ray's voice quivered with each animal noise and degrading word he was made to speak, designed to hurt Randy's sister. He stared down at her inert heap.

With unfazed resolve Moonpie obeyed her brother's orders and took Billy Ray's penis into her mouth. Billy Ray howled in agony, repulsed as he felt his penis stiffen in her mouth. Apologies stumbled from his lips–a litany that offered Moonpie a focal point. A chance to survive. And keep her a small step head of the same demonic madness that had already engulfed her brother.

The rest of the night faded in and out of Randy's memory in stilted images. Getting bottles of Jim Beam from the truck, making them guzzle. Moonpie retching. Sticking the muzzle of the gun in the crack of Billy Ray's ass until he mounted his sister. Her bulk bouncing in the dirt and then on top of Billy Ray. The thrill of them doing and saying whatever he commanded. Randy saw his hands float in front of him as he tied Billy Ray to an oak tree branch after he'd gotten bored of controlling him.

His sister's face–bloodied, disfigured–was underneath his. Images of her as he watched from the bedroom window became reality and was immediately disassociated in Randy's demented mind. Her wails of terror and pain were the frenzied cries of passion. Those sounds he'd heard her make on so many hot, drunken nights. She fought, tried to crawl away. He expected it. He'd seen her buck and rock, shake the entire trailer. Tonight she'd finally do this to satisfy him. She always knew what men wanted. He groaned and panted his lust.

He was high on the knowledge that he'd finally proven how much of a man he was. "Screw you, daddy!" He screamed. "You were wrong! I'm a man. Look at how good I am! I'm doing the things you said I couldn't do. And I'm doing it just like you, daddy. Just like you did to mama. And the women you brought home–showed off in front of us." He pointed to Billy Ray. "And mama's watching me, like you made her watch you."

When Moonpie and Billy Ray begged him, over and over, to stop, their urgency confirmed his actions, they were asking for more. The degradation of the night his father caught him with one of his cousins out on the tractor took control of Randy. He moved harder, faster inside his sister, trying to out distance the agony. He heard his father's horse whip crack in the air like a live wire. Faster, harder. His orgasm was peaking. He raised up, twitch-ing and bucking, feeling the sting as the whip cut into his flesh.

It wasn't until later in the work shed, after his father tied his wrists to the deer rack and took his time degrading and making fun of him, that Randy realized he wasn't being punished. Instead his father was laughing. That's the first time Randy could remember doing some-thing that made his father laugh. He was standing as he did before, crying. He smelled the long ago animal odors, saw the dirt floor stained in deer blood. His father's words echoed inside him, telling him he was no good at the one thing revered in his family. He watched again as two of his daddy's paid tramps yelped and giggled while his father romped with them in the dirt. He saw his mother's bloodied face as she tried to intervene. And watched as she crumbled to the floor. He'd learned long ago that his mother could do nothing to help him. "Mama, you dumb whore," he said as he took Moonpie's head in his hands. "Why can't you ever make him stop? Mama," he cried suckling on Moonpie's breasts. "He talks to me. All the time in my head. I can't make him stop." He went after her in a frenzy pushing her legs higher in the air.

Haunted by the memories Randy felt as the two women moved on him, the sounds of his father's voice as he gave them orders. He remembered each recoil as the trio jiggled the flesh between his legs, sneering, laughing, making cruel jokes about his size, his inexperience. They explored freely on his young body as he pulled at his restraints unable to break free. His back still carried the scars when he'd begged to be let go. It was time to make his mother kiss each one. Tell him it was her fault that she had never made her husband stop. Her time to ask, plead for Randy's forgiveness. His father was unequaled, forever unchallenged at manhood. He had pranced before his son, cocky vindication seeped from every pore. He'd never forgotten his father's lesson.

He hated them all! Especially their weakness. And the flesh between his legs. The need, the craving, what it drove him to do. But mostly he hated the memories taunting him. Driving him into a lunatic spin.

But *this* night's events were lost on Randy. He had succumbed to the vortex at last. To the hounds of hell that had nipped and licked at his heels ever since that long ago night. The brutality was like music in his head—violins prodding him and Satan was rosining the bow.

*Kentucky: 1985, Louisville–An investigation of arson at a black family's home uncovered a unit of Klan police officers called COPS (Confederate Officers Patrol Squad). California: 1993, Los Angeles–A black policeman allegedly was assaulted by several white policemen while he was on duty as a part-time bank security guard.–*Klanwatch.

Chapter Twenty-Nine

I emerged from the swift waters of the Savannah River pretty far from the bridge and the River Street area where I'd take my plunge. The current had pushed me at an angle, dragging me all the way across to the other side. It took hard swimming before I got far enough to the bank to stop drifting. I stumbled and fell shoeless out of the marsh, cutting my feet on broken glass and other debris. The docks here were deserted and the marsh bordered the entire complex. It was hard walking and full of sink holes, rocks, and other debris. I'm sure I managed to step on and trip over every one of them. I was exhausted and queasy from gulping river water and from the pounding in my head. I walked and rested. Threw up. Sent curses into the night. Started it all over again.

As I finally reached the highway that led to the bridge and back over into Savannah, I saw a security light from a building ahead in the dark. It was a closed fireworks store. So I was in South Carolina. Illegal to sell in Georgia, fireworks stores were a typical sight at the Carolina state lines. Dumpy buildings really, most of them painted in bright eye-catching yellows and reds. But no complaints here, they had a working phone outside. I read the advertisements on the building in the dim light–huge block letters about three feet tall. M-80s, Screamers, Cherry Bombs.

The cab driver eventually found Crazy Pete's and me, and drove me over the bridge into Savannah. He looked insulted when that I paid him in wet money that had managed to stay inside my shorts pocket.

A hint of dawn penetrated the dark sky as I finally made my way back into the hotel. I showered, arranged for my wet clothes to be laundered then scanned the Yellow Pages for a shoe store to replace the Docksiders I'd lost in the water.

Like bonafide white trash, I entered the shoe stores along River Street in my bare feet, but found only tall, spiky heels to wobble in or trendy, but uncomfortable. Heading back to the hotel, the sun was out, burners wide open. My bare feet sizzled on the hot cobblestones making me quick-step from rock to rock, frantically searching for shadows. The motion only served to make me feel worse.

Which is exactly how Al found me–swaying slightly with one hand against the building to hold me steady? "You look plum tuckered, Paloma." I didn't have the gumption to fire off a smart retort. He kept up his disparaging assessment until he was standing directly in front of me. "Why are you walking around on these stones in bare feet? You got a..."

I interrupted by purging my stomach of more river water. Unfortunately, Al was on the receiving end. My head was fit to burst causing my embarrassed retreat to be muddled. I stumbled into the wall and then into Al who had been trying to pull me somewhere. He gave up the struggle, scooped me up into his arms and headed toward his office. People stared openly as we made our way. "Al, put me down! I can walk by myself. Dammit!"

"Watch your mouth, little lady." He looked stern but his eyes were smiling, enjoying it! Each time I wrangled an escape he'd grab my limb as it got free. Which was how Aggie found us as we battled into the law offices, me slamming down on the floor finally free.

"Alvin Eason! What in tarnation have you done to her?" Aggie asked, voice full of consternation as she gave Al a cuff on his arm.

"Oww! You don't know your own strength, Aggie! She was wiggling like a jelly worm. I'm trying to help her!"

"You have a funny way of showing it! Move aside! She's sprawled like a lame horse. Lawd me!" She gave me a helping hand up. I took two steps and was covered with a blanket of sweat as my legs buckled.

"Alvin! Come here."

"First you send me away, now you want me back."

"Shut up, you old coot, and stop your polly-foxing! She's fainted."

"I haven't fainted! It's the heat and this headache. *Droga!*"

"I'll take her into my office." He scooped me up again. I opened my eyes but everything was still spinning so I closed them, admitting I'd need help on this one. Aggie was giving orders on just how to place me on the couch. Al had his own ideas. They bickered like children while they both hovered over me.

"I'm okay, people," I said firmly.

"Uh-huh." Al went into the bathroom, Aggie to fetch water. He returned taking the glass his cousin offered and tried to drown me with it. I wrenched it from his hands to sip without spilling. Peering above the glass, I noticed Al was bare-chested. Hmm, vomiting has its pluses. I took full advantage of the view. Nicely tanned, a bit muscular for a desk jockey, a dusting of chest hair bleached blonde from the sun. No hernia from carrying my hide. Hey big fellow. Could I be in lust?

"I don't know if I can stand any more water. I already drank the whole river." I briefly filled them both in on last night's shenanigans.

"How did you swim in that swift current?" Al queried sternly, moving my head around so he could look directly into my eyes. It was all I could do not to flinch and pull away from his penetrating gaze. It was like being in the principal's office, not because of trouble, but fidgety just because you where there.

"Ouch! Watch it, Al!" I pleaded lightly to have an excuse to wrench myself free. "I didn't really swim. About all I could do was stay afloat and slam into things. The current eventually pushed me to the Carolina side. I just had to walk *forever* to get back to civilization."

"You're a feisty little gal! Instead of being upset over the attack, you're mad because you couldn't beat the river." He shook his head in mock sadness. Dead on! How did he figure me out only knowing me a short time? "I'll call my doctor. I'm sure we can get you in–"

"No, Al. Thanks. That's not necessary. But aspirin would be handy." He and Aggie didn't move. I looked at them both saying, "Really! I'm fine. The worst that happened to me is that I lost my Docksiders and I'd just broken them in. But enough about me. Has anything happened with Dixie since last night?"

Al's feigned sternness. "Gee, sugah, it's still early yet. You might not have to rest, but I do need a few hours sleep once in awhile."

"Sorry," I said, properly chagrined. "It seems like forever since yesterday."

"The GBI will be hard at it this morning working out which members of the Klan were involved with the murder of Lemond."

"They already know for sure it was Klan?"

"It's pretty obvious. The mode of Lemond's death certainly has their sig-nature. But it all has to be checked out."

I nodded. Lemond. How was I going to tell Dixie? She had enough to worry about. And then I'd have to break the news to Mama Clarice and Beverly. People I loved where going to be forever devastated by what I had to tell them. I couldn't stand that. "*Porcaria,*" I moaned into my hands.

"Things really are set in motion, sugah," he said apologetically.

I shook myself more coherent. "Huh?" I looked at him. "I wasn't talking to you, Al."

"Who the heck were you talking to then?" He smiled and turned the playful wattage up in his eyes. That twinkling was *very* distracting.

"Who knows, Al." He rubbed my cheek, his hand warm and sensuous. No more hand patting? Had I moved up a notch? Or down? And why did I even care? I just met the guy! A dose of reality will sober my thoughts.

I was itching to move, get started again to find something to help Dixie. I sat up and the floor moved like it was a rug and every speck of dust was being shaken out. I flopped back on the couch, closing my eyes. Al lifted my head and slipped a pillow under it. When I opened my eyes he was inches from my face. His eyes were soft, moving like the hands of a clock as he scrutinized me inch by inch. He moved closer, hesitated, then pulled back, busying himself with the couch fringe. And me? He'd made me so jumpy I felt like throwing up again.

"Could one of the people behind the murder or what's happened to Dixie be a Jerry or Randy Beamon?" I asked him.

His eyes bulged. "How did you get those names?"

I told him about my visit to the Last Chance. "After I walked out of the bar, a guy named Jerry followed me and was very interested in making me go bye-bye."

"He said he knew Randy?" I nodded. "And you said he tried to *make* you go with him?" Al was one sharp pencil. Didn't miss a single word. "You could have gotten hurt."

"You haven't met the owner." He didn't smile. "I know a few things about taking care of myself."

"And the bruises all over you prove how good you are."

"I spent last night rolling around a river!"

"Some of those bruises look older."

"I participate in extreme sporting events."

He snorted disbelief and kept watching me like a parent. I grew uncomfortable. If a person could lay nonchalantly, I tried very hard to do so. Al had been sending out vibes that didn't have much faith in me doing something to help Dixie. I'm sure there wasn't much I could say to convince him. I'd just have to prove it to him. And to myself. "Those guys who broke into the hotel room..."

"You only heard his first name. Randy is very common."

"Obviously. On that list you gave me of known and suspected Klansmen in Rincon had two others with–"

"What list?" He looked like an ostrich, his neck stretched out in anger. "I didn't give you any list." I described that particular paper from the stack of information he'd given me.

He rubbed his head in frustration. "No! That was an intelligence report that no one outside this office was supposed to see."

"Why not?"

"Nothing has been substantiated. We must check, and double check, all the information. We get tips from informants, anonymously, any place. I don't take any of it seriously until my group or someone I trust confirms it. My pal at the GBI sends me just about everything they get, some I probably shouldn't. He trusts me and knows I have my neck on the chopping block. He thinks I should be aware."

"Yes, you should be. Your life has obviously been threatened." I swept my arm toward his outer office, indicating his security garrison.

"We also get dumps of information. Most of it takes a good bit of sifting through before it's gospel. My investigators created that list because their names came up frequently and we decided to check them out first. Then we could focus on the ones that the reports mention less or we thought fairly unlikely from what we already knew."

"I understand. But I'm not going to broadcast anything, certainly to people I don't know. Heck, I don't know anyone here to tell. I can check the list of names out. What I learn can help both of us." His neck muscles were still tight. I tried to reassure him. "Honest, Al. I'm not going to do anything to hurt Dixie." Wasn't that obvious?

He held up his hand stopping me. "No, I don't mean that. It's hard to explain. Some of it is, I'm a lawyer. I have to be extra careful what I do."

"I totally agree. But, Al, I'm not. I do know a little bit about investigations. If nothing else–I was born to gather data." I smiled.

Again, he didn't. "What?" No answer. Was he hiding something, or wrestling for explanations?

"I don't think you should do anything else. Just go to the hotel and rest."

"I'm fine, Al. Yes, I am planning on resting. But you can't expect me to just sit around after what has happened to me. Twice someone came at me. I want to, no, I *need* to find out why! Wouldn't you?"

"But I wouldn't go busting in like a wild horse."

"What makes you think I would?"

"You're young." Huh? I really couldn't believe it! How inane! A rarity, but I was at a loss for a comeback.

Aggie beat me to it. "Why are you talking nonsense, Al? What does age have to do with it?"

"Experience. Or the lack of it. He abruptly changed directions and shouted. "Did you take those papers from my office?"

"What did you just say? You have a lot of nerve!" I yelled back. Before I could remind him he *gave* me the papers, Aggie joined us in the bird pen, her whole body rigid.

"Now both of you calm down! Lawd me, Al! Don't bark at her! She's had a pretty rough time of it." Al verbally attacked Aggie for sticking up for me, so I came to Aggie's rescue. We shouted simultaneously until my head pounded harder forcing me to drop out.

"Aw! My head!" I massaged it, but my fingertips didn't zap any good feelings inside. The two cousins were still at it. Aggie was holding up well against Al. Probably had years of practice if his mood today was typical. The pain in my head was increasing. I took a deep breath and bellowed. *"Cala a boca!"* Shut up! It worked. Silence. All three of us went back and forth looking at each other, glaring, snorting and sputtering. I broke the calm. "Why would you immediately jump to the conclusion that I got information from your office without your permission?"

"You sat in the Pirate's House the other night and told us that you broke into computers all the time. It's reasonable for me to think you could do that with written data."

I was going to blow a gasket. "It really chaps my butt when a person lulls another into conversation during a social occasion, then uses it against them later. Not to mention, twisting the words around to suit your weak argument! You know exactly what I meant–it's controlled hacking. The companies know exactly what I'm going to do." I tossed in haughtiness. "I'm not even going to justify my work. It has nothing to do with this and you know it. You are so very unfair. And how dare you imply, no, you boldly stated that I–. " His phone rang and he waltzed over to the desk to answer it. And had the nerve to mosey through weather and baseball talk while I stewed! He finally hung up.

"Well, it's been *real* fun, Cousin Alvin, but I have to deliver papers to the courthouse. You just make sure your Neanderthal ways don't knock another one out the way," Aggie warned sternly.

"What are you talking about?" Al asked.

"You're so dang smart, you figure it out." Aggie left, a hushed click sounding as she closed the huge, thick outer door.

"I over reacted, Paloma. I'm sorry." He was contrite, soothing and convincing. I was still smarting from his accusations while his abrupt con-versational changes were keeping my head spinning–without the burden of a headache. The deep betrayal I felt surprised me. I really wanted to hurl inimical words his way. He kept up a litany of apologies while I sorted through my hurt. If he was going to make nice-nice, I would have to get myself in check. Now I felt like a baboon. Al was offering the olive branch. I'd be an even bigger baboon if I didn't take it. Oh, how I just wanted to walk over and flick him!

"Okay. Me too." I looked down and mumbled into my chest.

"What? I didn't hear you."

"I'm sorry, too." Al burst out laughing. My head shot up. The room was canted from my sudden movement. "You are a tease, counselor."

"So, I guess you are going to rest up at the hotel today. And forget about this ugliness."

He was doing it again. "Not so fast. First I thought I'd look into this Beamon guy or maybe check out the plant." You had to tell him, Paloma. Couldn't just sneak off and do it.

"There are some very bad men involved, Paloma."

"I've already met some of them."

"Yes, and look at what happened to you!"

"I know. You get a kick out of telling me about it. And I'm young. Stupid. Don't know how to chew gum and walk down the street at the same time. Look, Al. You are working on getting Dixie out of jail. Do you need me to help you with that?" I locked him in a penetrating stare until he an-swered me.

"No."

"Can I go help the GBI on Lemond's murder?" I didn't wait for his denial. "Do you think the Savannah Police will make an effort to find out who *tried* to break into my hotel room when they didn't take anything, didn't put anyone in the hospital or morgue? Will they bother with last night?"

"Maybe."

"Should I call them? Tell them about Dixie in jail, which is why I'm here. Explain about Randy from last night and the Randy on your list. What about the investigation as it goes over county lines. They will set up a task force over a few knots on the head, pot-shots at a tourist, broken latch on a hotel patio door?"

He took his turn mumbling down into his chest. "No."

"All those events happened to me. I think it ties into what's going on with Dixie. I'm the only one interested in who is after my tail. So I'm left to check it out. I'll be very careful. More so than ever! It never crossed my mind to ride into town firing a six-gun."

Al leaned over me. "You should go back to the hotel, young lady! There are trained professionals who can look into it."

"You overbearing bully!" I shouted, pushing him away from me. "I *am* one! I've been trained in investigative techniques."

"For computers!"

I stood so I could pace while arguing. It seemed the thing to do. "Not just computers! Okay, so I haven't any dead-on police investigative work on my resume. Doesn't some of your legal experience help you in other areas? If I catch people hacking, I've caught a *criminal*. People who break down hotel doors are *criminals*." I made an about-face, using Al's own technique against him. "Why are you shouting at me? How did things degrade so quickly? Oh, yes, you accused me of *stealing* your papers." Oops. That ignited that fire again. I cut off further conversation by out-shouting him in Portuguese until he finally comprehended that he had no clue what I was saying. "Now that I have your attention, counselor. I did not *take* that piece of paper! You *gave* it to me! It was in the stack of materials *you* placed in *my* hands. You owe me another apology. And this one better be sincere!" When he didn't answer, I bellowed out, "Well?"

He grabbed my shoulders yanking me to him. I pulled away. He mumbled something about strength like an ox before he wrapped a hand behind my head and planted his kisser dead center on mine. His lips were purposeful, searching. Mine woke up and started talking back. As quickly as he'd begun, he released me. I staggered back against the couch and plopped down on it. "What was that for?" I stammered.

"It seemed the only way to shut you up."

"Merda! Porcaria, Al Eason! Get out of here this instant!"

"You're in my office," he calmly replied.

In the 1970's, David Duke, founder of the Knights of the Ku Klux Klan and the National Association for the Advancement of White People, took the Klan from behind their sheets into three-piece suits. Duke promoted relocating minorities to specific geographical areas. When campaigning for public office, he claimed that he no longer had an affiliation with the Klan, although his phone number and the Klan's were the same. He was elected into the Louisiana state legislature in 1989.

Chapter Thirty

Randy Beamon woke up in a stinking black mood. He was bruised and sported one of the worst hangovers in his twenty-nine years. As he'd stumbled into his trailer just before dawn, he'd gotten his butt kicked by some brute Swartzman had sent over.

"Don't screw up again," the guy said, then left. Now Swartzman was riding him to get to the Gundersen plant. He hung up the phone and gingerly got out of bed. Dried blood spotted his body. That guy must have really kicked his butt bad. The phone rang again.

"R-Randy. Where have you been?" Wyman Hughes, Imperial Wizard of the Righteous Klans of Georgia, blared into the phone.

"I've been busy, Hughes. I gotta work, ya know."

"W-w-what work have you been doing?" Hughes asked, silently cursing his stutter.

"Da plant. Odd jobs an' stuff."

"It's the 'stuff' I'm worried about. What about that Lemond guy? You kill him?"

"I don't know who dun that!"

"Don't you lie to me R-R-Randy. I'll kill you."

"I ain't lying! What's got your drawers in a twist?"

Hughes ignored the question. "What's new with the white girl?"

"She's only half white, I keep tellin' ya! An' I don't know," Randy lied. "But I'm lookin' inta it."

"Hmm-huh."

"I'm lookin' inta it! It's gonna take a little finesse."

"F-F-Finesse? You can't even spell the word."

"And you can't even s-s-say it," Randy mocked and heard the deep intake of breath from the Imperial Wizard. The phone slammed down in Randy's ear.

*   *   *

"R-Red, get the guys together–those boys who did the Swansboro job. We got a Klavern rally tonight. We need to meet as soon as everyone can get together."

"Can't do it, Hughes. I'm fixin' to go somewhere."

"Where?"

"None of your business." Click. What the heck was going on? Hughes held the phone in his hand until the recorded message requested he hang up. He pulled at his mustache, worried. The police were gunning for the Klan boys because of the lynching, and the membership wanted to know what Hughes was doing about it. Rumors and panic were flying all over town. Some wanted the money the Klavern owed them and didn't have. And now he'd heard there was a new group in town. He couldn't get jack-shit for information on them. His accountant was phoning him. That always meant bad news. He rolled his head around in circles stretching the muscles in his neck. Might as well have it limber for the sword of Damocles above his head.

*   *   *

Billy Ray was straight as an ironing board, lying on the couch. He'd been up all night. Who could sleep after what Randy did? He only moved to light another cigarette, usually from the one he'd just smoked. He tried calling Moonpie, but there was no answer. She'd insisted on Billy Ray taking her to Savannah to the emergency room—once he'd caught a ride home, then come back to get her—because there'd be less chance of running into someone they knew. She swore Billy Ray to secrecy, but needn't have bothered. How could he *ever* talk about what happened? When she wouldn't stay in the hospital overnight, he half-carried her, drugged and crying for somebody named Brice, up the stairs of her trailer.

His mind drifted to Randy and he forced himself to focus elsewhere. If he didn't, he'd kill him. Hunt him down like a deer and shoot the shit right out of him. But he wouldn't sit in jail for doing something to Randy. He'd think of something else. In time, Randy would pay.

His phone rang startling him. He lay there listening, only his elbow moving and a finger to flick the ashes into an a bowl resting on his stomach. Screams crept into his head. He shut his eyes tight, tears threatening still. He smoked faster. Randy would pay.

*   *   *

Swartzman looked at the pathetic man in front of him. He'd been worked over well. "Nice to know I got my money's worth." He smiled broadly at Randy's bruises. "I trust you've returned all the weapons you've stolen." Randy nodded in a quick jerk. "I got a job for you. Screw it up and you're out." Randy took a breath to start his excuses. Swartzman waved a large hand and spoke vehemently. "You'll get in the car and not say a word the whole time. Not one damn thing. Is that clear? Just shake your head." He laid out the plans, not offering Randy a chair. He went over them again. "Understand?"

"Ye..."

"Just nod." Swartzman opened the case on his desk and offered the gun to him. Randy picked up the .9 millimeter admiringly. Swartzman's toys were always top of the line. Until that moment the gun had been clean of prints. Randy screwed in the silencer and aimed at the picture over Swartz-man's head.

"Don't point that gun near me, you stupid ass! I don't care if it's unload-ed. Now! Or you'll find out how well I can use one." Randy complied, then they left. Swartzman sipped J & B and listened to Vivaldi on the drive into Savannah. It was nice not having Randy's mouth ruining it. Traffic was light and they reached the hotel quickly. Randy parked in the back as Swartzman pulled an envelope out of his briefcase and handed it to him.

"Take this envelope to the hotel manager. Just give it to him and come immediately back to the car. I'll call when I'm ready. Room number's 202." He shut the door behind him and climbed the stairs to the second floor. He smiled, took off his sunglasses and knocked on Brice's door.

*   *   *

Moonpie didn't know how she did it, but she climbed out of bed. She stumbled, pained and disoriented, into the bathroom careful not to look in the mirror. Filling the dirty tub with hot water, she gingerly dropped her body down into it.

When she woke up later, the water had cooled. She drained and refilled the tub. When this water turned lukewarm, she tried several times to get out, succeeding on the third. It didn't occur to her to dry herself off. She pulled a shift over her head, slid her feet in sandals, scooped up the money she'd asked Billy Ray to leave for her, and slowly made her way to the car.

There was enough gas to get to Savannah. To Brice. She needed a friend now more than ever. Her trip was shaky, full of hysterical crying beside the road, swerving across the lanes as the painkillers took effect and eased the agony in her nose and other battered parts. Why hadn't anyone given her something to stop the pain in her heart?

During the 1970's and 1980's–Louis Beam, Grand Dragon of Texas and a lieutenant of David Duke's, ran at least four paramilitary training camps in Texas and North Carolina. The army was the brainchild of retired Green Beret Glenn Miller who trained his men for a revolution to establish a southern white republic by the year 2000. Investigators discovered active-duty Marines were recruited and they found a cache of stolen military weapons–grenades, dynamite, plastic explosives, rifles, gas masks, and anti-tank rockets. Miller, convicted for illegal weapons crimes, is now in the federal witness protection program in exchange for testimony against other supremacists.

Chapter Thirty-One

I had fallen asleep on the couch in Al's office and was awakened by an excited Aggie back from more Savannah appointments.

"Howze your stomach, Paloma? Can you handle a bite to eat? I have time before I have to skedaddle back to the office."

" Oh, I can't. At least yet." I pointed to my bare feet. "Lost them in the river last night."

"You only packed one pair?"

"Yes, ma'am. Docksiders. It's all I ever wear. If I can get away with it. I've been wearing them since I was a kid. I buy the next size up so they'll be real loose and comfortable. But the yuppies have discovered them and I may have to find something else." I sighed as if it were the end of the world.

"If you bought the right size your shoes might still have been on your feet. I wear size eight. I've got some scuffs in the car that'll keep the fire off your feet."

"I'm a nine, but I can wear something until I get to a store today. Thanks, Aggie, you're the bomb!"

"I guess you're welcome," she answered skeptically. She ordered me to stay in the doorway while she brought the car curbside and up to the front door of Al's Law Center, saving my last layer of foot skin. We decided on a restaurant that served breakfast all day.

"How're you feeling?" she asked later, as we climbed the steps.

"My head hurts like crazy, but no dizziness. I can deal with it. This looks like a country cabin," I commented as we waited for the hostess. Like most places in hot, humid climes, it was deliciously cold inside.

The restaurant was small and homey, shelves lined the walls and was loaded with goodies, like a home food larder. Although the items inside were preserved in jars, everyone referred to the process as home canning. The sun filtered through the window shining onto the endless colors of fruits and vegetables, creating a stained-glass window effect.

"I'm hungry enough to order a double of grits," I announced.

"Sounds good to me. But, Paloma," she said with mock serious-ness. "That depends on how you eat them." She looked at me through slitted eyes, testing me.

"Salt and butter."

"Good. Somebody stayed with me once, asked me to pass them the sugar!"

"No way! Eeww! I don't eat Yankee grits."

We ordered and the waitress slapped her order pad shut with a snap. "Three minutes 'til take and rake." She was true to her word. We were soon stuffing our faces with ham, bacon, eggs, and biscuits, homemade like the preserves we drown them in. I watched Aggie until she was a few bits from a clean plate and worked the conversation around to a lighthearted interrogation of her.

"What led you to working Fish and Game?"

She ate the last bite and slid her plate aside, folding her arms on the table. "This is gonna take a bit of explaining. My family owns a cabin between here and where I live on Lady's Island. I inherited the land when my parents passed on." Her eyes became misty, but cleared up quickly. "My husband, Matthew." She paused, sighed. "He's dead now, too. Well, we kept finding game senselessly slaughtered on the north part of our cabin land. It seemed everybody was doing it. Sometimes we'd catch a hunter stalking doe out of season. Why do people want to wipe all the animals out? What are they gonna do when it's all gone? Manage it correctly, and they'll be enough for everyone. We respected game laws and I decided everyone else would, too." She wiped a spot of grits off the table.

"I'd been working for the Wildlife Federation for almost ten years, amongst protest of every male in the department it seems. For the first three years I was cook, secretary, you name it. If it was women's work, I did it. Finally Matthew told me to check the federal laws, and we discovered a section that I used to get me out from behind the typewriter."

"Uh-oh. Trouble."

"I'll tell you what! I figured there had to be other women in the same predicament, so I called other federal agencies. I found three others—one in Customs, a civilian on the Marine base at Parris Island, and another was a game warden on the northern shores of Carolina." She stopped long enough to sip coffee. "We all had scored in the top ten percent on the required exams, but we couldn't get posted to any of those positions. We found a lawyer who'd won similar lawsuits in Baltimore. We hired him and let him go to it! I don't know what made those ol' codgers madder—the Yankee lawyer or us women stepping in a man's world." Aggie's laugh was deep and infectious. "Lawd me! I still have to butt heads today. I'm up for a promotion and someone has been trying to mess with it."

"How?"

"Sabotaging things, making me look bad, and undermining my authority. I need to keep a constant eye on my territory."

"Kick those chauvinistic men in the butt."

"I'm trying. Well, if you're ready, we best git."

After we'd climbed back into the hot federal car, Aggie turned to me. "I want to ask you something. How did things end with Al and you?" I hesitated, not knowing exactly what to say. "I mean, did he calm down or keep talking 'til you were ready to clap his trap?"

"Other than accusing me of theft and youthful stupidity, he seems to think I need a lot of rest. I saw a bit of the "old boy south" in him yesterday, but he was down right chauvinistic today."

"He tends to like more *feminine* in women. When I was kicking around the idea of the law suit, he was behind me all the way. I think he would have been disappointed if I hadn't."

"Was that because of the lawyer in him or support for you?"

"Now, now! I just want you to know that he means well." She continued beefing Al up for me. Then she stopped and grinned wide. "He doesn't often get so riled up about a woman and what she's doing. You sure put a bee in his bonnet! You know, it's a contradiction."

"What is?"

"Him. Al. He spends most of his time talking in court, helping people get out of trouble. He's created brilliant legal maneuvers and precedents. On a personal level Al's just as suave with everyone. Even females. Except the ones he is attracted to. He turns plum asinine. His mouth always gets him into trouble. And the more he tries to get out of the mire, the more stuck he gets."

"Kind of like B'rer Rabbit and Tar Baby," I supplied.

Aggie shook her head. "It's like Uncle Remus knew Al personally when he created the story."

Chapter Thirty-Two

"B-Billy Ray? You in there?" Wyman Hughes knocked again on the door. His eyes trailed the dried blood from the smear on the doorknob to the droplets on the steps. He knocked louder. He heard movement inside, then nothing.

"Are you okay, s-son?" He opened the door gingerly. "Where'd the blood come from? Jesus, s-son. What happened?" Billy Ray's lip was split, knuckles raw, his face, arms, neck swollen and bruised, and dried blood spotted various places on him. He'd almost teased Billy Ray, asking if the woman was worth it, but stopped himself when he saw the devastation on the young man's face.

"Are you hurt bad, B-Ray? Y-you need a doctor?"

"No." His voice was low, like he was sick. Billy Ray lit his last cigarette. Hughes sat in the folding chair and waited. The guy didn't speak. "You lived with me and my family for many years. You're like a son to me. Why can't you tell me what happened?"

"I just can't." Billy Ray's hand shook as he stubbed out the cigarette. "Because you are the daddy I never had–I want you to leave it alone."

"Okay." Hughes said slowly. "W-What d-do you w-want me to do?" His stutter, always worse when he was fidgety, defied the lessons he was taught at the speech clinic.

"Cigarettes."

"I got a pack in the car. D-Do you need some beer?"

"No," he said curtly, then softened his tone. "Thanks. I want a clear head." Hughes retrieved the smokes from his car and brought in a six-pack of Bud for himself. Billy Ray was limping out of the kitchen with a half-empty liter of cola. He took a long swig from the bottle as he made his way back to the couch. After lighting the cigarette Wyman offered, Billy Ray sat forward, resting his elbows on his knees. Billy Ray considered telling his father part of the story, afraid that small town gossip would get back to Hughes–then he'd believe the worst. He'd be ashamed of the orphan he took in off the streets.

God, how could he have gotten an...erection? Had being around Randy rubbed off that much? Made him able to do the disgusting things he'd been made to do? Coming home from the hospital, he'd told Moonpie he hadn't wanted to. Hadn't enjoyed it. What else could he have done with Randy waving that gun around? He thought he was going to be shot at any moment. He still couldn't quite believe either of them had escaped without taking a bullet. He'd told her all this over and over. She'd finally yelled at him to shut up, her fists flailing out blindly, uncontrollably. He'd stopped the car to comfort her, but she jerked away so fast she'd banged her head on the window. His mind kept coming back to Randy. The gun he'd shoved down his pants. Moonpie's mouth opening up as Randy shoved him forward.

He sobbed into his hands, no longer able to contain his pain, confusion, humiliation and disgust. Billy Ray turned away embarrassed, further shamed for his lack of manly strength. This time, mercifully, Wyman Hughes didn't chastise him for his tears. Instead, he wrapped his arms around him, holding him like a baby until the last sob died on his lips.

1981–Louis Beam and his army conducted violent campaigns against Vietnamese fishermen in the Galveston Bay area. The Southern Poverty Law Center filed a lawsuit against Beam and the Klan. A federal judge ordered a stop to the harassment and banned paramilitary activity. Beam later went to Hayden Lake, Idaho, the home of the Aryan Nations, to write Essays of a Klansman, *describing an assassination point system to attain the one point needed to become an Aryan Warrior. Point values: black people and police–one-tenth, the President–one.*

In retaliation for the harassment suit by the SPLC, the Klan fire-bombed their Montgomery, Alabama offices. Three Klansmen were later arrested and convicted.

Chapter Thirty-Three

My prayers that the wind would cool Aggie's bare-bones government car were futile. Heat waves pranced like a St. Vitus dance in the road. I tried to avoid thinking, which was as successful as not swatting a fly prancing on your picnic. I leaned back in the seat and let the warm air hit my face.

"Aggie, tell me about your husband Matthew."

She sighed deeply but contentedly. "He was a fine man. Don't think I'll ever find anyone to top him."

"How did you meet him?"

"When I was a junior in high school–never mind what year–I met a dashing young man. Philip Grainger."

I popped my head up and looked at her. It was a classically southern reply. Her answer was a story and it didn't necessarily begin where my question left off. We'd be covering delicious Aggie history now. "Grainger? Al's step-brother–the sheriff in Rincon?" I asked a little too loudly. She bobbed her head up and down and quickly checked on traffic.

"Grainger graduated the year before me. We began courtin' and probably would have gotten married. That's how it was done back then. But my pappy said I had a hitch in my git-along. I couldn't tolerate young lady clothes. I couldn't stand all those layers of under garments and in the summer! Lawd me! We couldn't walk around buck-naked like they do these days. No wonder women were supposed to just sit around and act pretty, we were too danged hot to do anything else!" Aggie laughed as much as I did. I'd already begun to realize how much she loved life and squeezed all the enjoyment she could out of each moment. I admired that quality.

"And I wanted to go everywhere my pappy did. Mama would tell me to stay with her, learn to cook and sew. I'd pitch a fit. Sneak out." She had a wonderful voice for storytelling. I shifted for comfort and let myself become immersed in it. "Grainger wanted me to drop out of school and get married. I talked my father into letting me spend the summer with a cousin up in Columbia. I wanted to see the state's capital. I mentioned that I own a cabin. It was my father's originally.

Black farmers were hired to plant and pick the crops. With the cabin so isolated, most of my friends were the farm hands' kids. Claretha and Toby, twins, were my best friends."

"Sounds similar to what Al told me about his childhood."

"Exactly. That's the way it was in most of the country areas. All so isolated. Al and I would spend parts of the summer with each other. He thought the world of Toby. They were always gettin' into something." She was in some far-away place as she relived her memories. "While I was gone that summer, a white girl blamed Toby for raping her and getting her pregnant. A mob of angry rednecks came to the cabin. They told my father they were there for Toby and his hangin'. My father refused, urging them to wait until the judge was in town at the end of the month. They wouldn't. The cabin was burned and Toby was taken away. When Claretha saw Toby tied up and on his knees in the cart, she went running after him. A man in the wagon whipped her over and over. But she kept coming to help Toby." The years had not softened the pain of telling. She finished the story in a ragged voice. "And getting whipped." She brushed a tear away. "It was a long time ago, but it still gets under me today."

I gave her shoulder a pat of understanding while she paused to struggle with the past. "What happened next?"

"Claretha finally got close enough to jump on the wagon. Someone kicked her off. She fell on some rocks and hit her head. She woke up once and asked for me and Toby. Claretha died two days later." Her freckled face pinched up in anger. "Damn Grainger." She hit the steering wheel.

"Grainger was one of the vigilantes?"

"No." She cut the air with her hand. I was getting the cart before the horse. Curbing my excitement, I let her unroll the story in her own time. "See, it was his sister who was pregnant! She was a tramp. He knew it. Everybody knew it! He also knew about a tacky white boy she'd been seeing."

Aggie had really made a strong denunciation of Grainger's sister. In the South, tacky *sounds* harmless enough. But we all know a secret. Southerners would *never* want their family, friends or personal tastes remotely attached to that one small word. Being called tacky straight to your face is grounds for self-defense.

"Although Grainger knew the truth he never said *anything* to stop the men! Toby was the scapegoat. They hung him in a tree right in his parent's yard. Just like Lemond. Claretha might have lived had she gotten the proper care. The only hospital close by was just for whites. So was the ambulance." I waited politely but she didn't continue.

"Aggie, that's dreadful. Who found him in the tree?"

She shook her head. "That's not it. Toby's parents were home when the men brought him there–barely alive. They held the parents back while the others put Toby on a milking stool, the noose around his neck. Then they kicked the stool out from under him!"

"*Bundões*! How horrible!"

"*Bundões* is right. Now tell me what does it mean?"

"A word that if my grandmother heard me say, she'd cram a bar of soap into my mouth to wash it out."

"Good! I'll use it." She tried it out a few more times, her head and neck lunging forward to emphasize each word.

Geez, I'm corrupting a little not-so-old lady. "Uh, Aggie, it means bas-tards." She gave a nod but had no further comment. I steered her back to the story. "I guess no one was tried for your friends' murders?"

She looked quickly at me, fire in her eyes. "Hell no! When the Grainger baby was born, he was as white as cotton sheets." I leaned my head slightly out of the window and closed my eyes. "My parents didn't tell me until I came home. I was devastated! About Toby, Claretha *and* my parents' silence–both while it was going on and not telling me right after it happened. I didn't speak to them for a whole month. Then only to tell them off. Grainger was angry, and said some nasty things about me and my choice of friends. He said he could never forgive me. *Me*!" She beat her fist in the air and gave a throaty *uuhh!* We listened to the sounds of the wind and the engine while we pondered the past.

I put my arm around Aggie's shoulder and gave it a squeeze. "Thank you for telling me. I now understand why you and Al get so riled just hearing the name Grainger." I leaned to one side and wiped the sweat off the back of my thigh and the car seat, doing the same for the other half–a rather unpleasant consequence of shorts, vinyl seats and Southern summers. When I lived here I'd always have a towel with me for the sole purpose of drying my backside.

Aggie cleared her throat. Goody, more was to come. "Al confronted each man involved. He wasn't much into his teens, either. He wanted them to pay for the burning of my father's cabin and to give compensation to Toby's family–a crusader even then."

"What did they do?"

"Laughed! Al was mad enough to spit fire! The men were in the general store, the gathering place of the time. Ol' man Grainger owned it. Al walked right in and took some flour and beans, and was going back for more when the ol' man stopped him. Al slipped around him and blew up! They dodged around trying to get Al and ended up trashing the store. He was a young thing then. Skinny as a rail, too. Of course they blamed us."

"Us? You were there too?"

"Yep. My parents never found out I was there with him." She stopped talking to concentrate on passing a man puttering along dangerously slow on an ancient tractor. The two-laned road with its constant traffic, turns and intersections made passing an art form not experienced in cities with multi-laned freeways. A long stream of cars was lined up behind us making des-perate and perilous maneuvers to beat each other to their destinations.

"Lawd, me! Most of the men did get a little pay back," she continued with a grin, once she had slung the car into the other lane, whipped the car around Farmer John and darted back to our side of the road.

"How?"

"First, we dumped soap detergent in their wells. We got a mule and pulled one man's outhouse down when he was out of town. We also took eggs and meat from the smokehouses. We opened the animal pens almost weekly to free the animal. And one time..." She laughed so hard she was weaving inside the lane. "We were hiding up in the hills, looking down on old man Grainger's farm. We waited for his family to go to bed. We got cold so we plundered around Grainger's woodpile. There was a bottle—we didn't know what it was at the time—but it smelled chemical. Al soaked a rag—we aimed to make a fire. There was a big iron kettle there. We turned it over accidentally and started a fire to beat all! Up went all the moonshine for the whole county! I tell you what! There were explosions all around us. We beat it out of there and almost outran our own horses!"

"Aggie, I don't believe it! There's enough in what you told me to blackmail Al for years!" Still giggling, she headed toward the ditch—on the other side of the road. Slowing down, she drove the car to the correct side, and laughed a bit more before picking up speed. "Did old man Grainger leave his wife or did she die?"

"She died in childbirth. Then Al's mother, Lubby, married him."

"Why? Al mentioned his father was a big influence on him for tolerance."

"Lubby's relatives were dirt poor and all Klan, clear back to Reconstruction. Lubby thinks as long as the, uh, colored people keep in their place everything's okay. She never took to Al Senior's ideas about people being equal. Al's father was very generous to his help as well. Lubby didn't like that at all. She wanted money, coming from poor beginnings. Al Senior died from a stroke. But he didn't have much even if he'd kept it all. So as soon as enough time passed after her husband's death, Lubby married it."

"I guess Al isn't very well liked by his relatives."

Aggie smiled. "That's a nice way a' puttin' it. Things have been strained between Al and his mother since her marriage." She sighed. "That's enough about me."

"Wait! You didn't say how you met Matthew."

"Lawd me! There I go flappin' my jaws about all this other mess. You sure you want more?" I was saying yes before she could finish asking.

"Well," she adjusted herself in the seat and checked the mirrors before continuing. "After Grainger and I broke up, I went back to Columbia the next summer. I met a Virginian named Matthew Dewitt. *Boy, was he something!* His father was an ambassador—that was almost like royalty back then, especially to my country roots. Matt had lived abroad a lot, giving him a different—and better–perspective on things–he was not at all like the times we were living in. He was very advanced about women's stations in life. My mother swore I married him just to spite her." Snort. Snort. "He urged me to paint. I have a little talent in that area."

"Are those *your* paintings in Al's office?" She nodded. "Lady Gauguin. I'm impressed."

"Thank you. I had a dream as a child to travel the South Pacific and paint the islands and the people. He sent me on a three-month tour to Tahiti, Bali, Bora Bora–you name it. He stayed behind and came out to join me at the end of the trip. That was before we had young'uns. Anyway, that was very unconventional in those days."

"You aren't kidding! How did everyone react to your trip?"

"Lawd me! They shore thought we were crazy! Except Al, of course. We've always been allies."

"I didn't know you had kids."

"Yep, Frank lives in Atlanta, and Susan's in Arizona. When I came back from the islands, I painted day and night! But after a while I got another hitch. I needed something else. Matthew loved to hunt and fish. He built another cabin, the one there now. We spent a lot of time there. Many wonderful years together. He was sixteen years older than me. He died a ways back. Cancer." Aggie sniffed and her eyes watered up again. She dug into her purse and pulled out a tissue.

"I'm sorry, Aggie. I'm sure it never gets any easier, especially someone who was that wonderful and loving. I didn't mean to make you sad." She brushed it off and I watched her body struggle to get itself contained.

"Almost there. I've got a minute or two, so howze about I give you the nickel tour?" We drove along azalea-lined yards of stately Southern mansions and wove through narrow cobblestone streets. "General Oglethorpe's plan when establishing the Savannah colony in 1733 was based around a series of public squares. Most survived today and are filled with beautiful fountains and endless plants and flowers. Nice places to stroll around," Aggie reported. The down-town area is laid out like Charleston's– on fairly straight and square streets if you have a chance to poke around." We drove by Wright Square and turned down a street where Aggie pointed out the Juliette Gordon Lowe house, the founder of the Girl Scouts. We zipped along, stopping to read a few historical markers before Aggie began checking her watch. As we passed the Pirate's House I decided to free her, saying I'd walk and I knew the way back to the hotel. We waved and I watched her clunker disappear into traffic.

Her stories had put me in a pensive mood. Shielding my eyes from the blinding sun, I gazed at a block of old mansions. White columns and old-styled storm shutters adorned the front, the yards blocked by wrought iron fences. Wreaths of flowers hung on doors and gates. At one elaborate his-toric home I spied a intricate chandelier through etched glass panels that framed their front door. The huge side pieces of glass were as large as my door at home. Further back I could see an enormous curved staircase, immediately bringing to mind Scarlet O'Hara images. The homeowners had even decorated the street lamp on the sidewalk outside their home. Styled like the gaslights of antiquity, but run by modern electricity.

Narrow, old streets played havoc with contemporary transportation. Romantic magnolia trees were everywhere, their wide-eyed blossoms taking in every moment, but revealing no secrets. I heard the clip-clop of hooves behind me. A horse-drawn tourist carriage–a stunning replica of olden times–wheeled by. The driver waved in friendly greeting, which I returned. Cameras snapped and whirled as a guide broadcasted history into a small microphone. Two youths clad in orange sanitation coveralls picked up Coke cans and McDonald's cups while another cleaned a bronze historical plaque.

This port has been witness to it all. From steamships and plundering pirates to supertankers and longshoremen. Thundering cannons of war, slavery, Reconstruction, segregation, civil rights. Well-mannered folk, genteel southern attitudes, hate mongers and bombings. Much of the South was different. But how easy it was to cling to the past when so much over the years had stayed the same.

Louis Beam's ally, The Covenant, had a two hundred twenty-four-acre compound on the Arkansas-Missouri border. The FBI raided the camp in 1985, resulting in a three-day standoff. Weapons found: rocket launcher with missile, grenades, land mines, antiaircraft guns, seventy-seven semi- and fully automatic weapons, dynamite, C-4 explosives, and a truck that was being converted into an armored car. The Covenant, including Louis Beam, was charged with seditious conspiracy. Beam became a fugitive and was arrested in 1987 by Mexican police. In 1988, The Covenant/Beam trial resulted in acquittal by an all-white jury, the defense contending the members' assassination plans were their right of free speech.

Chapter Thirty-Four

Swartzman waited patiently while Brice shuffled around inside her hotel room. Soon the door opened and he stared into Brice's face. It was a shame. Brice was good talent. "You're looking good, Brice, as usual."

"And you. You're right on time, too, as usual. Have you ever seen such hot weather? I'm wilting just standing in the doorway."

"Then ask me in." He gave her a Tom Cruise smile.

"I'm sorry. Come in. It's so good to see you." Brice shut the door and stood like always, giving Swartzman time for another appraisal.

"Nice clothes."

"Versace. I went shopping just before the trip." Brice moved to the mini bar. "I remembered you." She held up a bottle of his favorite scotch. "And I poured one for you as soon as I heard you knock." He drank long, letting the smooth liquor flood his mouth.

"Ahhh. That was fine." He held out his glass. Brice took the bottle and poured. "Come here." Brice moved in front of Swartzman. He reached out to caress her firm breasts. "It's been a long time, Brice. I don't find too many like you in these parts."

"I'll try to make it up to you." Swartzman pulled Brice into his arms. They stood together holding each other and he felt himself grow hard. They kissed slowly, rubbing pelvis to pelvis.

*   *   *

When Billy Ray awoke, his father Wyman Hughes was sitting on the trail-er floor staring at the wall. He started talking immediately, before Billy Ray had time to think. "I've got an idea. Don't worry, B-Ray, you won't have to tell me what Randy done." He was concentrating hard so he barely stuttered. "Something funny's going on. Has been for a while. I knew Randy was in the thick of it."

"You put him there!" Billy Ray snapped.

"What are you talking about?"

"The other night at River Street–with the girl."

"I think you better explain, B-Ray." Hughes's anger burned as he learned of Randy's trickery. "I ain't never sent Randy after no girl. Why didn't you check with me?"

"You weren't home!"

"He lied to you. That just makes it all the more important to put an end to Randy. As you were sleeping, I was able to round up a few men for a meeting tonight. You'll be there."

Billy Ray made a decision. "No."

Hughes looked hard at his adopted son, astounded at the blatant disregard he heard in Billy Ray's voice. They argued back and forth. Usually Hughes could wear his son down, wear everyone down. But there was a steeliness in his son that he'd never seen. It made him all the more curious about what had happened last night. He *had* to find out. He *would* find out. They continued their verbal rounds.

"I'm starting over, dad. I don't want nothin' to do with Randy or any of that hate stuff no more. Always spouting off about people. Beating on people. I'm sick of it and I'm sick of him!" He spoke with such vehemence Hughes didn't try to change his mind. That would come later. There was time.

"I ain't wearing no robes, dad. No more."

Hughes couldn't focus on Billy Ray's bombshells *and* keep his stammer at bay. His mind was stuttering, too. Finally he was able to speak. "W-Why don't you come home, spend a few days with me, B-Ray?"

"I don't want the kids and Wanda nosing around me."

"I'll get r-rid of them. C-Come on, son. It's b-been awhile since it's been you and me. L-Let me help you." It was nearly five minutes before Billy Ray moved. He got up and walked out the door. Hughes checked around the trailer for burning lights and cigarettes then went out to join the boy he thought he knew. Randy Beamon did something to make him change his colors. A son of his not in the Klan? That's what had brought them together. He couldn't figure for the life of him what that no-count Beamon had done now. But he was going to find out if it took him all of now and the hereafter.

"There will be an economic collapse, riots in the cities, famine, and war. People will kill each other for food, weapons, shelter, clothing, anything. It will get so bad that parents will eat their children...blacks will rape and kill white women...homosexuals will sodomize whoever they can...It is time that people woke up to the conspiracy in America and prepare themselves with weapons, food, and supplies, in a rural area far away from the cities."–James Ellison, leader of the Covenant–Klanwatch Intelligence Report #47/December 1989

Chapter Thirty-Five

Deciding to walk to the hotel hadn't been the brightest idea. Aggie's too-small shoes were playing hell with my feet when I got back to River Street. I passed the hotel looking for a shop I'd seen last night before my Esther Williams show in the river.

The Ship's Store was a mariner's dream. Filled to the rafters with at least one of everything a seafarer might need plus a well-stocked nautical gift sec-tion. I was soon selecting a pair of Docksiders and paid handsomely for them in this tourist area. But it was worth anything to have comfortable feet. I rummaged around, touching objects made for boats, reveling in the familiarity of them. I was hot and tired, but I still didn't want to leave the comfort of the store. It was the type of place I'd shopped many times with my parents and grandfather. Navigation charts were stacked in the corner. The Savannah River was displayed in various segments. I pulled out a detail of the downtown area. I stared, loving all the markings, finding where my night adventure started and approximately where it ended. I turned the map over. The river north of here was drawn with veined branches fanning out.

I bent closer, a plan forming in the back of my mind. The river went practically into the backyards of eastern Rincon. I traced the thin line depicting the city limits. The plant must be about here, I mused, tapping my finger on the spot. Since no one was able to get into the plant through the front doors, perhaps the back way would be easier. The chart didn't give me everything I needed. But I knew who could. I rolled up the chart, paid at the counter and sauntered out in the heat.

*   *   *

"Papa! It's your favorite granddaughter!" I said on the cell phone to the man who only had one granddaughter.

"Well, hello there, honey. You still in L.A.?"

"No, I'm in Savannah."

"Howze Dixie and her family?"

"Hmm, I'll fill you in later."

"When are we going to see you?"

"That depends on how you answer this question."

"Shoot."

"Do you still have the Core of Engineer charts for Georgia?"

"Of course, an old salty never tosses out his charts." I'd purchased a chart at the Ship's Store in Savannah, but it wouldn't hurt to check out Pop's.

"You used to do a little fishing on the Savannah, didn't you?"

"Yeah, before Nick drowned." Nick had been Pop's best friend for as long as I could remember. Mine too, because he'd always brought me something, usually sweat, when he visited.

"What about Rincon?"

"Been through it. I'm more familiar with the river a bit north of there. But I have what you need. How did I do?"

"Perfect. Can you get the *Pipsqueak* ready?"

"Can do."

"Thanks, Papa. I'll see you in an hour." Within fifteen minutes I had skirted Hardeeville, South Carolina and headed toward Hilton Head Island. I kept my speed down through the trap zones. At Highway 170, I was free to burn up the road again–providing I didn't get stuck behind farm machinery. The roads were clear and soon I was slowing down as I approached the bridge to the foot-shaped island.

I rolled the windows down and was greeted by a blast of warm air. But it was Carolina Low Country air! I was drenched in its perfume. I looked out over the Broad River and saw shrimp trawlers in the distance. I searched the metal towers holding power lines over the marshes for the osprey's nest that has been there for at least fifteen years. Old Gussie was still calling it home. My grandmother and I always gave her a wave as we passed the island's favorite bird. I felt good, down deep, for the first time in days.

I slowed the car to thirty-five as I crossed the bridge. A car with out-of-state tags zipped by. As I made the first bend, old Smokey was crawling out of the brush in pursuit. During my teens, the police came from Beaufort–forty-five minutes by car, twenty by boat. Crime had been almost nonexistent–especially in winter–petty theft of summer homes left empty for too long, and a few collisions on the twisting island roads. It had been no man's island in winter, six thousand residents until the silly season when the population rose to fifty thousand. More than that now even during the lean months.

The first views coming onto the resort island are quite humble–marsh shacks, home of the Gullah speakers, descendants of former slaves. In another mile the overtaxed land on this twelve-mile island bore new mini-malls, plush condominiums and the first of at least twenty golf courses. The Ghost Crab Resort had doubled in size since last year's visit when there hadn't been a hint of additional building. Shopkeepers and construction companies went bottom up almost daily but no one seemed to notice. As one foreclosed, two more applied for building permits. I took a good look at the stretch to the left and right. My old island home was looking raped and pillaged–as far as growth was concerned. Soon golf courses would be the only thing free of buildings. Each one now was ringed by the homes of Arnold Palmer wannabe's. The four-lane Highway 278 could barely sustain the traffic. But to visitors, the rustic tone, no neon signs allowed, the marsh grasses, lush flowers, and white sand beaches were paradise. Yes, Hilton Head Island was still breathtakingly beautiful. But long-timers had seen it even more so.

I passed the turn-off for Skull Creek, the location of many of Dixie's and my swash-buckling episodes. I negotiated my way carefully through the two traffic circles. They'd been created to quickly feed cars in the various directions but served to keep tourists in a perpetual state of confusion, the locals in constant ire, and when the two met, it was to the benefit of Trimmer's Auto Body Shop. There were more accidents here than the rest of the island. To island youth, the circles were an endurance test to see who could last the longest whipping around them in succession or how many could be completed–per gallon of gas–in each person's car.

On North Forest Beach Drive, as was ritual, I recited the names of all of the streets–named after Atlantic seabirds and in a tourist-friendly gesture, alphabetically. There were various cadences made up through the years. We'd even jumped rope along with a more elaborate version I'd forgotten through the years. Probably because I'd rather have picked locks or gone sailing than hit myself in the head with a flying rope. North Forest Beach Drive started at Coligny Plaza and the second island circle. Avocet, a long-legged shorebird with an elongated upturned bill, was also a street where rocker John Mellencamp had built a huge eyesore of an occasional home.

Bittern, Curlew, Dove, Egret, Flamingo, Gannet. Heron, where I blasted the horn twice and waved for Joyce Atkins, an old friend who lived there. She wasn't around to reply with her typical raised middle finger and wide Carolina grin. Probably skipping work, Bob Seger blaring while burning up island roads. The closer I got to home, neighbors and life-long friends of my family out doing various lawn tasks and home repairs, all responded in friendly gestures as I passed them with more bleeps of the horn.

I hung a right onto Osprey and goosed the engine so I could sling a bit of dirt and oyster shell as I finished the short block. The rental car had a good view overlooking the Atlantic where I parked. My grandparent's house is a two-story wooded island abode, raised on posts to avoid the occasional storm flooding. The backyard faced the ocean. Sea oats, pillaged by tourists even more since their recent endangered status, lined the perimeter of their property. I laid on the horn one last time and jumped out of the car, taking the stairs two at a time. My short and stooped grandmother was standing by the door when I reached it. I took her in my arms and twirled her around. She tapped my back with a wooden spoon.

"Paloma, glory be! Set me down and stop all that racket." She didn't mean a word of it. Giving her a few more spins before complying, I then took a long look at her face searching for signs of illness or age. A few more wrinkles, but grandmas could never have too many. Her weight was good, and the smile on her face was there because of me.

My grandfather burst through the back door as noisily as I'd entered the front, a string of fish in hand. "Who's making such a fuss outside? Sounds like a marching band. *Toot! Toot!*" He plopped the fish in the sink and tried to wipe his smelly hands on my shirt sleeve. I gave him a bear hug. It was good to be home!

While Papa and I went over the equipment I would need, Gran put down a spread big enough to feed the whole island. Although it was only a few hours since I'd eaten breakfast, I dove into lunch. All my favorites were steaming from large bowls–ham, collards, red potatoes, fresh corn-on-the cob, and cornbread. As we ate, we updated each other on the news and tales from the palmetto telegraph that spread island gossip.

Suddenly my grandmother bolted from her chair and raced into the living room. "Paloma, come quick, it's just about time." I looked at my watch. 12:03. Two minutes until time for "The Man". I ran to the bathroom, used the toilet quickly, dashed out and dove on the couch. My grandfather took the calm approach, ambling to his chair. The familiar sounds of *The Jaded Joker* announced the start of Perry Mason and, thanks to TBS and endless reruns, helped account for why I became an obsessed fan of mysteries. Once again ritual dictated. No one dared talk until the commercials. All stories hung unfinished in the air as the program came back on. When the last credit rolled, talking started spontaneously.

The show over and wanting to get a little background information on the Gundersen plant, I booted up Heathcliff and did an Internet search. I marked files that I wanted to check, sending them into a download queue. Starting with the usual–financials, ratings like Dunn and Bradstreet, general business information and people-in-business indexes. Any news articles for Gun-dersen? I typed in a search, skipped eye-balling the list of hits, instead placing them all into the queue. I left Heathcliff alone to finish his down-load.

I helped my grandmother clean up in the kitchen while unobtrusively wiping up corners and spots her old eyes missed. Girl talk began after Gran chased Papa out with his smelly fish. When the dishes were dried and put away, I went out to the back porch to watch Papa clean the days' catch. "There's an extra scaler in the drawer over there." He always said that. I gave my standard reply.

"Eeyy, no! I'd rather eat them than clean them, Pop."

"And you call yourself tough." His grin was as wide as a watermelon rind.

"Yep, and you better not tell anybody any different."

"How long you gonna be around?"

"I don't have an agenda. For the next few days I'll be in and out. Then you'll have me all to yourselves."

"And Dixie?"

"Still in need of help." I explained her situation, waiting until now as part of an unspoken habit we'd fallen into by our mutual love of my grandmother. *Don't worry Gran and woe unto those who do.* "She's finally getting her arraignment tomorrow."

"I'm sorry to hear about Lemond. Give me the details and I'll tell Gran later on." I relayed recent events and as I had anticipated, he understood my involvement and offered some of his simple wisdom. "This hating people for nothing has to stop. If there's anything I can do, you better ask. Do you need any money?"

"So far I don't, thanks. It's nice to know I have support. Hopefully every-thing will be cleared up soon. I'm sorry I'm running out as soon as I get here."

"Gran and I aren't going anywhere. Do what you have to and don't worry about us. Who does Dixie have for an attorney?" I told him about Al, the Waving Girl Law Center and Aggie.

"I saw someone over yonder at Pinckney Island, checking game licenses. She wrestled a drunk redneck to the ground and cuffed him–with one hand." I laughed, picturing it easily in my mind. "Is she about five-two, curly light hair, full of freckles, real cute?"

"Yep. But this cute business–I'll have to tell Gran." It's amazing how many people he knew along the islands and on the mainland. I could never get away with *anything.* Everyone knew my old guy, Mr. Sid. If you went to the store with him, make sure you have an hour or two to kill, because you can't go two steps without having to stop and chat with someone. But those same someones looked after them both very well, especially when I moved away for college and now in Seal Beach. They were well loved and respect-ed and they treated others the same way. Their church community had some of the most giving and lovable people you'd ever meet. But, in spite of the constant attention, I still harbored guilt in leaving them behind.

"I know that look on your face, child. Don't feel guilty over living your life."

"Taking up mind reading lately, Papa?" He pushed fish innards at me. I scooted behind him and pulled the straps on his coveralls shortening his pants about five inches. We could go on like this for hours. Kind of a country bumpkin' intellectual exercise. I solemnly spoke of my dear birth-place. "The island is just too over-built, Pop. I don't like what I see."

"Me neither. If I wasn't so old, I'd have left this place. Too many people. Remember when there were no cops? It was a good thing too, the way you were getting into every empty house. And when you learned those new-fangled alarms and showed old man Van der Hausen how fast you were able to get past that new security system he'd paid thousands for. I thought he was going to have a stroke! That alarm company didn't believe you could do it! Hah! You were fourteen. Foot, it wasn't that long ago. Cops're all over the place here now. There were no murders for over twenty-five years. Now, with drug smuggling and other such meanness, it's getting bad as Noo Yark City." I snorted with mirth.

"As I drove on the island, I saw a bunch of car tags from above the Mason-Dixon line. Somebody needs to kick all those snowbirds back up north," I commanded.

"And I got the boots to do it." He shook an unbooted leg at me, trying to look stern. Impossible. I changed the subject before I got choked and sentimental. "Done any fishing around Daufuskie?"

"Nope. I've been sticking around home lately."

"Why? Is something wrong?"

"No, chile, just getting old and I tire quicker."

"Papa, you're gonna live forever! When was the last time you and Gran got checked at Doc Miller's?"

"Just last week. Everything's fit as a fiddle–little worn perhaps–but for our age we're fine. Let's get the maps out and get you on your way." He cut a square in the side of several empty gallon milk jugs and filled them with fish and water and put them in the freezer.

"Where's the *Shrimp*?" I asked about my tiny first boat, so named because of its size.

"It sprang a leak. Too big to fix."

"Well, it did last a long time. The wood finally gave, huh?"

"Yeah. Look in that cabinet behind you. Everything is in there. Hugo blew out a lot of my old maps. Dang near took the *Katie* with him, but she held up well under the circumstances." The boat, obviously, had been named for my grandmother.

I dug in the drawer and pulled out rolls of navigational–nav–charts. I found one of Georgia and held it up against the wall. I located Savannah, then moved my finger up. "Wow, I didn't realize how big the river was. It splits Georgia and Carolina clear up to Tennessee."

"I have all of Georgia mapped. There's one of Rincon." I searched, bringing out memories with several of the charts. We reminisced about trips we'd taken. Fish we'd caught, all a bit bigger than the last time we told the same story. I found the nav chart that detailed a different part of the river north of Rincon than the one I'd bought. Chart-wise I was set for any thing and any where. We unrolled it for a quick look.

"Here it is. I was right. *Super legal!*" My hand smacked the table. Papa jumped at the sound.

"Land sakes, girl. What's got your gander up? I almost cut my finger off." He finished scraping the fish mess off the table. A few errant scales flew off and onto the floor. "Get that up for me, honey. Kate will skin my hide if she sees that down there." I wrinkled my nose at the task but cleaned it with a paper towel. "Go check on your grandmother then we'll plot you a course."

In the house, Gran was napping on the couch. I decided to slip on a swim suit under my shorts. It could get very hot today floating in a boat under the sun. I'd always kept a few bathing suits here so I wouldn't need to take a wet one back home after that one last swim before leaving for the airport. This suit was fading from navy to a lighter blue, but then, I wasn't strolling to a beach party. It would do. I shoved a pair of jeans–for the buggy night–into my overloaded pack. The last task as always–shutting down Heathcliff.

I looked out the kitchen window. It was *de rigueur* for island homes to have several outdoor tables, especially one used only for seafood purposes. My grandfather had set up the picnic table in the backyard under shade. I dumped ice in the tea pitcher, stuffed cups and other accessories under armpits and in pockets, grabbed the pitcher with three fingers and headed outside. The view from here was astounding–the true essence of the island. The sun was at the right angle for the palmetto fronds to cast a cooling shadow over us. Shrimp trawlers–themselves an endangered species–chug-ging in from Broad River Sound, passed in the distance. Low tide brought out the wonderful smell of the pluff mud–briny, slightly pungent–*home*. The afternoon breeze was strong enough to help with the heat as it moved inland. I felt it caress my cheek and watched it stir the moss hanging down from the ancient oaks.

I rubbed the glass of ice tea across my forehead. I listened for the whistle that the wind created as it moved under the stilted house. Dixie and I were convinced it was haunted. The resident good ghost, as we'd decided, aided us in our pirate shenanigans and helped in forming the tall tales of our adven-turous youth. I sighed contentedly. Familiar ground had steadied my inner turmoil from recent incidents. Here was safety, dependability, order, predictability. Out there was chaos, devastation.

"Yoohoo, *neta*! You've been out collecting seashells?" Our phrase for day dreaming and worrying.

"Sorry, Pops. There's a lot of 'em today." *Neta*–he'd called me granddaughter. He'd remembered the word I'd taught him, about the only one he'd learned. When I'd returned from Brazil, I'd had hopes, an obsession, with teaching Portuguese to my grandparents. I'd thought as one does in youth, that wanting it would make it so. Only Dixie succumbed, perhaps from having picked up a good bit of the language when she spent the summers with us in Rio. Then back to live on the island, I'd been disappointed and even angry at first, that my grandfather seemed almost against trying to learn Portuguese. Growing into adulthood, with the ability to see better the hows and whys of life, I was sitting on the bow of the *Katie* watching my grandfather at the nets. I'd been angry at him not remembering what I'd taught him the week before. In epiphany I'd realized that it wasn't that my grandfather didn't want to learn it. He'd have done anything to please me. For reasons I'm still discovering, Papa had considered himself not only an uneducated man but worse, an uneducable one.

He'd sacrificed to give my dad a great–good wasn't enough–educa-tion. Perhaps my father's great success in the import business had prompted his inadequate feelings. But he'd never let it show. My father's hero had been his dad. Geez, I'm going to start bawling if I keep this up! Instead, I walked up to the old salty and gave him a long, loving hug, followed by a smacker-roo on his cheek. "Papa, I love you. And Gran. If I've ever done anything that made you feel I didn't, please know that it was youthful stupidity. You both mean the world to me. It sounds trite but I couldn't have done it without you. Nothing. And I'd never have made it through six years of college without you and Gran." We repeated the hug and kiss. I know I saw mist in his eyes, but he quickly turned and busied himself with the charts.

How's shrimping?" I asked, as we weighted down the charts with conch shells.

"Bad to worse, *neta*. We've all but lost hope of it catching up with the '99 harvest. And we had the nerve to complain about that year. The storms stir the supply up, the droughts dry them out while over-salting everything to death. There's pollution, but it's being taken care of, so we've been told. I don't go out much anymore. I let the family men get the big loads. I still cast a net at our spot. That gives Gran and me enough to eat and freeze. Especially now that you're gone." His whole face crinkled in a smile. "You sure can put away the shrimp. I use to think you were hiding them somewhere in the house. All along, they were in your belly." I beamed at the memories–staying out all day at a little inlet that was deep enough to harbor shrimp, crab and fish. With the ocean ahead, inlet at left, the remains of Fort Walker behind us in the dunes that bordered a marsh, Papa taught me the art of catching my own makings for a Low Country cookout.

I successfully caught blue crabs without getting pinched and learned to bait a hook with Catawba worms–puffy, green with black markings that spit a lime-colored juice in defense and still grossed me out. The true test was learning how to hand cast a shrimp net, which, in gathering it to throw, required a third arm or one's mouth. After many tries I was able to fan the net out like a dancer's skirt as it sailed in the air. It rendered some big beau-ties as I hauled it toward me. I didn't think I'd ever get used to the taste of that soggy, salty net. Now I missed it.

We poured over the charts. My grandfather was an authority on any hole that had water in it. He drew the best route to get there. There, being what I thought was the backside of the Gundersen plant. My excitement peaked.   "What all do you need, honey?"

"The *Pipsqueak*, binoculars."

"Hitched the boat up right after you called. What else?"

"Well..."

"Spit it out. No time for you to stop speaking your mind."

"I was hoping to borrow your .357." I looked down at the charts anxiously.

"You think you really need it?" He peered over his glasses at me.

"I don't want to have to take it or use it. But Lemond was murdered."

"That is a consideration. Well, your daddy and I taught you to be responsible. I know you won't be waving it around to draw trouble to you or doing something dangerous that you'd not normally do just because you have a gun."

"Absolutely, Papa. It's better to talk your way out of trouble."

"Exactly. A pistol'll come in handy for vermin other than the two-legged variety. Lots of wild animals in the woods along the river. And snakes."

"Thanks for reminding me."

"Is Gran napping?" I nodded. "Go inside now then, pick what you need. Don't forget ammo."

I tiptoed through the living room and into the den, opening the gun case and sampled a few. I chose a Smith and Wesson .357, with a three-inch barrel like my Dan Wesson. Then I selected a .38 snub-nose. I opened the drawer and picked out two speed loaders for each of the guns and a box of ammo. I left the bulkier leather pistol cases and slipped them both into holsters. I tread quietly to the back porch, gazed out at the Atlantic Ocean pinning for a swim, then rejoined my grandfather. I emptied the two pistols to store them under the seat.

"Whatcha gonna do–say 'bang bang' when you point the gun at someone? Won't do you much good without them," he said indicating the bullets.

"Habit. California requirement, Pops. Have the ammo in a separate place in your car, empty pistol."

"Well, this ain't L.A.," we chorus together smiling. I stashed the pistols under the seat. I tossed my suitcase in the cab and anchored Heathcliff on the seat beside me. He needed to work on his tan. The sun would energize his solar battery charger.

"Paloma, boat's all fueled up. So's the spare tank." Pop laid some tackle and bait in the boat and secured them. "Props for cover while you're spying." Uneducated–not! He'd thought of something I hadn't. If I was approached about what I was doing around the plant, then I'd best be able to back up my story. He packed a few other essentials–Avon's Skin So Soft used as a bug repellent, sandwiches, flashlight and binoculars. There was also an ice chest full of Diet Pepsi–he gotten my favorite soda–and a first aid kit. Between that and the guns, I'd probably sink. As we finished loading, a car approached down the road.

"Oh, shit, Pop!"

"Where in the name of Sam Hill did you learn to talk like that?"

"It's Aunt Lilly." I moaned.

"Oh, shit," he replied.

"I don't need her sass right now. And I'll never get out of here!"

"Just get in the truck and drive off. I'll tell her you had to go." He urged me toward the door with hand motions.

"She won't accept that. She's going to be mad enough to catch fire. Make up something."

"We shouldn't lie, Paloma."

"Pop, I've always wondered something. Who in the name of Sam Hill is Sam Hill?"

"I don't have the slightest idea." I climbed into the truck. Aunt Lilly was at the stop sign, a short block away. "Paloma, just keep your wits about you. You're tough and smart. At the first sign of trouble–get out of there. Don't worry about my stuff. It goes without saying that I want you back safe above all else." I looked into his face. His skin was like leather, baked seventy-seven years in the sun. Leaning out the window, I hugged and thanked him, then eased the truck forward. Lilly's horn blared behind me, an obnoxious series lasting ten seconds or more. Sounded like she was tooting out Morse code. Long, short, short, short, long. I stepped harder on the gas.

"Why doesn't Paloma stop, Sid?" Aunt Lilly's shrill voice could be heard for miles. "She had to have heard me. What's the matter with her?" I winced as I coasted onto Dune Lane. She wasn't even out of the car and she was already complaining. Short, short, Looonnnggg! "I didn't know she was coming home. She should have called. You should have told me. You and Kate need to set a better example for her, Sid, and you know it. I tried. The good Lord above knows how I tried. Make her stop." Poor Papa.

"You know how loud she plays that music of hers," he said. I moved my head like I was jamming.

"Why didn't she drive down Pelican Watch? You're letting her go fishing at this hour?" I braved a look in the mirror. Lilly was talking up a storm. I saw Pop's hand reach up for his hearing aid. You didn't have to tell me which way he was turning the volume.

The Anti-Defamation League estimates the white supremacist movement has 20,000 members and 200,000 sympathizers–one-third women. The Aryan Nations, with around 500 members was responsible in just one year for firebombing churches and an interstate natural gas pipeline, murdering a Missouri state trooper and an Order member who talked; rob-bing two banks (netting $1.4 million) and three armored trucks (netting $3.6 million)–the largest robbery ever committed in North America (only $430,000 has been recovered). Louis Beam's share of the loot was $100,000, Tom Metzger's around $300,000.

Chapter Thirty-Six

Before heading off the island, I stopped at Dixie's family house. I wanted to check that no relative was there and ask some neighbors for any details on Clarice's vacation itinerary. I'd barely gotten out of the truck when Mrs. Bishop, a fellow teacher like Clarice, came across the street to greet me. She was a good friend of the Hightower's and I felt comfortable relaying information and knew she would trust me to divulge anything she knew.

News of Dixie's incarceration was met with expected indignation and upon hearing of Lemond's murder, Mrs. Bishop's toffee-toned face was saddened and outraged. She turned back into her house for a key to the Hightower's front door, severely rebuking my assurances that she needed not bother.

"We'll do this in a civilized way, chile." She swatted away my case of picks. Her husband had been one of the locksmiths who'd agreed to let a pre-teen commit legal lock picking when my grandfather realized my talent and energies needed a constructive direction.

Inside Clarice's spotless kitchen, Mrs. Bishop pointed to papers tacked to a little bulletin board that made up the call center. In typical Clarice efficiency, were copies of all the Hightowers' itineraries. During a brief discussion, we decided to track down relatives on the trip so that the news could be delivered as humanely as possible from family and not by a stranger or by me over a long-distance phone call. I found today's date on the list and the hotel where Dixie's brothers were staying. The cruise ship was expected to dock that afternoon in Bora Bora. Taking a deep breath for courage, I hit 00 for the international operator asking for all the country and city codes needed to call the South Pacific. Internally, I was a bit grateful that the family was not at the hotel and I could post-pone destroying their lives a bit longer. But that left me with how to eventually reach them while I was roaming. Mrs. Bishop solved that for me, too.

"You say you're on your way to help Dixie?"

"I hope so."

"Okay, I'll sit by the phone. Meanwhile, I'll get the bunch here working on things." I knew she meant long-time islanders ready to help the Hightowers however they could. I called the hotel back, asked for the front desk manager. I explained in general terms about a family emergency. He assured me he'd pass on the message himself. He was tactful and didn't delve too personally, but was savvy enough to extend his help, starting with a call to the airlines for available flights to the U.S. He'd have that information ready for the Hightowers when they arrived at the hotel. After relaying a few other ways he'd be able to help, I felt my friends would be in good hands. I hoped the hotel knew just how valuable a manager they had. I hung up more relieved than when I'd begun the call.

Mrs. Bishop was busy making a list of tasks that needed to be done on her end. Another competent soul. I promised to keep in touch and covering all bases I gave her my cell phone number and Al's and Aggie's contact information. She would have hunted down Al anyway–wanting an update on Dixie straight from the attorney's mouth. I knew she'd be dusting a chair off at the arraignment along with a group of supporters she'd enlist. Keeping her house line free, Mrs. Bishop had her cell phone out, speaking English and Gullah hurriedly, galvanizing some old-time islander into action. The wagons were circling and Mrs. Bishop was in charge. Look out!

As I maneuvered Papa's truck and trailer toward the mainland without knocking over a mailbox or hedge, neighbors were already walking over to her house. I waved at the small parade as I drove off.

*   *   *

Billy Ray waited in the car while Hughes went inside to talk to his wife Wanda. Ten minutes later the garage door opened and Wanda backed the Cadillac out. He ducked down not wanting the kids to see him. When he could no longer hear the engine he sat up and went inside.

He walked around looking at everything as if it was his first time in the house. Hughes tapped away on the adding machine in his office. The entire house had been redecorated, a task Wanda accomplished every other year, come hell or high water. Billy Ray went into the huge game room. It was complete now with a pool table in the center, *Happy Days*-styled jukebox in the corner. A big-screen TV dominated the far wall, and in front of it Nintendo games were strewn about the floor. The sleek, expensive stereo system Hughes had shown him at his electronics store a few months ago filled up the remaining wall. Movie DVDs, video tapes and game cartridges were stacked neatly on the top shelves. Music in various formats, collected through the ages, filled two long rows.

In Wyman Hughes' office, the phone rang and after answering it, he closed the door for privacy. An excited Willie was almost shouting into it. "Slow down, boy. I can't understand a word you're saying."

"He's really done it now, boss. I been tryin' to get you all day long. You ain't gonna believe what Randy's gone and done now."

"How about you tellin' me *what* he done instead of just that he done some-thin'."

"I just did."

"Willie!"

"Okay. Okay. Randy's gone and kilt him a black boy."

"Where did you hear that?" Could it be true? How could he use the news to his advantage? "What proof do ya have?"

"Well, I wuzn't there boss, but all the guys are talkin' 'bout it. One of the sheriff boys dates my wife's sister's cousin's daughter. And she..."

"I don't need to know your whole family tree. Get to the point!"

If the Imperial Wizard had kept his clap shut, he would already know what Willie had called to tell him. But Willie didn't say this to Hughes. Instead he took a deep breath and continued. "The police says it's true, so I reckon it be true. Out on Blanford Road last night they found him swingin' from a tree."

"Dead?"

"Deader n' a doornail."

"Randy done that?"

"Yep. Randy and one a' his friends. They lookin' for him real bad. Had the state G-bies out there pokin' 'round. And you know those state boys'll be turnin' over every stick and corn stalk to get 'em. That there nigger-loving attorney from Savannah done stuck his nose in it, too. What's left over when the state and that scab are done ain't gonna be worth a hill a' beans. And you know Randy. He'll be dumpin' all the blame on everybody 'cept hisself."

"You got that right," Hughes agreed. Willie had no other information to pass on, so Hughes thanked him for calling and hung up. "Whoopee!" He yelped. This was great news. Now he could talk with Billy Ray about making this work for them. Hughes grabbed the door knob, but as he turned it, his son's tormented face flashed in his mind. "Randy and a friend. Oh no! Did Willie mean B-Ray? Is that what has him so riled up?" Hughes spoke aloud. Willie would tell him if his son was suspected of being the friend with Randy, wouldn't he? No, that lily-livered pissant wouldn't have the guts. Wille would let him get blind-sided with it and then lie his way out. It couldn't be anyone else, though. Randy didn't have any other friends.

Deep down he knew his adopted son was soft. If he was with Randy when that lunatic kilt someone, then B-Ray would be all churned up inside. Just as he was now. Damn! And Willie had said that Randy was already taking the blame off of himself. He couldn't let Randy get away with it. Billy Ray couldn't stand up to Randy. He'd shown that over and over, year after year. Hughes had to make sure Randy took the blame. "All of it." His mind spun, thoughts coming to him so fast. Hughes owed Randy a lot of money. He never could figure out where that loser got that much cash. Randy had been pushing him lately, showing up all over town like he was shadowing Hughes. Getting in his face, saying he was going to talk to Billy Ray or his wife. He hinted that he was going to tell his father-in law. That would be *big* trouble for him.

So now he had the opportunity to make Randy disappear and not have blood on own his hands. And Hughes would then be free and clear. Things were definitely looking up. But if Billy Ray wouldn't tell him what happened, how could he work a plan? He thought about that for a few minutes. Another idea taking form. It might work. He'd just tell B-Ray that some-thing had happened and it involved Randy. But the slime was gonna get away with it. So if they didn't get the focus back on Randy, then they were going to... To what? Hmm. What would get his son fired up to help? Especially when he's been spouting off today about leaving the Klan, washing his hands of everybody? The kids! Yes! He'd tell Billy Ray that Randy was trying to get at Billy Ray by involving his younger brothers and sister. Billy Ray would do anything to protect them. And in protecting them, Hughes would naturally have to be included. A great plan and Hughes didn't have to do any of the work! Yep, it was a great time to be alive.

Standing on the patio, Billy Ray was surprised to see a hot tub. A screened-in room adjoined it overlooking the pool. It had happened again. His foster-father had sworn that it wouldn't. Hughes was always deep in hock and had probably used Klan money to cover it. Until now, Billy Ray didn't believe he could have felt any more dispirited, but as he stood there he felt the numbness deepen. He heard the screen door slide open and Hughes joined him on the patio.

"Dad, you've done it again, haven't you," he spoke quietly.

"Whataya think about the game room? And I put in the swimming p-pool just for you, son." He turned to his father and stared deeply into his eyes. Wyman Hughes looked away.

"How much this time?"

"W-What are you talking about?"

"When was the last time I went swimming, dad? The last time *I* wanted to?" His voice ended with a squeak, pain cutting off his vocal chords. "Whose money did you use–the store or Klan?" When no answer came, he yelled. "Tell me!"

"It's okay, s-son. I got a plan worked out. I'm getting out of it this time."

"How?" Billy Ray sat on the arm of an Adirondack chair.

"Don't worry about it. I got a good plan. We'll make it work."

Billy Ray's mouth was very dry, a white filmy line framed his lips. He wiped it off with the back of his hand. "Who's this *we* you're talking about?"

"You and me, son! Who'd you think I was talking about?"

"I told you the last time, I'm tired of bailing you out. Two times I paid off your bills. You gotta learn self-control! Wanda, too! You need help I can't give!"

"Don't you tell me how I gotta be!" The Imperial Wizard shook his fist in the face of the young man. "I told you I got it all worked out! I'm doing this whole thing because I love you like my own flesh and blood!"

"You were in debt way before you came to my trailer today," he spit out between clenched teeth. He couldn't deal with this now. Not after what Randy Beamon had inflicted on him. Randy had been a breaking point–or so he thought. But life again hammered Billy Ray down. Such a deep dispirited gloom flooded into him that he physically ached inside. His whole life had been lies and guilt that grown-ups–his own parents, real and foster–had dumped on him.

"W-what happened last night?"

Billy Ray couldn't tell the truth. Not yet, if ever! "I washed my hands of Beamon for good. Now you're trying to make me feel guilty for your lack of control!"

Hughes' face was twisted with fury. Billy Ray-The Manipulated had learned well from his dominating mentor. But his father was too dense, again, to realize his schemes never really worked. "I took you in, got you b-back in s-school, gave you a roof over your head."

"Don't." Billy Ray held out his hands as if he could stop the words from reaching him. He spoke softly, but with a new determination that made Wyman Hughes freeze. "It. Has. To. Stop. Dad." His eyes bore into the haggard face of the older man. "Can't you see? I'm dying here." Billy Ray tore out of the house running as fast as he could.

*   *   *

I found the river launch and slid the boat in the water with ease. No one else was around, although there were several trucks and campers in the lot. I found even more gear stashed in the boat. My grandfather kept it there all the time. A metal box held a flashlight, knives, various fishing gear, kitchen utensils and who knows what was stored underneath that layer of goods. I loaded the handguns and placed them in my backpack.

Next, I stuck Heathcliff and the cell phone into a water-tight container inside the boat. I phoned Aggie at work but she wasn't in. When asked to leave a message, I relayed a brief "check your home machine". I called her home, leaving a recording of my plans and the location.

All of the problems Dixie had, and Lemond when he was living, involved the Gundersen plant. And the people there were serious about keeping others out. That meant they were hiding something and I wanted to find out what that was. Donning an orange life jacket, I put on my disguise as such–a khaki fishing hat pulled down low, a few of Pop's prized lures attached, and dark sunglasses. I picked up the oars, rowing out to where the river was deep enough to drop the engine. It sputtered to life with a puff of smoke.

I'd memorized the directions–which branches to take–but pulled the chart out to have at the ready with an extra life jacket on top to weight it down. I estimated it'd take about fifteen minutes to get there. The river water was dyed burnt orange from the surrounding Georgia clay. I munched on Jordan Almonds while steering. At the first bend in the river, I took the left branch. A large motor boat passed pulling a skier. Their wake was strong and I moved my boat away from it.

I approached a wooded cliff. And just past it, almost invisible by a sheer curve in the river, was the Gundersen plant's landing. On the opposite side of the river, the bank showed definite signs of erosion that created several small lagoons. I picked the middle inlet and tossed out the anchor. With the fishing pole strapped to the side of the boat, minus a juicy worm since I was faking anyway, I settled back and inspected the Gundersen landing from a distance.

A metal shed, about three hundred yards long, was built on high ground. The company name painted on the side in large black letters. A cement boat ramp and dock jutted into the water. A picnic area with a canopy, tables, and chairs rested under the shade of a group of trees, along with two brick barbecues. Inspection completed. I packed my mouth with Bazooka Joe and deliberated on snooping around the building, but decided to hold off. I waited.

And lasted about five minutes before my butt went to sleep and my legs cramped. My skin was cooking in the heat, so I splashed river water over my legs and arms. I shifted for another five and checked my watch a thousand times. *How does Dixie do it?* This was as exciting as reading the phone-book. I was bored, hot, irritable. I started singing, tonelessly, picking songs appropriate for the occasion. "Old Man River", "Rolling on a River", "Cry Me a River", "Summertime." To stretch, I put my head down between my legs, getting an upside down view of the rear of the boat.

I pulled out a canvas case so sun-bleached I couldn't guess the original color. This was the last container of gear I hadn't yet pilfered. I wondered if you can tell a man by what he kept in his boat. I opened the case and peeked inside. Galoshes inches too big for my feet were stowed on top amid sticks of beef jerky, a pack of Juicy Fruit stuck together in one mass, a deck of cards and a plastic bag of poker chips. Night fishing, huh pop? Now I knew better. Still bored with surveillance, I made a tent of my windbreaker to shield the sun's glare and booted up Heathcliff to peruse the information I'd gotten on Gundersen. Still unable to see the screen well in the brightness, I pulled out the tiny Bubblejet printer and single-sheet fed in the paper. Now, wasn't I high-tech cool! New Docksiders, non-frills boat, pretending to fish while computing my little heart out miles from an electrical outlet? Slam! I jumped, making small waves as the boat pitched from my rocking. "You're cool, all right," I said aloud to myself. Seeing no attention directed at me, I used the binoculars. At the landing, two white cargo vans with Waltco lifts were parked with their rears facing me. Crates were shoved out one at a time, like candy in a Pez dispenser, then moved into the shed. I snapped a few pictures with the tiny digital camera, counted crates. As the trucks were leaving, I used the binoculars again to peek at their license tags, and was only able to see one clearly.

I typed the tag number into Heathcliff, adding a summary of the men's actions. I debated putting on jeans as the sun, even with my skin used to lots of tanning, was getting a work out. Perish the thought of not wearing shorts. I dove into the water to cool off.

Nineteen minutes later the two trucks came bouncing back along the rutted dirt road and the men unloaded. I climbed back into the boat–a delicate maneuver with no solid ground under my feet and without tipping Heathcliff and gear into the drink. I only bothered to dry off my arms so the PC wouldn't get waterlogged. Checking the men out with the binoculars again, I typed in the time, number of trucks and how many crates they unpacked. They had to be getting them from the plant to be gone such a short time. I heard a faint whistle.

A guy walked around the rear of the shed and stopped with his side toward me, to take a whiz over the cliff. He made a zipping motion when he finish-ed and turned toward the river, picked up a stick and tossed it. That's when he saw me.

I pulled up the rod, my heart skipping. As I cast the line I followed the arc as an excuse to sneak a glance across the river. I watched the guy watching me. *Go away, nosy man!* After an eternity he returned to the shed. Thirty- three minutes later the trucks came back. And two more times. I noted this and took pictures again. Then not a creature stirred for two hours so I spent the time studying the information I'd printed.

The first sheet described Gundersen's businesses, none dealing remotely with computer electronics and no information why the company had ventured outside of their domain with the Rincon electronics plant. The company was based in Boston, subsidiaries everywhere northeast, assets galore, stocks doing well.

The Rincon plant was not yet a year old and a man named Swartzman was in charge. I browsed through the short biographies on upper management, stopping to read Swartzman's in length. Two years ago, he'd been the head of security, now he was in charge of a new highly technical venture. Quite a promotion there, dude. The information stewed in my cerebrum until the chug of a diesel engine broke the thinking process.

A small barge slowly inched up river to the Gundersen dock. As I jotted down the name and registration number painted in radioactive orange on the bow, the men came back in two panel trucks and unloaded twelve crates onto the barge. This, too, was a Kodak moment, which I took during various stages of loading. The barge transported the crates up river. Time to go snooping. When saving the files, I clicked on the encryption function before Heathcliff was told to snooze. No one would be able to read the file. Unless they got the pass code from me. I reeled in the line, stowed the rod and followed a safe distance behind. The barge stopped at a split in the river. I passed it discovering the split had created an island.

The near side of the bank was populated with mangroves, their S-shaped trunks hanging over water, moss dripping from their limbs. Testing their strength, I stepped up on the bottom curve of the trunk and pulled the boat underneath. Excellent cover.

On the bank, I stretched my body, working out the stiffness and watched a group of squirrels play tag as they dashed from limb to limb. I finished reading the Gundersen data, which rendered nothing more enlightening. The eight men from the landing roared up to the barge in a speed boat. They boarded, unloaded it, then disappeared into the brush. Not much on efficiency–all this toting equipment–but nobody asked me. With my camera, I clicked away. When the barge was empty, it chugged back the way it came. The dockhands, as I'd dubbed them, soon appeared and sat on the bank of the island sipping a few cool ones before they boated back, to the landing I assumed. I waited forty minutes but the island had no other visitors.

I climbed back in the boat, made a wide circle to the opposite side of the island and tied off. I put Heathcliff back in his case and out of the sun. It was getting close to bug time, so with regret to the heat, I unrolled the jeans I'd stashed in the pack and slipped them on. I worked out the stiffness with a few knee bends. Next I slipped the .357 in the side holster, and tossed the backpack over one shoulder. The walk was riddled with obstacles of nature, but I made good time. I stepped to the edge of a clearing and saw a small building made of aluminum siding. It had a screened-in porch, typical of river dwellings. I picked a spot by the front door and watched.

Giving what I hoped was sufficient time to notice anyone lurking about, I took pictures of the building, put the gun in the pack, slung it over my shoulder and walked to the door. It was padlocked. No problem. My picks were with me–never leave home without them! In short time the lock slipped from the clasp. I opened the door and let out a breath when the still air stayed quiet. I entered.

I stopped dead in my tracks, surveying the room. Signs and symbols of White Power colored the walls. Large white letters—WRF–framed in black stretched corner to corner. WRF? White Racist Farts? I crept to a table with cardboard boxes stacked on top. I rifled through them and was surprised to find it full of Klan propaganda. Scanning the hate material, no WRF was mentioned. I slipped copies into my pack. What interested me the most were the crates and boxes against the back wall.

The wooden boxes had THIS SIDE UP stamped in red. I tried to lift the lid on one, but it held fast. I looked around and saw a crowbar on the floor. I went to work prying off the lid. The box contained computer circuit boards, in rows of threes. I lifted a Styrofoam tray, saw the same underneath, but noticed the sides were chewed from shoving the oversized foam into place. I tugged and tugged until I'd worked it out.

"What the heck?" I said aloud, almost starting at the sound. Night vision goggles were hidden underneath. Each pair had white letters stamped on the sides–DPD, BPD, MPD. It wasn't until I saw LAPD that I made the connection. Could this really be? The lettering indicated police departments? I knew that Dixie's police equipment, what she hadn't shelled out of her own bank account, had spray-painted departmental identifiers on them. I thought about the data I'd read this afternoon. A listing of Gundersen branch offices. The cities fit the initials on the goggles. I needed new toys. So, one for the authorities and one for me! I slipped two small pairs into my pack, thinking how brave–or stupid–I was shopping in a den for white supremacists. Underneath the goggles were ten night vision scopes. And then there were eight.

I moved to a smaller crate and pried it open snapping photos as I worked. Sweat slid down my body. This box held items encased in silver bags. Slitting it open with my knife, I pulled out a slim black box. I dug deeper in the crate finding the same thing. Eight on the top. Estimating the depth, I guessed thirty-two mystery boxes. I took two off the third tray for later examination and covered up my theft. Since I was pilfering everything else, why leave another waist-high stack of smaller boxes untouched? I opened the one on top and found rows of chips– the micro kind.

Plain cardboard boxes were stacked to the ceiling along another wall–two rows deep of cell phones. The last two crates were flat and long. These must be important–the wooden tops were nailed every few inches, more than the other crates had been. I worked up enough nails to peek and shone the flashlight inside.

"Merda! Puta que o pariu! I don't believe what I'm seeing!" I whispered. An AT4–one of the U.S. military's disposable rocket launchers was neatly packed inside. My breathing was faster. *What the heck is going on in this town?* This wasn't the usual Klavern equipment and with a launcher in their midst, these guys were definitely playing for keeps! *And* they would be very irate if they thought their domain had been compromised. I needed to erase my tracks. I used the knife handle to hammer the nails back down on the lid. I moved back to the other crates, taking the time to do a neater job of resealing them.

In the corner, almost obscured were boxes looking like over-sized foot-lockers, military olive drab in color. I flipped the lid up. "Whoa, again." M-16s, AK-47s, AR-15s! And conversion kits to make the guns fully automatic. From the U.S. Army. The WRF–whoever, whatever they were–had enough fire power to invade a state. Or country.

I made a quick inventory check, my nerves telling me I should have left a long time ago. Six large crates and from their size, probably all goggles. Mystery black boxes, twenty-two crates. Cellular phones, nineteen. Anti tank weapons, two. It was probably too dark inside the room, but I took photos of all four sides. I left the way I'd come in, my stomach knotted until I reached the clearing. Just to be safe, I made myself walk. Being stopped by Gundersen men while out for a day of crashing wildly through the brambles wouldn't do. Once I'd reached the boat and gotten away from the island, I quickly typed everything I'd discovered into Heathcliff and encrypted it.

My trip back to the plant was made in the dusk. I steered the boat over to the Gundersen side and tied off before I reached their landing. Watching again for signs of life, I decided it was clear and risked a quick look.

Ditching the pack behind the shed in case the boat or I was spotted, I stood on my toes at the window and shined the flashlight in. Eight crates of the mystery box size were stacked in the corner, four plain cardboard, and two goggle-sized. Then my vision was marred by the reflection of four people–each wearing the white robes and cone--shaped hats of the Ku Klux Klan.

South Carolina: 1993, Great Falls–A twelve-year old black boy was arrested for beating a nine year-old white boy; 1993, Hilton Head Island–A sixty year old white man was beaten by two black men.–Klanwatch. *1994–Marchers protesting the state's reluctance to take down the Confederate battle flag still flying atop the capitol have promised to demonstrate in other cities if the flag isn't removed in a month. The Coalition for Unity and Progress contends the flag can be flown anywhere else, but tax-paying citizens who feel it a symbol of racism shouldn't have to see it flying on government property. The marchers are targeting the state's tourist industry by marching on Hilton Head Island, a popular resort, on Labor Day weekend. South Carolina is the last southern state to display the flag at the capitol.*

Chapter Thirty-Seven

Brice was a mechanical sex partner, which suited Swartzman. Her "let's just get what we came for and get out" philosophy matched his. A compatible lover was hard to find. He stood up from the bed to dress then made a quick call on his cell phone. "Busy," he lied, flipping the phone closed. Brice was being unusually lazy staying in bed. He crossed to her and sat down. Brice enveloped Swartzman, offering kisses.

"What do you want to do now, Swartzie?"

"Why don't we talk about the plans? The reason why you are here."

"General business. Just like last time–a progress report and what you need from Boston in the coming months."

"Then will you tell me your plans?"

"I'm going to do a little touring this time. I love those old Southern mansions." The slap came as a surprise. Brice's head reeled back, banging into the headboard. Seconds later there was a knock on the door.

"Room service."

Swartzman quickly strode over, unlocked it and went back to Brice. But it was Randy who entered, sporting his unctuous sneer, hunger for the kill evident on his face.

"What the hell is this, Swartzman? Can't you wait until I'm dressed before you parade your hoodlums into my room?"

He laughed, moving close to her face. "It's a shame about you, Brice. I was really getting to like you."

"You have a strange way of showing it."

"That's your fault, babe. Didn't you hear about me in Boston? What I've accomplished? Don't you know why I was sent down to this stink hole?"

"What are you talking about?"

Swartzman leaned over, his face directly in front of Brice. "You don't screw with me and you don't screw with the men."

"What...?"

Swartzman watched Brice's face tighten as she finally realized how much trouble she was in. "I saw the women! I *heard* you!" Swartzman spit out, then laughed. He reached behind him and Randy placed Brice's files–the one's Red had copied yesterday–in his hands.

"It was for you and me, Swartzie. I swear! That's what I flew here to tell you. It was all for us."

"Then why the games? Regular visit? Take in some sightseeing?"

"I wanted to have a little fun, too. And surprise you."

Swartzman's eyes held a dead-end stare. "Brice, you don't play those kind of games." As he was leaving the room, he snapped his fingers. Randy pulled out the .9 millimeter.

"We could have done big things, you and me. But you didn't stay in your place. It's almost laughable. A *woman* heading the race war in America? Ha-ha!" He put a hand on the door. "Randy." Taking his time between shots so he could enjoy it longer, Randy pumped the trigger three times. The silencer did its job, the shots sounding more like loud spits.

"Randy, bring the car around." As soon as he was alone, Swartzman climbed up on the dresser and pushed the ceiling tile away. He reached for the tiny mini camera disguised as a sprinkler nozzle and slipped it in his pocket. He patted it, smiling at his insurance policy. Swartzman turned and looked the room over. All material evidence gone. The manager would give the room a wipe down, no fingerprints for the cops to find, if the cover-up was compromised. He gave one last look at Brice. Yes, a compatible lover was hard to find.

* * *

Moonpie had trouble finding the hotel and was afraid to stop and ask for directions. With the strapping for her broken nose and all the bruises, she couldn't cope with people staring. Driving back to Broughton Street, Moonpie retraced her route and found the hotel at last. She sank back into the seat with relief when she saw Brice's rental car. Resting a few minutes, she laboriously got out of the car and climbed the steps. Using the key her friend had given her, she opened the door when Brice didn't answer her knock.

"Aaagh!" Moonpie crashed against the door, sagging to her knees as she saw the red stains on the sheet and Brice's unblinking stare. Moonpie's body seemed no longer capable of shouldering her burdens. She fell over sobbing, wondering where the additional tears came from when so many had already fallen. She crawled like a sick turtle to the bed. She tenderly righted the dead woman's head. Moonpie rested hers beside Brice, placing her lifeless hand on her cheek and holding it there. "I wish it was me instead of you."

* * *

"You didn't say nothing about another broad being up in the room," Salvador, the hotel manager, told Swartzman over the phone. He spoke tersely but kept his voice low, so he wouldn't be overheard.

"We agreed on keeping the dead woman up there until this evening, but what about her friend? She could call the cops!" Salvador's wife had nagged him to distraction that the extra money he received from Swartzman for the occasional use of the hotel and his silence wasn't worth it. If she'd been there at this moment, she would have crossed herself religiously several times, planted a hand on her hip, glared at him and sighed. Salvador hated that sigh. He scratched his five o'clock shadow and belched into the phone.

"You trying to screw with me?" Swartzman asked as he waved the guys out of his office.

"You're the one humping, *amigo*. There's this fat chick upstairs, babbling about the dead woman. She's beat up and stuff."

"I'll call you right back." He dialed Evan at work, saying the code: "It's your brother." Swartzman tapped his fingers on the desk impatiently.

"Call you right back," Evan promised.

Swartzman buzzed Mildred while waiting, ordering her not to disturb him, even if the Gundersen plant was on fire.

"What's up?" Evan asked pleasantly.

"When can you get away?"

"Half an hour. I don't have much time left on the shift."

"I need a pick up at the Country Inn. Go to the desk for a key. Code name is Cisco."

"What kind of pick up?" Evan asked.

"Two women. I need you to take care of them."

"No problem."

Swartzman hung up and called the Country Inn. "Yeah, Salvador. Some-body's on their way to take care of both problems. Code name G Man. I'll send a guy over with something extra for your trouble."

"Pleasure doing business with ya, *amigo*," he said trying to sound much calmer than he felt.

More than 20,000 people have been murdered in Yugoslavia and over two million people displaced because of the war. Croats have raped over 20,000 women and girls as part of their ethnic cleansing program.

Chapter Thirty-Eight

I spun around to face the three Klansmen feeling like doing a very childish act in my jeans. Their faces were covered, except for eyes and mouth holes. I pressed my back against the Gundersen shed. "Come with us," the one in the middle spoke.

"Ah, no thanks, ya'll. I have my own ride."

"We aren't giving you a choice." And they proved it by advancing quickly for men in long dresses. I tried a fancy evasive move–running like crazy. But they split up and blocked me. I figured I was a goner. So I decided to check out of this world like I lived it. Mouthy.

"You guys too chicken to show your faces?" I asked. "The flaps are il-legal. But then none of you were bright enough to go to law school."

"High school was good enough for this." I saw a rather large school ring head toward me and attempt to shove my eyeball through my head.

"Gee, thanks. Never had a black eye." *Never had your eye hurt this bad, either, smartass.* The three hooded figures formed a circle around me like witches at an altar, me their sacrifice. I heard a tear–one of them came at me with duct-tape. I spat at them, opened my mouth and locked my jaw, squirmed, limboed–anything to get away or at least make their work harder. In the end they won, taped my mouth then placed a cloth bag over my head and pulled the drawstring closed. My hands were tied in front, then my feet. They picked me up and I started the gyrations again as they carried me a few steps. For revenge they knocked me around, but I, being a woman who knows her own mind, still wormed around while they still retaliated. From the noise–slamming of metal in the rear, a high step into the vehicle and the sardined conditions between my abductors–I figured we were in a truck. "Get down."

"Where?" I asked through the gag, only coherent to me. The answer was a headlock and a push down onto a lap. I tried to work the bonds free. The truck bounced, one side going down, then the other, as we traveled over rough road. Several minutes later we drove over smoother pavement. I estimated about twenty minutes were spent before more bumpy surfaces. Meanwhile, I squirmed, employed my head uselessly as a battering ram on whose ever lap I'd been borrow-ing. In return I was cursed, punched, and my clothing, I could hear, was ripping in various place. This was a first for me–abduction. Just sitting there doing nothing seemed so sissy, so reconciled to what was happening to me. When the engine stopped, hands none to gently helped me down.

"I t-told you not to rough her up."

"Hey, we couldn't help it. She's a little hellion, sir."

"Take that thing offa her h-head." It took a few seconds for me to focus in the dimness, especially with the injured eye. A pale light mounted on a pole lit the night in an eerie pastel of ash. "You are not in any d-danger." Ha! The man stood before me, his flap held on with white strips of Velcro. Yank it off and instant law-abiding citizen exercising his First Amendment rights. Probably when a cop was around as it was now illegal for Klansmen to have their faces covered in public when in uniform. He wore a patch that I recognized from Al's literature as the insignia of Imperial Wizards every- where. He was chief bigot and I counted nine more hooded and robed figures, heinous ghosts who seemed to glide along in their long dresses. The summer of evil, the old man had said.

We were in a clearing in the woods. That narrowed it down. The Wiz pointed to a man and made a slicing motion. The guy whipped out a large hunting knife and came toward me. I jumped up trying to kick out with my tied feet. I did nip the guy in the leg, but I was descended upon and soon lost the fight. They held my wrists while the knife-wielding Klansman cut the ropes that bound them. They all had a good laugh at my unnecessary fright. I found myself on my knees and didn't like the connotations so I sat down. My chest was heaving, I couldn't seem to find my breath. Be mad, not fearful. Right! The Wiz's outstretched hand came toward me. With effort I appeared stoic. *Be mad!* I repeated it like a mantra.

He tugged at both ends of the tape on my mouth. Ouch! My body tingled like a live wire, as if evil could flow from his fingers to me. I placed my hands together in a *sampeah* gesture, looking like I was ready for prayer, raised my hands between his arms then separated them, whacking his away. With a good hold on a corner, I ripped the tape off in one clean motion. Needles of pain pricked my lips, like I'd just shaved them with a dull razor blade. I licked my lips, tasted blood and spit it out. *Now* I was mad!

"*Bundões!* You assholes." I croaked, dry-throated. They laughed.

"Was all this necessary, Exalted Cyclops?" the Wiz asked looking at a particular conehead. How he could tell them apart was beyond me.

"She was screamin' and wiggling like a sack full a' cats! I'll tell you what! You could hear her clear down to the Okeefeenokee." A Klansmen near me shifted his feet. Ah. Sticking out from the bottom of his robe were well-worn leopard print boots. Okay. Not the biggest clue. But I'll find you. Tear this town apart until I find you in your silly boots.

"Now," the Wiz said. "He's going to cut the ropes at your feet. He will not harm you."

"Hmm-huh."

"You are so distrusting," the Wiz said acrimoniously.

"It's your track record, Wizzie."

"Brother." The Wiz pointed. Bro' had been standing in front of a child, similarly attired. I stared, horrified at the small, stony figure, hatred showing in the tight little fists planted on his hips.

"You mystagogues start them out early, when they're impressionable and can't make up their own minds," I accused. A few men took steps toward me but Wizzie lifted his hand and all movement stopped.

"We are not here to explain our actions. But we are willing to help you see the error of your ways. We'll accept any misguided sister or brother into our Klan."

"Thanks, guys, really. But I choose to hate someone for a real reason, like the kind of person that they are, not what they look like."

"You'll see the light one day. You'll get sick and tired of the country being defiled by infiltrators. Your neighborhood will be slowly choked by lazy, thieving..." I tuned it out quicker than disco music. A thump into my back urged my attention. It was more of the same drivel.

"You keep repeating yourself."

"Come join us in the fight to save the almighty white race!" He trumpeted. His voice was evilly passionate, yearning to convert another into the fold. He reached down, conjuring, arms arcing upward, like he was scooping up the beasts from hell to release them into the night. Next he launched into a tirade of Biblical fire and brimstone interwoven with his racist theories–a common theme of these groups, based on the materials I'd read so far. How they could meld hatred and murder with Christian values like "love thy neighbor" was a quandary I was still sorting through.

"Can we get on with it?" I asked, making sure I sounded bored, world-weary.

He advanced suddenly, his white flap inches from my face. "It's inevitable. A race war is coming. You'll want to join us. To save your sorry hide!"

"I'll burn in hell first."

"That you will, Sister, that you will."

"From the looks of things," I scanned the Klanhood, "I'll have plenty of company. Look, we could go on like this all night. I'm bored with your jeremiad world. You said you brought me here for a reason. Get on with the program. Please," I added stupidly, like that would make all the difference for ordering Captain Hate around.

"Come." He beckoned.

"And don't call me Sister." I couldn't help myself.

He'd turned and walked toward the small building. One man stayed behind me to make sure I complied, babysitting me with a Remington rifle. I helped myself up, chivalry dead in this crowd. Standing was painful at first so I completed a few squats to work out the stiffness. I examined my knuckles–scraped badly. Extending my fingers, I found a few ragged nails and one missing. Oh well, I never was one for manicures and long painted talons. I glanced down at the ground.

The gunman wore Docksiders. Like me. First the yuppies. That was bad enough. What next? Terrorist running around in boat shoes?

Besides the Chevy pickup I had been limousined in, there were a few additional trucks and one huge car, white of course. I peered at it through the darkness. "Let me guess. That's Wizzie's car–Satan in a white Cadillac." The gunman fired a round into the air startling everyone.

"She has a mouth like an open mailbox." the gunman spoke defensively to the Wiz who'd come charging back.

"No more shooting!"

"Let me shut her up, boss!" the shortest Klansman begged. He turned back looking for approval. What the heck. I was dead meat anyway. I put a foot behind Shortie's knee. He buckled and dropped like a sacked quarter-back. When the man stood, his lovely white sheet was caked in black mud. Childish? Yeah. But I was sporting my Chessie cat grin. He pulled the middle of the robe between his legs *dhoti* style and shook the mud off.

The Wiz chastised us, sounding out his words with the command of a tra-veling preacher. He put a hand on my arm and steered me along as we entered the building. The Klavern looked more like a hunting camp. They were a clean crowd. Another thought just blossomed, it was new construction. A clue to the latter was a few bags of cement stacked in the far corner. The room had a small kitchen and two doors, which were closed, and was joined by a large screened porch that had canvas covers rolled and tied at the top. Plastic tables and chairs were placed in a circle. In the middle of the far wall stood an altar complete with insignia. Their sacred whatever, I guess.

"Sit down." We all did. "Want something to drink?"

I was trembling again, thinking this was my last night on earth and still trying to hide behind my mouth. "How about *Absolut* with lime? And a side of water." The Wiz pointed a heavily bejeweled hand of gold and diamonds and a man fell out of the circle.

"We have it, but there ain't any lime." he said, and placed two glasses on the table. Color me surprised! I picked up a glass, sniffed, and took a tentative taste. Absolutely *Absolut*. I decided to push it. What can you do?   "Since you're so accommodating, do you have a first-aid kit?" The Wiz pointed to another Kleagle who went to work on my hand. I pulled away to do it myself, but he held my wrist down, pressing it into the table.

"Be still. I'm a doctor." Color me astonished! He went to work gently tending the scrapes and cuts.

"I guess your Hippocratic oath only works for white people."

He ignored my mordant comment. "I can't help you with your eye. Put some ice on it when you get home." I was in a schizophrenic play. Klans-men serving good vodka and attending the wounds of their abducted? I didn't get it.

"The r-reason we brought you here is that w-we want to talk." *So that's why he sounds out his words so loudly. He stutters. File that away, Paloma, in case you live.* Once I noticed it, I couldn't help but focus on it. He had to repeat himself. "I think you'll want to know this information."

Fear thundered through my body and my mouth was on overload. "You wusses don't have anything I want to hear! Hiding behind your sheets. You don't have the guts to show your clown faces. Murderers! You killed a bright young man who was no threat to you. I hope civil rights groups eradicate every last one of you!" A white draped arm shot out but I was ready. I grabbed the arm, yanked it toward me. This Klansman was shaped like a punching bag, a cone-headed Mr. French. I gave him one in the stomach.

"You nigger-loving slut!" Make that a cone-headed *Mrs.* French.

"And we were getting along so nicely." I shook my head, pretending hurt.

"You s-should learn to s-sand that tongue of yours," the Wiz advised me, holding up the duct tape roll threateningly.

"Oh, that's how it works. I can exercise freedom of speech as long as what I say agrees with you."

"The problem with you is—you exercise it too m-much." It's strange, but I almost laughed. He wasn't the first to accuse me of excess opinion expression. "We will explain something to you and then you'll be gone." He motioned to the child, who performed the Klan salute—arm out, palm down, bringing the hand to the heart then out by his side. The kid completed another salute, this one borrowed from Hitler. Nobody's born a bigot. He'd learned well so far. Spinning smartly on his heels, the lad opened one of the doors. A man in a ski mask came out of the room.

"Don't tell me. The Ski-Klux-Klan," I said, my fingers thrumping a comedic rim shot on the table. "What's the matter? You flunk Klan college and can't get your bed sheet until you pass Hate-Pimping 101?" The Wiz held his hand up again to ward off retribution.

"Let's move forward. As I have said, we will not harm you."

"Just like Lemond?"

"That's why you're here. He wasn't killed by Klan." Ski Mask spoke between sucking on a cigarette. He gave the room a continual once-over with furtive glances, hands shaking, body jumpy. He was scared. I liked that.

"And with your sterling character references, I'll believe you." The nauseating smell of chewing tobacco wafted over and I braved an unobtrusive look. A few of the men were chewin' red and spittin' black. Those enjoying a pinch leaned over to let their flaps dangle, legs spread plopping the juice into an empty coffee can between their feet. Like a bench full of linebackers—they just sit and spit. "The Klan, noted for its hatred of minorities and their love of the noose, didn't kill a minority citizen by hanging him? *Right!* It seems, Wizzie, you have some renegade Klansmen." I shrugged my shoulders. "It happens."

"No." Ski Mask touched my arm. I jerked back. "Listen to us," he pleaded. This dude really wanted a sell. Why?

"This Klavern isn't responsible, nor is any other. I'm assured of their innocence," the Wiz said.

"Why are you telling me this? This whole thing is weird."

"The forces of this country have been working very hard against us lately. Several Klaverns were shut down by communists and ignorant Kyke lawyers–like your friend Al Eason." I envisioned brownish-haired, Protestant Al in a yarmulke. "And them dyke feminists. We are only trying to save the white race," the Wiz droned. "We are busy supporting our brothers elsewhere and cannot divert our attention to these false accusations. Our plans to rid this country of its abominations are merely postponed until our forces are ready."

He spouted the party line with vigor and not an inkling of a stutter. He probably practiced in front of a mirror like Hitler did. I yawned intentionally. "Spare me the rhetoric. If you just wanted to have a coffee-*klatch*, why kidnap me? Whine to the press. Or the cops–Grainger's in your pocket." The Wiz seemed to freeze for a few seconds at the mention of the Sheriff. Or had I imagined it?

"It wasn't really kidnaping."

"I beg to differ on that one." I drained my water.

"Would you have come any other way?"

"And miss the social event of the year?" I wanted to be able to find these guys when this was over. If I got away. I scanned the group, yearning for anything–however small–to recognize them later. But it was impossible to get a handle on anyone behind the white covers. Only Boots and Ski-Mask. And my big clue was his addiction to tobacco. And he wouldn't live long the way he was sucking down smokes. He hadn't stopped since he joined our party and his unsteady hand was lighting his third from the second. I wondered why he didn't have on the Klan garb. Forgot to pick it up from the dry cleaners? And why was he feeling so hinky? This little party was one of the reasons for joining up. Meeting me was a benefit of membership.

"I think we ought to teach that mouth a' hers a lesson," the guy who sounded like the Exalted Cyclops spoke.

"Patience! We'll be rid of this pest soon enough." Wiz made several motions in the air. Probably a secret code–shoot her in the back next time you feel like it.

"Wiz, I've been meaning to ask you, is he called Cyclops because he only has one eye?" They were finally fed up with my pithy chatter and their retaliation site was the lower left side of my face. I'd read that extreme fear produces adrenaline that makes you impervious to intense pain–like being able to walk ten miles on bullet-riddled legs. I was obviously doing something wrong. My jaw hurt like hell. I wouldn't have been surprised if I now had a portable jaw–like a set of dentures that I could slip in or take out. It had been beat on enough to dislodge it. I shook my head to clear my stupefied brain and worked my open jaw in tiny circles. It still hurt like hell. Now maybe I'd keep it shut.

"Now, back to matters," the Wiz continued as if nothing had happened. "We do not know who set us up, but we'll find out. Until then, the killers of your colored boy go free."

"Has it ever occurred to you that white is also a color?"

"Please, miss! You stray once again from what's important! You must tell your associates about this error in justice. We must not be scrutinized when we are innocent."

"That'll be a first. Okay, if I'm to believe you–the Klan is coming clean?" I bet my good eye was bugging out on this one. "And you want *me* to help? I still don't believe this. You're worried about your reputation?"

"Here we are tryin' to hep this gal an' this is the thanks we get!" the Exalted Cyclops spoke with such venom I'd need a snake bite kit. "No wonder more white people are joining the Cause."

The Wiz faced me. Ski Mask put a hand on the man's shoulder. The Wiz nodded. Ski Mask stood. He wore a huge belt buckle, about four by two inches. It bore the silver silhouette of a naked lady. Truck drivers had the same figure on their mud flaps. A class act.

"I'm not Klan, as you can see." I heard low murmurs in the back of the group. Someone in the crowd called Ski Mask a traitor. Wiz's head snapped in their direction. With faces covered I could only guess that he was miffed. Ski Mask cleared his throat and repeated his statement. Although he spoke louder, his voice quivered. He lit another smoke with trembling hands and talked on. "I know these people did not kill that boy! You *must* believe us. Isn't it worth checking into?" He licked his lips leaving moisture on the wool around his mouth.

"What's your interest?"

"I can't tell you."

I looked at the Wiz. "Do you know how ridiculous all this sounds?"

"Just do some checking," Ski Mask urged.

"Let me get this straight. Someone is killing people and blaming it on the Klan. The Klan is pissed and wants to clear the air. For the good of humanity. Right, so far? And you want me to look else-where, but you won't tell me who or why."

"You are trying the Imperial Wizard's patience."

"Don't talk to me about patience! You send your stupid patrol to sneak up on me. Their faces are covered and they're too dumb to realize I won't be able to identify them. But, they threw a hood over me anyway. Then tied and gagged me." I was heating up for the finale. "All the while sniggering like a bunch of children. And now you want me to be sympathetic? Let me give you a tip. If you want an adversary to be receptive to you, you should be kissing ass, not kicking it."

"She brought it on herself. It wasn't my fault," said the sheeted man in leopard boots, while another Klansman heartily agreed.

I watched Wiz's diamonds shimmer in the light as he moved his hands. "We made a decision to cover our faces as protection. Otherwise, we could not have talked with you. We can only hope you are receptive to the fact that the real murderer is going free." The Wiz folded his arms on the table. There was no sound but the shuffling of feet. "The Imperial Wizard has spoken." The silence stretched past a full minute.

Hmm, now what? "If I'm so free, I want to leave," I said to the Klavern. Wizzie nodded. "We'll finish our meeting, then you can go. Remember," he pointed a finger at me. "You would be wise to do as we asked. Others won't be as easy on you." I bit off my reply.

They filed outside, shoving me along with them. I was ordered to stand with a guard while the men went forward a few yards. I watched them struggle to upright a cross which was wrapped in papers. Once the cross was in place, they lit sticks, circled the cross and gave a salute that looked like an exercise for nursing home aerobics students. Their arms went out to their sides and I lost the rest while staring at their backs. They mumbled some Klan oaths, then deafened us all with horrible hate music, the band ending their tomes each time with choruses of "white power". Meanwhile, the Wiz and Grand Dragon worked the crowd like cheerleaders. "Louder, boys! I can't hear you!" After a few minutes they quieted.

The Grand Dragon issued further orders. "Klansmen, say the code and the ending salute." One at a time the Klansmen spoke it quickly, sounding like "hooga booger" then gave the Nazi salute. The Grand Dragon then lifted up a robed child. I wondered if he was going to be tossed onto the fiery cross as sacrifice. The Dragon faced the kid. "Where does Hitler live?"

"In my life," the young voice replied. The men clapped, then stood at attention. I was getting bored. I turned away, as if I could just walk off and hop a ride back into town. My captor pulled me toward him in a vice grip and clamped an arm around me, this time going for a nerve in the shoulder to stop my squirming.

On and on they spewed their racist beliefs and slogans. In my mind I sang Jimi Hendrix's "Purple Haze," complete with guitar riff sound effects and wondering when this crap was going to end.

The Dragon spoke of their small numbers and compared their group to the Last Supper saying, "Two thousand years ago remember Jesus coming down the mountain to Judea with only twelve followers. One of them was an FBI agent traitor."

Huh?

He droned on about thirty pieces of silver and ended with a warning that the white holocaust was coming soon to a city near you. "We must show power. White power!" Cheers lifted up from the group. "Not a simple parade around town, but a show of arms and force!"

"Yeah! White power!"

"I mean fucking guns!" The Grand Dragon added. "TSS," I think he said, which galvanized the men into a chorus line of *sieg heils*, shouts of hooga booger and after a few hearty "white powers" we were dismissed.

Now I assumed was chit-chat time as the guys mingled and I tried to figure out what TSS could possibly stand for. Totally stupid shit? Nah. Totally shit-stupid. Had a better ring to it. I listened as one member compared their Grand Dragon leader to Hitler. A few guys joined in the conversation adding what they admired in him that echoed traits of their Nazi hero. Even though he was hidden by costume, the Grand Dragon sported an "I'm just a laid-back, good ol' country boy" air while he looked down modestly and shuffled his feet. I'm sure he would have kicked a can or tire if one had been around. "Oh, gosh, guys, don't compare me with Hitler. I'm not worthy."

The bodyguard beside me spoke suddenly and I jumped. "I wish I had you for my biological father. I coulda' used your guidance while I was growin' up."

Enough! The grip on my shoulder kept me focused on pain instead of a retort. I gave the guy the elbow and as other members noticed our struggle, they closed in to hold me still.

"Take her back now. We have done what we can. If she is wise, she will act on our message of help. You," he indicated Ski Mask, "will go with them. Remember your orders," he said to his followers. He turned back to me. "For your safety you will leave here tied. They *will* release you, but they have orders to subdue you if you make any trouble. Put her in the back with him." He tapped Ski Mask's shoulder.

I was bound again in a replay of earlier. Everyone was there to see me off, except the Wiz. The night sky was very clear, brilliant with stars. Out of a sailor's habit I looked for a cluster of celestial lights for bearings. I spotted the handle of the Big Dipper and played connect the dots until I spied the North Star. The Klavern was northwest. "Here's the hood, bitch. If you try anything funny, we'll kill you." They sniggered. Something tugged in my brain. *Hey, Paloma, the Klavern is northwest.* I paid more attention to my surroundings. It wasn't much, but maybe I could direct Al back to this place. At least the general area. Once hooded, I heard the crackly sound of Velcro as they took off their masks.

"Come on you guys, let's get her in the back." I recognized Ski Mask's voice. The tailgate creaked down and something slid against metal, then sounds of wood on wood. And laughter as the goons lifted me up. Such a happy bunch. "What the heck do you guys think you're doing?" Ski Mask's voice was urgent. Alarmed, my heart kicked into high gear as I thrashed my limbs and butted with my head. For a moment, we grunted and jostled *en masse* until they were able to subdue me again.

"Let's hog-tie the ol' heifer," was the general consensus.

"Put her in the back a' the truck! Leave 'er alone!" Ski Mask ordered.

"Shut up, you traitor!" A new voice angrily spoke. "If you weren't kin to the..."

"You're talking too much!" Ski Mask warned just as sharply.

"Get this heifer still, for chrissake." There was a scuffle behind me, but I was more worried about the positions I was being forced into. "Bend your knees." I locked them. Someone chopped them from behind then shoved me roughly. Wood on wood again, then I heard a metallic click. I reached out with my fingers. Wire shapes. Animal smells penetrated the hood. A dog cage. The engine started, the truck rocked as the men boarded.

"Lady, don't worry. It's not worth the fight to get you out. It won't be long. They don't like it when people get the best of them, especially pushy broads," Ski Mask elaborated. I let that one pass.

"Can I take off the hood?"

"Yeah, I got my mask on." I managed to push it up with tethered hands. He was the one I needed to find again. I watched him, and as we passed under streetlights I tried memorizing the shape of his nose, cheek bones, his voice, physique, sneakers and especially the belt buckle. Anything to fish him out later. Then I read the stars. We headed south about five minutes at slow speed, bouncing around on a dirt road littered with potholes. Several times I repeated all the turns and distances we'd taken to help me remember. "Are you guys going to kill me?" He seemed surprised I even entertained such a thought.

"No lady. We're doing just as the Imperial Wizard ordered."

"What's really going on here?" I asked quietly so as not to draw the attention of the bozos in the truck cab. He rubbed his temples in circles as if he had a headache. I hoped it was a blinding migraine. I waited. "Please tell me. No one else will know what you..."

"Shut up!" The truck turned left and increased speed about ten minutes east on a smooth paved road. "Listen, just do what we asked."

"I'm not the police or GBI. I'm not sure anyone will listen to me."

"You were the right choice, lady."

"Why? Why me?"

"Please, just shut up," he begged. "I didn't even want to tell you this much."

"Then why did you?"

"You talk too much!" We turned onto another dirt road, my head banging as they negotiated the first bump and drove for north-north-east. I could smell the river. "Put the hood back on, we're almost there," Ski Mask ordered quietly. I grabbed the ends above my head and pulled it down, tugging the drawstring slightly. He tapped on the cab. "This is a good place, guys. Put her here," he called loudly.

The boys decided to have a little fun. The truck stopped suddenly. Me and the cage slid forward. It smacked into the cab as the trucks' rear slid around. The driver completed several more sharp turns to bang me around because I had the nerve to dis' the Klan. Finally the truck stopped.

"Thanks for the ride, fellas," I said as soon as they had lifted me down from the truck bed. For an answer they punched me in the gut, carried me down to the landing, and tossed me into the river. My butt painfully whacked the cement ramp bottom. The water was shoulder high and filled with the smells of boat oil and gas. I stood stoically as aluminum cans and debris flew by or pelted me. They soon grew bored and drove off into the night. I pulled the hood off and stuffed it into my front jeans pocket. I reached the river's edge and sat in the dark trying to free my feet. It was a simple square knot, which I undid quickly. I stood and promptly slipped in the mud. My hip took the brunt of the fall and I lay there a moment coughing up river water and cursing every bad thing I could think of. When I recovered enough, I gingerly tried to climb but slipped again. Okay, I get the hint. Not mud, clay. This time I crawled up the bank on my hands and knees.

A little late, I looked around for interlopers, of the Gundersen variety. I tried to get my wrists free with my teeth. It was hopeless. I hurried to the back of the shed, relieved to find my backpack undisturbed. I dug for the knife, used my teeth to get it open and sawed at the ropes with difficulty. Finally unbound, I shook my hands to reignite circulation. Damned if I was going be a victim again. Who knew what the night had in store for me. I pulled the .357 out as I moved into the dark cover of the woods.

Drenching myself with SSS in a dim hope to drive the blood sucking mosquitoes away, I pulled out the penlight, a small notepad and pencil and quickly wrote down the approximate directions from the Klavern and anything else I could remember about tonight. It was a very rough guess on how long we drove on each type of pavement and between the few turns we made, but at least it was *something*. From my pack I retrieved the night vision goggles I'd taken earlier and donned a pair. Everything was illumi-nated in bogeyman green. I scanned the area not spotting a two-, or even a four-legged creature about. With the goggles, the boat was easier to find. I started the engine and hightailed it. When I had put a good bit of distance between the Gundersen landing and me, I stopped the engine. Slumping down in the boat, I hung my head and shook long and hard with relief.

Utah: University professors and the co-president of the Lesbian and Gay student union received letters with swastikas and "death to gays, thank God for AIDS" during a campaign to get an anti-discrimination clause added to the student bill of rights.–USA Today 12/90. *Keith Ogden, a gay man, was beaten to death. Joshua Swindell, twenty-one and Steven Mateus, seventeen, were charged with murder and committing a hate crime.*–Klanwatch, 1995.

Chapter Thirty-Nine

"The woman in that hotel room was dead! You didn't say a thing about that when you called me at work." Evan had dared raise his voice to Swartzman, his superior in the WRF, ignoring his motions to sit down. "You said there were two women who needed taking care of. Not dispose of a dead body." Swartzman didn't move a muscle. "Why didn't you tell me?"

"If I'd told you beforehand, you wouldn't have handled it as well. And here," he slid a stack of bills over to him, "I'm giving you double what you got for the last job."

"The last job was just giving you lousy information!"

Swartzman stared coldly at the man before him. "Okay. We'll call it quits right now, Ev." He walked to the opposite end of his office, taking time filing.

"You can't do that! I got to have the money. You promised!"

Swartzman sat down. "Well, well. You're in a bit of a quandary." He made a tent out of his fingers and tapped them at intervals. "The motel job is the kind of thing that crops up now and again." He dipped his head side to side casually. "Next time it might be information, tail someone, or a bit of house cleaning. You have to make a decision if you're in or out. No hard feelings." Swartzman poured himself another drink, not bothering to offer Evan one. "Now, I have to take care of this broken woman in the next room. Let me know what you decide." He watched Evan storm out of the building.

"Do you know where Randy is?" Moonpie mumbled when Swartzman finally had her composed and sitting up. He pulled a chair over and faced the large woman. He leaned toward her as fatherly concern, so easily faked, filled his face.

"Moonpie, I have no idea." He paused, screwed his face up playing the game. "I'm sorry to tell you this during such a traumatic time." He indicated her wounds. "But, your brother has gotten into a big mess." Moonpie stared at him so intensely her eyes didn't blink. "The police are looking for him. Me, too. He has proven himself dishonest." He didn't know if all of what he said was exactly true, he hadn't verified all the rumors flying around Rincon, but he'd never let that hold him back before.

"Did he kill Brice?" she asked bluntly.

He nodded. "I'm afraid he did, Moonpie." The bandages formed accordi-on pleats as Moonpie's face drew up, lips quivering. Her legs shook as a low rumbling wail started in the pit of her stomach and spewed out.

"Do you have some medication?" She made an attempt to get her purse and dropped it. He searched it for pills and saw the small vial. Brice had a thing about using nose candy to aid in her manipulation ploys. He'd been baffled by Brice's visit to Moonpie's dump–bewildered at the connection between these two unlikely females. Brice had gotten this dumb woman hooked. He replaced the vial of cocaine, found the pain tablets, doubled the indicated dosage and gave her a Jim Beam chaser.

"He always takes the good things I have. Why did he do this?" The thought hit Swartzman that she wasn't referring to Brice.

"Randy did this to you?" she wailed again. He reached out to touch her and she jerked away, her face changing from sorrow, to fright, then disgust. This woman who threw herself at any man was now repelled? This night was full of startling revelations. Leaving Moonpie to guzzle herself into a stupor, Swartzman used his secretary Mildred's desk. Flipping through the employee roster, he stopped at each WRF member debating who would be the best soldier to contact.

"Willie, come down to the plant. I have something I need you to do."

"I was just about asleep."

"The sooner you get here, the faster you'll be back." Willie arrived six-teen minutes later, Swartzman noted.

"What the heck happened to her?" Willie indelicately asked.

"Randy," Swartzman reported very pleased.

"Randy beat on her? Well, that's one thing that sorry ass is good at. He shore did a number on her." He stepped closer. Moonpie was feeling the effects of the booze and pain medication. "What's she saying?"

"I'm not sure. She's been babbling ever since she got here. Something about Randy taking the very best away from her."

"What does that mean?"

"I don't know. Do you have any idea?"

"Nope."

"I ga-ga fin' Ra-Randy." She slumped over.

Willie reached out to steady her back to the couch. "Woo-wee. She's a goner."

"Have you seen Randy?" Swartzman asked.

"Nope. Don't wanna. Thangs go missin' when he's around. That boy can steal the hat offa' your head and you lookin' right at him."

"Take her home." Willie's face blanched.

"Nooo! Hefinme." Moonpie half rose and stumbled into the two men. "He do me 'gin."

"What?" Willie asked. "I can't understand you."

"You. Help me," she begged. Willie took her arm to steady her. "Don't you touch me! Don't you put a fu-finger on me. Everybody takes. Every. Body." She broke into sobs and collapsed on the floor.

1991: Germany, Saxony–two skinheads clubbed to death a middle-aged man because he called Hitler a war criminal. Austria–A planned reunion of Waffen SS officers was cancelled due to public outcry. The reunion marked the 40th anniversary of the Kameradschaft IV and was to be addressed by an SS major general who was responsible for locking six hundred people in a church and burning them.

Chapter Forty

After I put the boat back on the trailer, I took stock of personal damage. I was cut, sore, wet, bug-bitten and beyond tired of this river. I yanked the soggy bandages off my fingers. Red clay covered most of me. In ankle-deep water, I stuck a finger in a clay pile on my arm and scraped it off. Splashing water over the remains did nothing to help remove it. As I bent over, my brain pinged. Something shifted in my memory chips. Deep in thought, I rubbed clay between my fingers.

"That's it!" I blurted out loud. "Clay! *Merda*! Was the Wiz really telling the truth–the Klan was not responsible? "I've got to call Al." Pulling clothes out of my suitcase, I tugged my wet jeans, which were more like a neoprene wetsuit, off my body. The hood fell out of the pocket onto the ground. I picked it up and threw it into the cab. I changed clothes while swatting a swarm of no-see-ums that buzzed around me. I climbed into the truck and dialed Al's home number.

He shouted into the phone. "Where have you been?"

"Al." I held the phone from my ear.

"I've been calling you for hours."

"Al, why are you..."

"I was worried about you after Aggie called and told me where you'd gone."

"I have new evidence..."

"You shouldn't go hot footin' around by yourself." And on he went, as long-winded as Aunt Lilly when she was on a tear. I tried a few attempts of butting in on his butting in. "Where the heck are you?" Silence. "Well?"

"I didn't know I had permission to talk. Do you always start a conversation by yelling into the phone?"

"I don't know why you couldn't go back to your hotel room like a good lit..."

"Oh, no! Don't you dare tell me you were actually going to say 'a good little girl'! Aggie is right. You are a Neanderthal." I hate the new phones. You can't slam them down to disconnect when you're angry. You simply press down. Not much of a statement. I tried, nonetheless, by stabbing my thumb heavily onto the off button. Very soon, the phone rang. Even though I expected it, I started at the sound.

"Where are you now, Paloma? Are you safe?" That's better.

"Relatively so. I'm near the Gundersen plant."

"After what happened to Dixie, I'd think you'd exercise some common sense..." He was off again, yammering away.

"Al, I think the signal is getting weak. What?" He replied and I pretended I couldn't hear. "What? Al? Are you there?" I scraped the keys across the mouthpiece. "I'll have to call you back, Al."

"You are one stubborn, mule-headed woman."

"Al Eason, this week you have compared me to a horse, an ox, and now a mule's head!" I lowered my voice to playful. "Are you trying to seduce me?"

He sputtered into the phone. "Nothing's wrong with the signal now," he finally said.

"It's nice to know something can make you blush," I told him. "The phone's getting warm."

"So what's this new evidence?" he asked, making another of his abrupt changes in conversation. I smiled.

"You're a bit like that stubborn mule, too, Counselor Eason." I told him I didn't think the Klan was responsible for Lemond's death.

"And where did you pick up this information?"

"From the Wiz of the local Klavern." I said it casually, like "ho-hum, toodle-dee".

"There is no Klavern!"

"There is now." I went on in a rush, my excitement growing again. "At first I didn't believe him, but then, when they took me back to the Gundersen landing and threw me in the water, I slipped on clay. Remember the clay? Al! Don't talk so loud!" I pulled the phone away from my ear again. "I was trying to explain but you interrupted me." He still was. I counted to ten. Did it again. Enough. *Calla a boca!* Al, please! How can I explain anything to you if you don't stop talking? You're still talking, Al. Al? Al! You obstinate overbearing bully." My second language came in handy again. I blared out a string of Portuguese phrases my mother *never* taught me, peppered with an 'Al' thrown in to let him know he was the subject. It drives the other person crazy not knowing how badly they are being told off.

"What?" He finally stopped long enough to hear me. "I have a feeling you've told me something I wouldn't like."

"So stop interrupting. Now. First of all, I didn't barge into the Klavern. They grabbed me–. Al. Al!" I hung up.

"I'm sorry," he said when he called back.

"This is your last chance," I teased.

"I *can* worry about you can't I?"

"Yes, just don't do it so loudly. You sound tired. I just realized how late it is. Sorry. I'm so excited. Hang on a sec. I want to get my tail out of here." Once I turned the truck around and headed out on Willow Pea Road, I relayed the day's events to Al. He called Vontana, then phoned me back. Al directed me to his farm off Quacco Road in the hinterland of Chatham County for a rendezvous with the GBI. His farm was so far down in the woods, they had to pipe in sunshine. This time when I hung up, I said goodbye.

* * *

Willie made a quick call to Hughes before he rejoined his sleeping wife. "Sorry to wake you, but I've got somethin' you'll be all a'buzzed to hear. I saw Moonpie down at the plant and she was a'stumbling and a'bluddering like a dying cow. I asked her who broke up her nose. She said it was Randy! Can't nobody even put a finger on 'er without 'er jumpin' clean outta 'er britches."

"Where is she?"

"I toted her over to her place. She was mad enough to hem a bear. Didn't want to be taken there. Said Randy kilt her best friend."

"Is there any truth in it? I mean Randy's an idiot but all a sudden he's takin' out people right and left?"

"Hmm." Was Willie's short reply.

"Who's that friend Moonpie was talking about?"

"I dunno. It could be a figment of her imagination. You know how skywinding she gets sometimes. Next thing I know, she's limp as a dishrag. Slobberin' and stuff. It's the dangdest thing I ever saw."

"Where's Randy now?"

"I don't know."

"How did she get to the plant?"

"Don't know that neither."

"What *do* you know?"

"What I just told ya."

"Thanks for calling, Willie. I'll call you back tomorrow in case something more develops. You've proven yourself to be an honored member of the Rincon Klan."

"Thanks." Hughes just *had* to remind him about the Klan. Willie's stomach turned sour. Between telling Hughes what Swartzman wanted him to say, letting Swartzman know what Hughes was up to, and keeping track of what was *really* going on so he could tell the GBI, was getting harder for Willie to keep straight. Was the extra money worth it? In the beginning he thought so. Now, he'd turn it all in for a good night's sleep. But that money had long been spent.

* * *

Swartzman had just stretched out on the couch to snooze in the half-light of his desk lamp when the phone rang. "It's Red. I'm near Randy's dump now."

"Great. I'll call you after Randy leaves here. Shouldn't be long. I'm out." He moved to his computer and scrolled down the listing of car phone numbers. "Evan." He pressed Enter and listened as his auto-dialer went into action.

"Yes," Evan answered.

"Where are you?"

"I have the surveillance detail on Al Eason's house tonight. Same thing as sayin' I'm in the sticks. Why does he live so far outside Savannah? Hey, wait a sec. The woman just turned onto Quacco Road. Why they paved this road out here is unknown to me. I counted only six houses in the last ten minutes."

"Shut up! You're yapping like a girl," Swartzman testily ordered. "Listen to me now. He's secured up to his eyeballs. Don't even pass his driveway. Hang on." Swartzman went to the map drawer and flipped through them until he found the Chatham County map.

"Evan, there's a house about a mile from Eason's. 4356 is the number. Stop soon after that. That clown has lasers and a couple bodies protecting his ass."

"I can handle it."

"That's why I picked you. It's late. We're set for tomorrow morning. I'm sending two men. One you know–Randy. Should be here any minute. I'll brief them and send them to you." Swartzman had a plan in action to turn the screws a little tighter on Randy. Meanwhile, he had to get Randy and keep him busy while a second plan was set in motion. This one to silence Randy. For good.

Red got the call from Swartzman to get mobile. He drove behind Randy's trailer, made a quick check around him and slipped on rubber gloves. The cheap lock was easy to jimmy. He went to the phone first. That was the most important–if Randy was stupid enough to come back here with all the heat on him. He unscrewed the mouth-piece and placed the cylinder where it wouldn't dislodge. He surveyed the small place. Bedroom first, then living room, kitchen, bathroom. He worked swiftly but carefully, taking anything that could jeopardize the WRF's plans for a safer America.

As he had learned from the video on effective property search and hiding techniques, he examined cushions, pillows, and the mattress, looking for any signs of a secret place. Now the fun. He tossed out the contents of every cabinet, shelf and closet, letting the contents crash onto the floor. Red trashed the few electronics Randy had managed to acquire. Pickles, ketchup, orange juice splashed on the floor and wall as he used them for baseballs. He hammered the cheap walls, stripping away the material and pouring soda and flour down the holes. He surveyed the damage. Scribbling Randy's code name on the same death calling card he left when scaring a black, Jew or other riff-raff, Red left it taped in plain view on the front door. He checked his exit and drove off, singing along with Hank Williams, Jr.

Japan, 1992: The newspaper Shukan Post *attributes the recent Nikkei Index plunge to be the responsibility of Jews. "Some observers speculate that given their need of U.S. markets and the impolitic of openly attacking their customers, some Japanese use the word "Jew" as a code for "American".*" Response, Fall, 1992.

Chapter Forty-One

What I could see through the darkness of Al's spread was impressive. The house was older, rambling, country fare. A porch circled the structure on both stories, complete with swings and a jungle of hanging baskets. Beside the tractor, a water pump stuck up from the ground, a bucket hung from the curved handle. I could smell hay, corn, and horses in the air.

I estimated about two acres of land were cleared for his yard. Red and yellow indicator lights of security equipment glowed in the night. I pulled up next to Al's car and fell out of the truck, none to gracefully, onto my feet. I was as tired as Al had sounded. I made my way toward the house.

"Good evening, Ms. Paloma."

"Shit," I said, nearly did, and cleared the ground about two feet. My head whipped around. I didn't see a soul. "Hi, Gus," I said into the darkness. "Busy night?" He gave a two-ha laugh. Al came out on the porch, the clap from the screen door echoing as it closed.

"Did you say hello to Gus?" he asked.

"Among other things. All this sneaking up on me is making me lose my religion." I stopped at the door and looked down at my filthy legs and shoes.

"I better hose off before I traipse into your house. Geez," I said peering in. "It's so neat and clean. Especially for a guy."

"Don't worry, come on in."

I hesitated. "Do I have time to take a shower?" He guided me upstairs and showed me the facilities. "I need my things from the truck."

"I'll put them in the adjoining bedroom." He pointed to the second door in the three door bathroom.

"What's that door?"

"Linens."

"In the bathroom?" I pretended surprise. He smiled and shut the door behind him. *Too late to ask him to scrub my back.* Probably shock the tan off him if I asked. I stayed under the warm water until my skin looked mutant. He knocked on the bedroom door as I completed my fourth costume change of the day.

"Come in."

"Feel better?"

"Yes. Thank you so much!" His appearance stopped me in my tracks. He was barefoot, wearing jeans rolled at the cuff, and a T-shirt advertising Law Center softball. His curls were tousled. All he needed was a piece of sweet grass hanging between his lips. "Hey, Al, no vest!"

"My only time to relax."

"You know, when you are at work, the suit, tie, the office–it looks right. So does this place. If I didn't know any better, I'd call you Farmer Eason. How do you do it? I get uncomfortable when I spend too much time on land."

"It wasn't always like this."

"Yeah, the plastic wife."

He stuck his hands in his pocket, leaned back against the wall and crossed an ankle. The pose gave him a sexy "aw shucks" demeanor. I successfully batted down the urge to fling myself into his arms. Being alone with him and with the electricity I felt in his presence made me feel self-conscious. Uneasy. And that means my mouth gets busy. I babbled insignificant small-talk and Al let me take the lead, not offering any conversation except polite replies. When I finally ran out of babble, I switched to nervous action, vigorously towel-drying my hair until I risked needing Rogaine. *Geez, do or say something, Al,* I wished silently.

"I've got your jeans washing." Finally! He pointed outside the room. I could hear the machine working somewhere in the house. He motioned to the dresser. "And this is about as good as I could do with your shoes. Want to dry them?"

"Nah, they're boat shoes. S'pose to be wet. Thanks again, Mom." I took the shoes and put them on. "You look tired. I should have waited until morning."

He shook his head. "I was working on a few cases."

"Getting ready to kick butt tomorrow in court for Dixie?"

"You got it!" he said with rah-rah. He gave me a penetrating stare. "You sound pretty chipper."

"Not really."

He came closer, scrutinizing. "I saw some bites and scrapes earlier, but now, woo doggie," he said, sounding more like Jed Clampet than Attorney Man.

"Woo doggie?" I chuckled then faked a serious tone. "So I look that bad?" I took a cautious peek in the dresser mirror. "That bad." I agreed. "You should see the other guy."

"Who gave you the black eye?"

"Actually, a big mosquito flew at me. It was loud as an airplane engine." I stuck my arms out flying, dipped the right wing and made engine noises. "Al, if someone–" I looked at him. "I'm babbling. I know it."

"If you can make jokes after the day you've had, you're allowed, tough lady."

"It's an act." I blurted the truth.

"I'm beginning to learn that about you," he said quietly.

"That's almost as scary as my meeting with the Klan." There is no silence in a Southern summer. Crickets and bullfrogs serenaded us with an occasional whinny from a horse. I was wired and feeling that familiar need to do something so I could skip the one-on-one with Al. I wanted a man to love me, but *getting* to that point always made me want to flee. And Al's presence always filled a room. It was impossible *not* be aware of him. "I was so tired when I got here. Not now. Do you need any hay tossed or the stalls raked?" I was bouncing from foot to foot.

"Paloma, the first time someone took a shot at me, I felt the same way you do now. Your world gets tilted, and it eats at your confidence."

"It wasn't that bad tonight," I lied and straightened my belongings that didn't need it. "Knocked me around. Threatened." I didn't mention that just seeing those guys in white sheets scared the daylights out of me. They could have just stood there, turned around and driven off. It would have had the same impact. Their history, reputation, spoke for them. Loud and clear.

"You can't be tough all the time. That's too much of a drain on your system. Most people eventually calm, but I'm still waiting on you." He smiled briefly. "Release it. I'll certainly understand." I packed my things again and tried to block out the intimacy that seemed to fill the room. He took the shirt from my hands, and stepped even closer. His hand gently caressed my face. His eyes were potent and seemed to look deep inside me–places I feared anyone to tread. I skittishly looked down at the floor. "Did the Klan do all this to you?" He indicated my body with a sweep of a finger.

"Some. I did enough on my own, as usual. I got most of it when they put me in the cage..."

"What cage?" I flinched at the rise in volume. "What did you get yourself into–I'm sorry for shouting, Paloma." He looked at his feet. "I seem to do that a lot to you."

"And I'm always thanking you," I one-upped him, then explained about the dog pen.

"You've done a lot for Dixie. Put yourself through a lot."

"Not really. She'd do the same for me or my family. And has done in the past."

"After all that you're still charging ahead. You won't stop."

"I *can't*. Dix is my friend–has been since the beginning of time. Her kind doesn't come along that often. She needs help. I can give it." I gave him the Reader's Digest Condensed version of our lifelong friendship, how both our families were practically merged together. "And if it were me locked up..."

"I understand." His words were as soft and caressing as the hand still rubbing my cheek.

"Al, why do you get so bothered by me checking a few things out?"

He took his time answering. "I guess I feel like I'm not doing enough."

Sounded doubtful to me, but I let him off the hook for further explanation. "You are–getting Dixie free! And you have other cases,

other people depend on you." *Porcaria!* Those eyes of his! From the
first, my reaction to them was surprisingly intense. I'd never met
anyone who had attracted me so quickly. He kissed my forehead–about the only place free of injury.

"But no one wants the truth in exchange for the sacrifice of you."
I let the crickets fill the silence. "You've gotten some good information tonight. You'll pass it on and let Vontana take care of it."

"If he will."

He didn't speak for a moment. "You *entrust* people, Paloma, but
you don't *trust*."

"Why should I? I haven't found too much in most people *to* trust.
Besides. It's a mean world."

"What about me?" He took my hand and squeezed. I pulled back,
injured fingers throbbing.

"Woo-doggie, Al." I flapped my hand to fling away the pain.

"You're bleeding." He grabbed a towel and wrapped it loosely
around my hand. "Come on downstairs. I'll patch you up." The
moment was over. I asked him to bring the evidence I had placed on
the bed and my backpack.

Al carefully medicated and bandaged me while I downloaded the
pictures I'd snapped today with the digital camera. After they were
saved onto my notebook, I made a copy for the GBI. Al dumped ice
cubes into a sealable plastic bag for my eye and offered Vaseline for
my raw lips. Neither of us found the courage to resume our upstairs
conversation. Just as he finished with the scrapes on my arms,
Vontana and friends arrived.

The Office for the Protection of the Constitution reported in 1992 that violent extremist activities increased seventy percent. Youths under the age of twenty-one committed seventy percent of those acts, with males committing ninety-seven percent of the crimes.

Chapter Forty-Two

It was electrifying telling the agents everything I'd discovered. I happily gave them a copy of it all–the barge and boat names, registration numbers, the approximate island location, a list of weapons and equipment, images taken with the digital camera, the Klavern details, a pair of night-vision goggles, and one mystery black box. I pushed the items across the table. There was a lot of shrugging among the agents as they fondled the device, but they wouldn't dare admit to me that they, too, were puzzled.

From a map that Al fished out of a neatly arranged cupboard, we determined that the Klavern was in the woods between Rincon and a neighboring town, Springfield. There was a huge tract of government land in that area of possible Klavern locations which helped narrow down the expanse. One agent scoffed at the usefulness of this piece of information. But I thought if one of their purposes was to gleam as much intelligence on hate groups, this was definitely a start.

"These aren't illegal," one of the agents quipped as he fingered the goggles.

"Why do they have them?" I countered.

"Maybe they varmint hunt with them," another agent suggested in a tone that hinted I was a dunderhead. I leaned over to peer at the plastic ID hanging from his shirt pocket. Stabenski.

"With police logos on the side?" The room was silent. "You're stupid if you think I'm *that* stupid," I told him. Stabenski passed everything but the CD of photos on to the next man. I showed them a few pages of Gundersen data I'd downloaded.

"Paloma," Vontana said, not bothering to look at the information. "Maybe the company doesn't hang all of their wash out on the line."

"You mean dirty linen." They stared politely.

"They could be *legally* manufacturing all kinds of items that we don't know about," Vontana added.

"What about the way they treated Dixie? How did those racist cops find her so quickly the night she went to watch the plant? With *these!*" I pointed to the goggles. "Why are they being so secretive about Lemond?"

Agent Stabenski leaned across the table toward me. "Lady, I gotta say your imagination is admirable." He leaned back, superiority blazing.

I counted to ten. "What about the AT4's?" I was pleading so forcefully it sounded like I was yelling. "Everybody has a few rocket launchers, I guess. For home or office. I'm *so* behind the times." Mt. Rushmore, these guys.

"And what about the hate material? That's worth checking out. This stuff," I held up the leaflets I'd taken from the shed, "is being sent all over the country. Look at the addresses. That becomes FBI territory."

Stabenski grinned like a fool. "Hey guys. Get this chick. She's telling us the law. We'll pass this on to the proper agencies." Vontana apparently had never seen his hands. Head down, he kept examining them.

"And why is a supremacist group stockpiling another's hate material? It's not like they are sharing. The Klavern didn't have any material on the WRF. Besides, its not like there are tons of membership fees to go around in a town the size of Rincon. I don't think one would encourage interest in the other. Especially the Klavern. They have *nothing* like what I saw in the WRF place on the river."

"That doesn't mean the components plant is connected. What's the name?" Stabenski asked.

"Gundersen" Al and I chorused.

"Or that any of it has to do with Lemond's murder."

"I don't believe this! Lemond worked for Gundersen. He became distant to his family–a family he's always been close to–then disappears." I sipped at the soda Al had placed in front of me. "Okay. Forget Gundersen. What about the Klan?"

"You know how many people claim they're innocent when the heat's on them?" Stabenski asked.

"That's not the Klan's style. They like to parade their transgressions in public. Right?" I looked at Al for support.

"Yes, sugah." Al scanned the men's faces. Silence.

"I gave you an estimation of where their Klavern is. They kidnaped me. Take these," I said, snatching up the goggles, " to help you find it."

"We're noting your complaint and will check into it. We can't run rough-shod over the citizens–"

"You can't seem to run anywhere!"

"Missy, you need to remember that you got this information illegally. We can't use this."

"I know!" I was shouting, but couldn't help myself. "I just wanted you to *see* it and know that something is going on at that plant and in that meeting house. Now it's your job to find out what–legally! *Droga!*"

"Paloma," Al said placatingly.

"Al. Don't! *Somebody* thinks I'm onto something. Since I came here, why else would all of these things happen to me? The hotel break-in, Jerry at the Last Chance, River Street." I had stumped the crowd indoors. The insects outside filled the silence.

Al tried again. "Don't take it out on them, sugah. "They're just doing..."

"Just doing their job? Is that what you were going to say? If they were doing their job, they'd get off their butts and investigate. They're so disin-terested in my kidnaping, I'm not even worth making jokes about." I stood quickly, flipping the chair backward with a loud smack. I turned to flee. Al grabbed my arm while I tried to dodge his grasp. We did a brief taffy pull before I slipped outside to commune with the tractor. Al followed me.

"I know you're upset about Dixie."

"This has nothing..."

"Shhhhhh," he said, turning me around then touching my lips lightly with his fingertips. "Let me finish. I'll talk to Vontana alone tomorrow and see if he'll reconsider."

"Excuse me if I don't hold any optimism," I barked, then lowered my voice. "I don't mean to yell at you. They're acting so condescend-ing."

"Yes, they are. I'm not sure why. We've always had great rapport. Why are you more worried about the plant and the WRF than the fact that you were kidnaped by the Klan?"

"They let me go! If they really killed Lemond, then kidnaped me, why would they then let me go? I'm what they detest. I'm a half-breed, have black friends. Hey, I even like you! So rid the white race of another deviant! Maybe I'd feel differently if they'd done more than make fun of and humili-ate me–although it really chaps my butt when I think about it." At least Al was listening. He took my injured paw, careful of the sore spots, and held it gently in his. "Al, I've had a lot of time today sitting in that boat thinking about everything. I let it all flow through my mind however it comes. That often works for me. I'd like to tell you what I came up with thus far. So would you hear me out first? Then tell me what you honestly think? Please don't treat me like those guys in there–no games or feeding me crap."

"Sugah, I promise!" He folded his arms across his chest and looked at me, ready to concentrate on what I was about to say.

I took a deep breath. "It's not any *one* thing. Or incident. It's a lot of little things together." I gave him a cookbook list of the day's events that stood out, starting with me spying at the plant's river landing from the john boat. Next, I briefly shared the computer data I'd gathered on Gundersen. "Now!" I looked at Al to make sure he was still with me and he was. "Effingham County has two hate groups–the Klan and the WRF. We'll take the oldest hate group first. I don't have to go into the reasons why they could be guilty of lynching a black man. It's practically their reason for living. So, then. Could the Klan be innocent?" It sounded strange just saying it.

"I saw their Klavern. It's not an outhouse, but it's nothing special. And there weren't enough people there tonight to play a game of Yahtzee. The Klavern is new, so they're getting *some* money from somewhere. But the whole Rincon Klan doesn't compare with even just that WRF place on the river–and they didn't have members there when I visited." I almost said "broke in" and while Al would know that's the only way I could have gotten in, I didn't have to air my dirty undies in public. At least not all the time.

"The WRF already outclasses the Klan. Just looking at their equipment, I can see that they are a bigger, well, more improved hate group." I put my whole body and expression into selling my theories, looking quite spastic, I'm sure. "Their equipment is like Space Age versus the Stone Age. The Klan's three to five shot hunting rifles versus what our military takes to combat. They had a barge take them and their equipment to their place down river–although not an earth shattering event, it is telling. More planning, equipment and money involved. There's a lot of variety in their sophisticated equipment–all those types of weapons, boxes, scopes, goggles. And the PD equipment. Were there a ton of dirty cops pilfering or donating their own equipment? Stolen? Whichever way it happened, they both cause the price to be jacked up. So even more of a cash outlay. A lot more. And imagine all the manpower behind it all!

And you may ask," I said smiling. "What shows us Gundersen could be in cahoots with the WRF?" Al nodded, enjoying how I told my story. He was relaxed, the strain gone out of his body. "Let me tell you why! It was Gundersen plant equipment that transported the weapons. At least on land. Lemond worked there. He's gone. Dixie was captured when she went to check out the plant. It's got to be something big to risk repercussions of all her rights that were ignored and laws broken during and after her arrest. Even a first year law student could point that out. Sorry, Al. No offense."

"None taken, sugah." And he patted my arm to back up his words. "Continue, please."

I exaggerated a deep, noisy breath. Dug in. "The WRF. It appears they are more organized than a handful of Klan. And what little I've seen of the WRF, it matches the information you gave me and what I've read on the Internet. From reliable sources," I added so he couldn't point out that just because you read something doesn't make it true. "It's not that I simply believe what the Klan told me. I've analyzed it, and I do believe it carries enough weight to check into. If that little corner of the WRF world is that 'impressive', imagine what we haven't discovered. They're new in town, but too organized not to have a counterpart somewhere else. Boston, probably which is their headquarters."

He nodded, still listening. Still giving me a chance. What a dude.

"I came up with two reasons why there's Klan literature at another white supremacist headquarters." I ticked them off with my fingers. "They are in cahoots or the WRF is up to something against the Klan. You told me that Randy was handing out Klan leaflets after he shot at me. Gundersen's people are WRF. Randy works there. That's not an astounding piece of circumstantial evidence," I rushed on in case Al was preparing to refute me. "But add to it the fact that the plant's Personnel Department has no record of him working there. Ever."

Al did a double take. "How did you...Paloma you didn't do something illegal with that computer of yours?"

"Al!" He braced himself for a tongue lashing. I decided to keep him guessing and turned on the charm. "Of course not, honey pie!" I replied sweetly. "His buddies say he works there. I called to confirm. Nobody there by that name. Why the lies–whoever it is that's telling them?"

"Tell me about the Klavern."

I went over my actions, what I saw, the Wiz's speeches, what the others said and did, sparing Al my witty repartee with the bedsheet brigade. "I don't know if this means anything. I had nothing but eyes to stare at and what I saw in Wiz's was fear. Same with Ski Mask. I know that look. I've become friends with it."

I let Al chew on that for a moment. "You're still antsy, Paloma. There's more. "

Yep, there was. It was disarming that he'd pegged me so dead-on, having only recently met me. I'd been pogoing without the stick. I stopped, revved up my mouth instead. "The plant, it keeps coming back to the plant. What better way to hide their agenda than with a *legitimate* business! It certainly has helped the mob for eons. Go ahead and scrutinize! The products or services could be completely legal. It's what they *do* with the funds that's the crux of it. I've heard that they haven't hired locals for top jobs. That could be innocent or they don't want locals involved because they would find out too much." I told him about security supervisor Swartzman now in charge of a high-tech operation. That didn't fit logically either.

"And it helps having the plant in a small town like Rincon. They don't need or have sophisticated law enforcement. Heck, Grainger is the perfect cop for this scenario. That's what I think is going on. What do you think, Al? Hit me."

He took his sweet time replying–the little terror. "You apply your computer logic everywhere. I guess you're used to breaking things down and looking at the pieces." He cuffed me lightly under my chin with the back of his hand.

"Don't cajole me." I pushed his hand away.

"I wasn't."

"Then it's my time to apologize. *I'm sorry.* I've had enough mockery tonight so I'm a little sensitive in that area. Some tough lady, huh? Those jerks in there," I stabbed their way with my finger. "Treated me like a dumb female. I'm onto something, Al. I can feel it from my Brazilian heart down to my Polish toes."

"Anything else you remember?" Al asked.

I closed my eyes to review it all. "It's nothing big. When they were putting me in the cage, a guy said something to Ski Mask that made me believe he and the Wiz are related. He stutters by the way. The Wiz does." I opened my eyes abruptly, looked directly into Al's. And like the counselor, I changed conversational direction just as quickly. "Your buddies showed up at Lemond's house. Why didn't

they just wait and get a report about his murder–let the locals handle
it or attempt to?"

"They were doing me a favor."

"Why can't you do one for me?"

"Paloma! It's not that simple..."

"Now *you* listen to me, Attorney Man." I brought his chin front and
center with two fingers. "There's one more thing." I paused dramatically until I saw Al's face perk up with interest. "My clothes tonight."
The perk moved into a quizzical expression. I cracked up. I'd been
saving the best for last.

"When the Klan dropped me back at the plant–they literally did. I
slipped on clay climbing up the embankment. And I kept slipping.
Red Georgia clay, Al! The same as on Lemond's body." I knew what
he was thinking. Trying to narrow down red clay would be tougher
than finding the Klavern.

"It's all mud and woods around the Klavern! I shoved one of those
yahoos down and he came up covered with black mud. The Gundersen river landing is surrounded by cliffs of clay!"

"You said you didn't go in and bust up the place." He playfully
checked my forearm for muscles. His hand stayed there, finger tracing
a path to my shoulder.

"You're distracting me," I said sing-song.

"Uh-huh."

I was so into trying to get Al on my side I ignored his shy attempt
toward a little romance. I'm so hopeless. "I know–Lemond could
have been murdered anywhere, but maybe something's on him to link
it with the land-ing or Gundersen. Forensics, trace evidence.
Something! Can you find out from Vontana? We *have* to find out
why Lemond died. If it wasn't a hate crime, then what? Maybe he
knew something he shouldn't. He wasn't a doper. No enemies. He
was a nice guy, so the usual reasons he could've been murdered don't
apply."

"I agree with you there. Lemond looks clean. But Vontana does
have to check it out. Sometimes the family is the last to know of a
loved one's other life."

I'll give him that and told him so. "I don't know if it's enough."
He used his head to point toward the kitchen, meaning the GBI inside
it.

"I don't see why not. You know what any good investigator
does–pokes, sifts, until something shakes loose. But the shaking has
got to start. Why aren't the GBI, or any enforcement group for that
matter, *doing* something?"

When he didn't readily reply to my grand idea, I got a little hyper
and began to feel stupid. I immediately saw holes in my postulating.
I felt the heat rise up my neck and head to northern latitudes. "It all
fits, Paloma." His tone changed to doubtful. "You *may* be on the
right track."

"But?"

He looked down at his shoes and shifted uncomfortably.

"What, Al?"

"Nothing, sugah. I'm taking it all in." He stood like Goliath, no expres-sion on his face. I waited. He couldn't look at me. He must not believe me. Despondent, I turned and tiredly trudged to his back door. "Sugah, you want a job?"

I stopped. "I don't come cheap," I warned over my shoulder.

"I didn't think you would." I turned to face him. "When we go back in-side I want you to tell them what you just told me." He joined two fingers together. "Everything down to the infinitesimal detail. I believe your per-spective does have merit."

I beamed at him and finally gave in to my desire and flung myself into his arms. "Here I am thanking you again. I'm so glad you believe me!"

"Paloma, I believe *in* you." We stood for a while, together. A cooling breeze embraced us. He rubbed my back in slow, soothing circles.

"Sugah?"

"Hmm?" I murmured into his chest.

"While you were stomping Klan fanny, someone invited the TV news to Rincon's park for a try at a cross burning."

"A try?"

His body shook. I looked into his face alarmed, but saw that he was trying to contain laughter. "The newspaper was wrapped too tightly around the wood. It wouldn't stay lit. And you thought *you* were humiliated tonight!" We enjoyed the moment, our laughter boosting our spirits. He gave me a soft kiss on my ground beef lips. A kiss as sweet as the first strawberries of summer. I returned the compliment with a Rio lip-locker hot enough to melt Georgia asphalt. When we came up for air, he adopted a leering attitude. "Let's go back to something you said before. If your toes are Polish and your lips Brazilian, what does that make your hips?"

"Definitely all my own. But it's better if I show you." The screen door slammed.

"Yo, Al," Vontana yelled. I think I actually heard Al mutter a damn.

"Let's go back inside and get things rolling," Al said to me, then called to Vontana that we'd be right in. "Will you stay after our guests leave?" I nodded, that ol' Chessie cat grin reaching from ear to ear.

Al tried to help me. It was US and THEM. In the end, all informa-tion, theories, and suppositions were duly noted and would be acted on when *more* evidence was uncovered by law enforcement. Al was baffled by his friend's lack of interest. The agent was still not saying much.

Musical chairs commenced with THEM out in the yard smoking while Vontana, the only abstainer, conversed upwind with his fellow agents. Probably making rude comments about me. Al and I weren't

privy to the conversation. We even had an agent babysit us at the table–the type of guy you wouldn't want to meet in a dark alley. When THEM came back inside, Al and Vontana went out. After a few moments the agent yelled out. "They want more evidence!"
"If that's want you want, then *I'll* go and get it!" I exclaimed to the remaining agents who watched with boredom while I ranted. I stormed into the kitchen, grabbed my pack and other materials and in a definite huff, went out the front door into the night.

Wisconsin: Kenosha–Two Skinheads fired shots into a black church during their Bible meeting. California: Mariposa–Three armed Skin-heads were arrested after they attacked black families in a public park. Westminster–A Skinhead parade resulted in a cross burning, vandalized homes, rocks with racial threats attached thrown at Asian-owned shops.

Chapter Forty-Three

It took a few wrong turns on long pitch-black roads that had no street signs that I could see, before chance provided the paved road back to civilization. I searched the radio channels in the truck, sorry my grandfather's crawl into the electronic age hadn't progressed at least as far as a lousy cassette player. Finding nothing but advertisements, twang, and wimpy, I twisted the knob to off. I took an eye off the deserted road, dug around the truck for the notebook computer, booted it, popped in Queensrÿch's *Empire* CD, rolled the volume control up and deafened myself.

So there I was, Ms. Big-City, angry, chaffed. Burning up the road doing seventy in a ten-year-old pickup truck with a gun rack, pulling an even older john boat. *Gee, ma'am, where ya' going in such a hurry? Gotta get to that fishing hole, officer.*

"Now what, Paloma?" I asked out loud. I drove another ten minutes, realizing again, how exhausted I was. And homeless. It was past 2:00 A.M. I sped around a curve and saw a billboard that claimed Southern hospitality at the Port Wentworth Inn. Savannah wasn't that far away, but a bed one mile at the next left sounded better.

In spite of my need for sleep, I couldn't. After an hour of tossing in the bed, I gave up. I retrieved handfuls of gear, Jordan almonds and only the clothes I'd need from the truck, remembering to get a dress ready for court tomorrow. Using Heathcliff as a diary, I entered all the events that had occurred since the last entry, then read and reread them until I got sick of thinking about it all. I saved the file and scanned the game subdirectory. Perhaps a mindless hour annihilating bad guys in *Quake* or *Half-Life* would help–at least it would make the time pass faster.

As file names scrolled past, I saw the game subdirectory I'd created for Dixie's youngest nephews and nieces. They'd wanted to be like their older siblings, spending too much time in front of a computer. I'd offered to find some pre-school packages that wouldn't warp their brains too badly. Surfing the Net, I'd downloaded a lot of share-ware–free or cheap software–games and dumped them all in a subdirectory to later copy onto diskettes. I'd never finished doing that. The games that were ready, I was supposed to have mailed them. That's what I thought Dixie was calling me about that evening when I learned she was in jail. Finally making good on my promise, I began transferring the game files, letting my thoughts drifted from one subject to another.

It seemed like a year ago–not a few weeks–that I'd driven Dixie to LAX for her trip home. When I'd arrived back at my house, the LED on my answering machine was flashing. Much to my chagrin, as soon as I'd left my house for hers, Ms. Dixie Hightower left what was supposed to be a funny, smart-assed message. She spoke like the machine was human–imitating me because she says I treat electronics like friends. She was so positive I'd take off in typical head-in-the-clouds fashion, the games still on the counter. Could Mr. Phone Machine let Her Majesty know that Dixie knew Paloma would forget? Her smugness oozed through the tiny speaker. Sometimes I loathed technology. But Dixie had been right. I'd spent the night before her flight coding my little heart out for BOB, the robot, sucked into the computer, oblivious to life and time passing around me. I'd made sure I set an alarm to wake up, but I'd left the house, games on the counter. *What?*

My nerve endings came cactus-prickly alive. The disks. Could they be the key? Something was niggling in the back of my mind. I typed what I'd just been thinking about, getting the days and times sorted in my PC and in my brain. How had I first learned Dixie wanted games? She'd telephoned me. Ooo. Ooo. I'm onto something! My fingers smoked up the keyboard detailing what we both did and said next, dates and times. Then Lemond disappears. He's a software engineer. Computers again. Did he have some kind of important data? On diskettes? Where were they? The Voice had wanted diskettes. He was prepared to beat their location out of me. Why did The Voice think I had them? My thoughts were flying along with my fingers. It was there. I just had to slow it down and grab on. Details. Break it down to each single component. My excitement exuded heat, warming up the room.

The message. Someone there at my house that day? Got the wrong idea? Good, go with that. Take it to a logical conclusion. After I beat that angle to death, it didn't feel right. But the message kept niggling at me. I decided to call my friend Grant in Seal Beach, owner of Counter-Surveillance, Inc., the spy toy shop.

"This better be good, or I'm gonna hurt you when you get back to the seals," he threatened. Through the phone, his yawn sounded just like one.

"You'll love it! I want you to find out if Dixie's house or phone has been bugged." He expressed total surprise as I knew he would. Once I convinced him I was serious, I gave him instructions on how to accomplish this with my house in disarray. I described Dixie's spare key and the rack in case it was no longer where they'd been before The Voice's hurricane housecleaning.

"I'm giving you the keyring version of the Clapper for Christmas. I assume this is important and not the ravings of a drunk, paranoid customer."

"Both. Grant, can you go do it now?"

"What about your house?"

"I wouldn't think so. I'd been playing with the detectors a lot there. I think that I'd have been alerted."

"It wouldn't hurt to check."

I grinned, knowing he was easy to hook. I gave him my hotel phone number as back up to the cell phone. He asked about Dixie. "Honey, we'll explain it all when we get home." Grumbling about being left out, Grant bid me goodnight. I was so excited when I hung up the phone, I slipped on my bathing suit and went to the pool. Picking the simple lock on the gate, I swam laps until my arms couldn't bend on their own.

Back in the room, I showered and dressed in shorts. With the hotel coffee pot, I cooked more of the Brazilian herbal remedy for my new set of bruises. It could steep while I ran to the store. The brew seemed to be working as the herbalist promised–chasing out the free-radicals. Sounded like a rock group. But the purpling of the bruises never appeared, only a light discoloration. Whatever works. I left the room again. This time, in search of a late night store that sold cosmetics to cover up the damage the Klan had done to me that my clothes couldn't hide.

1993, Birmingham, Alabama–Once a battleground for the civil rights movement, a Civil Rights Institute has been built that depicts historical racial events since World War I, and present day progress towards tolerance. The Institute overlooks the 16th Street Baptist Church–site of the 1963 bombing that killed four girls–and Kelly Ingram Park, site of demonstrations and confrontations. 1994, Los Angeles, California– The Simon Wiesenthal Museum of Tolerance opened with exhibits of modern-era genocide, and has state-of-the-art learning and research facilities.

Chapter Forty-Four

"How does the defendant plead?" Judge Hill asked Dixie.

She answered with a confident, "not guilty." Each cop–Pepsi, Toothpick, Singleton, Grainger–took the stand and brazenly lied about the cause of Dixie's arrest and blamed her for her own injuries. Pepsi was the first to describe her "unruly behavior" despite their friendly demeanor. The district attorney asked that no bail be set due to Dixie's out-of-state status.

"Bail is set for one million dollars." A chorus of disbelief sounded in the courtroom. The judge banged the gavel twice. Aggie and the Hightower neighbors and friends, who'd come along as an informal support group, all turned to look at me. A few reached out to brace me as if any moment I would need restraints. Okay, I admit I was ready to knock some heads around. "Acting the fool", as Gran would say, would only make things worse.

"Your Honor, my client has not been charged with a crime to warrant such high bail."

"Counselor, you should be happy I set bail at all."

"We respectfully ask that your Honor consider the extenuating circumstances."

"I'm aware that your client's relative was found dangling by his neck from a tree in his yard." Dixie's knees buckled and Al reached out a hand, but she steeled herself and sat down slowly amid whispers and gasps from the spectators. I ran to Dixie's side, soothing her, apologizing for her finding out about Lemond in such a heartless manner. We clung to each other and I whispered words of encouragement before the judge snarled at me and the deputies advanced to separate us. "Your client should have thought more carefully before she assaulted the officers. Court is recessed for fifteen minutes." He breezed away from the bench reeking of self-importance and biased victory.

Aggie kept turning to each of us, patting arms, trying to calm nerves with placating words. She soon ran down, stomped her foot twice and bellowed, "I don't believe what just happened! That judge! *Bundões* is too nice a word for him, Paloma! You'll have to teach me something worse that fits that putz. I'm so angry I could spit nails!" Al

looked ready to fly over the railing, I assumed to *try* and shut her up.
I was momentarily stunned into unnatural stillness–body and tongue.

Behind me I heard someone question what had just occurred. "How
does he get away with it? Aren't there investigatory groups, a
committee, *anything* that makes sure this type of thing doesn't
happen?"

"Paloma, I'll met you outside. Away from them." Al motioned
toward the enemy–the group of cops, prosecutor and court deputies.
"We'll figure out our next move outside."

Dixie turned to look at me. The friend who imparted strength,
clarity and erudition, was pale now, shaking and seemingly so small.
I reached out for her hand and babbled. "I am *so* sorry that you aren't
going home with us. You know we'll be going nonstop until you're
free! Be strong, Dixie. I love you."

Her island neighbors echoed my sentiments. Dixie was still in
shock, unable to comprehend what had just happened. She barely
blinked and her body was stiff, leaving movement to the deputies
tugging her along. I watched her retreating figure until she was
swallowed up in the same hallway she'd passed through earlier.

* * *

"Paloma! Wait!" I turned and watched Al sprint toward me. He
looked as unhappy as I felt. I wasn't quite sure how to act around
him, experiencing a case of the morning-after-our-first-kiss jitters. A
real kiss. That one in his office when he'd said it was to shut me up
did not count. He gave me a hug and kissed the top of my head. "I'm
sorry, sugah. I failed."

"You don't need to apologize for a bigot judge."

"There is that, but I was talking about last night. When I came back
inside, you were gone."

"I was angry at your buddies, not you."

"I worried about you driving around in an unfamiliar place with the
Klan after you." His eyes had bags underneath so large I could have
let him borrow a bra to hold them up, looping the straps over his ears.
I told him so. "You don't look so hot yourself."

"Oh, yeah? What do I look like?"

"A female version of Joe Hollywood." He indicated my sunglasses
with a tip of his head. I'd worn them indoors to keep the gaping of
strangers at a minimum, even though I'd piled on a thick coating of
pancake makeup that threatened to slide off my face from sheer
weight. As the chatter subsided, we mumbled "hums" for a while. I
hate beginning relationships. They're like new shoes–uncomfortable
and they pinch. By the time you get them broken in, you're out-of-
style and alone. While shopping in the next season, you find each new
pair exacts a higher price.

"I'm glad you aren't mad at me."

"No, but I am at that *bunda* in there." I jerked a thumb in the general direction the judge had slithered away. "One million dollars! Is there a law against excessive bail?"

"Yes, but Judge Hill obviously thinks he can get away with it."

"Can we see her? She needs to be with at least one family member especially after that judge slapped her with the news about Lemond. How can people be so cruel? I feel so helpless, useless and, and–*defeated*." My voice broke and I was surprised that I was seconds away from crying.

Al's eyes revealed deep compassion. He scanned the hallway and with my elbow in his hand, steered us into a windowless supply closet. When he closed the door, I was almost sightless. I leaned against a shelf of cleaning supplies. Al had no choice but to stand close–very close to me.

"Not fancy, but more private," he explained quietly, his warm breath floating past my ear. "Paloma, talk to me." I panicked, thinking he wanted me to confess in romantic verbiage. I stuttered. Al emanated a confident, sexy persona that from our first meeting had aroused my stale libido. But my initial bravado is soon tossed into the bags of garbage I drag to each relationship, breeding insecurity, mistrust, and a dozen other feelings that only get in the way. I ended up a few beats behind his conversation as my brain flapped around trying to think of something that would please both of us–Al to feel warm and fuzzy and me not to talk myself into being a fool. During catch-up, I realized Al was eyeballs deep into attorney mode. He wasn't referring to romance, but to Dixie and today's setback. Relief! I gave him my full attention. He was listing what angered him about the legal sham perpetrated today.

I told Al, "I think that until now I figured Dixie's situation would be cleared up–that it would be–I don't know–perhaps an easy legal matter. I mean–*come on!* Dixie's an honest person, never hurt anyone! Even if she weren't a cop, she wouldn't have done anything so wrong to end up like this!" Frustrated tears spilled down my cheeks.

He used his hands, as he usually did, in consolation. While he talked, he gently caressed my skin, then moved to my hair and stroked it. "I am truly sorry, Paloma. I never doubted that I'd get her bail today. I totally underestimated things. Can you forgive me?" In the darkness his soft voice was so plaintive, so needy. So sexy. Our physical closeness in the small room awakened a yearning that slowly flooded inside me like a sip of splendid wine. Totally out of character, I made the first move, leaping as usual without a thought. I pulled him closer for a kiss, slipping my arms around his waist. His hands remained on my face. Yummy. Ever so gently he moved his lips to my eyes, kissing the tears away, murmuring ever so quietly.

Oh, the heck with the pain! I crushed my lips into his, letting the fiery passion ignite and surface. A low-throated moan escaped me and I wantonly grabbed his rear pulling him even closer.

Leaving lips for my neck and ears, Al's breath blanketed my shoulders. I shivered wonderfully in the warm room. "Al," I whispered and moaned again. He abruptly pulled away. "What's wrong? Why did you stop?"

"I didn't." But his cell phone had. As he pulled it out of his pocket I heard the low hum of the vibrating mode. Perhaps I was a bit jealous. At least something was buzzing in this tiny closet. Aggie was outside the courthouse looking for us. *Droga* and double damn *droga!*

It was like being doused with cold water—Al already flipped back to all-business the instant he flipped his cell phone off. It was hard convincing my lust to smolder.

As we descended the wide white cement stairs—typical of many U.S. court-houses—Aggie ran toward us, her short legs pumping for all she was worth. Dixie's support team trailed behind her, leaving the shade of an oak tree that bordered a park across the street.

Aggie stopped before us panting. "Lawd me, I've worked myself into a dander!" No one seemed interested in what had sidetracked Al and me. I wasn't prepared to confess.

"Can we see her before she goes back to jail?"

"I'm going to find that out in just a sec, cousin dear," Al advised. "I wanted to speak with Paloma to discuss bail."

"I have it all set, Alvin," Aggie said in a tone that admonished Al to catch up with events. "I made a few calls, have people checking some things out. I had to go to the car for some phone numbers, then the dang phone battery died, so I had to go back. And..."

"The bail, Aggie? And who is the lawyer here?"

Aggie smiled or grimaced, it was hard to tell. "I'm gonna put up my land—both places." Mrs. Bishop's mouth dropped in surprise. "And I got some in savings. That'll be a start. You guys work on the rest. Clive, my banker, promised to have everything ready if I can get there by noon. It'll be close. I have to get to Beaufort *now!*" She looked at her watch, waved, and took off.

Shaking his head, Al mumbled, "Sometimes I could throttle that woman!" I coughed an incoming laugh away.

"I'll help Dixie anyway I can. You just tell me what I need to do, Mr. Eason," Mrs. Bishop, island neighbor to the Hightowers spoke up. The rest of the supporters agreed.

"Al. Call me Al." He flipped open his phone while stepping away for the call. I heard murmuring among the islanders and caught the tail end. Both Al and Aggie surprised them. He for his casual folksy manner, and Aggie for signing all her properties to bail out a black girl she barely knew. Mrs. Ella, at least eighty years young, claimed she'd need to buy a pack of smelling salts if peculiarities would be the norm for the day. Her friend Mamie Lou, suggested a slug of her home-made peach wine would work just as well and they wouldn't have to stop at the store to get some.

"If you have Aggie's permission," I teased once Al rejoined us, "I've got property and count my grandparents in. We'll show those bastards!"

"Paloma, such ugly words from a pretty young lady." Mrs. Bishop stared sternly at me and when Al agreed, she wore that smug look that adults get when they've shown up a kid. "We don't have to go down the toilet just because we're russ-lin' with trials and tribulations."

"Yes, ma'am. I'm sorry," I replied, knowing when I was whipped.

"Let's go to that sandwich shop over yonder and get a bite before we leave," she offered.

"Great idea. Paloma, here's Aggie's cell phone number. Get her to keep you posted on what she's doing. This afternoon I'll be working on a change of venue for Dixie's case. I'm going now to see a judge in Screven County." The group headed to a small deli at the end of the block. I took my time following them, hoping that Al would lag behind with me. It worked. "What plans do you have this afternoon, Paloma?"

"None."

"Tonight?"

I smiled on the inside and out. "Same."

He grinned back. "I'll call you when I get back to the office. It'll be late afternoon. I'll try you at the hotel, okay?" It was more than okay with me. Al said he would stop by the courthouse to see if Dixie could speak to her attorney and perhaps, one of us, although it was doubtful. Al left us at the sandwich shop, taking his lunch with him in a white bag while we all peppered him with "tell Dixies"–well-wishes, supporting comments and that we were working on her bail. Dixie would be waiting at the courthouse until all detainees were ready to go back to jail.

I picked over my lunch, not pleased with life, and grew more restless by the second. I heard a muffled ring, realized it was my cell phone somewhere deep in my backpack. I frantically dug it out. "Paloma, it's Grant."

"Hello, pal," I said warmly, all eyes at the table on me. "Hang on."
"Excuse me," I good-mannerly informed the crowd. I walked outside so I wouldn't be yelling out "you're breaking up" throughout their meal.

"What happened to your house, Paloma? Did you know it's in shambles?"

"Yes, I warned you. It'll take too long to explain now. About the bugs."

"You were right, Paloma. One's in Dixie's phone. It's a very sophisticated model. Pretty big league. How did you know?"

"I'll tell..."

"Me when you get home. You've got a lot of telling to do. What do you want me to do about it?"

"Nothing. It won't hurt to leave it. Grant, I owe you a month of prime rib at the Chart House. No, two months."

"I'm gonna bankrupt you."

I now had afternoon plans. After I hung up, I zipped back into the deli and laid a ten on the table, grabbed my pack, and announced I had an errand to run. I left before anyone could ask me any questions.

* * *

As soon as Aggie cleared the Effingham County line outside of Rincon, she pushed down hard on the gas. For once she was glad she had the federal car. She could speed, especially in her state of Carolina and most likely not get hassled by a cop. She flew down Highway 21, her tires squealing into a left turn onto I-95.

Off the multi-lane interstate, Aggie slowed for heavy traffic on the two-lane road into Beaufort. A military convoy was inching toward Parris Island. She begged the opposing lane to open up so she could pass. When she had her chance, she slammed the gas pedal all the way down, almost standing straight up in the car. As she passed the convoy's last two vehicles an oncoming truck rounded the bend.

"Dang federal piece of shit." She pumped the gas uselessly. The truck drove onto the shoulder, fighting to keep from sliding down into the ditch. The horn blared. Aggie replied by sticking her hand out the window and giving them the finger. The Marines who witnessed the feisty older lady tornado gave her an honorary salute as she disappeared around the bend.

* * *

Realizing no one knew which hotel I'd stayed in last night, I went back to the Port Wentworth Inn to think and plot. Instead I fell asleep. I awoke at dusk. I checked in with Mrs. Bishop on the island. Clarice and Beverly flew into Jacksonville, Florida early afternoon and drove the four hours to Lemond's house. They needed to start funeral arrangements and decided to do it from there. I phoned Aggie next, who angrily told me that when they'd gone to bail Dixie out, the judge had reconsidered. No bail. I felt like pulverizing something. Then someone. Hearing the news decided my next moves, but before I put them in action, I made a few more calls.

I dialed my grandparents, let them know I was still alive, then phoned Lemond's house. Clarice answered. I could hear the steel reserve in her voice. She brushed aside the sympathies, heading straight to Dixie and what had been happening. I filled her in on everything Mrs. Bishop hadn't known to tell her and then discussed my theories that I'd tried to pass on to the GBI. She listened intently, not interrupting even for an occasional "hmm". Lastly, I explained to her what I wanted to do. In essence I'd be helping a group whose every existence I wholeheartedly detested.

"I don't believe *my* black behind is gonna help you prove the Klan is innocent. But if they didn't murder my nephew, I wanna know who did. Come on over. I need the company. Beverly is totally blown away, as she has a right to be. I've got her knocked out from a sleeping pill. That lawyer you got for Dixie sounds like the real thing. I'm going to meet with him tomorrow." I brushed aside her thanks. Quid pro quo. "Then his cousin Aggie called. We talked a long time. She's already family. Said she may stop by in a few. That won't be a problem, will it?"

"No, ma'am."

"Al's looking for you. Said you weren't at the hotel on River Street."

"No, I'm not. Look, Mama-Clarice. He won't like what I'm coming there to do. He's got to do things by-the-book. That's the man he is, even if he wasn't an attorney. If I find evidence tonight that could help Dixie's case, we can work on a way for Al to use it. They've been fighting dirty while we've been playing it straight. This hasn't gotten us anywhere. Maybe it's time to play by their rules. If Al isn't a part of what I do, then it shouldn't jeopardize Dixie's case."

"I agree. Come on over. We'll sneak you in the back door if we have to."

* * *

I made it to Lemond's in good time, glad for the darkness to hide the tree. I kept my eyes diverted anyway. Beverly was still asleep on the couch. "What about you, Ma?" Clarice pushed her feelings aside. Her maternal sonar played out for anyone in need, while sacrificing herself in support of others. In between catching up on news and bear hugs, Aggie arrived, getting her own strong hugs from her new friend Clarice. Lemond's house was neat and clean, the exceptions being a layer of dust expected in an unoccupied house along with fingerprint powder necessary for a crime scene. Cleaning supplies stacked on the coffee table told me that Clarice would soon rid the place of those nuisances. I plundered a bit. If someone had searched the house before, they'd done a very neat job of it. I asked Clarice if she noticed anything out of place.

"I couldn't say, honey. I wasn't here that much. He mostly came to the island. But I don't see anything obvious. I knew he had a small TV and stereo, they're here." She shrugged her shoulders and looked pained, like it was her fault she couldn't provide a list of missing items.

"I didn't think we'd find anything here in that respect. But there is one place I definitely can check. She led me to the back of the house and pointed to a room on the left.

Lemond's bedroom was a small, neat, masculine abode. Memorabilia from Illinois Tech hung on one wall, a dresser and large desk crowded the other. There was no chair, so I improvised by sitting on the bed's edge, Aggie and Clarice sat on either side of me like bookends. Flipping the PC on, I drummed my fingers on the desk while I waited for it to boot up. I clicked away on the keyboard, "getting my fingers wet" peering into the many files on Lemond's hard drive. It took a while, as I knew it would, and I explained this to the women beside me. "And it can be boring, too." They chatted amongst themselves while I ignored them, all too easily sucked into my task.

File peeking complete, I slid the computer out and peered behind it, to check out the communications options. "He's got an internal modem." I said to myself. I pushed the PC back toward the wall and followed the phone cable coming out the back of the unit to a cabinet on the hutch. I opened the little door, found the phone and checked its connections. Aggie asked what I was up to.

"It all started with Lemond," I explained, and continued with the same theories I'd been broadcasting to Al and the GBI. Like Clarice, Aggie agreed with my speculation. "So we–I guess I should say I–will start there." I patted the CPU. "I haven't found any files that were important or dangerous enough to, ah..."

"Get him killed," Clarice finished gently.

"I checked for hidden files, and there weren't any that he'd created on the hard drive. I'm going to check his CDs and diskettes. Let's just hope he didn't hide them in another location." We dug around the hutch, each of us pulling out all the media we found. I searched the contents of each disk and CD that he'd created himself. Luckily there weren't many. I slid another diskette in the A: drive.

"Paloma, that's a Microsoft disk. That means Lemond didn't create the files on it, right?"

"Yes. And no. If there is room on a disk, you can copy files onto it–even a commercial software disk. Like this one." I waved one for emphasis. "These commercial–or proprietary–software disks are useful places to hide data . While it's not full-proof, most people would check the disks with handwritten labels and skip the other ones. Hide it in plain sight."

"Brilliant, Paloma!"

"Not, really, Aggie. A few years ago, mainly because I was too impatient, I copied a file onto a WordPerfect disk. Later I needed that file and didn't remember I'd used a commercial one. I never had before. I spent days searching for it." I continued checking disks and CDs. No luck. "I'll have to hack into Gundersen's computers," I announced and began doing so.

"Will they know you are plundering in their computers?" Aggie asked.

"I won't know until I get into one."

"Don't you need a password for that?" Aggie asked.

I grinned. "Lemond did it all for us." I definitely had their attention. "We need a modem to dial up and get into the plant's computers. The phone and PC don't speak the same language, so the modem converts data back and forth for each machine. They need communication software, which Lemond has, and it has a script option that recorded all the keystrokes necessary to log onto the plant's computer. It saves time and retyping. All I have to do is select which of two accounts he has. Please pass me a glass of tea, Mama-Clarice. Now, here goes."

I crossed my fingers and drank the cold, refreshing tea while I waited for the high-pitched squeal from the modem. "Come on, baby, talk to me! Great, we got a handshake!" The screen filled with cheery words welcoming me to Gunderson's Compaq Alpha system. "They have an Alpha!" I yelled, excitedly holding a fist up in minor victory.

"This is good, right?" Aggie asked.

"Yes. The Alpha and I go way back, when it was DEC's VAX system. Compaq bought them and changed their name to–. Sorry! I'll keep it brief. In the Alpha world, if you want to delete or copy, you type 'delete' or 'copy'. That's as simple as it gets." Aggie was politely looking interested but I didn't believe it for a second. "On some other systems, the commands aren't that straightforward. They can get confusing." I dug in my pack for Jordan almonds, offered them around and popped two into my mouth.

"I'll say a big 'amen' to confusing! I'm still getting used to the computers at the school where I teach," Clarice spoke in my left ear. "I don't think I want them taking over my life like some of my students and other people that I know." She gave me a poke in the ribs with her elbow.

"Me neither!" Aggie agreed in my right ear. "So, Paloma, what are you going to do first?" The conversation was coming at me in stereo.

"See if anyone else is logged onto the computer. Then find out if their security and auditing have been set up." I typed in SHOW USERS while Aggie clucked her tongue nervously. "We're alone." Relieved sighs filled the small room. "Okay, now their security." I typed SHOW SECURITY and explained. "That command does just that. And another one, SHOW SYSTEM, will display all the applications running on the Gundersen systems, including any independent programs or third party software that would monitor additional security concerns. SHOW ACC is the shortcut command for their system accounting. You can set flags for the system to notify you when certain instances occur. For example, how often somebody logs in and out, what terminal was used, if a certain file was utilized." I actually cringed until the answer flashed on the screen. "Whew! They only have minimum security, and are only concerned with major system plundering."

"A large plant like them? They don't have good security?" Aggie asked incredulously.

"Only when you are Dixie and want to check them out from the bushes! Anyway, friends, Gundersen's computer security is set up to block anyone from deleting data, but there are no cyber roadblocks to stop us from copying or reading. That can be just as destructive. This situation is not that unusual, even with all the hype about computer break-ins. It's the same thing as locking your door and leaving the windows open."

"Right!" Aggie said gleefully. "You could find out what your competitors are up to, without removing physical property. They'd never know."

"Aggie," I chided "I'll have you addicted to computers yet."

"So no more sneaking into an office late at night and cracking the safe, like they do on TV."

"Why bother when the safe is online. Ladies!" I laughed low and throaty, giving them an evil look. "Now for some snooping. It's party time! I'm gonna check a few things. Just for caution."

"What?" they choroused.

"I'm looking for the batch queue–it's a way to run programs and not have to be at the computer. Most people create one to start backing up the system. This gives them a duplicate set of records in case the originals are damaged in some way. Since backups eat up most of a computer system's resources, companies schedule them at night when the employees aren't around to use the computers. A batch file will reliably start the process at the same time, every time. Computer operators often have to be there to change tapes or make sure all goes well. If backups start running, it will slow us down and probably kick us out of the system. The longer I'm in Gundersen's computers, the more risk of getting caught. A hacker's motto–get in, get your business done ASAP, get out."

"I agree. My stomach's doing flops as it is," Aggie said, holding her gut.

"Hmm. There's nothing in the queue to run automatically. I'll check a few files. Uh-oh."

"What?" came their panicked chorus.

"They back up their files every night. As they should. Nine o'clock. We have one hour." I rubbed my hands together, a willing pirate ready to plunder for booty.

"They'll notice, won't they?" Clarice chimed in.

"The system could–but they don't have it set up that way. I only have to check periodically to see if someone has logged on."

"If someone comes in and checks the system how will you tell?" That was Aggie.

"They could send me a message. Who are you and what are you doing on our system? Or they could just pull the plug."

Clarice asked uneasily, "Can it be traced back here?"

"From what I've checked at the beginning, I'm almost certain that I won't leave a footprint. I'll erase my tracks if I do. If tonight goes okay, the next threat would be if someone at Gundersen checks the access logs tomorrow. Those logs will show that someone was in their system tonight and at what time. It will also let them know that the 'someone' was Lemond. Because it's his account. They can't trace the actual call, the logs will only show which phone company was used. To keep this location–Lemond's house–from showing up in that trace, I've bounced the signal through a hacker site in Indonesia. That should cause a few head scratches when and if they look at the logs in the morning. The only way to discover me in their system tonight is if a plant tech gets on a computer and types the SHOW USERS command. They'd see that Lemond is logged on, trace where that is coming from, which would show Indonesia, not this house. Don't worry, this is all happening on the Internet, so it's a local call. But unless they suspect something, they won't even look. The phone company would have to be involved *if* Gundersen has a tracing mechanism and *if* they already are suspicious about this. But I doubt they will because their security is so poor. They obviously aren't concerned about hackers."

They murmured polite ahhs, and hmms. I didn't add that someone else could have been lurking in the system and had already sounded an alarm. But from what I could ferret out, I didn't think that was the case. I munched another almond, lined a few up on the desk.

No true computer nerd could avoid checking out the cyber-muscle of a company's systems their first time inside. I let out a whistle as I determined the Gundersen computer inventory. As I paged down, the screen filled. "They have a ton of computers." I pointed. "See, these are areas, each one named after a city. Each area has at least one very large system, like the Alpha which can support a lot of employees. And to get a rough estimate on total employees per area, you could count the number of PCs. This means they have..." I kept my finger close enough to keep my bearings but not leave prints on the screen.

"Twenty-two cities," Aggie said, interrupting.

"Boston has the largest collection of equipment, but that could be because it's the home office."

"You better check to see if anyone is watching us." I did. "We're still safe." Clarice hallelujahed while Aggie thanked the good Lawd.

"Each employee that needs to use a computer has their own directory–or a bit of space on the system. I'm checking Lemond's now and will look for any hidden files. When an employee leaves–for whatever reason–a good system's manger locks access to that person's personal account, but they keep the files in case they are needed. Most companies work it that way."

"How are you getting in?" Clarice asked.

"Through a general access account. Systems operators have two accounts–a main one with maximum privileges and one with only a few of them. Lemond's personal one is where he'd type letters, create files and such. And for his work in the computer department, he'd need an account that allows him to do functions like maintenance or solve problems that occur on the system. But companies sometimes forget about that second personal account. Every person's account should be shut down before they are canned." Both women nodded.

"If I were Lemond and I had very important data, I would have made a copy of what was hot, moved those files into my account, then hidden them. Right now I'm checking Lemond's personal account. I just brought up a listing of all of his files. If we look at the amount of space the files are taking up, we get this number." I pointed to it on the screen. "But if we look at the space the computer has allocated for his account, we get a larger number. That implies he has hidden files."

Aggie sat up excitedly. "Let me see if I got this straight. It's the same thing as if you take the total square footage of a house and deduct the size of each room, any big difference in amounts could mean there is a hidden room."

"Exactly!" We high-fived. I dabbed at fake tears and spoke in a quivery voice. "I'm so proud of you!"

"I'm beginning to like this computer stuff." Aggie admitted.

"Me, too! "I've always been very proud of Paloma. And my Dixie," Clarice appended, like a good mother should. "Does Lemond have any hidden files?"

I'm sure we were all holding our breaths. I furiously typed in the commands to reveal the files. We waited impatiently. "Yes! Here they are. Now ladies, let's go see what is so important that Lemond had to hide them."

"This is so thrilling, but I feel like someone has to know what we're doing." Aggie was jiggling her legs in excitement, creating a vibrating bed while I checked to see if anyone had logged onto the Gundersen computers.

"Now back to Lemond's hidden files." I displayed a list of the files. Names scrolled down the screen.

Clarice leaned over my shoulder. "Look at these cities. There's Atlanta, Bosie, Boston, Charlotte."

Aggie couldn't resist joining in. "Columbus, Dallas, Houston, Jackson."

What the heck. We trioed along. "Los Angeles, Miami, New Orleans, Portland. RINCON!"

"I think we should look at that file." Aggie suggested.

"It wasn't created in the Alpha's operating system so I need to find out which software created it."

"Hurry!" she ordered.

"I'm working as fast as I can!" Aggie rubbed my shoulder blade in contrition as I tried to increase my typing speed. I used the TYPE command to take a peek at the files. It looked like word processing text. Seeing that Word Perfect was the only word processing software Lemond had, I used that program to open the Rincon file. "This is going so smoothly, I'm getting worried." We all gasped.

"Lawd me!" Aggie cried. We crowded together on the bed like we were posing for a photo. We were looking at the mission statement of the WRF as it concerned their Rincon camp. I scrolled through the document. It contained their mission statement–your everyday white supremacist schlock and their goals. We didn't need to go any further.

"Well, I'll be horn swoggled!" Aggie exclaimed breaking the silence. "Look at this, Paloma!"

"I'm looking, I'm looking!" The file contained a list of equipment, including weapons, operations plans and ideas, existing site information, locations of future acquisitions. Everything you need to know to run a hate group. Most importantly, there was a list of names.

"We have to show this to the police. Or call Al," Clarice said.

"This is going to salt the bottoms of the whites," I said, doing an Aggie by jiggling my legs.

Aggie started to agree, then looked at us. "You're forgetting we haven't come by this information legally."

"Details!" Clarice gave a haughty shake of her head. "Paloma'll figure out a good lie."

"Thanks! What about my reputation?" I dodged Clarice's swatting hand. "Let's get the data first. I have to get the files off of the Gundersen com-puter. There's two ways to do this and both are going to be cumbersome."

"Why?"

"Because Lemond doesn't have enough disk space."

"He hasn't had this computer long and you're telling me it's full?"

"He's got a lot of software–graphics packages and such. They're very big files that eat up a hard drive. That's not including the games and he seems to have every one of those. I just tried deleting some of them, but he has the 'delete' function password-protected. I can most likely hack it, but it'll take time." They both nodded. "Lemond's PC has the communications software I need. I can copy the communica-tions information from Lemond's PC to mine and use another phone to connect with the phone of the plant's computer. The drawback is I'll have to break the connection we have now. We might not get it back."

"How would you get the other number?"

"I'd try numbers one up or down from the phone number that is set on Lemond's PC. Most companies buy a block of consecutive numbers."

"*You are so sneaky*," Aggie exclaimed, tweaking my cheek.

"What's the other way?" Clarice asked.

"Copy the files from Lemond's PC, then to diskette, take the diskette to my PC, copy the files down to it. This way is slower, but we won't purposely drop the modem connection. It's your call, girls." They both looked like Christmas choir ornaments sitting with their mouths opened into perfect Os.

"Let's play it safe," Clarice said. "Wouldn't it be better to have *some* information than none?" I nodded while looking at Aggie to see if she agreed. She bobbed her head.

"I need Heathcliff–my computer." Aggie seemed to levitate off the bed, and as soon as her feet hit the floor, she was running out of the house, my keys in hand, to the truck.

"Paloma, honey, what do you need? These things?" Clarice asked.

She held up a stack of CDs. "I wish. But no, I need diskettes. I have to use them because the CD's can't be over written with other data. Once I burn–which is sort of like copying–data onto them, it's permanent. Unfortunately diskettes don't hold nearly as much data as

CDs. And they take longer to load up with info. We just don't have any blank CDs."

By the end of that explanation, Clarice had fished out a large box of diskettes. "Shoot. The dang box is big but there's only three inside." I created another session so I could snoop further in the Gundersen system, if time allowed, while the copying process was going on.

Then a tap came from the window.

Clarice shrieked, tossing the diskettes she was holding into the air. I jumped twice—once from the noise and the second from Clarice's arm zooming dangerously close to me.

"It's me, Aggie."

"You scared us to death!" Clarice scolded as she slid the window up.

"Here, quick, Paloma," she said and shoved Heathcliff through the window. I just managed to keep it from thunking onto the floor. "Somebody's prowling around in the front yard."

Britain: Rolan Adams, a black teenager, was stabbed to death by a group of nine whites. Five were acquitted. The Adams family was told by callers they were glad their son was dead.–Time 8/12/91. The number of hate crimes from 1988-1990 rose from four thousand to six thousand, and the violence is increasing, British police sources say.

Chapter Forty-Five

Aggie struggled to get inside. I pulled her roughly through the window. Clarice grabbed a baseball bat from under Lemond's bed. "I don't think I was seen. I ran behind the fence." Wham! Wham! The door resonated the knock. The two women hollered but I didn't. I was too busy stuffing my heart back down my throat. I was fairly certain I wasn't traced as a hacker from the Gundersen plant to here, but in the tumult, I never got a chance to tell the ladies. Then I thought of Lemond and the hate crime data I'd been reading. It made me wish for a machine gun for protection.

"Girls, I'm going behind the easy chair. Paloma, you ask who it is. Do it from back here," Aggie commanded, "so they don't know someone is in the front room." She crouched down and disappeared into the darkness. Two more knocks sounded on the door.

"Beverly? You there? Are you okay? It's Esther. From down the road."

"I'm gonna kill that woman," Clarice threatened, sounding more sickly than fierce. "I've just lost the last of my good years." She stalked out of the bedroom to answer the door.

"I heard screaming. Is everyone all right?" Beverly asked as she groggily lifted her head up from the couch. Sleep had done nothing to soften the devastation her son's murder had etched into her face.

"You nearly put me into orbit," Clarice fussed to Lemond's neighbor before Aggie moved to close the bedroom door.

"Paloma, get back to the computer." Aggie pushed me gently, no trace of fright apparent. We both moved back to the desk.

"Okay, I assume the other files with city names are similar to the Rincon one. So we can just mark them to be copied instead of taking time to read them now." She nodded. "We can poke around other files and see what more we can get to nail those guys."

"Paloma, those ACC files could stand for accounting–"

"That's what I was thinking." I checked the system for a spread-sheet package, found Excel and started it. Meanwhile I booted up Heathcliff, created a batch file to copy the data from the diskette to the hard drive, then the diskette would be wiped clean. That way Aggie would have less PC tasks to do and it would hopefully save time. I cleared the diskette, then gave Heathcliff to Aggie. I downloaded information from the Gundersen computer until Lemond's PC ran out of hard drive space, then I compressed the files so they would take up less space and need less time to move them. That done, I copied them off of the PC to the diskette in the A drive then passed it to Aggie.

She shoved it into Heathcliff, ran the batch file which copied the data onto my hard drive and cleared the diskette. Lastly, she gave me back a clean disk for me to start the process over again.

"This is slower than molasses," Aggie reported.

"A watched computer never processes," I said.

"What is that, a high tech version of a watched pot never boils?"

"Yep."

"Not bad, honey." Pat, pat. We worked and waited, only the drone of computers and the window air conditioner could be heard.

The bedroom door opened and Clarice entered. "That heifer is just too nosy! She saw the lights on and came to see what was happening." No one spoke for a few moments, lost in watching the process.

Soon Clarice stood up and threw her hands in the air. "I can't take this, I have to clean out the refrigerator or something." She left the room but soon came back, sighing and tapping the floor with her foot restively. I checked the time. Backups would be starting soon.

"I have to go to the bathroom," I stood, my legs groaning from the movement. As I was zipping up, I heard a high female call, shrill enough to blow the wax out of my ears.

"What?" I yelled as I ran back into the room.

Clarice pointed like she'd found a body part in the Sunday salad. "We've lost connection." My elation, like a speeding train, slammed down into hell. Climbing over people and furniture, I bumped the keyboard and the screen lit up again. I collapsed onto the bed.

"The screen saver." I could barely talk.

"Clarice!" Aggie yelled.

"Aggie!" Clarice replied.

"Both of you!" I added.

"I didn't know!" they chorused.

"I think I damaged a valve," I admonished and stuck my hand between my bosom feeling my heart threatening to leap out of my chest.

"Lawd me!" Aggie interrupted. "Has anyone gotten on the machine?"

"No rest for the wicked," I jeered good-naturedly. I sat up, cracked my knuckles, flexed the fingers then clicked in the command. "Nope."

"That's good," Clarice said relieved.

"Yes, ma'am but the bad news is that only a few files have been transferred because of this laborious process we are going through. Someone should be getting to the plant for backups any time now. Let's hope they're late."

"Can't we try again tomorrow night?" Aggie asked.

"It's possible, if no one has realized I was in the plant's system. Tomorrow someone could be waiting for us. And they could have a trap set that traces back to me. They'll do more than just slap my wrists."

"I don't want anyone else hurt. What's an easier plan, honey?" Clarice asked.

"For the night operator to have a delay. I'll copy down what I can. We'll figure out the rest later. I'm going to ignore you for a bit–to try some things. I'll need good concentration. It's the time limit that is throwing us a curve ball." No one spoke as I mentally climbed into the system, fingers flying over the keyboard as I poked and peeked more heavily into the Gundersen computers.

In the corner of my mind, I heard whispering, saw movement, but didn't pay it much attention. I glanced up a few minutes later. Clarice was whis-pering to Aggie as the two women left the room. I heard them speaking to Beverly in the hallway. I turned my concentration back to the computer. It wasn't long before the front door slammed, then a car started up and drove away.

"Was it something I said?" I asked the empty room.

In 1980, TV repairman Tom Metzger won the Democratic nomination for Congress in San Diego. When defeated by his Republican opponent in the general election, he formed the White Aryan Resistance (WAR) and began a cable TV show called Race and Reason *(seen in more than thirty-five cities), created a racist computer bulletin board, and installed a toll-free hotline.*

Chapter Forty-Six

Clarice and Beverly sped down Blandford road, neither having a clue how to give Paloma the extra time she needed, both knowing they *had* to do something. They turned onto Highway 21, slowing only because of their fear of the local police. They pulled into the Walmart parking lot.

"I should be the one to do something."

"Like what?"

"I don't know, sister. You're the smart one. You're better at these things than me." They sat in the darkness, motor running. "I know!" Beverly shattered the quiet. "You drive down the road and park the car. I'll call in a bomb threat, a fire, anything. When the emergency vehicles come, you'll put the car in the middle of the road and block them," Beverly said uncharacteristically blasé, as if terrorist shenanigans were a family routine.

Clarice peered over her glasses at her sister. "A bomb threat? Girl! You crazy! I'm not sure the cops here would even know what one is. What if they don't take it seriously?"

"They have to. Fire and bombs are the only sure reasons they would clear the entire building. If they don't, I'll think of something else. You'll have your hands busy with the road watch. Come on now, keep your daubers up." Beverly walked resolutely to the pay phone and watched the car drive off and disappear down the road. She dialed the emergency number. When a female voice answered, she pinched her nose and spoke. "This is the Puritan White Army."

"What?"

"Shut-up and listen, girl! This is the White Puritan Army, I mean the Puritan White Army! We have placed a bomb in the Gundersen Plant in Rincon. We are doing this in the name of white people across America!" She repeated it two more times.

"Who are you?"

"It doesn't matter. Just know that we are gonna blow up the plant tonight! Right now!"

"What kind of bomb?"

"A *real* big one." Beverly almost giggled. She slammed down the receiver and left the lighted sidewalk to stand in the shadows.

Meanwhile, Clarice's teeth were chattering from fear. "I'm doing this for you Lemond and Dixie," she spoke aloud to have something to do. She parked the car at an angle, blocking most of the road. Rummaging under the seat for a flashlight she opened the trunk and

took out the road flares, lighting two and placing them a few feet away
from the car. Clarice hurried to the front and popped the hood. She
pointed the light at the main starter coil. Last year she'd lost the coil's
cap when it had come loose. She'd been stranded on a dark country
road for hours. That was the only thing she knew about cars, other
than where to put gas. As soon as she heard sirens, she yanked the cap
off and removed the coil.

Back in the parking lot, Beverly heard sirens and her heart leaped
with fear. She ran to the pay phone and dialed 911 again.

"I'd like to report a fire."

"What's the address?" An authoritative voice asked.

She gave the street name. "I heard this big boom and then I saw
smoke and fire." In the background she could hear the emergency
operator.

"Lieutenant, the bomb at the Gundersen Plant has been confirmed.
I have a caller reporting an explosion and fire." Into the phone he
spoke, "What is your name?"

"Oh, sweet Jesus! Look at the fire!" Beverly screamed as she hung
the phone up and collapsed against the wall. "I'm going to jail for
falsely reporting an emergency and then to hell for lying," she said
aloud.

As Beverly walked to the end of the parking lot, the wail of sirens
was closing in. She hurried through the fields that ran alongside the
road and just made it into the woods for cover when the police cars,
fire engines and ambulances turned onto the road.

She watched Clarice get out of the car. A parade of trucks and cars,
lights flashing, turned down the plant road and drove toward her sister.

Clarice waved her hands in the air and hurried toward the police
car. "What are you doing, woman? Can't you see we have an
emergency?"

"My-my car. It broke down. I can't start it."

"Sheee-it! You're blocking the road." He took a step toward
Clarice's car then stopped. "What are you doing down here anyway?
This road only goes to the plant." Clarice had no idea what to tell the
sheriff. Under his breath, just barely, she heard him utter a disgusted
"nigger", and watched him shake his head. She now had the nerve she
needed. She'd box his ears good, if she had to.

"Hey, sheriff, you gonna get that car outta the way so we can get to
the fire?" asked one of the paramedics who was walking toward them.

"I'm gonna need some help, sonny."

The emergency vehicles had pulled too close to the stalled car and
more time was lost as everyone backed up, the fire trucks taking the
longest to maneuver. Meanwhile, Clarice locked the car, slipped the
keys into her pants pocket. When the sheriff tried the door and it
didn't open, his ire was so evident on his face, even the EMS guys
chuckled as they watched him strut and swear.

Clarice made a show of searching her purse, not finding the keys,
searching again and again. Finally Grainger grabbed it and up ended

it onto the hood of the car. Her lipstick rolled into the darkness. She wasted more time hunting for it.

"Ma'am, check your pocket," the ambulance driver suggested with kindness.

"I don't ever put the keys there, young man." She didn't have the nerve to hold them up much longer. She patted the pockets then sheepishly grinned. "Well, I declare! You are a smart man. Who are your parents? Do they live in Rincon?" It was the Southern thing to do, inquire of the family lineage and profusely thank any and all who came to assist–no matter how small the contribution.

The technician started to reply but Grainger inter-rupted, ordering the young men to push the car onto the shoulder. While the heavy work was being completed, Grainger found other tasks to do. After checking a notebook that Clarice noticed was blank, he flicked his flashlight directly into Clarice's face, blatantly staring.

"Do I know you?" he asked gruffly.

"No, uh, sir." She looked squarely into the eyes of the pudgy man before her, knowing her body was visibly shaking. She thought of what he'd done to her daughter so that her edginess would slowly dissipate.

"All you coloreds look the same anyway."

"Yes, sir! I'll just call home for someone to pick me up at the Walmart." She made herself thank him and slowly walked toward the store. She heard the trucks drive off and waited a few seconds before looking behind her. The emergency vehicles were racing toward the plant. She ran back to the car taking the coil from her purse. She replaced it and burnt rubber getting away. It wasn't until she'd turned onto Blandford Road and was heading back toward Lemond's house that she remembered Beverly was not with her. She stopped the car in the middle of the road and debated. "It's too risky to go back there." Nevertheless, she turned the car around.

Racing out of the woods, Beverly ran down the road, yelling and waving, trying to get Clarice's attention. She had just reached Hardee's restaurant when an additional stream of cars, traveling from the north and south, turned onto the plant's road. She ducked down and hid among the azaleas lining the building. Beverly sat trembling, expecting Rincon Police to come riding into the parking lot looking for the person who'd called out the army. She didn't have a quarter for a call, but was not sure she'd risk walking into the open even if she'd had one.

"My stars and garters, my crazy sister!" Snorts of laughter shook her, turning into full-blown guffaws. Beverly was still cackling, tears streaming down her face, when Clarice returned to the parking lot to find her.

*   *   *

I wiped a few tears from my eyes when the two women finished telling their story. My stomach hurt from the strenuous laughter.

Beverly and Clarice stood in the living room, hysterically stomping their feet like Hungarian folk dancers and finished their tale.

"Beverly 'bout made me bust a gizzard string," Clarice managed to say between guffaws. "That and finding her sitting on the ground between two azaleas, making a devil of a racket! I'm about to wet my pants!" She hurried to the bathroom.

"I hope we gave you enough time," Bev said.

"I'm almost done." With the important data.

"I think this calls for a snack," Clarice announced, on a pit stop from bathroom to kitchen.

"Like what, friend?" Aggie asked.

"Something fattening. Let's get busy in the kitchen." I went back into the bedroom to check both activities I'd set up concerning Gundersen's records. Being an incurably nosy person, I'd played on the system and hacked my way into the plant's financial records–the legitimate ones. That's what I wanted to plunder now since I had more time. I was alone in Lemond's bedroom and the temptation was overwhelming.

I scrolled through the SWARTZ subdirectories, stopping at one named PERSONAL. Time to take a peek. The rent-a-cop turned plant manager may have been savvy enough to jump over a few rungs in the corporate ladder, but savvy computer user he was not. There was too much vital information on the system. He used a popular personal finance software package, but it was an older version. That meant the programs had been on the market long enough for cyber-punks to hack it to pieces. And share with other computer geeks, like me, worldwide.

Upgrades had changed with the times, adding security functions that his version did not have. Swartzman assumed his data was protected because the main computer systems had a few security checks. A typical assumption. But once you broke past the front door of the palace, the kingdom was yours. I checked the time, wanting to know how long it was going to take for me to crack Swartzman's accounts. I could brag later to my hacker friends–if I got through in good time.

As my usual hacking habit, I started with easy tricks, not really believing they'd work, but covering all bases. It was almost sad, Swartzman's vulner-ability. And this inadequacy was going to make him very angry. I just had to make sure he didn't find out that he should place his wrath on me. I checked the status of the download of the WRF data, flipped to the second session and I let my fingers do the walking through his personal data. Bingo! I was in. I noted the time, not one of my fastest hacking efforts. I clicked around the system until I found his stock information. Swartzman was wealthy– he owned an immense amount of blue chip stock. I spared a moment to reflect briefly on the principles of my profession. Then I initiated the actions that would allow Swartzman's assets to serve a better purpose for humanity. I transferred a portion of his stock into an account in

Rio de Janeiro. The transaction would be noted, of course, but the trail would stop at the bank. And they ain't talking. But Save the Amazon Rainforest and some of those orphans wandering the streets in Brazil would be.

Intent on quickly getting in and out of Swartzman's financials, I also needed to watch out for any coding that would jam me up later, like unknowingly leaving my footprint. I was so into the task I had leaned forward almost nose to screen with the monitor. Fingers and mind melding together to become one with the computer.

"So, almost done?" Aggie asked as she suddenly materialized in the room like an ectoplasmic entity. I was beyond tired of people sneaking up on me. If I'd been a cat, I'd have only one of the nine lives left.

"Paloma, you look as guilty as a fox in a hen house!" I'm not sure if I stuttered or sputtered. "What in tarnation are you doing?" I begrudgingly confessed then assured her I'd undo the deed.

"Put it back?! Are you stupid?" She sat on the bed beside me and gave my head a light thunk. "Close your pie hole, young lady. You're gonna draw flies." I gave her a friendly shove. She asked me for details. "Is that all the stock?"

"No. The plant shareholders have some," I told her.

"Let me see." We looked at the records. "Let's compare these names to that roster for the WRF." I found the information quickly. There were seven shareholders also involved in the hate group. Checking their personal information, they lived in three of the states where Swartzman had set up camps. "The government is just gonna seize all the assets when this meanness is exposed. The majority of the money will then be wasted. More eight hundred dollar toilets and such. At least this way some good's gonna come out of it."

"Are you sure, Aggie?"

"Now I am. Twenty years ago, maybe even ten, I'd have said no way. There's been times since then when I've wished I could do something like this–even things out. Make justice work when it hasn't for such a long time. And you aren't taking any of it for yourself." When she sighed, her shoulders slumped in resignation. "What have you got in mind to keep us outta jail, Robin Hood?"

"I'll take full responsibility–" was as far as I got.

"I'm in this up to my boobs like you. And I have a few ideas to keep us out of the poky." She wagged a finger at me, but it was a mean finger and I didn't argue further. I couldn't waste the time if I was going to continue hacking.

"Paloma, why is it so easy to wipe him out financially? I mean, if it's that easy, then why does anyone put anything on these darn contraptions?"

"It all depends on how the person sets up their software, their accounts. There are levels of protection–but you have to employ them. Also, you have to stay on top of the ways the systems are getting hacked. A man told me once that there is always someone staying up all night long, dreaming of ways to screw you over."

"A wise man. Who was it?"

"My father." I smiled briefly and continued my explanation. "I'm sure Swartzman wanted things simple for himself. Especially if he doesn't understand much about PCs. When he played around with stocks, he wanted to do just a few nifty things by computer. But he didn't protect himself by keeping others out. He should have set up roadblocks, even if it was something simple like needing a password to open the program. You can also block access to subdirectories and even files. I'm in his account as if I was he. I can do *anything* I want. The software doesn't know who is really accessing the program. Whoever has the code gets in. I have his.

"By the time Swartzman discovers the money is gone–it'll be too late. And then he'll only be able to trace the transaction. It'll point back to him and only show *what* and *how much* went *where*. He could raise a stink. I just have to make sure the smell does not point to me or Lemond's family."

"Besides, who's he gonna cry to!" She rubbed her hands together gleefully. "Let's do some more. What charities should Swartzman help out?"

"We need the account numbers for donations."

"Here's Al's." She pulled out her pocket planner, flipping through it. "I often have my bank transfer money into the Waving Girl Law Center fund." She gave me the numbers. "He uses that account for the *pro bono* work and to help clients who've been injured or had their business or homes wiped out by a hate group. That often takes a lot of money. If they are able to sue, you know how long that takes in the courts.

Sometimes there isn't much to get from the hate groups anyway. Al turns all the 'winnings' over to the client, but often they are left so destitute. And having to wait for years for a lawsuit to make it through court makes it a worse strain. The racists try everything to keep from having to turn over their assets. Some groups go under, over and around the law every time they blink.

"Last year a group who'd been instructed by the courts to turn over their land and building destroyed their Klavern then sold the land. It was illegal, but it was all over before they were caught. The guy who bought the land didn't know what had happened. He lost it and his money. The land wasn't worth that much. In another case, the hate group beat-up a couple who initiated a lawsuit. The victims were a family–husband, wife, three kids. Both parents suffered multiple broken bones and such. The woman lost her job–her dang boss wouldn't give her the time off to get better or keep her job open.

Sorry, Paloma, I'm wasting precious time. But suffice it to say, that was only the beginning of that families' problems. All because they wanted to raise their kids in a safe neighborhood. Cases like this are what Al uses some of the funds for."

"Good enough for me, friend. He needs all the cash he can get. What will he do when he finds the gift?"

"Can Heathcliff send a fax?"

"Of course," I said in mock indignity.

Aggie rolled her eyes. "Can you send an unsigned letter without Al knowing who sent it?"

"Yep. I could also send an email."

"Without it telling Al who it's from? At work it always says who is sending the email."

"It tells you what account is sending you the email."

"I thought you'd say something like that. And you have an 'un-Paloma' email account?"

"Several."

She snorted. "Don't know why I bothered to ask."

"I'll use a throw-away email account."

"What is that?"

"Throw-aways are the freebies that all Internet companies offer these days. They are very limited in functionality, but you don't have to give any personal information to have one."

"So it can't be traced back to anyone."

"Exactly. I can add and close as many throw-away accounts as needed, but my true email account is guarded and stays the same. Unfortunately, a *real* hacker, one intent on theft or damage, uses the same anonymous accounts. Pedophiles and other criminals use them, too."

"Let's use a throw-away to tell Al he's getting an anonymous donation. And, let's instruct him to give some of it to Lemond's family for burial costs and whatever."

"You're so bad, O Freckled One! Al would die if he knew." Where had I heard that before? Swartzman and his friends of hate appeared to sell a few more slices of his stock holdings. Aggie became so enthused about our criminal acts she was practically sitting on my lap. "Who's next?"

"Nobody, unless we have more account numbers."

"It says at the bottom of the screen, F2 is More Info." She pushed the key.

"Okay, who's doing this?" I asked in a good-natured growl. "You aren't supposed to read the instructions." She hurmpfhed in reply. Bless those programmers, a drop down menu listed several hundred non-profit and other types of organizations. Every social ill, every disease, every helpful idea, plan and cause was there from Green peace, March of Dimes to Save the Beach, Whales and Redwoods. I wouldn't have been surprised if Save the Mutant Ninja Turtles had a charity group.   The list contained contact infor-mation, banking instructions with electronic fund transfer availability. It was all set up, including bank routing numbers for deposits. I only had to click on money transfer, select how much, where-from and where-to. It was that easy.

"Let's choose some that Nazi will get real pissed about," Aggie suggested, an evil glint in her eye. We made a list from what we'd dubbed as Charities The WRF Is Least Likely To Support and transferred stock. As I logged off of Gundersen's computer, we discussed the chances of us sharing a cell in a federal prison.

In 1985, Tom Metzger was an invited guest of Louis Farakhan at a Nation of Islam rally. Metzger and his son John are the most successful recruiters of Skinheads in the movement. Metzger's daughter, Lynn, is a senior member of the Aryan's Women League, which helps WAR stop the "demasculinity of men by Jew-dyke feminists".

Chapter Forty-Seven

Aggie spoke to an attorney friend she trusted, relaying a stripped-down version of my hacking caper, leaving out the stock transfers, of course. We needed to know the best way for the data to be handed over to Al and Vontana. Because my hacking was illegal, the results from that would make it impossible to waltz into Al's office to present it. The attorney said something about fruit from a poisoned tree.

"What would happen if I had records of illegal doings, but the stuff was illegally obtained? Is there a way to get the information to law enforcement so that they could use it?" I waited impatiently for Aggie to complete the call. Even if Al couldn't use the information–I could. It let me know that I definitely was on the right track.

A few minutes into the call she offered her profuse thanks, snapped the cell phone shut and gleefully reported we were still in business.

"It's like we already thought. We can't let anyone know who sent the information."

"That may be hard to do. Al and Vontana will probably interrogate me as soon as they realize the data came from a computer."

"It's *us*, Paloma. I'm in this just as deeply as you." She grabbed my hand and squeezed. "We're going to send a copy to each of them. Agreed?"

"Agreed."

"I'm glad we don't have to mail them copies in an envelope. Knowing Al, he'd run over to the GBI and get Vontana to spare no resource in looking for trace evidence to find out who sent it. Speaking of the devil," she said as she answered her ringing cell phone. "Al," she mouthed to me. I was so excited about the data we'd gotten, it was hard not to grab the phone and spill my guts.

He had equally exciting news. Dixie was getting a special hearing tomorrow in another county. Al was petitioning that charges be dismissed and he would make every effort to get the violations of her rights into the court records.

"Sugah, I'd love to see you tonight, but I've got tons more work to do on Dixie's case."

"You're off the hook. For now." He hung up with a chuckle. I had plenty to work on myself. Besides getting the data copied and ready to send to Al and Vontana, I wanted to nose into it again.

The phones quiet, we retired into Lemond's living room. As the three women discussed funeral plans, I felt a tightening in my gut. The sadness and panic rising inside me. Beverly broke down each time she tried to speak–a distinct change from her earlier charge through the night with her sister outside Gundersen's. Clarice and Aggie administered to her superbly while I felt incompetently in the way. They finally convinced her to rest. She had to be steered into the bedroom and taught how to lie down. She eventually cried herself to sleep. I made light conversation for a few minutes, dramatically noticed the late hour, and drove back to the hotel.

My bare legs gave the bugs something to nibble on as I climbed out of the truck and hurriedly searched the cab and under the seats for needed items. In my haste, I jerked the pack out and when I slung it over my shoulder, the items tumbled out of the unzipped bag and onto the pavement. Not a toe seemed to have been missed. It only made sense that I bang my head on the way down to collect the gadgets. The phone rang. I fumbled around for it. "Paloma?"

"Aggie?"

"Well, I'm glad we've figured that out." She snickered. "Al called back. Do you want to ride with him to the arraignment? He..." A high-pitched sound came from around my feet. It was a foreign tone and it was loud.

"Wait a minute, Aggie!" I whipped down, quickly picking up the gadgets one by one, until I found the offending source. The little black box, one of two I'd taken from the WRF camp on the river, was the culprit. I gaped stupidly at it.

"What in tarnation is that noise, Paloma?"

"I'm not sure," I replied, shoving the phone between my shoulder and ear and turning the box over in my hands. Numbers flashed on the digital readout. Then I was sure. *"Merda!"*

"Lawd me! You keep yelling like that and I'll be gettin' a hearing aid."

"Aggie call me back immediately." When I answered her call I ignored her questions. I gripped the box, waiting. I shook it, like that would make it hurry up and work. "Hang on, hang on, Aggie. Let's see if..." Ting! Ting! "I think I got it. Call back again."

"All right, but you *better* tell me then."

I leaped several times in the air joyfully. I'd felt guilty not letting the GBI guys know that I'd snitched two of everything that night on the river, keep-ing one set to play with–to dismantle and discover it's function. Now I was glad of my foresight. I'd just figured out the impetus of what was happening in Rincon. The phone rang again.

"HallelujahthankyouJesus! Ag! Talk to me, *Mama*!"

"Ag? Mama? What are you carrying on about?" The box sounded. I stared eagerly at the LED panel. The same numbers flashed again.

"Yes! Yes! Honey, we ain't just a'cookin', wez a'cookin' grits!" I bossa nova-ed around the truck and salsa-ed backwards waving the phone and the box over my head. The desk clerk checked me out warily through the front glass. I gave him a Brazilian boob shimmy while I squatted and shook my hips. I ended by blowing him a kiss. He didn't attempt to catch it.

"Wooo!" I calmed, leaning against the truck.

"Paloma! Are you there?" I jerked my head up, put the phone to my ear. "Sorry, Aggie."

"Now if you don't tell me what's going on, young lady, I'm going to come there and beat the stuffing out of you. You'd make a preacher cuss."

At the risk of making her more angry, I giggled at her colloquialisms. "Aggie, the black boxes are used to defraud."

"Okay. So?"

"It's picking up cellular phone signals."

"Will you explain it–in English?"

"The black box was on when you called. A few seconds later it beeped, gave a digital readout of your ESN–electronic serial number–and did it again when you called back."

"It's that easy? You mean, someone could be getting my signal and calling their drug connection in Timbuktu?"

"Basically."

"How?"

"You asked," I warned.

"Explain it simple, Paloma."

"Okay. When you make a cell call, your phone broadcasts your ESN."

"Right. The sales rep said it was uniquely mine."

"It is. The ESN verifies the phone call and its billing. But, the ESN periodically broadcasts, making it stupidly easy to defraud by using those numbers."

"So how does the box work?"

"It bites the info right out of the air–your phone number, the ESN, manufacturer, and the number dialed. All you need to do is reprogram a counterfeit chip and plug it into another cell phone."

"By the time the fraud is discovered, the crooks have moved on to another signal," she joined in.

"Right," I agreed. "Besides, with each new gadget designed to make life easier, there's always someone staying up..."

We finished together. "All night dreaming of a way to use it to screw you over!"

"So the plant in Rincon is making illegal devices to pick up that signal?" Aggie asked.

"They could be doing it legally."

"How?"

"The same boxes could be used to program and repair legitimate cell phones."

"And I thought I only had to worry about brain cancer. Is this fraud the newest thing in criminal behavior or have I been living in a closet?"

"The cellular phone companies don't want to make the fraud public because their consumer market hasn't been saturated."

"Money!" she spat it out. "It all comes down to cash and they haven't made enough of it yet."

"Exactly. But it's not such an issue that you should throw your car phone away. On newer phones there are improved security options. But most people don't employ them."

"Why not?"

"Well, Aggie, did you activate your security?"

"I don't know what you are talking about. When I bought the phone, it wasn't mentioned. Why is that? Wouldn't that be a great sales feature?"

Most sales people push convenience over security, because most cell phone users want just that. I can help you secure your phone later."

"What else do you know about cell phone fraud?"

"The largest cell companies in California wouldn't give me the time of day when I called for information, even though some have their own fraud department. I had to pester the Secret Service. And they haven't learned yet how to return a phone call."

"You are plum full-up with useful info."

At least she didn't say it was useless. "It's fun to learn and the toys you get to play with are fabulous."

"Let me see if I got this right. Some turd gets one of those boxes, turns it on and when someone uses their cell phone, this machine picks the ID number out of the air.

"Yes, ma'am."

"How do they then get the number?"

"I'm looking at yours right now on the read-out!"

"Lawd me! How can it be so easy to do so much damage?" Before I could reply the line clicked. "Hang on, honey. Someone's on the other line." Call-waiting. Yes, I hate that. While I'm placed on ignore, the person is determining which caller is more important. I busied myself with the backpack. "Paloma?" Aggie's voice was high, excited. "Al's on the other line. I was telling him about that box thing. He wants me to give him more information. Hold on."

With another flick of her finger, I was forced to endure more waiting. I laid the phone on the seat, turned the black box off and squeezed it into the bulging pack. That's when things turned wiggy.

Uh-uh-um. A grating sound behind me. Human. Suddenly my mind was propelled back to Seal Beach. On the couch. The mere thought of that night violated me again. A sudden degrading stench washed over me. The pack slipped from my fingers. I froze.

I was jerked around, shoved backward, pinned down on the seat. A hand cupped my chin, fingers spread out like an umbrella, then tightened.

"Look at me." He spoke in grunts. I could feel his chest against mine rising, falling. My face was squeezed like a melon, nerves sliced pain down my cheeks.

"*Look at me!*" That sound–clearing of the throat in short quick bursts. My eyes focused then locked. I was toe to toe with The Voice.

1988–Greg Withrow of Sacramento, California, was the head of the Aryan Youth Movement (part of Tom Metzger's White Aryan Resistance). When Withrow had a change of heart and resigned, his former friends broke into his apartment and beat him with baseball bats, warning him not to talk. Several weeks later, he was kidnaped, hung crucifixion style, and nails were driven into his hands. Withrow was succeeded as president by John Metzger, the son of Tom.

Chapter Forty-Eight

Aggie alerted Al, who alerted Bruce Vontana of the GBI, who alerted the police about Paloma's disappearance. Al found his cousin sitting beside Paloma's borrowed truck, sobbing. He let her vent her anger and did not speak until the last accusation died on Aggie's lips and sobbing took over again. The parking lot of the small inn soon filled with official vehicles. They used the manager's office for a command center and were packed like bait into the tiny space.

The desk clerk didn't have much to tell. "I saw her dancing around the truck, talking into the phone and I went back to my paperwork. A few seconds later, I thought I heard something outside. I glanced out the window–saw the truck with the door open, the dome light was on. That was it. Then I heard a car tearing out the parking lot. As it passed out of the driveway, I thought I saw the girl in it. I glanced over at the truck, saw the door was still open, the light on. I went to check it out. When I made it to the truck, I heard a woman howling through the phone. I gave her directions here. Then all you guys showed up."

"What about the type of car?"

"It drove away so fast, I couldn't get any details."

"Aggie," Vontana said gently taking her hands. "Tell us everything again, every detail Paloma said about the black boxes." Aggie relayed the information.

"Do you know what it means, Bruce?" Al asked. The GBI agent shrugged. They all took turns dissecting the information Paloma had discussed with Aggie.

Aggie stifled a sob. "Why are we standing around supposing and mighta' being? Where the hell is she and who has her? The Klan again?" No one spoke. "Y'all are to blame." She pointed to Stabenski and Vontana. "You wouldn't give her an hour of your time to check anything out. You brushed her aside and belittled her. Bruce, you better pull out all the stops to get her back. And do it now!" After a brief penetrating glare at both agents, she rose and walked wearily out of the room.

*   *   *

Leroy Anderson, the head of finance for Gundersen Enterprises, stood facing Swartzman, whose color had drained from his face.

"Boston had the stocks transferred with my authorization to sell. I confirmed it last night before I went home. I get here this morning and nothing."

"Nothing?" Swartzman asked.

"Zero. *Nada*. Zip."

"I get it. What I don't get is, what happened?" Swartzman stood, but this time the man didn't cower.

"You can *not* blame this on me! There is a system for auditing myself and my employees. It'll prove that *I* didn't do it."

"Then who could it be?" He talked through jaws so tight he'd need dental work.

"My guess is somebody in the plant."

"I know that, idiot! Who else could it be? The little old lady down the street?"

"You don't have to get snippy with me."

"If you don't have anything useful to tell me, get out." He snatched the phone up so fast he spilled his morning coffee. "Damn!" Swartzman slapped at other articles on the desk and sent them flying. He phoned the assembly line manager. "Send Willie in here now!" He watched the clock until the man arrived.

"When was the last time you talked to that Imperial Whatssit?"

"Hughes?" Willie asked.

"Who else?"

Willie adjusted his cap nervously. "Coupla days. Why?"

"Call him. I want you to find out if he called in those bomb threats. Act like you're enjoying the fact that I'm pissed as hell." Swartzman turned the phone base so that it faced Willie.

"Sorry you had to wait, Willie. I had a customer," Hughes apologized when he answered the call. "Have you heard anything else on this Moonpie-Randy situation?"

"Nobody's said pea turkey to me. That ain't why I called. I wanted to know if you and the guys did something last night at Gundersen?"

"What do you mean?"

"I just saw Swartzman." He explained about the bomb. "He's got a swarm of bees in his bonnet." Willie took the note pad Swartzman held out to him. "Apparently it cost him a heap of money in lost production," he said reading the first line his boss had scribbled. "The cops are giving him the devil."

It was a moment before Hughes spoke. "So he's really upset?"

"I ain't never seen him like this. He's got veins a' popping outta his forehead," Willie sniggered. "And his face looks like a tow sack a' turnips." Swartzman shot his employee a warning look. "So, did you do it?"

"Why do you want to know?"

"Whaddya mean? I'm Klan. I know I ain't been to meetings lately but that ain't my fault. It's Swartzman. He's a real slave master." Willie spoke truthfully but looked down at his shoes so he'd have nerve to continue. "Besides, I cain't stand the man. This bomb thing made my entire day. That was real smart, whoever done it."

"Weeelll," Hughes said, drawing out the word. "It wasn't nothing big, but sometimes it's the little stuff that does it. Now you don't breathe a word of this to anyone, you hear?" This was a bonus for the Imperial Wizard. Let that Kraut see that the Klan could push his buttons for a change. Calling in a bomb, that *was* clever. He wished he'd thought of it himself.

"Not a word to anyone, Hughes. I appreciate you puttin' your confidence in me." Swartzman made a cutting motion across his neck. "Well, Imperial Wizard, I best be gettin' on."

"What did he say?" Swartzman asked a split second after Willie hung up.

"He says it was his idea, but he wouldn't say who done it."

"You handled that real good, Willie. Now get back on the line. Close the door behind you." He leaned back into his chair and closed his eyes. Just what the hell was the Klan up to? Did they have the brains to get into his computers? Not the Klan boys he'd met. But somebody had been up to something last night.

"Mildred, get somebody from the Computer Department in here this instant!"

Oregon: 1988, Portland–Mulugeta Seraw, an Ethiopian student, was attacked by Skinheads as he got out of a friend's car. They beat him to death with a baseball bat. The Skinheads were arrested for murder. In 1990, the Southern Poverty Law Center filed suit against Tom and John Metzger, of the White Aryan Resistance on behalf of Seraw's family, charging they were the masterminds of the attack. A $12.5 million judgment was won.

Chapter Forty-Nine

The morning sun blanketed the land. Al had finished the dawn chores for his small farm as soon as he'd come back from the inn. The cow, three horses, seven pigs, eleven chickens, and one macho stud rooster had all been fed. He set the timer for the lawn sprinklers and the four acres of crops that stretched out on the east side of his house. He checked the time. Almost 6:00 A.M. He had a few minutes and would squeeze out every second.

He enjoyed the smell of freshly misted crops in the morning and evening. He often wound down from a long day by standing in the spray. He'd lean on the fence and just breathe deep–the aroma of Mother Nature–the smell of the land. A Southern man was nothing without his land.

He loved helping people, worked hard at it. But he also needed the farm. Both were a part of life, of him. Al could not endure the long hours, frequent travel, threats against him, the loneliness, and the steady stream of cases illuminating all the pain and injustice, without this peaceful refuge to soothe his mind and soul.

All it missed was a family. He only had Aggie. His mother's marriage to Grainger, Sr. had driven a wedge into his heart. As much as he loved her, he could not accept her life. Nor could he count a Grainger as family. In the beginning he'd tried, but he always left his mother's new home feeling the need to bathe. And, too, he felt he was deceiving the people he helped.

Al sat in the gazebo, shaded from the sun by a cluster of magnolia trees. Their blossoms were big and beautiful. Like Paloma's eyes. Where did that unexpected thought come from? Paloma. Gone in the night. His temper flared. He gazed at the crops and the forest beyond, telling himself to be calm. Southward, he could see the tip of the large pond–a lake, Aggie called it–one of the best features added since he took ownership of the property. He yearned for a peaceful day of fishing from the bank of that water.

Quiet times would elude him for a while. He knew this, it happened often when he was knee-deep in a case. But it wasn't Dixie's problems he was thinking of this early morning. He had other things weighing on his soul. Al, whom many considered almost saintly, had an enormous case of the guilts.

He often lay awake at night, keeping old wounds festering, and flogging himself for his mistakes. Last night another weight was added to his overburdened shoulders. Paloma. This hard-headed, vivacious young woman who'd barged into his life. And awakened a yearning he'd believed he'd quashed through his long hours at the Center.

Thinking of her, he made a thin attempt at a smile. How strong–no, fierce was a better word–the friendship and loyalty was between her and Dixie. Paloma. Demanding, challenging him, shouting Portuguese curses one moment, laughing and looking at everyone vivaciously wide-eyed the next. And she was mouthy. That full mouth, he wanted to kiss it, to crush his lips into hers. To hold her and be held. Smell the scent of her perfume. It had been so long. Why had he sold her short? Al looked at his watch. It was time to leave for court, to help Dixie. Time to pick up Paloma at the hotel. But that was useless. She wasn't there.

He stood and punched the post, accomplishing only physical pain. But it was nothing compared to the emotional and mental pain pressing down on him. Damn your soul to hell, Al Eason! Admit the truth. Above all, he'd betrayed her.

*   *   *

Did I face Randy and The Voice with the tough girl persona I generally hide behind? Yeah. For a while. A cover was on my head. The Voice shoved it over me as soon as I got in the car. I was blind to what was happening, where we were going. We drove over bumpy roads then went inside a building. The room became the Chamber. They forced me into the chair–the condemned–strapped in. My shirt was ripped open. Randy giggled like a kid, making lewd comments.

I was more concerned with the darkness caused by the hood than any degradation this yahoo could come up with. I think it was Randy's idea to use me as an ashtray. In time, the additional burns didn't seem to increase the pain, just spread it around.

The Voice was good. He had to be a graduate of the Dr. Joseph Mengele school. Knew exactly what to do. I lost it then–after the first jolt. My throat was dry and raw from the screams. My body was out of control, muscles seemingly ripped away as they clenched violently. After an appropriate interval, I got it again. That's when I smelled smoking skin. Mine.

Later, I remember bucking and jerking–it came from out of nowhere– although no volts were being applied. Only my head was free. I thrashed it around like a weapon, striking everything that came near me. I was wild. As they righted me and the chair, I revved up again. I knew it was useless. But every cell inside me shrieked alive. I couldn't stop. To stop was surrender. Acceptance, defeat.

Randy loosened the ties on the hood. My head aimed toward the smell of him. Thwack! He cursed me, said I nearly broke his jaw. Wish I had. My head smarted where I'd made contact, but I liked that I'd hurt him. He grabbed me in a headlock and with his free hand, fondled my breast. When he didn't get the reaction he wanted, for revenge he smeared his thumb around the burns like he was mashing pesky ants. Then he pulled the hood up, just enough so I could see. Once my eyes adjusted, I looked around. The Klavern. A third guy was in the corner. Just standing there with his mouth open, beady eyes darting around. One hundred percent goober. The type of guy who, no matter what age, would fart loudly in a crowd, then snigger about it with his buddies.

I stared at him with loathing, used it as a diversion from what was happening around me. The goober glanced at me, looked at Randy. Then to The Voice, back to Randy. So gutless, he couldn't stare at either one with any conviction. I spit at him once when his eyes flitted my way. No saliva, my throat and tongue swollen and desert dry. But he knew what I meant. Still tied to the chair, I lunged, snarling, eyes locked on him. Every fiber of my being sent out my loathing and hatred to him. I wished it could be tangible, to seep into him. Like poison. Injure and hurt. He jumped slightly, growing pale. Good. I hoped the image of me in that chair haunts him until his last painful, rasping breath. He just stood there, staring.

Randy and The Voice fought over who'd get me first. And it was going to be bad because I wasn't cooperating. "Let me have a turn wid' 'dose thangs."

"You don't know what you're doing," The Voice told him. "You have to be very careful or you'll kill her–before we need to." Randy didn't like to hear the word no. The Voice tried to make a deal. "We'll get the information, have our fun, then you can do whatever you want." They slapped at each other, then a full-blown fight ensued. Randy pulled a gun. With his tail between his legs, the goober in the corner ran out of the Klavern. I heard a car crank and drive off.

"Randy, put the gun away," The Voice hurled out angrily. Randy took his time. The Voice went for his legs. In the tussle, the gun fired. The Voice let out a yelp. As I watched, I silently hoped they'd shoot each other dead. Randy broke away after kicking The Voice in the head a few times. That gave him just enough time to drag me, tied to the chair, out the back door of the Klavern. He pulled the cover down over my head again and tied it.

*   *   *

"You know lately, Mrs. Aggie, just as soon as there's some good news, something bad happens to take that happiness right outta my heart."

Aggie understood Clarice all to well. Dixie's change of venue was a good sign. They were carpooling to the courthouse. But the good news was tainted by the sadness of Paloma's disappearance.

"Vontana will find her. They have a lot of people looking." Aggie turned into the parking lot of the county courthouse just as Grainger was escorting Dixie into the prisoner entrance. He was sweaty, his face sunburned and set in anger. *"Good for him,"* she thought and smiled. Arm in arm, she and Clarice climbed the steps.

* * *

"Don't you jerk me around, Swartzman. Where's my money?" Shawn Munson spoke tersely into the phone.

"Leprechaun, you'll get your money. There's been a little snag."

"And what might that be?"

"Damn computers. I don't know why everyone raves about them."

"The money, Kraut!"

"Now there's no call for that. It's not my fault! There's been some kind of computer problem in Boston. It'll be fixed soon. You know how these things are."

"I *don't* know. You got till 1700 hours."

* * *

Aggie sat beside Clarice and turned around, looking the spectators over. The support group was there, three rows of people strong. News had spread around Lemond's neighborhood, and many of them had joined the islanders today. Those just meeting Lemond's family expressed their sorrow, many commenting they'd liked the young man's cheerful, helpful way.

The eyes always told the story. It broke Aggie's heart seeing so much pain in all of them. Aggie scanned the other side of the courtroom, noticing all white people sitting on the opposite side. She could almost hear the thoughts of people as they entered the room, scanned the crowd, then sat on the side of their color. Sometimes she believed the only thing that had changed since desegregation was that the signs were no longer posted.

She scrutinized every face, wanting to remember as many as possible. Whoever orchestrated Paloma's disappearance would probably be here, looking smug. It was all she could do to sit still. She wanted to snatch up each and every spectator. Slap them until one talked. And she'd start with Grainger. Then his silly deputies, two of whom stood proudly beside him.

"Al, look at those three over there," Aggie whispered as she leaned toward him. "This ain't a court, it's a simp convention."

He smiled wanly at his cousin. "You should have brought your cross-stitch."

"I did. But I can't concentrate today." His eyes showed the devastation he was feeling. Dixie, so scared and sad sat, head down, beside him. They'd broken the news to her about Paloma, knowing she'd be looking for her as soon as she entered the courtroom.

"The judge made good on his promise for extra security," Al told his cousin.

"That's one thing you don't have to worry about." She patted his shoulder encouragingly. Turning sideways in his chair, Al took Dixie's hand and reached across for Aggie's. The rows of friends formed a chain.

*   *   *

I could hear cars passing by. That was all I knew. No. It wasn't.
I was in a car trunk. There was a cover over my head. Randy Beamon
had been there. Or had I dreamed it? So dark beneath the cloth hood.
It was hot. When was daylight? It'd be even hotter then. Oh, God,
no! I was trapped inside a trunk!

Austria: 1992, Vienna–Five teenagers, sixteen to eighteen years old, were arrested for the desecration of a Jewish cemetery. Pamphlets with semantics and misspellings common to German Ku Klux Klan groups, suggest help was received from across the border.

Chapter Fifty

"They're on to you, man. You better clean house pronto."

"Huh? What are you talking about?" The agent hurriedly explained that their secrecy had been compromised. Their group and present actions were known to the GBI. Swartzman felt his stomach drop to the floor. It was all crumbling around him. Everything he'd worked so hard for. "How, Evan?" He could barely get the words out.

"I'm not sure. The big shots have been in a meeting all morning. All's I heard was they'd found out there was a new group in town. I'll tell you more as soon as I find out. I gotta go."

"You call if they move on this."

"Yeah."

Swartzman would have to be surprised later. He called for the WRF boys and while he waited for their arrival, he retrieved a file of mobilization plans he'd made just for a time like this. He thought he'd never have to cut and run. So much work and planning to make sure he wouldn't fail. And now to leave, hide, start it all over again. Damn! Well, before he left, he'd be sure to take no prisoners. Whoever got in his way would die.

He asked Red to come in alone. "Watch the GBI building for any signs of mobilization." Red left, proud to be considered for the special task. "Send the others in."

"Okay, we have a lot of work to do." He gave orders as he moved down the list. They had trained for this. He was confident that when the cops came, he'd have the pleasure of looking at their shocked faces as they found just what he'd told the whole town he was running here–a computer components plant. His only worry, really, were the weapons. There was no law about having a group like the WRF. That was his right under the Constitution. Most of the guns weren't. He set up extra security at all the gates and surrounding areas while the men worked.

*   *   *

Fish rose up in the air, gracefully arching forward to disappear back into the water. The dolphins could talk. Papa was shrimping. The wind blew his hair. Gran was there. We finally talked her into going on the boat with us. She couldn't swim. But then she could, the dolphins said so. She dove in the water, laughing, and became a mermaid. The dolphins chattered and swam with her. I called after her, "Gran, can I be a mermaid, too?"

* * *

The judge visibly winced as he looked at the color printouts of Dixie's injuries. Al laid out the other evidence, or the lack of it. Peering over his glasses, the judge stared at each person as they took their turn on the stand. Then the judge called Grainger before the bench. Dixie's body shook like it was ninety-five below, not another sweltering day.

Al whispered in her ear. "You're doing good. Just take deep breaths." He rubbed her back for a moment, then kept his hand there to comfort.

"She attacked two officers," Grainger said. "I bet she was doped up."

"Did you take blood or urine samples?"

Grainger crinkled his nose at the thought. "No."

"Then let's stick to the facts–if you have any." Al had assured everyone that this judge was "color blind". Dixie kept cautioning herself not to get her hopes up. "You mentioned attacks on your officers. What were their injuries?"

Grainger leaned toward the judge whispering as he rationalized Dixie's beating. "I think you'd agree, your honor, that you would even go after Mother Teresa if she was beating you to a pulp." The deputies sniggered in response.

The judge said loudly. "I think I have enough information to study. The court will..."

"Your honor, may I speak?" All heads turned to the aisle where a man, slight of build, walked resolutely toward the judge.

"Look who it is Al!" Aggie tugged his shirt. "What's he up to?" Al shook his head and tensed, already forming an objection.

"Identify yourself."

"Lester Abrams, Federal Marshall in the Rincon District Court. I have information you need to hear before you make your decision on this case." Dixie leaned over the table, her sobs echoing in the courtroom.

* * *

Talk at Bessie's Styling Salon focused on one, and only one, subject–Randy and Moonpie. "I heard tell that Moonpie was carryin' Randy's baby." The women squealed in horror and denial.

"That can't be," Martha said, not wanting to believe it for Moon pie's sake but knowing anything could happen when Randy Beamon played a part in it. "My husband Kyle's first cousin, once removed, is related to those Beamons. Mind tell you, ain't none of them act like that Randy." She wanted to be sure that these ladies knew that neither she nor her husband had close kin who were *that* tacky.

"Go on with the story, Bessie." Enid urged.

"I heard tell that when Moonpie told Randy about the baby he off and went berserk."

"Oh." they chorused.

"Y'all know Randy, he has his way with everything. He's been coming over to Moonpie's trailer," she glanced down in what she hoped was a modest and ladylike manner. "He's been gettin' it from Moonpie for a long time."

"Eeww! Gross! Lord'a mercy!" In high-pitched echoes around the shop.

"Why didn't she call the cops?" Enid asked, then added, covering her mouth daintily. "Maybe she likes it." Another chorus of yucks and eews was the reply.

"Would you call the cops on Randy?" Martha asked. The women shook their heads.

"He threatened to kill her if'n she did." That part wasn't really true. But it sure did sound like something Randy would do. "Well, just look at what he did to her when she tolt him about the baby," Bessie added as if someone had challenged her contribution to local gossip.

"Poor Moonpie," Martha murmured. "I guess we should go visit her. Take her a casserole or somethin'."

"You're crazy if you think I'm going over there," Enid said resolutely. "Randy might come by and no telling what he'd do to us." The women agreed. "She'd probably hiss at us, throw the food in our faces."

"Well, truth be told, I was hoping y'all would say something like that. I ain't never cottoned to that girl," Martha confided. "She bein' loose as a goose, most of her life."

"My husband says talk at the plant is she got what she deserved," LouAnne offered. "I'm gonna tell you the God's honest truth. As sure as the sun'll shine, you can always count on that Moonpie to be slinging it out of both drawer's legs."

"Maybe this will teach her to behave like a Christian lady."

* * *

Al hugged Dixie, who was still stunned that the ordeal was over.

"I'm sorry what happened to you, Miss," Marshall Lester Abrams said to Dixie. "I had to overlook it when it was just their mouths spoutin' hate, but there ain't no call to do what they did to you. I would have contacted you, Mr. Eason, but I only found out about the change of venue this morning."

"At least you got here. We can't thank you enough. Do you realize that with testifying about racism in the Rincon court system–especially that judge–and Grainger and his deputies, that you may be in danger?"

"Yes, sir. I got my pistol on me. Me and the misses are taking a few days off 'til the ruckus dies down." They shook hands and quickly left the building. When Al turned to talk to Aggie, he saw her brown head disappearing through the door. He bade a hasty "be right back" to Dixie and followed his cousin. Outside, he rushed up to her and Gary. His partner shook his head.

"I'm sorry, no word on Paloma."

Al looked at the ground as he felt hope vanish. "I'm such an idiot..."

"We promised, cousin. You did good today for Dixie. She'll be leaving here with us." Aggie squeezed his shoulder and stood up on her toes to give him a peck on the cheek. "Let's use our energy to find Paloma."

* * *

But I was Catholic in Brazil, Aunt Lilly! We went to Mommy's church in Brazil and Daddy's church in America. So I can pray both ways. Why can't I be Catholic and Baptist, too? I'm sorry I knelt down in church and embarrassed you.

"Bless me Father, for I have sinned. It's been four years, no five. Six? Let's just say it's been a long time since my last confession." Darkness.

* * *

"Sheriff Grainger, a man named Swartzman's been calling the station for you about every half hour. I didn't tell him where you was."

"Good job, Shearhouse."

"You comin' back to Rincon?"

"Eventually. I have to run a few errands."

"What you want me to tell that guy when he calls back?"

"You haven't seen me. I'll check in later." Grainger left the courthouse, planning to drive as far from Rincon as possible.

* * *

"Chinaman, where's the girl?" Swartzman growled to The Voice.

"I told you Randy took her after he shot me. Ohmygod it hurts! I thought you didn't care about her."

"I do as long as the diskettes are missing! What happened?"

"Can't this wait? I got a bullet in my ass." He squeezed his eyes tight.

"That's better than one in your head. Talk to me. You and that other idiot were supposed to get the diskettes and kill the girl. What went wrong at the Klavern?" The doctor hurried into the examination room, shocked that the man before him helping the WRF supremacists group was Asian.

"Man, I can't believe you brought me to this quack. He's just a sot."

"You want me to take you to a hospital? Then you can explain everything to the police."

"Give me something for the pain. I can't take it anymore. Please!" Doc turned his back on the men and prepared a syringe.

"I'm losing blood big time. How bad is it, Doc? Oh man, the pain! Hurry up and give me something for the pain!"

"Shut up, you pantywaist. It's not that deep of a wound. You weren't shot point blank." Doc took a step toward The Voice, holding the syringe out before him.

"You quack, that needle's big enough for a horse!" The Voice laid his head down wailing loudly as Doc made the injection as long and painful as possible.

*　　*　　*

"I got the diskettes, man. And I got the girl."

Swartzman stopped cleaning out his file cabinet to talk to Randy. He wasn't in the mood. He'd just left Doc's and was knee deep in his office bug-out procedures. "Bring the diskettes to me. *Now!*" He shouted into the phone.

"Uh-uh."

"You're too stupid to play these games, Randy! You're gonna get your ass blown away."

"Fifty thousand dollars."

"Eat shit." Swartzman disconnected the call.

Randy called back immediately. "Forty thousand."

"I'll give you ten and might let you live."

"I'll call you."

*　　*　　*

The tire iron. I awoke with it digging in my back. I turned sideways in the cramped space, pushing up with my bound hands. Pain rippled through every muscle of my tortured body. When my torso cleared the floor, I swept my hands across, pushing the tool as far as I could before I collapsed exhausted.

Thirst took my mind momentarily away from the heat. I feared I would suffocate soon in the stale, thin air. I moved against the rear of the trunk and grappled with the tire iron until I got it in my hands. On my back again, I took the tool and carefully tried to pry the tape from around my neck. I quit after doing nothing more than scraping skin and drawing blood. In frustra-tion I lashed out at my small tomb, hitting, kicking and banging my head. I screamed until my voice became twitches of hoarseness.

*　　*　　*

No one was speaking anymore, Aggie noticed. When one of the phones rang they'd all look up expectantly. Then the answerer would shake their head. No news. Paloma's grandfather had called. He'd wanted to come there, but Al finally talked him out of it. *No telling what we'll find,* she thought, *I know that's what Al's thinking.*

In the short time she'd known Paloma, she'd grown to love the girl. She liked people who were forthright and sincere. And Paloma was impatient, like her. *Where are you, girl?* She walked around, searching for Al, even-tually locating him down by the river. "Honey, you beatin' yourself up again?" she asked, joining him.

"I've been such an ass to her."

"Yep. You have."

Al's eyes misted over. "Thanks. You certainly tell it with the bark on."

"You didn't say that to get my pity." She sighed and kept her voice level. "Al, honey, you get along with people of all races. You just have trouble with other sexes. Paloma knew you'd be mad."

"Then why did she keep on digging?"

"Her friend, doofus! Besides, who are you to dictate what she does? Why do you take her snooping around as a personal assault against you?" When he didn't answer, she continued. "Poor Al. You've been consumed with saving the world. You and Vontana. Have you forgotten that you aren't the only ones who can do it?"

"Is that what you believe?"

"Yes. Only Vontana's not as eat up with it as you are."

"What I've done for others, or tried to, has never been to assuage my ego."

"I never thought that for a minute. For so long, it's been you, then your small Center battling people, hate groups, for the government to take a stand. It's warped your thinking."

Al almost laughed. Could she be correct? "Aggie, I never thought Paloma couldn't help out. She has her own skills to bring to the situation."

"Right, but you keep wanting to control her and how she utilized them." Aggie snorted. "And Paloma won't have none of that offa you!"

"I'm not like that all the time. Or am I?"

"Doesn't Gary and Kevin have to reign you in every so often?" He signed and nodded. "Then you went bonzo and told Paloma she was too young."

"I said she was young."

"Glad you cleared that up! Make you feel better? I'm sure it will to Paloma, too."

"You are a pain in my backside, cousin."

"You wouldn't have it any other way."

"I can't understand why she kept digging when her life was in danger."

Aggie stood rigid in disbelief. Al looked back at her puzzled. "Dang, Al. I'm waitin' for the punch line. Did you *hear* what you just said?" He nodded. "Well?"

"Well what?"

"Lawd me!" She clapped her hands together and roared back in laughter. Al's bafflement deepened. "My stars and garters! I don't believe you! *You* can't fathom why any one would help out another when danger's involved? That's you, Al! You're up to your crack in security. You got a target on your back and a boat load of white guys begging to be first in line to pull the trigger. Now don't go gettin' your bowels in an uproar! There's more I got to say and you're gonna listen."

Al crossed his arms against his chest, settled in defeated.

"You help people you don't even know. When you first started lawyering, you had to practically beg hate crime victims to let you sue the groups that were responsible. That put them in a whole lotta danger. Now, think what you would have done if it had been me or a friend in trouble? You'd get rabid. Paloma and Dixie's bond is like kin. You tell me what the difference is in what you do for someone who walks into your law firm, right off the street, and what Paloma has been doing for Dixie?"

"I think..."

"I wasn't looking for you to answer that. At least not right now. I'm on a tear."

Al smiled and almost relaxed. He could always depend on Aggie. What a dear soul, his cousin. "You have the floor."

"Thank you. What those two girls went through, good or bad, growing up made their bond even stronger. Paloma moved to another country when she was young. That's tough. Then she lost her parents and had to go live with that kooky racist aunt. Dixie took a lot of crap offa that old lady, but she was always there for Paloma, or writing and calling to help her."

"How did you find this out?"

"I asked Clarice. What is it with men? It's not a national secret. I just went up to her and asked her to tell me about Dixie and Paloma."

"Paloma evaded talking about herself every time I asked."

"It must be painful for her. Tell her you'll be there when she's ready. Instead of making her pay for not acting how you want her to act. The second thing hanging you up is Paloma just wanted to be taken seriously–even if all her theories were discounted later."

"I took her seriously."

"On your own terms."

He held his hands upward, pleading. "Because I was worried something like this would happen."

"Paloma knew the risks."

"Aggie, I believe Paloma thought nothing bad could happen to her."

"You're trying to make sense of a bond between two people. Cops put their lives on the line for their partners. Fire fighters run into burning buildings for strangers."

"She..." He stopped talking as Vontana walked up.

"What were you saying, cousin?"

Al spoke loudly. "She might have stopped looking into the WRF if the GBI had treated her differently. And she'd be here now!" He spun on his heel and walked away not once looking at his friend.

"Bruce, he'll come around," Aggie said and put her arm around him.

The agent was as pained as the rest of them. "Not if we don't find that girl alive."

*   *   *

You are going to die, Paloma. Get yourself together. I don't care anymore. His hands are all over me! Get away! He's coming at me again to hurt me! *He's gone. They are both gone.* I don't believe it. I'm tired. I hurt so bad. Give up. I. Give. Up. *If you don't do something now, you will die.* But it's too hot. *Do it!* I'm so sleepy. *Now!*

Aunt Lilly is coming at me. Screeching my name. She was so intent on hitting me, she nearly wrecked the car! *Aunt Lilly it's new. I just bought it! I knew you'd be so critical about what I was wearing, so I bought something new yesterday. But you aren't even listening. Why is it that when you fly off and accuse me of something and I try to explain or clear up your mistake, you don't even give me a chance to do so? Why don't you calm down and just hear me out? Why do you hate me so? Stop hitting me! It is new. Ow! Why don't you calm down! You don't have to punch me! I can prove it when we get home. The fish designs are airbrushed. That's why they look faded. Stop! Don't hit me! Watch the road, there are cars! It's not my fault you overreacted. What you did was your own doing. Not my fault. Hitting me! Ow! Stop! Stop hitting me!* Blackness.

I fought off the haze. I didn't want to be awake. It was so terrifying. Sweat made the hood cling to my head like skin. I stretched the cloth as far away from me as possible. I stabbed the tire iron down at the stretched out material, the tool clanking against the car and gouging my skin. I yelled in frustration and pain, banging away at my metal tomb. I felt myself slipping back into the haze. *CALM DOWN! CALM DOWN! CALM down. Calm down. Calm.*

Later I turned on my side, pulled the hood away from my head. Holding the tire iron like a big pencil in my fist, I anchored the hood with the sharp pry-end. Summoning up all the strength and determination I could, I moved my head away, straining, bending. Back, and back. Finally, I heard a small, brief ripping noise. Fueled by the crumb of success, I tried again, but the tool kept slipping out of my sweaty hands. I felt around, searching for the tear and worked a finger in. I yanked down feverishly, over and over. *You did it, Paloma!*

*   *   *

"Al, dammit! Will you stop?" Vontana stepped up his pace and circled in front of his friend. "Just talk to me. We're best friends."

"I seem to be the only one who thinks so."

"That's not fair." He grabbed Al's shoulder to stop him. "I told you more about the case than I was supposed to. You don't want your professional confidences put in jeopardy. Please respect mine. I was under orders not to say anything. Yes, I think it was handled wrong. I was all for letting her think she'd stumbled upon the greatest national secret and we'd take it from there."

"You're telling me now that she was right. You sat there and watched her walk away feeling the way she did!" Vontana saw the search volunteers staring as Al shouted. "Why? What was so important that you could sacrifice a woman who was just trying to find some justice for a friend?"

He shuffled his shoes in the dirt. "I'm sorry, Al. I can't tell you." He saw the punch coming and stilled to take it.

"Get out of here. Go do your job." Al's voice was foreign to him, a low-throated rage usually reserved for the hate mongers he fought against. Vontana walked to his car, shoulders sagging as he rubbed his chin.

*   *   *

Reality. The first look inside my dank tomb sent me into another fit of panicked thrashing. As I quieted, exhausted, I closed my eyes. Despair weighted me down along with the hot air. *Time's running out. What's your plan?* I went to work on the trunk latch. With the tire iron, I pushed, pried and beat it. Nothing. I freaked out again. Each episode was more chilling and terrifying–that loss of reason and power over the situation. And my own mind.

Come on, Paloma. You've got people who depend on you. Keep trying! You're an analyst, start analyzing. I thought briefly. Okay. The biggest threat is air and heat. Remedy? I scooted around and tried kicking the back seat out. It tantalized me, moving inches, but it always flopped back into place. I kept at it, the effort heating me up even more. I stopped, rested briefly, then felt around my tomb. Just like those idiots who put you here– find the weakest point. Then exploit the hell out of it. I pulled the carpet down from the side of the trunk, sliding a corner of it under me to hold it in place. A flimsy piece of metal covering the taillight base gave at the edges. I pried it away and smashed the lights and plastic covering.

"Yes!" I cried in relief. My spirits soared. I took deep breaths as I pressed my face up against the hole. The air outside was almost as scorchingly hot, but it was *fresh* air! And it offered a tiny ray of hope. But soon I felt despair creeping up again. Unless someone found me soon, I would cook to death anyway.

Think. Imagine the inside of a trunk. What can you try? I envisioned the latch, the standard way the mechanism works. Thought about what I knew of cars. How they were built. Lost cause, there. My only interest in autos–did it have a rag top, how good was the sound system. Some padding was bunched up under me and the bear metal was cooking my skin. I lifted my right shoulder and tried to scoot it out from under me. It was a struggle, like everything else I did inside this metal tomb. A finger caught on a loose carpet thread, painfully wrenching it sideways. I tried to shake the thread off. Wait! Not thread. Wire?

I followed it, my fingers gobbling up the length as far as my arm could reach. Stereo wires? I felt along the wire the other direction.

No. Better! The trunk's electric source! Checking to see if I had any bit of a fingernail left, I worked my thumbnail to scrape the plastic coating away. It was cumbersome, made harder by the sweat and not being able to see well. I felt a slim piece of exposed wire. Slid it up against metal. Nothing. My desperation was pitiful, my thumb unable to move now from numbness and cramps. I moved around and shoved my face up against the wire and chewed. I felt a raw jab shoot through my nervous system as my tooth hit the metal. I ignored it and continued biting. Then I brought the exposed wire again to the metal trunk. *Click!*

*   *   *

Ezeriah Jackson had just finished hoeing his front yard. It was time to go inside and rest during the worst heat of the day. He smiled at the work he'd accomplished, walking over to the tall hedge that separated his yard from the Ride Share lot. The shrub needed watering. In another year, it would be tall enough to help block out the highway noise.

As he was turning, a movement caught his eye. A trunk in the lot lifted up all by itself. He marveled at the new-fangled gadgetry of cars these days. He'd always dreamed of owning one with push-button everything and a lever to open the trunk while sitting in the front seat. Pretty soon, cars will drive themselves. He waited to see who was getting out. And he waited. When no one exited the car, he figured it was just as well his retirement earnings couldn't afford him such a vehicle. He'd be the one to buy a lemon. He could imagine walking to the car and finding doors open, trunk exposed to the elements.

With all the thieving these days, he'd best go close the trunk. He couldn't leave a note to let the owner know of the problem with the car, because Ezeriah had never learned to write. He put his hoe down and walked across the yard.

When he peered into the trunk, Ezeriah thought he was going to have another heart attack. The thing, that woman! Aiyyy! It, she moved! "My sweet Jesus, please have mercy on my poor soul!" The woman turned slightly. Her head was framed with wet, dark material. Her face was red, bruised, bleeding, lips swollen.

"Help," she croaked. Her eyes closed as her head rolled over.

"Lord a'mercy! Don't go and die on me, chile!" Ezeriah stepped forward, then back, then forward again, his mind and body out of sync. "I never in all my born days!" He closed his eyes and stretched an old, skinny arm toward the poor woman. Good, golly, she was blistering in this heat! He opened his eyes and saw his hand rested on the woman's rear. His arm shot back like an eel going into its hole. He swallowed and reached out again to pick up her limp wrist. He applied pressure. A weak pulse. Should he cover her? No! She'll blister more, but it's so hot! He looked up to the sky as if he expected the clouds to give him instruction.

He moved, focusing on Tom's Restaurant across the highway. Ezeriah was galvanized. He shuffled his eighty-eight-year-old body across the four-lane highway, a heat sandwich covering him as the sun beat down and hot waves from the asphalt rose. He didn't waste time trotting around the deep ditch for the driveway. His feet slid down the deep, grassy slope, and he panted as he climbed the other side. He paused a few seconds for breath, wishing he had worn his hat to shield him from the sun.

Inside, cold air enveloped him. It hurt his head, made him dizzy. Ezeriah swayed as he walked to the hostess. "Ee, there's a woman." He tried to point but instead, collapsed on the floor. The hostess, Sue, squealed in terror when Ezeriah fell. She bolted to the rear of the restaurant, babbling inco-herently.

"We're being robbed?" Robert, the head cook whispered and took her bobbing head as a definite yes. His years of Army training kicked in. It was his duty to warn the others. While Brenda attended Sue, another noise sounded from the dining floor. Nadine, a frequent customer, saw Ezeriah on the floor. She was emotional, prone to hysterical behavior. She let out a weird noise and pointed.

"What's the matter with you?" Asked her husband Fred. He stared in disgust as pieces of waffle fell from Nadine's mouth.

*　　*　　*

The Ride Share parking lot was almost directly across the highway from the front doors of Tom's Restaurant. Margaret Feldman used this spot to meet her lover. Both married, they frequently trysted in out-of-the-way places. Bill Shipman would be here in a few minutes and they'd be off to a nearby hotel. She got out to stretch her legs.

Three cars over a trunk was up, but Margaret didn't think much about it. Until Paloma sat up. She moved faster than she had in years. Blubbering her fool head off, she raced across Highway 21. Cars were forced onto the median and shoulder to avoid crashing into her.

Margaret smacked the doors of the restaurant with enough force to make the windows rattle. As she spied Ezeriah on the floor, her voice cranked up a few octaves. Waitresses ran in circles, hollering and crying. Customers didn't know whether to dive for cover or vacate the premises.

At this moment, the restaurant owner, Tom Babjak, was in his office deep into dreamland. His snores were loud enough to strip the siding off of the building. The hostess could occasionally hear him, even from the rear of the restaurant, and with the office door closed.

The man had a right to be exhausted. The night cook had run off with the head waitress. Both owed everybody in town. They'd lay low for a few days, then show up on payday. Probably ask for their jobs back. It had happened before, it would happen again.

Meanwhile, Tom was severely short of help and was stuck working an eighteen hour shift, most of it over a hot grill. It had been awhile since he'd had such a long day. His daughter, until last month, had split the duties with him. But she, too, had flown the coop. Having the time of her life, she was gallivanting around the world. Everybody having a good time, but him.

Twenty minutes ago he'd stacked clean hand towels on his desk as an impromptu pillow. Just a few winks, he figured, and laid his head down. He was soon deeply asleep. That's when all hell broke loose in the dinning room.

The cook, Robert, banged on the office door. "Open up, Mr. B!" He rapped again, then kept up a steady pummel. But nothing roused his boss from slumber. Robert dug frantically in his pocket for the office keys. It took precious seconds before he found the right one. He fumbled at the knob and soon the door swung open. He looked around, searching for the phone, lifting up reports and opening drawers. Suddenly it rang. Robert followed the sound. The towels. He raised up a corner, spying the curled cord. Mr. B was asleep on top of a few towels and a ringing telephone! He gently pulled his boss back and leaned him against the file cabinet. Mr. B's head dropped down onto his chest.

Robert snatched up the handset. He had to stick a finger in his ear to drown out the snores. "We have an emergency, please call back later." He immediately pressed the hook down. With the line clear, Robert dialed 911.

Denise charged into the tiny room. "Call 911! Call 911!"

"I am, Denise. Calm down! Is everybody alright? I smell food burning. Check the kitchen! Move!" This was enough to make *him* run shrieking out of the restaurant.

"Call 911! Call 911!" She snatched the phone away from Robert in mid report. The two struggled over it. Robert had almost won when Denise stomped on his foot, hitting one of his corns bulls-eye! He staggered back, knocked into Mr. Babjak, whose arm slid off the desk, hit Denise's rear and swung down beside him. Denise, believing she was being goosed in her rear end, went berserk again. Robert took full advantage, commandeering the phone while shoving the hysterical woman out the door. It slammed shut behind her and he quickly locked it. Now his only competition was the saw mill snoring beside him. He finally completed his call.

As he hung up the phone and opened the office door, Mr. B lifted his head a few inches and looked at Robert through droopy eyelids. "Do you have to make so much noise, Robert? I'm trying to sleep." He leaned over, aiming for his makeshift pillow. He missed, but didn't even notice. Mr. Babjak was snoring again before Robert shut the office door behind him.

Canada–Anthony McAleer violated a court order to shut down his hate phone line, Canadian Liberty Net, *while a federal tribunal conducted civil rights violation hearings. Meanwhile, McAleer moved his operations from Vancouver to Bellingham, Washington, changed the name to* Canadian Liberty Net in Exile *and used the Vancouver phone to forward calls. McAleer has ties with a Vancouver-based neo-Nazi group called ARM Skins, the Canadian branch of the Church of Jesus Christ Aryan Nations and the Ontario Heritage Front. Douglas Christie's (McAleer's attorney) clientele includes nearly all Canadian neo-Nazi or alleged neo-Nazis who have been brought to trial in Canada.*–Intermountain Jewish News.

Chapter Fifty-One

"It was a professional," Doctor Morgan said, facing Al, Aggie, Dixie, and the GBI agents.

"Why do you say that?" Vontana asked.

"They knew where to put the leads, for one. And a defibrillator on a live person causes a multitude of problems beyond basic electro-torture."

"Explain." Aggie moved between the doctor and the agents.

"I don't think that's necessary, cousin," Al interjected uselessly. She was resolute. The doctor scanned the room and with an outstretched arm swept them into a corner.

"Skeletal muscles contract upon electrical impulse. You have to know what you're doing–and know it very well. It can cause many problems. For-eign electrical currents zapping a working heart, it's like getting struck by lightening. A defibrillator just compounds it." They stood in grim silence.

"Especially if you want to be effective," Stabenski interjected. Even the doctor joined them in showing displeasure at the agent's unnecessary comment.

"Doctor, you can't be getting too many of these types of injuries," Vontana asked, thinly disguising his attempt at establishing his level of expertise in electro-torture.

"Army," he stated simply, not offended by the question.

"We had a guy once," Stabenski said casually. "An informant who got nabbed by the dudes he was ratting on. They put wires around his chest." He made a breaking motion with his two fists. "Snapped the rib cage, the muscles just froze up. Asphyxiated the dude. He was..."

"Enough, Stabenski," Al snapped and Aggie chorused her agreement. The agent shrugged his shoulders like he'd been extremely helpful to an ungrate-ful group.

The doctor continued. "She has several burns. Probably cigarettes. Contusions to the face and abdomen." He glanced at the initial report and continued listing injuries. "Each of these, in themselves, is not life threatening, but taken as a whole, she's pretty banged up. Paloma's doing well for what she's been through. From her view point though, that's like saying she got hit by a car, but it was a small one. She was lucid when she came in. I don't know how. That's how we were able to notify you so quickly. Most people would be zonkers. Right now, she's in and out."

"Can we see her?" Al asked.

"I'm waiting for someone to take her to a room. We're pretty busy. One person only, for now, please. A nurse will be out shortly. If you'll excuse me." The doctor hurried off to another emergency.

"Dixie, you go," Al said. "It'll help her knowing you're free."

* * *

Dixie believes only doctors could possibly like hospitals. They're paid ungodly sums to whack people open, patch up the maimed, and leave the pain and healing for the nurses and patients to deal with. I'd only visited the unfortunately incarcerated before. Now I was surrounded by cold, silver bed rails and giving credence to Dixie's theory of medicine.

Aggie came for a visit alone so she could fill me in on what happened with the data we'd downloaded from Gundersen. We'd anonymously emailed it before I left Lemond's house the night of my second kidnaping, but I hadn't gotten an update. Aggie assured me that no one had mentioned anything to her. We seemed to be in the clear and so far I'd covered our tracks well. Al did allow to her one night, that some new information had come in about a new group, so at least the WRF would now be investigated. The problem is, in all our excitement of hacking into the computers and not getting caught, we'd never found any evidence to let us know who really killed Lemond. The GBI were still working on the Klan theory.

But my probing investigation would have to wait for a while. If it wasn't nurses asking me tons of questions, the GBI agents were, and swearing they were making progress on the case. I was miffed they were listening to me now. It got a little dicey when Al expected he would be allowed to sit in on my interviews–interrogations, really–but I wasn't ready to have Al and those close to me know the intimate details of my time at the Klavern. That's just the way I am. And this was different than anything I'd experienced. As I assume most people are, when faced with your own lack of control, your own cracking up, it was sobering and humiliating. I had to accept it before I could expect others to. So I assured them all–doctors, agents, family and friends that I was OKAY.

It was obvious, to my way of thinking, what had happened to me. Just take a look. Of course Vontana needed more details but the repeated ques-tions over the week were taking its toll. I wanted to focus on getting over the incident–not always dredging it up. Lying there, I developed a theory of criminal justice, which Dixie basically pooh-poohed.

First, the cops visit you at the most inopportune time–hands occupied, gown with flaps open, bare behind aimed at the door.

Second, they are more suspicious of the victims. Third, you have to repeat the same story several times. She said it was for accuracy and sometimes people remember things later on. I replied that since cops don't trust anyone, they hound you to see if you slip up.

The Secret Service made a cursory visit, asking minor questions about the black boxes and seemed surprised when their lab people confirmed what I told them, that the equipment was for cellular phone fraud. Well, the agents reminded me it was the *"alleged"* commission of fraud. Alleged, hell. Those boxes couldn't do any thing else. Let's call a spade a spade.

I talked Dixie into wheeling me out to freedom, which brought a stream of previously scarce medical staff to my side. "So this is how to get a nurse quickly," I joked as a stern one whisked me back to my room. She didn't laugh but she did call for a doctor. Five minutes later a man in the customary white lab coat entered. This medicine man was quite different from the older doc who graced me every so often with his surly disposition. I liked doc number two better.

He was young, with long, curly blond hair tied in the back. It was natural, I checked his roots. I have a thing for men with long hair. Looking like he stepped off a California beach, he was bronzed and muscular. Maybe I wasn't feeling as good as I thought. Nonetheless, I was able to woo Dr. Morgan with promises to come rushing back if I began to fall apart. He gave me instructions, had no trouble convincing me how miserable I'd be feeling for a few more days, and blessed me on my way.

Recovering on the island, Al wormed his way into the good graces of my grandfather–a feat accomplished just after introductions. He and Pop went fishing at his pond and had plans for terrorizing the wildlife in the adjoining woods.

The next few days were peaceful and almost fun. I awoke daily at the crack of noon. GBI inquiries about my kidnaping were waning. Al's schedule was light, and thanks to a satellite dish I had installed at Pop's a few years ago, I could watch *Perry Mason*, with an occasional *Rockford Files* and *Simon & Simon.* But mostly I slept, complained and slept more.

Tired of the couch potato routine, I paid Al a visit at his farm. The time there was just as relaxing. The day before I was to leave, he came home from work announcing a new case to investigate in North Georgia. He'd be out of town for a few days. I dropped Al off at the airport, then headed back to Hilton Head Island. Driving on I-95, the interstate highway that connects Maine to Miami, I watched as the big rigs flew by. And then the truck with the fancy mud flaps nearly blew me off the highway.

Silver silhouettes of a naked girl adorned each set of rear tires. My skin began to tingle. Images flew by in my mind. I'd seen the same silhouette image on Ski-Mask's belt buckle! At the Klavern. As soon as I got to my grandparent's house on the island, I called Dixie.

"The cops are still blaming the Klan for Lemond's murder which the Klan denies. I'd like to know for sure the correct killers have been caught," I told her.

"You know my family and I agree. I know Aunt Beverly, above all, would want to know the truth."

"She deserves that much."

"How are you holding up, Paloma?"

"I'm feeling like I'm running three hundred baud in a DSL world."

"What are you talking about?"

"If I gotta explain it, it's not going to be funny."

"It's not funny now."

"Kiss my butt!" I laughed, aggravating sore places on my body. "Baud rates are the data conversion speeds on the modems. Three hundred is *slow*."

"Guffaw, guffaw," Dixie spoke, but there was laughter in her voice. It had been too long. "And DSL is that new super-quick speed."

"Excellent! I'm so proud of you. Now, Dixie," I said, getting back to the events in Rincon. "We have to get something on Randy. And I can find him through Ski Mask. The best place to do that is the bar that's just over the county line. The Last Chance."

She sighed. "I'll help all I can, but there's no way I'm going into that bar."

"Why not?"

"It's a honky-tonk."

"We've been in worse."

"Speak for yourself," she said with false indignance. "Paloma, the Last Chance is a *redneck* bar. My black ass goes in there and some Billy Bob and five buddies will be escorting me out. Limb by severed limb."

I started to say something, but didn't. The ugly truth hung in the air.

California: 1988, San Jose–Skinhead Michel Elrod pleaded guilty to killing a local rock musician, Scott Vollmer, when Vollmer tried to keep him from stabbing his black friend.

Chapter Fifty-Two

Friday night at the Last Chance. Wallets were flush, perfume heavy, and men postured to be noticed. I entered charged, my skin on continual crawl. Like being sunburned during a Santa Ana–the extremely dry, often strong desert winds in southern California.

I found a table in the corner with a good view and a wall to protect my back. Nobody just beats the crap out of you these days. You got a beef with somebody, you pull out a gun. So if you're going up against them, they're going to be armed, so you do it too. And the cycle begins and propagates. I'm sure it says something about our society. Even so, I stuck my hand in my jacket pocket, felt the gun and relaxed.

No one seemed shocked I was alive. Nancy sailed by chomping heartily on her gum. She stared at me an extra few seconds. I wondered if it was because of my previous visit when customer Jerry tried out his escort service on me, or the tons of pancake make-up Beverly had used on my face. In spite of what she had to work with, she'd done a masterful job. In the dim light of the Last Chance, I looked more like a woman who's overly fond of Avon than a fisticuff victim. Nancy scooted over to take my order, delivered it, sallied through the droves with no talk.

Lulene came out from the pool table area in the back. She hooked four long-neck beers through her fingers, spying me as she left the bar. "Come back and play pool if you want."

"Thanks, I will in a while." As she walked away, people, mostly males, lined up in front of the bar like a firing squad. The previous song played again. The locals were gyrating various body parts, yelling at each other above the din of music. I looked at their shoes, searching for Docksiders and leopard-skinned boots.

A woman sitting alone at a table in a nightclub is open season. Although I'd be less apparent at the bar, I was afraid I'd miss something with my back to the crowd. Like a bubba with a sharp dagger lunging at me. I was overdone with make-up, wobbling stiffly and sporting an angry look I hadn't been able to erase for days. Even with all that going against me, my female hormones beaconed throughout the jungle where hungry males sniffed out my scent.

I couldn't have attracted more men if I'd bathed in Spanish Fly and served the whole place raw oysters. I had two Coors lined up in front of me I hadn't asked for. People came and went for over an hour. But so far, no belt buckle, Docksiders or boots.

When *Achy, Breaky Heart* played for the sixth consecutive time, I realized I now possessed the answer to the age-old question of what, exactly, is hell like? Answer: a song I found obnoxiously irritating plays for all eternity as cigarette smoke swirls around my head and burns my eyes, only warm domestic beer to drink, time moving as slowly as a postal clerk, sweaty good ol' boys eyeing me like this evening's pork chop, and an uninvited goober, high as a Georgia pine, sitting too close beside me sporting a tattoo that said "Screw the Navy," complete with a pictorial demonstrating how.

Sometime later, the door opened and two guys entered. I felt the flush of excitement as they passed. The large belt buckle. Ski Mask! They headed for the pool tables. I stuck my head around the corner and watched him line up a quarter to play. Lulene untangled herself from a guy's lap who stood and shook Ski Mask's hand. I counted out two minutes. As I stood up, I'd neglected to excuse myself and barely escaped Popeye's octopus arm, which shot out and pulled me back. I dodged him, then pool sticks as I made my way, stilted in the jeans rubbing the burns, toward Lulene. "Has your boss given you any trouble?" I asked conversationally.

"He's outta town. Be back ta-morrow. I'll know then." She held up her hand, fingers crossed.

"Just keep your cool and move quick." She nodded gratefully. "So. Who's the guy?" I made a motion toward the one she'd used for a chair.

"Just a guy." She spoke flatly and sadly, as if her pet dog had croaked on Thursday. "Don't look now, but my ex-boyfriend and ex-best girlfriend's in the corner over yonder. This here guy kinda likes me. I'm just bein' friendly so they'll see." The hurt showed in her face.

I nodded. Lulene made me sad. So did this entire place. "Who are these people?" I jerked my head toward the group where the Ski Mask/Belt Buckle stood. She flipped through their names. "And those two good looking guys are Buddy and Billy Ray." Ski Mask was Billy Ray. I stared until he noticed. If he recognized me he hid it well behind an expressionless face. He held a cigarette at his mouth.

"I'm learning how to shoot. Want to try?"

I thought of pistols at first but figured it out when her pretend boyfriend handed me a pool stick. He introduced himself as Slim, but wasn't, and moved behind her to help. Her shot was a straight scratch.

I didn't do much better, except the cue ball did impressively bang the sides a few times before it disappeared into the hole. I grinned and shrugged my shoulders. Billy Ray looked at me intently. After Lulene's beau helped me flub again, I planted myself next to Billy Ray.

"That's an unusual belt buckle." I said. He was mute.

"Hey, help her out," Slim ordered Billy Ray, who begrudgingly showed me how to make the shot. His hands trembled as he pointed and explained pool science. I actually sank the solid-colored ball I aimed for. I grabbed his arm, tried to look like I was cruising for a pick up and batted my eyelashes. Still ignoring me, I rubbed my left one against him "hey, big fella" style.

"Billy Ray, we have to talk."

He pulled away like I was a hot burner. "How'd you get my name?"

"I asked around."

"How'd you find me?"

"The bar wasn't hard to figure out. Then I looked for that belt buckle."

"Damn. What are you doing here?" He lit a Marlboro.

"I have to get more information. Please! Otherwise nothing is going to happen. I won't give anyone your name. You're scared witless. Let me help you." He took a drag off his cigarette, parked the filter on the bank of the pool table, lit end barely hanging off the edge. He moved up behind me to help me make the shot, like lovers spooning. I played a ditzy female to hide my uneasiness of his body so close to mine. He sank two more low balls and distanced himself from me. When my turn came again, I looked at him. He made a decent show of pointing out possible shots while I spoke to him.

"I'm sure this makeup doesn't cover up what happened to me. Along with getting the crap beat out of me, I was stuffed into a trunk to die. *It was Randy.*" Billy Ray jerked back like he'd been slapped and closed his eyes for a few seconds.

"Make your shot," our competitor commanded.

Billy Ray looked up. "Women!" Then to me he said, "Hurry up!"

I shrugged my shoulders again, and gave a dumb blonde giggle. Billy Ray leaned over me, helping me sink another solid.

"You alone?" I nodded. His breath smelled like an overused ash tray. "If I'm seen with you, it'll be my tail in a sling."

"When this game's over, I'll go to the bar or something. When you leave, I'll wait ten minutes. We can meet wherever you choose."

He took his time answering. "Do you know the Willow Pea Cemetery?" He cocked his head southward.

I nodded again. I'd seen the entrance sign off of Highway 21. "Thanks."

"Make your shot. I want to get this over with." He burnt down half his cigarette with a last drag, dropped the butt on the cement floor and ground it out with his boot heel. We finished the game, solids winning. I hit the bar as agreed.

Half an hour later, Billy Ray walked past me and out the door. Just before it closed I saw the flash of gun fire.

New York: William Stump was waiting with his wife and three-year-old daughter for a train to their Bayonne, New Jersey home when four Skinheads began to shout racial slurs and beat Stump. One Skinhead took the baby's stroller and was about to push it down a flight of stairs when Stump jabbed a lighted cigarette into the Skinhead's face. Another Skinhead smashed his face with a bottle fracturing his cheekbones. Port Authority police intervened and arrested the Skinheads. Their ages ranged from seventeen to twenty-three.

Chapter Fifty-Three

I knocked people out of the way and kicked open the front door. Dodging to the side, I telescoped my neck around the corner peering into the night. I'm not sure that proved or prevented anything, but no other bullets came in that direction. Billy Ray was lying on the ground, fetal position, a hand at his gut. He was so still. I ran over shouting his name. A car skidded to a halt, half on the road, half in the parking lot. I looked up. It was loaded with people, only silhouettes in the darkness. I saw a shadow move at my right. Jerry. I'd last seen him in this parking lot. He'd tried to make me go with him. Tonight he pulled a pistol out of a shoulder strap. My hand went into my pocket and gripped the gun. A few people came out of the bar. He dropped the gun to his side.

Deciding quickly that he wouldn't shoot in a room full of his friends, I back stroked into the Last Chance keeping an eye his gun and a hand on mine. Inside, pandemonium had erupted. Nancy was yelling for quiet while she talked to the 911 operator. I made for the pool tables. Jerry followed, gun still at his side, and tried to close the distance between us. I vaulted over chairs and tore out the back door. A truck was pulling out of a parking spot. I ran to it.

"I need a ride fast," I said to the surprised driver as I jumped in. "My ex is a mean ol' cuss and he's right behind me with a gun."

The man tipped his cowboy hat. "Hang on." Using four-wheeled drive, he shifted out of reverse. Down a ditch and a few hundred feet of rough terrain we went. I looked out the back and saw Jerry trying to get his bulk closer to us. "That him?" The guy asked looking into the rearview mirror.

"Yeah."

"No problem," he said in an even tone. "I'm Ronny with a y. What's your name?"

"Scared senseless. Can we talk later?" He gunned the engine and sailed through three backyards, a field and onto a dirt road. Ronny with a y wound down dark country roads even more desolate than those leading to Al's farm. About ten minutes later he stopped the truck. "I think we're in the clear. What do you want me to do now?" I had my arm out the window gripping the door and my other hand was locked on the dash. "Relax," he said in the same easy tone. He pried my hand loose and laid it gently in my lap.

It's hard to check out your hero when your eyes are glued to the side mirror in blind panic. Ronny with a y was a semi-good looker, tan cowboy hat perched on his head, long black locks underneath. "Where are we?"

"I don't have the slightest idea." Same even tone.

"You mean we could have just driven ourselves into a dead end with Lard-Butt following us?"

"But we didn't." His smile came, then left as quickly.

"I just like to know when I'm suppose to be really thankful."

"Thissa be one of those times." He pushed his hat brim up slightly. "Did your ol' man shoot that guy at the bar?"

"I don't know. Probably."

"Will you tell me your name?"

"I guess I owe you that much. Name's Candy."

"Candy. If you want to talk, I'll listen 'til you're done. If you don't, I won't press you."

"If I talk, I'll lose it."

He nodded. "It won't be safe to go back to your place. You're welcome to bunk with me. I'll be good."

"Thanks. Uh. Give me a second." Going back to the Last Chance would be stupid. I thought of Al, then remembered he was out of town. Dixie was dealing with her own demons. "Are we anywhere near Savannah?"

"West of it, I'm pretty sure."

"Would you just take me to Savannahs' airport?"

"Sure." Half an hour later we emerged onto a highway my hero was familiar with. He'd kept his promise of not talking after asking if I liked country music. Not deterred by my resounding no, he slipped a tape into the deck. I possessed a severe aversion to twang, but this singer didn't have it. I had to admit I like the smooth, soothing female voice filling the truck cab. Five songs into the tape we arrived at the airport.

"That singer was a good choice," I told him.

"Mary-Chapin Carpenter. I thought she was the best one to help out." I handed Ronny a handful of twenties.

"I think you need it more than I do, Candy," he said.

"Not really. Besides, this can't even cover what you did for me. You could have gotten yourself hurt tonight."

"But I didn't."

I smiled back at him. "Well, Ronny with a y, you're about as laid-back as a hippy from a California marijuana commune. What's your secret?"

He kept his smile. "I did time in 'Nam. Da Nang. After surviving that, I figured everything else would be smooth sailing."

I stuck my hand out for a shake. On impulse I switched to a brief hug, pulling back before he could clamp down on a wound or three. "Makes sense, dude. Thank you for your help."

He tipped his hat. "Good luck, sweet Candy."

I went inside heading straight for the phones. I dialed Information for the number of the Last Chance, getting a busy signal each time I dialed. I phoned my grandparents, thankful that Papa, as usual, didn't question my skittering around. Last time I'd checked in, I was at Dixie's house on the island. I told him I'd be home late, and pawned off on him a request to call Dixie to say that I'd see them later. 'Fraidy Cat, I am. I didn't want to hash out tonight with anyone. I tried the bar again–still busy. I abandoned the booth and went in search of the van service to Hilton Head Island. A safe haven. A place to sort out another horror. This new one, the image of Billy Ray in the parking lot dying.

Chapter Fifty-Four

"*Bosta*," I cursed. The vodka bottle slipped from my hands, bounced painfully off my foot, soaking me, before it rolled around the deck into a dark corner. I slipped my drenched shoes off and headed below deck to find something else to wear. Taking the express route, I never touched a step on the way down. Deciding that was just as good a place to be, I stayed sprawled, drunk and sobbing.

Sometime before first light, I crawled out of the boat onto the splintery pier. With much stumbling, I untied the *Katie* and got her under way. But no matter how far I sailed her, nor how many shots I downed, I couldn't out run the shadowy darkness that continued to chase and engulfed me.

My memories were vividly real playing over and over in my mind. Facing pain and torture blind–with Randy and The Voice on either side of me. The suffocating dark trunk, and the terror I felt when I'd finally freed my face and saw my metal tomb. Billy Ray wanted to stay out of it. But I'd pushed him. Some investigator I am. I got him killed the first time around. Billy Ray. It was my fault he'd been shot.

I anchored well past Port Royal Sound and drank down another vodka while Korn and Lincoln Park CDs blared. I'd found another bottle in the cabin, half-empty, but it was enough to shut out the demons. At least long enough to get into a stupor. Recriminations. Self-loathing. Guilt. I knew when I awoke the demons would be back. But so would the rest of the vodka. I'd start the exorcism all over again.

* * *

"I took away what liquor was left on the boat. Wasn't much anyway. She wouldn't tell me what happened. I found out when Dixie called looking for her," Paloma's grandfather, Mr. Sid, told Al over the telephone. "She blames herself for everything. And I think the stuff that happened to her–what put her in the hospital–is keeping her up nights. I gave her a day to get it all out, but she didn't come back. That's when I did it–went to the boat. I've never seen her quite like this before."

Al kept his voice controlled, not wanting to heighten the concern that was apparent in the old man's voice. "What do you mean, sir?"

"She was all busted up. I mean worse than when she got here. But she didn't want me to help her. I don't mind her taking pity on herself for a bit, but enough is enough. So I took 'em. As soon as I left, she sailed further away. Problem is..." His voice trailed off then came back. "Good, Kate's sleeping. We hid a few pints around the islands and marshes for when we visit our secret spots. We have a sip or two, cast a net or rod and then be on our way."

Under other circumstances, Al thought what the old salty revealed about the bond between them would have been charming. They worked the ocean as he did land, familiar with every wonder it offered. But now the place where she found refuge left her wide open for Randy or anyone who wanted her out of the way. And in the state she was in, she wouldn't see it coming until it was right down on her. "Would it help if I came over to assist?"

"That would be right nice of you. I was fixin' to go look for her. I'll wait until you get here. I don't like leaving my wife for too long. She's not well."

"I'm sorry to hear that, sir. I'll leave right away."

"Good, I'll have the boat ready and drop you off when we find her. Maybe somebody else talking to her would do her some good." Al hung up, a sinking feeling in his gut—and not all for Paloma. She *would* have to use the ocean for an apotropaic ritual. He went to his medicine cabinet and swallowed several sea-sickness tablets. The last time he had been on a boat, the sea was nearly as smooth as creek stone. But that didn't matter. He'd begged Bruce Vontana to feed him to the sharks. He'd been greener than a tit on a bullfrog.

Canada: 1992, Toronto–Richard Manley, twenty-six, was arrested on suspicion of importing parts used to convert weapons to automatics. The police seized 13 guns, 2200 rounds of ammunition, including hollow point and armor-piercing bullets. Manley has ties with the Florida-based Church of the Creator and Canada's white supremacist Heritage Front. Manley, denying membership in either group, was captured on video before his court trial holding the COTC flag during a speech given by George Burdi, Canadian COTC leader.

Chapter Fifty-Five

"Paloma. Paloma!" I swatted feebly in the general direction where pesky noises endangered my coma. I refused to crawl to the end of the long tunnel that was consciousness. "Wake up. Come on." Thump. "Ow! Shoot! Dang boats." I opened one eye. Al was vigorously rubbing his skull. He glared down at me. "Well?"

"Well, what?"

"You came to say I told you so?" I asked, taking care to move nothing but my lips.

"I came to help you."

"Did you bring a bottle?" I closed the eye. Sonic boom!

"No."

"Then you can't help me."

"Paloma, sit up and talk to me." I moaned in response, peeking with both eyes this time, deciding it was safest to keep them shut. "What's that groaning noise? And I'm not referring to you," he added.

"The lines." I managed another lid lift to see how seasoned he was in sailor-ese. "Ropes," I explained. "Pop and I call it boat chatter." My lid slammed shut, vibrating my head like an earthquake.

"Have you been in the water?"

"Beats me."

"You could have drowned, commode-hugging drunk as you are."

"If you knew the answer, why'd you ask? And it's were. I ran out of booze a while back." My mouth tasted like someone walked across it with turkey crap stuck to their boots, I mused as I ran a dry, thick tongue over equally dry teeth. For some reason I shared this revelation with Al.

"You look like it, too."

"Thanks for cheering me up." I looked down–eyes only, minimum lid movement–to see that my last choice in boat apparel was a tank-styled T-shirt of my grandfather's and, thank goodness, I'd also managed to keep my drawers on. Just your everyday company's coming attire. I'll hasten to mention I was lying on top of the tiny table. I turned to look out the porthole. It was as bright as if someone had tossed me into a roomful of klieg lights, their brightness tortured and blinded me. Pepper dusted my shoulder and parts of the polished wood surface my body was not distressing. I sneezed twice.

"What are you doing on the table, Paloma?"

"Giving it a good shine." Al decided that I needed to stand and without an ounce of gracefulness, I did, while the boat rocked, ever so slightly. Al crashed into me. I fell, hitting my head as I went down. "For crying out loud, Al! The boat barely listed an inch. Why'd you go all wackado?"

He knelt beside me. "Paloma! Are you okay?"

"Not really. But you can't make my head hurt worse than it already does. Ha-ha," I faked. Now that I was awake, so was my emotional and physical pain. It came at me full force as I tried to keep my tears rumbling around my chest. I choked on a sob.

"What is it?" Al quietly asked.

"Everything." He lifted me to stand. My body was doing the limbo.

"You're a mess, sugah. Look at you. You're awful."

"Then don't look at me," I bawled. "You don't have to stay here. You can go." I flopped down into the rack and flung an arm across my eyes.

"That's not what I meant. You're beautiful–except you obviously felt that you needed more injuries. I go away for a few days and it goes to hell. And look. You're bleeding all over. You've got glass in your hands, mascara's run down your cheeks, your hair is knotted worse than my stomach, and it looks like you mopped the floor with your shirt."

"Oh," I said dully. "That all?"

"No! You don't have to get...Look at your feet. No, those are mine. I don't wear rings on my feet."

"Neither do I, Al. They're toe rings, not foot rings."

"Okay, Miss Sarcastic. Tell me why."

"Why what?"

"Why you are here. Why you disappeared then came here to hurt yourself." I couldn't answer. It was like I'd gotten so used to grief my body didn't remember how to feel anything else. I turned my back to him and tried to clamp my feelings down. "Let it happen, Paloma. You hold everything in. So much has happened and you don't open up."

"How do you know? Leave me alone. I'm too tired to talk." The effort to speak used up all my will. I wanted to hide. I needed to stay balled up, alone, angry, hurt, sad. To wallow in self-pity. Keeping my back toward him, I breathed deeply to summon up another plea. "Go away, Al."

"No."

"Yes," I weakly begged. He gently slipped his arm under my neck, scooting up behind me, his body barely brushing up against mine. His other arm was unsure where to park. Masses of bruises, scrapes and burns covered my side and thighs. "Oh, sugah, look what they've done to you," he murmured softly into my ear.

Later he said he wanted to talk about that night. I burrowed as far into the corner of the rack as I could. He kept bugging me. I got up to move and he followed, pushing me to talk.

"Dammit, Al! Can you swim?"

"Yes. Why?"

"I'm going to push you overboard! I'm serious! Leave me the hell alone! Please!"

He relented–for a short while. Al coaxed me out eventually and ministered to my injuries as conscientiously as he had days before, throwing him-self into nursing with total concentration. An occasional murmur intermingled with the boat chatter. Sterilizing a needle with a lit match, he picked the largest splinters of pier wood out my feet. I slept fitfully in minute clusters of time.

The smell of eggs frying and an occasional thump from Al bumping into the cramped quarters of the *Katie* woke me. It was dark outside.

"Good evening," he said good-naturedly, as if the last time I was awake was a fantasy. His shrewd eyes searched me from head to toe, then stopped at mine, drinking me in. I tried a smile. He moved the pan to the unlit burner and came toward me. I let him wrap me in his arms although I ached like hell.

"Are you hungry?" I nodded into his shoulder. "I found eggs, cheese and shrimp. I mixed them all together. And I made grits, they're not Aggie's, but I did okay. Let's get some food in you. I think I have the coffee maker figured out." He motioned for me to sit as he served me. "The shrimp were fresh. Did you net them?"

"Yeah. Bottle in one hand, net in the other."

"That takes a bit of co-ordination."

"I'm not a sloppy drunk." I looked at the mess around me. "It was like this when I moved in." Dodging the overhang, Al sat across from me taking my free hand in his. I ate slumped over, all the posture of the letter O. When I'd finished, I summoned the courage to talk.

"Do-do the c-cops know who k-killed Billy Ray?" I stuttered suddenly feeling cold in the hot night air.

Al brought his head up quickly in surprise. "He's not dead! Did you think..."

I nodded. "I couldn't stick around." I explained about Jerry chasing me.

"Billy Ray was only in the hospital a few days."

"I've sort of lost track of time."

"Oh, sugah, you've been beating yourself up because you thought he was dead."

"Among other things."

"It's those other things I want to hear."

"Why? Why is that so important to you?"

"I care for you, Paloma."

Manners forgotten, I put my elbow on the table and sunk my head into my palm. I used my fork to play with, staring intently while I counted the grits on my plate. "I know, Al. But why is it that with you caring means I have to rip myself open? Do you know how hard it is to close it all back up again?" My voice had gotten high and female-whinny. I put some air back into it. "Now is not the time." Al started to protest. "Sometimes I can't just start talking. My head's unclear now, and will be for awhile. Can you wait until I'm ready?" It really wasn't a question. Thankfully, he nodded. We sipped coffee in silence.

"I think I'd better take a shower," I announced when we'd depleted the java. "There should be some clothes here." I dug out an old shirt of my grandfather's and held it up to me. It reached close to my knees.

When I emerged, skin feeling fresh, but nothing else, Al was topside. He'd taken the mattress from the small rack and laid it on the deck. A cresol lamp was burning to ward off insects. He held his hand out to me as I joined him.

It was a wonderfully clear night. The lamp gave us enough light to see each other, and in spite of its bug-zapping purpose, draped us in a comforting softness. "Almost a full moon," Al ventured, pleased. Moon beams unfurled down from the sky to dance across the tiny waves on quick piano fingers. Just for us. Water lapped gently against the boat, a thirsty kitten coming to drink. I lay feeling the gentle tug of war between the boat and tide, concentrating in desperation on each sound, yearning for solace in things familiar.

"Paloma," Al said in that tone. In my mind I gave it the finger and an eye-roll. *Here it comes.* I started before he could. I tried to teach Al a bit of celestial navigation, pointing to the night jewelry of the cloudless sky. But he wasn't up to a class. He pouted a while in silence. Then he came around, telling me a story of the myths of Orion, Canis Major and Gemini. I mentioned I was born under the sign of the twins.

"That explains your behavior. Two people in one body."

I spotted Taurus the Bull. "And that must be your sign."

"I owe you one." He playfully grabbed at me, puppy dog happy on his face. Then it pained over as he stopped himself. He'd poked a few of my injuries. I bet he's going to bring it up again. We didn't talk for a long time. I rolled over and looked at Al, overwhelmed with emotion. I lay my head on his shoulder. We lay intertwined. "Paloma, it's not your fault," he finally said.

I nuzzled into his chest hiding. "Please, talk about something else. I feel like I've been eviscerated by pain." He tilted my head back, gently kissing my raw lips. We were silent again for a while. I was so lost in the feeling that I started when Al spoke. "Paloma?" I waited for what would come after. When I didn't speak he turned looking at me.

"I have some things to tell you." Pause. "It's not about that." I braced for more bad news. He lay back down and stared into the sky. "After your talk with the Klan, when we met at my farm, Vontana and the others were under orders to only listen to you, not offer any encouragement." He suddenly seemed uncomfortable.

"What?"

"I knew more about what was going on with the GBI than I let on. At first, at the farm, I was just as surprised as you were about the way Vontana was acting. We've always swapped information. The next day we met. He was risking his job talking to me. Sugah, you stumbled across something big. They couldn't figure out how you were getting information so quickly when they'd been working on it for months."

"I just went looking."

Al's face showed the anticipated argument he was so sure would come–me angry at him for hiding information from me. It's best for women to be unpredictable–it keeps men on guard wondering what you'll do next. They should not be able to put their finger on it. I ran my hand along his cheek. "It's alright, *meu querido*. My dear."

"That sounds nice. Doesn't sound as sexy in English." He took my hand off his cheek and held it. "I wanted to tell you everything. Not keep any-thing from you anymore. And, that I'm sorry."

"Thanks. Really."

"And I wanted to tell you that you have good instincts. You're young, but you catch on fast." I was glad he added that. I'd almost readied for a cat fight. "What you don't know, you'll probably find it on that computer of yours or read about it. On that web stuff." He crunched up his nose in distaste.

"One afternoon with me, and I'd get you loving your computer."

"Hmmm," he drawled huskily. "I bet you would," he leered up at me.

"Anything else you want to praise me for while you're on a roll?" I teased. A moment of panic, as Al hurried over events in his mind, unsure if he left out anything important. Something that would get him in hot water if he didn't mention. I left him dangling helplessly. "Om, well, you're good. Real good. At investigation, I mean. You can tie a drunk on full-throttle as well."

"You're so funny, Al." I put meaning into it. "Thank you. For telling me this."

"I just wish I'd told you the other things before tonight."

"It's okay."

"But if I'd told you what I knew, you might not have been taken to..."

I kissed him.

"I went along with Bruce while I let you wander off..."

I kissed him again. "So this is what it takes to shut you up!" I told him, barely hiding my mirth, giving him back the line he tossed to me after he surprised me with our first kiss. I added my own twist–no stalking out the door here. I shut him up again, this time a lot longer.

"I thought you'd be upset," he said when he got a chance. Coming up for air, I rested on my elbow while I gazed down at him.

"None of that seems important now. Not with all the..." He nodded, knowing which events. "And Billy Ray could have been killed because I pressured him into meeting me."

"You don't, you can't, know that. Why was that Jerry guy there with a gun? They must have been itching for a fight." My face was under cross-examination. He watched me carefully, searching for signs of crack up. But I was feeling stronger, vindication breathing new fire in me. I smiled. "I really had the GBI running?"

"Yeah." He playfully nipped my nose. That body part was malady free.

"Did Vontana tell you why all the secrecy?"

"I wouldn't know."

"Why? What happened?"

"He's still hiding something. We've had a falling out."

"Oh, no! It's all my fault."

"Now don't go taking that on your shoulders, too. This has nothing to do with you." I knew he was being kind. He pulled me down closer. It wasn't until the sun peeled away the darkness layer by layer that I felt able to talk, albeit briefly, about what had driven me to the boat.

After the 1992 L.A. riots, rap singer Sister Souljah said "Blacks could be justified in killing whites'" and that whites had "a low down dirty nature".–Response, Fall 1992. *Alabama: Anniston, 1993–A white teenager was allegedly killed by a group of blacks because of his race. An eighteen year old was charged with murder. California: 1993–A disabled Pacific Islander allegedly was kicked and punched by five black youths. A white student was attacked by two Asian youths.*–Klanwatch Intelligence Report 2/94.

Chapter Fifty-Six

We sailed back to Pop's pier and walked along the beach listening to the wind sing over the sand, sea oats shaking in the breeze. I made amends with my grandfather. He was unusually light with his reprimand. Could be because he had a fishing pole in his hand. We waved goodbye to him as he headed down to the water. "Al, are you okay with everything?"

He enveloped me in a hug. "Yes. And you?"

"Hm-huh."

"Do you want to talk to Billy Ray?" I pulled away and looked at him. His face gave me no help in how to answer. Was he really no longer angry with me investigating? He pulled his tiny cellular phone out of his waist pack, flipped down the bottom and punched buttons. "Gary, did you get the address? Okay, give it to me. Thanks. Yeah, she's well." He looked at me. "We're going to talk to him now." I nodded.

They discussed office matters, Al pacing to have something for his body to do. I assessed the back half of him each time he passed by. It was good entertainment. "No, I don't want Vontana's help!" He straightened sudden-ly, his rigid back facing me. "The boy was shot. We can't show up at his home with a Mongolian horde. I expect he's already jumpier than a virgin at a prison rodeo." Suddenly remembering I was there listening, he reeled around, cheeks coloring, embarrassed he'd said a naughty in front of little ol' me. I kept my face averted but laughter gave me away. Cackling, to be truthful. "I'll call you when we're done. Bye."

"A virgin..."

"Hush. Let's go."

Just under an hour later we found Billy Ray's address, but had about twenty mobile homes to choose from. We stopped at a yard where a couple sat in the shade watching their children run wild and make one heck of a racket.

"Sixth on the right," the man shouted over the shrieks of his offspring.

As soon as Al parked, I was opening the door. "Don't be so quick." He held my arm. "Wait for me."

"Al, I think I should do this alone. I'll convince him to talk to you."

"It may be dangerous."

"I won't go in. I'll get him to come outside."

"I don't like it."

"Billy Ray treated me decent. Stand nearby and you can come to my res-cue if I need it." He got out of the car, gun and phone in hand. I slipped on my grandfather's jacket, gun in pocket. When I knocked on Billy Ray's door, my heart beat doubled. I slipped my hand inside and gripped the gun, hopefully ready for any situation.

"You keep showing up like a bad date," he said as the door swung closed. I stuck my foot in its path and marveled at how much pain I was willing to subject myself to these days. My Docksiders were no protection, the metal trailer door seemed to rip right through the leather. "I only came here to get my mail and here you are."

"Billy Ray, please!" I saw the gun on his hip, and the large bandage on his midriff. "Do you want to live the rest of your life in fear?" He eased the pressure on the door. "Someone in the bar that night called the goober posse. And the shooter got there so fast, he must have been on standby. You need help. And I know somebody good."

"I don't want to get involved, ma'am. Things are bad enough."

"And they'll only get worse."

"So you want me to be in your pocket when they do?" He scratch ed the stubble on his face. "That was cruel, ma'am. I apologize." He was a few years older than me, calling me ma'am. I chalked it up to Southern manners. And how he reconciled it was okay to take part in kidnaping me to the Klavern and now felt it prudent to apologize for rudeness, I'd ponder for a long time.

"Billy Ray, you might as well be with the good guys."

"And just who are they?"

"The one's who want the truth, want to end this. Me. Al Eason. He's an attorney who..."

"I've heard of 'im."

"Let us help you."

"Like you helped me the other night?"

I tried another tactic. "How are you feeling?"

"Only hurts when I laugh," he said dryly. "Give me a minute to think. I'll come out and tell you what I decide." He pulled on the door. I grabbed it.

"Al's with me now. I just wanted you to know I'm not hiding anything. If you say no, we'll leave." He nodded and locked himself in.

"Okay, I've decided," Billy Ray said when the door opened again. I walked toward the tiny steps. "Leave me alone." I managed to slip Al's business card into his palm, Al's home number and Vontana's office number hastily scribbled while we were waiting. The door slammed once more in my face. I walked dejectedly to the car.

"Sugah, I had made plans to meet Beverly today. I need to talk to her. She said that they'd be at Lemond's. Do you feel like a visit?"

"Sure. I haven't spent much time with them." We were quiet while we headed down Blandford Road. We stopped at the stairs to Lemond's front door.

"You're taking Billy Ray's refusal well, sugah. Am I reading this right?" Off to the side I saw Dixie's lopsided grin glued to the window. I jerked my thumb indicating her to beat it. She peeped on. "Billy Ray may come around. He was willing to talk to you before."

"Yeah, he didn't shoot at us this afternoon. Maybe I can dress up in a slinky black number, shove my cleavage out and seduce the information from him." I looked at Al. "I wasn't serious," I confessed to his beet red face.

"With you I can't always tell."

"Good." He grinned lasciviously and got especially amorous. Dixie observed it all, that is, until her mother peeked out then snatched her away. I'll never hear the end of this, I thought as I entered the house. I was right.

"Dixie, you better hush your mouth!" Clarice scolded. "You're a grown woman. I raised you better. You act like you don't have a lick of sense." I stuck my tongue out at Dixie and mouthed ha-ha.

Al had Beverly by the hand, patting her as he spoke. "I wanted to see you about Lemond. The Center received a considerable donation. There were instructions to give you a large portion of it."

"Who did this?" Beverly asked. I held my breath.

"It was anonymous. We often get donations in that manner. They're bonds. You can cash them in or keep them."

"I don't know anything about that stuff."

"The Center has staff, as well as myself, who can give you advice or recommend another firm."

"Thank you, Al." I checked the seams on my shoes to hide my face. I couldn't wait to tell Aggie. He pulled out his well-used cell phone, the tone getting louder until it he answered it. His head bobbed as he talked. It was a short conversation and when it was over his body language said for us to be quiet.

"We all need to get out of here." Instead of moving we were frozen by his urgent tone. "Vontana called the Center to give me a heads-up. The GBI is raiding the Gundersen plant tonight." Whooping noisily, I jumped into the air, grabbing Dixie in the process. We stumbled around the kitchen, bouncing off things like pinballs, Al patiently waiting. "He's worried about retaliation. There's sure to be WRF members who'll miss the sweep. My farm is secure. Not so long ago we both received anonymous information about the plant being a front for a new group. It was just as you thought, Paloma." He went on to explain what most of us in the room already knew. Now that everyone was on the same page, I wouldn't have to worry about opening my big mouth. "If you need things from here, pack them now. We have time before the raid, but I'm still calling Gus to come here. Paloma, call Aggie and tell her to meet us there." We shifted into motion, each diving into our assigned duties.

Gus arrived well under an hour. He'd brought additional guards and we all sorted ourselves into separate cars. Feeling presidential, we motor-pooled to our safe house.

New Jersey: 1992–Grand Dragon Joseph Doak and Klansman Harold Patterson were convicted of plotting the murder of two rival Klansmen. Mary Doak pleaded guilty to conspiracy to commit aggravated assault.

Chapter Fifty-Seven

Before Hughes left the electronics store, he called home to see if Billy Ray had returned there after going back to his trailer on an errand. "I'm gonna meet with my Klan brothers tonight. Do you feel well enough to come along?"

Billy Ray, still shaken about Paloma showing up at his trailer, answered glumly. "Nah, you go ahead." Hughes hesitated, so tempted to yell at the boy, demand that he attend the meeting. Remind him of all that he had done for the ungrateful delinquent. Instead he asked for his wife, Wanda.

"Are you gonna tell me what's the matter with that boy?" Wanda snapped into the phone.

"He's been shot, for chrissakes."

"He was acting weird before then."

"He don't want to talk about it," Hughes snapped.

"Do you know what's going on?"

"He's my son. This is men stuff."

"Is it drugs?"

"Wanda!"

"He's knocked up some girl. You better tell me..."

"No! Shut up, Wanda. Man you got some imagination! And don't you go interfering with him while I'm gone."

"Where are you going?"

"I've got official Klan business to take care of."

"How long are the kids suppose to stay at my parents?"

"Until I say different!" Wanda slammed the phone down and sat down on her new couch in her newly decorated living room and flipped TV channels by remote. Nothing caught her attention. She tried chatting with Billy Ray, thinking it would help keep their minds off serious matters. Not only did he make a poor conversationalist, he was down right rude. She called a few friends, exhausting her sources for gossip. Wanda grew more restless as the clock ticked away. Deciding Wyman Hughes would pay, literally, for upsetting her, she grabbed a few mail order catalogs from the coffee table. First she'd tackle Neiman Marcus. The pages that interested her were flagged with colored sticky tabs. The phone rang and she snatched it up preparing to gripe to her husband again.

"Hello." She couldn't figure out who was calling at first. "Hang on a minute." She walked into Billy Ray's old bedroom. "Randy's on the phone," she snapped at him. He bolted up from the bed as if someone lit a firecracker under his butt. Wanda was going to get to the bottom of this and it was going to be tonight. She folded her arms across her ample first silicon- then saline-implanted chest and stalked down the hallway. Spiked high-heels clicked on the hardwood floors, the sound like a call to her poochie, Miss Powder Puff, or Pooh-Pooh for short. The dog scampered behind her, tapping her movements on claws painted to match her mommy's nails.

Billy Ray poked his head out of the bedroom door to see if she was eavesdropping. The pair of them clicking grated on his nerves worse than nails on a chalkboard. *Focus.* He had bigger problems. He swallowed the fear-induced bile so familiar to him since that night. *Dear God, what did that jerk want now?* He couldn't believe the guy could call him up, like nothing had happened. Now Randy couldn't take a hint or a straight-out plea to get out of his life. Billy Ray just wouldn't answer the phone! Let Randy get cobwebs waiting for Billy Ray to answer it. There wasn't anything in the whole wide world that he needed to know bad enough to talk to Randy.

Billy Ray headed down the hall. He'd take a walk. Walk off his fear. His hand on the knob of the front door, he stopped. His dad. He had to talk to Randy because he needed to know what the jerk was up to. And Wanda would surely tell Wyman, soon as he got home, that Randy had called. And if they could only guess at what Randy wanted, instead of knowing exactly, before long his father would be planning something stupid in retaliation. And screwing it up as usual. Like Billy Ray didn't have enough on his mind.

His insides were twisting and pulling. He wished that awful burning in his stomach would go away. He lit another cigarette and begrudgingly headed to the phone, thinking of another way to mentally kill Randy Beamon.

Saudi Arabia–John Schwartz, a Los Angeles businessman dealing in scrap metal learned of a pending sale of excess U.S. hardware from the Gulf War. Marhoon Nasser Auctioneers, the Saudi firm contracted by the U.S. Defense Department to head the auction, answered Schwartz's request to bid at the auction, saying "send someone else who is other than Jewish". With help of the Wiesenthal Center and a major article in the L.A. Times, *Schwartz did receive a visa but the word "Jew" had been stamped in it. Schwartz, a Holocaust survivor and Korean War veteran, stated that "having once before experienced having official papers stamped with the word "Jew", he declined to travel to Saudi Arabia."* Response, Fall 1992.

Chapter Fifty-Eight

Willie wished that his boss Swartzman had never asked him to contact Wyman Hughes, Klan Imperial Wizard, about the false bomb threat at the plant. Needing a boost in respectability from his dwindling group of evil-doers, Hughes snapped up responsibility for the hoax quicker than greased lightening. There wasn't more to tell, but Hughes kept calling for details. And Swartzman was bossing Willie–no, bullying–him around. It was like having two additional mothers-in-law. When Willie got home, his wife was worse. Tonight she nagged him so badly to change the baby's diaper, he actually got up and completed the offensive task. But it had slowed him down. He was finally ready to escape. He was almost in his truck when Hughes turned into the drive. Willie's stomach soured. He was trapped. He silently cursed his wife.

"Howdy, Willie." Hughes stepped out of the car, chatted about rain, and the last time he went fishing. Willie wanted him to get to it, but he smiled politely.

"What's new at the Gundersen plant?" Hughes asked, finally tipping his hand.

"Nothing." Willie looked quickly down at his feet and kicked the dirt.

"Son, you acting all a'quiver."

"I ain't."

"Why don't you look at me?"

"No reason."

"You've been acting a mite strange. What's the matter?"

"You're hounding me," he exploded. "What do you want?"

"Nothing. I didn't know it was such a bother for you to help your Klan brothers."

"That ain't it and you know it."

Hughes looked around the yard. "You got a car?" He asked surprised. "When?"

"It ain't much. It's used."

"How'd you afford it and the truck?"

"My wife's parents gave us the money." Hughes knew better. His in-laws were poorer than lizards. He propped his foot on a cinder block. "Now, Willie, why you lyin' to me?"

Willie scrunched his face up until it looked like it would disappear down his own throat. "He made me. I didn't want to! He said he'd hurt the wife and young'uns if I didn't tell him Klan secrets," Willie lied, hoping he sounded in genuine fear for his life.

"Who did?" Hughes asked, surprised at the information that fell into his lap.

"Swartzman. And I ain't got nuthin' to do with pinnin' the Hightower lynchin' on Mack and Rodney. I didn't even knowed he was doin' that. I heard it on the news and you could've knocked me over with a feather." Hughes gasped. It had been a hell of a few days! Now he knew who'd set his boys up! That Kraut–Swartzman! The two men coughed, took interest in different objects until Willie broke the silence. "Want a beer?" Hughes nodded. When he returned, Hughes was roosting on the tailgate of Willie's truck. He looked too comfortable, ready to stay a spell. Willie again internally railed at his wife.

"Okay, Willie. Start at the beginning."

Willie told a story that was about as much truth as it was a lie. "You can understand why I did it, can't you?"

"Sure, son. If somebody threatened my Wanda and boys, I'd be set to kill."

Willie relaxed for the first time since seeing Hughes in his driveway. "I've been tryin' to think of a way to tell you, but I been flummoxed. That man has all kinds of gadgets to find out what you're up to. I think my phone is bugged. That's why I didn't accept any of your calls. You ain't gonna do anything to me Imperial Wizard, are you?"

"That depends. How you gonna pay?"

"I ain't got no money."

"I meant, how you going to redeem yourself. Make it up to the Klan?"

Willie rubbed his head, but no useful information came out of the spot.

"Here's what you'll do. Along with reporting everything that goes on at the plant to me, I want you to tell that faggot communist some things."

"Who?"

"Swartzman," Hughes said a little testy.

"He's gay? I don't believe it!"

"Willie, come on! Keep up with me."

"What kind of things do you want me to tell 'im?"

"I'll let you know soon. You and I are going to put the WRF outta business." Willie's stomach did another flip as Hughes slapped him companionably on the back. Once he was in his car, the Wizard grinned back at him. Willie couldn't even find the strength to crack his lips apart. He was too busy worrying about how to keep both Hughes and Swartzman happy while he stayed alive.

Before he shut the front door, he looked out at his half-acre. He and his wife had cleared out the land themselves, put a trailer down, and worked like coon hounds to save for a house. This was supposed to be their paradise–a piece of the American dream. Lately, paradise was stinking like Rincon's city dump.

France–President François Mitterrand rejected a request of two hundred of Frances' top intellectuals to make an official apology for the treatment of Jews in wartime France. Mitterrand stated that the Republic should not be held accountable for the Vichy regime. Jewish protesters booed the President when he laid a wreath at the Velodrome d'Hiver, the site where French police turned over more than thirteen thou-sand Jews for extermination camps. More than four thousand children were deported. None came back.

Chapter Fifty-Nine

"Howze Billy Ray?" Hughes asked his wife on the phone.

"Worse now that Randy called."

"That blood sucking leech! What did he want?"

"How am I supposed to know? No one tells me a cotton pickin' thing around here!" Her tone warned of impending trouble. She could pout for weeks.

"Sweetie pie, things are a bit strange now, but something big is happening. It's best you stay out of it."

"Are you in trouble?"

"No," he said smoothly. "I'm just doing my job for my country and as Imperial Wizard."

"I'm bored and all B-Ray does is stare at the ceiling."

"I'll make it up to you."

"How?"

"Hmmm," he said like he was giving it thought. "Howze about a night on the town?"

"Which town?"

"You pick it."

"Atlanta."

"How'd I guess you would say that? You pick the date. Now put my boy on the phone." After Wanda screeched his name several times, Billy Ray finally picked up the extension.

"Randy wanted me to help him," Billy Ray explained to his foster dad's question.

"How? With what?"

"I didn't ask. I was so surprised he called, I couldn't think right. I told him people were around. He's gonna call later."

"Is he at home?"

"No. He wanted to know what I was doing here. I told him you were out of town and Wanda didn't like staying by herself."

"You did good, son. I trained you. You're a thinker like me. When Randy calls back, go along with him. We need to find out what he's up to."

"Why? I told you I don't want to be around him, not even on the phone."

"A good soldier keeps tabs on the enemy."

He was wasting his breath. "This better be worth it, dad."

"It will be, son. Trust me. I'll call back after the meeting. Tell Wanda I won't have the phone with me until afterwards. You know how she likes to call." Billy Ray murmured something meaningless and hung up the phone.

*   *   *

"I'm sorry, sir," Mildred said. "Mr. Swartzman gave me explicit instructions for you. The message is–do not disturb me. That's exactly what he said."

"He'll want to talk to me."

"I'm sorry. He said not to bother him, especially if Mr. Leper Khaun calls."

"You stupid woman!"

Mildred flinched. This day was just too much! Her boss was mad as a hornet, people were running around like ants on fire and nobody was where they said they'd be. And who did they come to for everything? Mildred! How was she supposed to hold things together under these circumstances? "Excuse me, sir. Those are my instructions," she said with a forced pleasantry. "If Mr. Leper Khaun calls, Mr. Swartzman has nothing for you.

"It's Lep-*pre*, not Lep-*er*!"

"Well, sir, I'm so sorry, it's a very unusual–"

"Shut up! Just shut the hell up!"

Mildred took a deep breath and sent a prayer of help skyward. She was a professional. She would survive! "Sir, is there a message?" Her pencil was poised, ready. What spewed from the other end of the phone would have Mildred in shock for hours and spreading her tale of woe for days.

"And you tell that Kraut his deadline has past. I know where he lives and I have contacts in Boston. *I want my money!*"

The phone slammed in Mildred's ear. "Heavens to Betsy! How rude!" She wondered how she'd report this message to her boss. "What a funny name Lepre Khaun."

*   *   *

"Yeah, Randy. Whatcha' want?"

"I need your help, Billy Ray." Randy sounded desperate. "I ain't got my car wid me. I last rode in that California dude's rental."

Here he goes again–talking big. Randy'd never been out of Georgia, much less the county. Now he was buddy-buddy with someone from the other side of the country? Right! Billy Ray was tempted to hang up.

"Drive it to the WalMart, okay? Park it close to the store entrance and put the keys under the driver's mat."

"That's it?"

"Buy a box of computer diskettes."

"What kind?"

"I don't know. Do you know anything about them?"

"I can ask my dad."

"No! I don't want you to talk to anyone about this!" Randy yelled.

"I hear you! You don't have to bust my eardrums. You're the one asking for favors."

Randy waited before answering. "Just get any kind."

"What else?"

"That's it. I'll call you tomorrow morning, after ten. You still gonna be at your dad's?"

"Yeah."

*   *   *

A door in the rear of the bar slammed, sounding like gunshot. Willie was surprised he'd kept himself from diving under the table. He was jumpier than a long-tailed cat in a room full of rocking chairs. No sooner had he gotten the Wizard off his back, Swartzman wanted him. Then he got the call to come to Savannah for the GBI. He had too many roles to play and was bound to mess up. Now Vontana was late and he wanted to rid himself of the papers before someone found out and he ended up like that Hightower boy. He kept his head down and sipped his beer.

"Hey, Willie." A hand grabbed his shoulder.

"Uh! You scared me, Vontana" he said irritably. He mopped up the small puddle of beer that had spilt by flicking it off the tabletop with a swipe of his hand. "My ass nearly cleared the seat." He wiped his damp hand on his jeans.

"My mother always told me only the guilty act like that."

"Har-har. I didn't see you come in."

"I used the kitchen."

"You're late."

"I'm worth the wait. Whatcha got for me?" Willie slid the yellow envelope across the table, breathing easier with each inch it moved away from him. Vontana slit the envelope open with his thumbnail, looked inside and came up grinning. "Whoa. You have certainly earned your money." Wetting an index finger, he rifled the papers, never taking them out of the envelope. "This is what I need to shoot the monkey off my back. And put an end to that girl's meddling." Vontana slipped Willie a small brown paper bag under the table. "Here you go, my boy. Keep in touch." Willie watched Vontana disappear through the kitchen. He finished his beer in a better frame of mind.

*   *   *

"Mildred, I told you I didn't want anyone to bother me for the rest of the day."

"Yes, sir. But, Mr. Anderson from Finance called to say he has the information you've been so upset over."

"What is it?"

"He wouldn't tell me. He wants you to call him."

"I'm the guy running this place and everyone is giving *me* orders! Get him on the line."

Mildred breathed deeply. "He's not here, sir."

"When that pansy-ass gets back, tell him to give you the damn report!"

"Yes, sir!" The offensive language today! Mildred quickly called Barb to cover for her on the phone. When the young girl arrived, she slipped her bottle of aspirin and Bible into her purse and hurried to the break room. Mr. Anderson was stretched out on the couch, a cloth over his eyes. "Oh, there you are, sir." She placed her purse on the table. "Excuse, me," she said loudly when he didn't acknowledge her. "I'm talking to you!" Anderson pulled the cloth off, gawking at the usually docile Mildred. "Mr. Swartzman is upset because you wouldn't relay your entire message to me. I *am* his executive secretary, you know. He wants you to tell me now."

"Fine! I've about had it with this place. Tell your boss that all the stocks were transferred to charities and cannot be undone." The man must be stupid, she thought. You don't take back money you give to charity.

"And their names?" Mildred pulled the phone bill from her purse and wrote on the envelope. She was nothing if not efficient and thorough.

"The African American Education Fund, the Waving Girl Center for Tolerance, California Asian Youth Association, Native American School Foundation, the Mexican-American Job Coalition, Save the Music." He covered his face again and lowered his head. Then he reversed his actions. "Oh, yes, there's one more. Jews for Jesus."

"Now that's just wonderful!" she said. "I had no idea Gundersen was supporting so many worthy causes." Anderson rolled his eyes and collapsed back on the couch with a groan.

*   *   *

Swartzman swung the ax down like the log was attempting his murder. He'd chopped enough wood for two Massachusetts winters. In Rincon it would barely be used, but he kept splitting the wood and heaving the pieces behind him.

The Klan had pulled one over on him, and he couldn't figure out which one of his men was guilty of helping. He'd grilled everyone. The problems were popping up as fast as he could take care of them. He swung down, missed the log, and almost caught himself in the thigh. *You're a soldier,* he told himself. *You can handle this.*

Randy. He had to go. He worked on his own agenda and was lying about having the diskettes. The problem with Randy in a nutshell–he didn't realize just how stupid he really was. Randy planned on snatching the girl all along. Swartzman would play his game and put the screws to him at the worst possible moment.

Leprechaun. He'll let the man wait. What could the guy do if Swartzman didn't pay him? Call the cops? He only had to worry about himself and keeping the boys in Boston happy. He wiped his face with his shirt tail and swung again. How could he quickly raise some cash? Sell some of the equipment the Leprechaun shipped him? Yeah, skim a crate of goods here and there. It wouldn't be noticeable while he accumulated cash. Maybe hit the WRF guys up for another donation.

But how did they get into my computer? Someone must have taken advantage of all the pandemonium when the bomb threat was called in. Everybody was running around in a panic like chickens with their heads chopped off. Did he just say that? Geez, he's been down here too long. Gotta get my WRF units back to working order and get out of the South. He wanted to be back in Bean Town, where "yous" can drive a "cah".

To recover his own money, he'd scale back WRF operations. Set up books for Boston like he did for the nosy IRS thieves and other communist government officials. That would only work short term. He got anxious when he didn't have a nice cushion to fall back on. Thanks to the Klan, his cushion was diverted to every minority group he'd worked his ass off to eradicate from his beloved country. A smile crept across his lips. There was always somebody who could use a little device to make some cash. And he had the money makers–the cellular phone detectors! Best of all was the fact that the unknowing, hardworking folks of Rincon were cranking them out by the crate load every day.

Barney the dinosaur may love us, but the feeling isn't mutual in some circles. When members of a white supremacist group learned that David Joyner, the actor inside the purple suit, is black, many forbade their children to watch the show. "We feel that blacks and their ways are dominating the performing fields," says a Ku Klux Klan member who would speak only anonymously. "Barney is no exception just because his true identity is concealed." You mean like under little white hoods?–Esquire, April 1994.

Chapter Sixty

Imperial Wizard Wyman Hughes didn't see Jeffery, a Kleagle, coming into the Klavern until it was too late to dodge him.

"I'm sorry to bother you again," Jeffery said. "I need the money for the work I done on the Klavern. At least some of it. "I'm sorry for having to bother you, but my wife quit her job on account of helping with the Cause. So things have been tight for us money-wise."

"Come here, son," Hughes urged the man. "I need to share something top secret. I don't want the boys to think anything's amiss. You know how people get the wrong idea. And it's your chance to do something for the Klavern."

Hughes held up two empty KFC chicken buckets. The word "kollection" had been scribbled in thick, black ink on each one. "I'm asking for a big one tonight. I wasn't able to get to the bank today. Time slipped up on me. I'll give you tonight's draw and I'll go to the bank tomorrow, square the accounts," Hughes lied. To get rid of Jeffery, he shoved the two chicken buckets at him and ordered, "you be in charge of this." He faced the group of men and raised his right hand to get their attention.

"Take a seat. The meeting is called to order! I have news of utmost importance, brethren. I'll get straight to it. Communist lawyers have been gunning for us lately and are trying to pin a nigger's lynching on us. Although we wholeheartedly agree with such disposal of the Mud in our great nation, I'm sad to say a rival group, posing as God-fearing Americans, have framed two of our leaders." He spoke louder. "We need lawyers to fight the people who dare frame us. We have to dig deep into our pockets to help our Klan brothers and fight the forces which try to undermine us." He signaled for Jeffery to pass the buckets and put in a wad of ones, holding them so the group would see him giving up a good chunk of bills, not their small denomination. He reminded himself to take them out before he gave Jeffery some of tonight's take.

"I want to talk to you about Randy Beamon. He's a renegade, a cheat." No one argued with the Imperial Wizard about that statement. "He's doing things in the name of the Klan that ain't been sanctioned by this Klavern. He's been threatening to hurt me and my family. Because I stood up to him and wouldn't let him attack any of you, my Klan brethren. He's gone and done some heinous crimes and I caught him trying to finger you guys." He stared at a few of the more weak and skittish members, knowing these new lies he was telling tonight wouldn't have to be substantiated. They'd take what they heard tonight and run with it. "And! Now, that ain't all! He's bringing communist federal agents snooping around to tear us apart."

"He's nothing! We're not scared of him! Let's get him!" The group roared.

"I've got a plan," he said when the men quieted. "I have intelligence trying to locate that fraud Randy who is somewhere out there hiding in fear." He flung a robed arm outward and pointed. "When we find out where that is, we must be ready at a moment's notice to fight for our Klavern and defend our families."

"I heard tell Randy done raped his own sister 'cause she's with child. His."

What else will be revealed before the end of the night? Hughes thought. *Could this be true? Randy's done enough now to hang himself. That is if I can bring him in. Is that what has his son Billy Ray so boxed in? While the news might be upsetting, it didn't make sense unless...No, please. Not that. Could it be that his son was upset about Moonpie? Could he have feelings for that tramp?* He pushed it out of his mind.

He looked out over the group, false sincerity oozing from every pore. "Yes, that story about Randy has been confirmed," he lied. "Randy has dared to bring an illegitimate retard into this world which breaks apart the sanctity of the family. Now Moonpie must live in shame for flaunting herself to her own kin! This is what happens when you don't live as God has put forth!

"Remember, brothers, we must be generous tonight! You must put your country and your Klan above yourself." He paused and looked each one in the eye. He didn't move to the next guy until each one squirmed in his seat–when the guilt and discomfort made their wallets loose. "Tonight is the time we need to get ready! The call to save our nation's freedom has sounded! We've been working long and hard for this." Shouts of agreement rose up from the group. "It's time to put our lives on the line to wipe out the evil forces invading the sanctity of our homes, our work, our children, our town! Blood must be spilled!"

"Yes! We're with you brother!"

"Think of the enemies that must be eliminated! We must be prepared to kill for what we believe in! Now can we have our closing scripture read?"

*Alabama: 1989, Montgomery–Maya Lin, who designed the
Vietnam Memorial, was commissioned by the Southern Poverty
Law Center to design a monument–the first of it's kind– depicting
forty ordinary people killed in the civil rights movement. The
monument faces the State House–where George Wallace, in 1962,
pledged he would uphold segregation.*

Chapter Sixty-One

"So much for quiet, small towns! There's more activity going on
in Rincon than in the whole state! The WRF thinks they'll head a race
war, and if that isn't busy enough, they run a computer plant making
components to finance the operation," Dixie said. She covered her
face as her hands gently massaged her cheeks and forehead. Her
fingers created bizarre shapes of her lips. Clarice glanced at her, did
a double take, shook her head sadly and looked away. I giggled. We
were sitting around Al's big kitchen table talking about the last
month's events.

"And the WRF is framing the Klan. I guess they want to shut them
down. I hope this raid finally ends things," I added. Everyone
nodded.

"I need to do something to calm my nerves. I don't want to think
about the WRF or KKK," Beverly spoke, her hands fluttering about
nervously.

"Let's play cards," Aggie suggested. Poker was the only activity,
we discovered, that Aggie would trade for her cross-stitching. Elbows
deep into a hand of lowball and the feisty game warden set the pace
by making us eat her dust. Moving on to the stud varieties, we began
to treat the night like last call at a single's bar. We ignored the
problems and events that festered around us with a determined
desperation. Al, finished with tending his animals, tried hanging out
in the "casino". We put him to work as waiter amid catcalls and good-
natured ribbing. He soon announced he'd had enough of wild beasts
and joined Gus in the quiet shadows outside. I folded–again–and
Aggie was a hair's breath from being accused of cheating. Nobody
wins *that* much. I just couldn't figure where in her sleeveless top she
hid the aces.

Dixie picked the next game, having a fondness for Mexican stud,
in which I fared no better. While wearing the wax off the cards, we
attacked Al's freezer. We inhaled the ice cream, Sara Lee, and a box
of goodies from Gotlieb's bakery he'd tried to hide in a far corner of
the frig.

Gus and Al braved indoors just before 1:00 A.M. as we ladies,
delirious on sugar and lack of sleep, were placing bets on who would
be able to stay awake waiting for news from Vontana. I chickened out
first, pretending sleep was the reason when in truth my heart was still
occasionally beating erratically thanks to The Voices torture tactics.
I led the exodus with everyone traipsing upstairs behind me. Dixie

and I paired off for the first bed-room, Clarice and Beverly for the second and Aggie took the third.

"Paloma, come here, quick!" Dixie urged.

I climbed out of bed complaining. "What?"

"See that door?" Dixie pointed across the hall, two doors down. "That's Al's bedroom." She bounced from foot to foot on the creaking floorboards. "Hear that? I'll know if you slip out of here, young lady."

"Kiss my butt." I went zombie-like back to bed. Dixie bogarted the covers as she tried to cover her almost six foot frame. We played tug-of-war with the top sheet. "For a skinny hussy, you sure do hog a lot of the bed linen." She denied it and pointed. I looked down at her feet. "You need a few more inches of bed. Serves you right." She tried to tickle me until she banged her head on the headboard and let out a snort.

"You may have gotten enough sleep in jail, but I haven't. Cut the crap or I'll tell your mother." She turned out the lights while the crickets sang a lullaby.

"Paloma?"

"What, Dixie?"

"You're my best friend."

"Are we having a moment?"

"Yeah."

"Okay, Dix. You're my only and best friend."

"And Al? You didn't think I'd forget."

"Heavens no, you're a cop." I grew pensive. "He was great. After–you know. I really lost it for a few days on the *Katie*. Maybe he's being nice to help me out."

"And once you're on your feet, *ciao, baby*?"

"Um-huh."

"I don't think he's that way. Not the way he chewed on your lips on Lemond's front porch." I gave her an elbow. She persisted. "So what about him?"

"I'm scared."

"It's at that stage?"

"'Fraid so."

"Hmm. Bad pun. Goodnight, John Boy."

"Night, Mary Ellen."

University of Illinois, Chicago–A penis severed from a medical school cadaver was placed on a door of a black female dorm resident. One in four minority students has been a victim of a hate incident (up to one million a year). University of Wisconsin, Madison–Twenty-three anti-Semitic incidents occurred in seven weeks.–USA Today 12/90.

Chapter Sixty-Two

"Willie, wake up. Someone's beatin' the front door down." His wife was rocking him with her foot and a bony elbow. He looked out the window, but didn't see anything. Pulling on the boxer shorts he'd snatched up from the floor, he stumbled down the hallway, wiping sleep from his eyes.

"Who is it?"

"Bruce Vontana."

The GBI agent had never come to his house. "What the hell you doin' here?" He asked as he opened the door.

"Come on, I've got something to show you." The agent didn't wait for an answer. Willie peered out at Vontana's car, didn't see anyone inside and trotted to catch up to him "Check this out," he said and opened the door. Willie bent over, sticking his head inside. The agent had his hands cuffed and his backside kicked before Willie's first yelp of surprise. Vontana rested his cocked revolver against Willie's temple. "Want to die?"

"No-No. Don't hurt me! What's the matter with you?"

"I'm pissed, Willie, and I think it's because of you."

"I swear! I ain't done nothin'!" Vontana taped Willie's mouth and eyes with blue duct tape and bound his ankles together. All he could do was lay there humiliated. Vontana slipped into the front seat and took Willie for a ride.

The car stopped later on. Willie had lost track of how long they'd driven. "Vontana you ain't got to do this! Talk to me! We can straighten this out," Willie begged after the agent ripped the tape off his mouth and eyes. "Please!" He sobbed shamelessly. "Don't kill me, man. I thought we were partners."

"Shut up, Willie. I'm not losing sleep because I wanted to listen to you." "Okay, just don't hurt me 'til we talk this out. Man, you actin' like Dirty Harry!"

Vontana slung the guy over his shoulder and entered a small hut. He squatted in front of the man, tethered him to an old wooden chair and checked the binds. He moved back a safe distance and brandished the gun.

"Me and the guys, we spent a long time planning this, shall we say, visit to Gundersen tonight. After all this time, we finally think we have the evidence, got the timing right. Why do we think that? Because, my friend Willie has been giving me information." He waved the gun for emphasis.

"Please, don't point that thing at me."

"Why not?" Willie didn't answer. "You are in no position to give orders. And why is that, Willie? Is it because you are tied to a chair, begging for your sorry life?" He turned away from him to slip the gun in his jacket pocket. Suddenly he advanced on Willie. In short, brutal moves the agent knocked him over with a backhanded slug and immediately righted the chair roughly. Willie felt he was being jerked in every direction at once. Like that monster ride at the county fair. It had made him sick then–his head was splitting, his stomach inside-out. Like he was feeling now. "Is it because Willie tipped someone off?" he yelled right into the man's face. "So when we went to the plant tonight it would be a complete waste of time. Is that what you did?" Willie's face froze in fear, spittle ran down the left corner of his mouth.

"Did Willie think about what he did to his buddy Vontana? I don't think so, because I got a gun and I'm gonna point it right at your head until you tell me what you've *really* been up to." The gun was in his hand in seconds. He aimed it dead center at Willie. He cocked it. The tick sounded like cannon fire.

Willie was too scared to swallow. "I-I-I ain't done nothin', man." Willie's pleas were convulsions of terror, red-faced and wide-eyed. "I don't know how they found out!" Vontana watched a few moments while the man lost control and sniveled. "I'm 'bout to crap my pants, Vontana. I ain't kidding."

"I believe you," the agent said stepping back and fanning the air. "About that part at least."

"Please, let me take a dump."

"You have such a sophisticated vocabulary. I'm beginning to think you're not worth the trouble." Still tied to the chair, Vontana dragged Willie outside, handcuffed one hand to the base of an old water pump. Then he untied his legs.

"I need me some toilet paper."

"Improvise, you screw up."

Back inside, it was more of the same. Vontana believed Willie would run to him if things got too hot, but he had to eliminate him as a suspect. Willie confessed he'd been getting money from both Hughes and Swartzman to spy on each other. Randy had suggested the idea to him. Willie snitched about Moonpie being at Swartzman's office, battered and incoherent. He also revealed that Hughes was up to something and wanted Willie's help.

"You better tell me as soon as you find out."

"I will, Bruce. I promise."

"Is there anything else you haven't told me?" Willie shook his head furiously. Vontana stared at his snitch.

"I swear on a stack of Bibles. What now?"

"You go back to your wife and act like nothing happened. And don't breathe a word to Hughes or Swartzman. Business as usual. You report to me *every* time one of them breaks wind." To emphasize his point, he shoved the gun into Willie's crotch. When Willie's hysteria mellowed, Vontana popped the clip and showed him the bullet-empty gun. Willie's crying, contorted face froze. Vontana thought he looked like a stroke victim as he untied him. He sighed and wiped the sweat off of his face with a shirt sleeve. Why did getting at the truth take such long, dirty paths? "Willie," he said quietly and slowly. "Let's go. I'll take you home."

"Where am I?"

"That empty shed about a quarter mile from your place."

"But we drove for a long time!"

"Willie, not everything is like it seems. You just make sure you are."

To get his manhood and pride back on track, Willie declined the ride. Vontana left him in his skivvies, mumbling and wobbling along the road. Willie was unsure of whether he should be very angry or deeply relieved.

New Mexico: Farmington–Three teenagers on a routine "Indian rolling" venture murdered a Navajo male. He was beaten, stripped, genitals and head hair burned, a firecracker set off in his rear, rolled down a hill, beaten more and pelted with branches. With bound feet, the man was able to walk about sixty-six yards before he died. The youths killed two more Navajo men that month. A white judge rejected trying them as adults. Their punishment was reform school.

Sixty-Three

I woke slowly, like I was swimming in gelatin, then quickly became conscious. Al, illuminated by the hallway light, was standing over me. I stretched out locking my hands behind his neck, wanting to yank him down with me. Remembering I already had a bed partner–Dixie–I pulled myself up and kissed him instead.

"Come downstairs, sugah." he whispered directly into my ear, hot breath making my neck tingle deliciously. I followed him out the room, pulling the door behind me. Naughty thoughts created a watermelon grin ear to ear.

"What time is it?" I asked once I entered his kitchen.

"Six."

"I presume A.M. You better make this very good," I teased, suddenly realizing we were in the kitchen. Farmer-attorney Eason getting a little kinky? Hmm. I hung my thumbs in his belt loops filled with anticipation.

"We're going to meet Vontana."

A cold slap again in my libido. Did this man ever let business matters sleep? "Vontana? Did you get a sudden urge to mend fences?"

"No. He called saying he has the lab reports on the car you were left in. And the other guy who helped nab you."

"He wants to see me now?"

"If you want to," Al said lightly, like this was a perfect time to traipse off to face demons.

"What about the raid?"

"He didn't say."

"Let's go find out."

"I'm ready. I don't think you want to go dressed like that."

"I ran around the courtyard of the Riverfront Hotel in a shorter tee."

"I'm sorry I wasn't there."

"Mr. Eason, you are such a flirt! And that's about all," I added at a lower tone. I tiptoed into the bedroom, tempted to wake Dixie just because. Instead, I pulled the least wrinkled shorts out of my pack and dressed in the adjoining bathroom, stifling groans and checking bandages as I moved around. I'd been staring into mirrors a lot lately, each time what stared back looked increasingly worse. This morning's reflection made me appreciate that Al could be enamored at all. I slicked down a few strands of hair to look less punk rocker, slapped a touch of makeup on the worst spots, brushed my teeth and went outside.

At the GBI building, Bruce Vontana was downstairs waiting for us. We were silent on the elevator ride to his floor. The Bias Crimes Division was small–three agents' desks crammed against each other with mountains of papers smothering the tops. Yellow ceiling lights painted everything a dim weirdness. Or perhaps it was the hour.

"Let's go where we can talk privately." He ushered us into a room with a two-way mirror. I looked through it seeing a carbon copy of the room we were standing in. Gray and dented metal tables and chairs, a standard in all government offices, made the pale painted walls appear even more dull and battered.

"Would you like coffee?" We both nodded. I sat at the end of the table, Al to my left. Vontana brought java, the aroma already perking me up. It tasted like house shingles. Old ones. Unable to handle it straight up, I drowned it in powdered creamer and sugar.

"Thank you both for coming. I'm sorry about the hour. I barely noticed it until the sun was coming up. That's how bad a night I've had. I'll make this brief. Hewson goofed in how we dealt with you, Paloma, and he knows it." I didn't mention that Al had already told me as much.

"Who's Hewson?" I asked.

"My boss. I've got a lot to explain." He looked and sounded so haggard, I knew the news wasn't good. I felt my hopes slide down, like me that night in Georgia clay. "I've been wanting to tell you some things, Al, for the last week. I couldn't track you down and then I found out that you were in Carolina for several days. On a boat." Bruce's smile was quirky. Al softened briefly. There was hidden meaning, some secret exchange between the two that I'd have to ask Al about later. I wouldn't waste the time at the moment.

Vontana sorted the folders and pulled one out. After briefly thumbing through the papers he passed one over to Al. "Ballistics report from Billy Ray's shooting. The bullets are .308's and match the ones from the River Street parking lot where pot shots were taken at you, Paloma. Randy Beamon and the two others with him that night are wanted for questioning. The local cops are working on that. I got an update faxed to me yesterday. The woman in the back of the pickup was probably his sister. She's apparently a rather large woman. She'll be found soon, I'd expect. The latest rumor from the Savannah Police is that Beamon beat up his sister. Bad. And an unconfirmed rape."

"Rape?" I looked at Al, floored. He imitated me.

"The lab is still analyzing the car you were in," Vontana said, focusing on me. "We were able to lift a print off the tape that was around your neck. That'll help cinch things. The car was rented with

a phony license. Now." He paused. "The picture's in the folder."
My heart thudded. I wasn't sure I was ready.

"The raid, Vontana?"

"You are the most impatient woman I've ever met," the agent said
lightly. "The raid. It was a dud, nothing out of place. Not even the
WRF letters Paloma saw painted on the walls. Of course, when the
techs go over everything, I'm sure they'll find *something*." Disap-
pointment was a very inadequate description of how we all felt. It was
palpable, filling up the room.

"Right afterward I went straight to my Rincon snitch and scared the
shit out of him–literally. He wasn't the one who tipped them."

"How can you be so sure?" I asked.

"When I finished with him," Vontana spoke quietly. "He would
have confessed to anything." He rubbed the bags under his eyes. We
were all a sorry looking mess!

"Now. Al. There were suspicions of a leak in our section in the last
few months. Nothing concrete or even that dangerous or important
was being compromised. Then it suddenly got worse. Hewson didn't
know which of his men he could really trust. To clear me, I had to be
checked out, so he gave me a special assignment. I didn't know I was
being tested. If I'd shared the details with you, Al, I would have had
to turn in the towel. It wouldn't have made a difference if you did
nothing with the information. Al, he was watching to see if I did
anything at all. There was something in the way he was talking that
day that felt hinky. The scary thing is I would have told you, right
away, but you were out of town for several weeks, so I couldn't talk
to you. That was the only thing that kept me from trashing my career.

"Anyway, after I was cleared, things were sailing along. But then
Paloma here, comes in and stirs up the pot." He put up a hand to ward
off any retorts–but I hadn't planned on giving him one. I didn't think
I'd done anything wrong. I checked some places and people out like
any investigator would do. Al told him exactly that.

"I agree. I never thought I would be telling someone to get lost who
came to this agency for help. That's what Hewson ordered me to do
that night at your farm."

"So what type of thing is being leaked out? Information only?" I
asked.

He shifted in his chair uncomfortably and shook his head. This
obviously bothered him. "Some of the items Paloma turned over to us
are missing."

"Since when?" I asked.

"That's what I'm tasked to secretly check out." He sighed wearily.
"Frankly, I don't remember when I saw them last. I haven't been here
in the office hardly at all. It hit me the day after I picked up what I
thought were photos of my daughter's birthday party. My son is into
computers, all that stuff. He told me that the photos were on disc.
That's what I picked up at the store. I think we can put them on the
computer, email them to relatives. Does that sound right, Paloma?"

"Yes. The CD of photos that I gave you is gone?"

He nodded. "I know you kept a copy." I slid on my poker face. I will neither confirm nor deny. Vontana continued. "I don't think they're that important now–thanks to your doggedness and additional information. But what the hell happened to them?" We batted this around a few moments–hemming and hawing–in Southern parlance. Another niggling in the far corners of my mind. It had to do with more damn disks. I thought over that night at Al's farm. Who was doing what. Oh well, later. I focused on what the agent was now saying.

"With this loss and now the raid tonight, there has to be a dirty agent in our section. Probably other incidents that at the time we didn't connect to a rat. I went to Hewson after I left my snitch. He assigned me the task of flushing the rat-bastard out. Now I'm feeling like a creep myself, spying on my coworkers." Vontana grimaced as he belted down the last of his coffee like a shot of whiskey. I almost shuddered in sympathy. That stuff was dreck! "I feel like I've been rode hard and put away wet." He took a breath and barged on.

"Al, I was getting flack for including you so often in GBI informa-tion. My plan was to lay low for a while, then tell you. But Paloma disappeared. Al, my gut was in that trunk, too. I never had a brother until I met you. Can we let the disasters pull us together instead of apart?" He paused, searching for something from Al. "I hope your silence means you're considering it."

"Who knows we're here?" Al asked.

"Hewson."

"Why the change of heart?"

"I told him I would quit. Our friendship means more. I never thought I'd be in a situation where I could lose it." I looked at Al, his face was stony, but I could see in his eyes that his brain was busy.

"Paloma, have you collected any additional information?" I shook my head. "Okay, I have a photo and some information you can look at." I picked up the folder and hesitated like I was about to find out how long I'd live with an incurable disease. I steeled myself, then dove right into the situation–like I always do.

"What's his name?" I asked, a flat affect in my voice. Inside I was filled with contempt and loathing tinged with fear.

"Tom Richards." The Voice.

"Filho da puta!" I called him every name I could think of and made up a few more. I spit on The Voice's face and sent the photo sailing toward the other end of the table.

Vontana flipped open the file. "His prints were in AFIS. That's the national database for fingerprints." He looked up at me. "You already knew that, didn't you." I nodded. Any mystery lover knows what AFIS is. "All the bad guys have priors. No surprise there. His sheet shows arrests and jail time in New York and California. Assaults mostly. Some thefts."

"Now we have to find the third man," Al said, moving to put an arm around me. A knock sounded on the door and Vontana stepped out. He leaned back inside to tell us that he had to talk briefly with his snitch. I heard the door opened on the other side of the window, then muddled voices.

"You doing okay, sugah?" Al asked with requisite hand patting.

"*Yes*. I really am. With a name, he can now be traced." I stood, needing to walk out the stiffness I was prone to while my body was healing. I paced around the table and retraced my steps but in the opposite direction. At the two-way mirror, I froze.

"Al, that's him!" I stabbed at the window.

"Who?"

"The other guy at the Klavern."

"You're sure?" Al asked rushing to the mirror. I gave him the would-I-make-something-like-this-up look. Vontana was pointing the man to a chair. Through the mirror the snitch talked with urgent, jerky mannerisms like he was trying to save his own soul. Or get Vontana to. Once more my insides jerked into panic mode. I clutched Al's arm. "It's a trap. Vontana says that man's his snitch. Al, he could be lying. Maybe he's the dirty agent." I was ready to rabbit out of the building.

*   *   *

Hughes left for his appliance store right after a very bad breakfast. Wanda, who was still not privy to what was happening around her, had run out of patience. She purposely burnt the toast, the eggs had bits of shell in them and she'd waited until the plate was banged down in front of him before she poked her little finger into the three yolks in his over-easy eggs. There was more. The coffee was weak and grinds floated on top. Her look dared him to complain and the last time he'd walked away with her mess untouched, he ended up wearing the vittles. Hughes ate in silence, not daring to push his wife further.

Billy Ray camped in his old bedroom, sullen and even more uncommunicative. Randy called. Wanda threw open his bedroom door, catching him in the buff pulling on underwear. She blatantly stared at his maleness. She snapped out of her sexual reverie, haughtily announced the caller, and slammed the door behind her. Her heels pounded quick thumps down the hallway. Billy Ray used the phone in the hallway.

"Man, I got problems like you wouldn't believe." Randy sounded both scared and thrilled. "Did you move my car?"

"Yeah, I thought you'd have gotten it by now."

"I told you I got other problems. Listen, I need my bowling bag. It's at your place."

"Since when?" Billy Ray asked.

Randy sniggered. "A ways back."

"Where?"

"Under the trailer, toward the back where we patched that water hose last winter. You'll see the spot. I cut away a piece of the insulation."

"Thanks for asking for permission, asshole."

"Don't get your boxers in a wad there B-Ray. Bring it to me. I'm gonna be gone a while. And don't open it. I'll be able to tell if you did. I got it set up that way."

"Where do you want me to meet you?"

"Logs Landing. That old cove where you and I used to hang. Come tonight right after dark." Billy Ray hung up. Wanda too, without a tell-tale click, from the living room.

Would Randy ever leave him alone? Billy Ray wondered. *What kind of person could do what he did, especially to his sister, and act like it never happened? A demented person! And Hughes wanted him to play along with Randy for a while. Why? It could only make more trouble for them all.*

His father seemed really tainted to him now. Was it because of Hughes's recent comments, making him feel obligated for taking him in? Billy Ray felt he'd settled any debt he owed the Hughes' when he borrowed ten thousand dollars to pay back the Klavern. Money his father had used to upgrade his home and a small attempt at taking care of Wanda's insurmountable credit card debts. Besides, Billy Ray had to promise that he would never tell Wanda. And he didn't. But she'd known something was up, and he'd had to lie for his father. Billy Ray thought that was wrong. Not necessarily the lying part, but he thought she needed to know there was a bottom to the well. Billy Ray had worked two jobs until last summer, paying the loan back. All for nothing. Whatever his father was up to, he was finished with it! He was tired of the violence, tired of being tired. He'd get the bag alright, he wanted to see what was so important Randy wouldn't hide it at his own place. He left the house, ignoring Wanda's questions.

Billy Ray felt like a thief even though it was his own house he was crawling underneath. Nothing felt normal anymore. Randy was right, for once. It was easy to see his hiding place. The bowling bag almost fell into his hands. He unzipped it and looked in. And stared for a long time.

You've gone completely over the edge now, Randy. A door shutting somewhere in the park snapped him to attention. He replaced the piece of insulation and as he crawled backwards, noticed a section beside it was bowed. "Damn, Randy, you mess with my home, the one thing I got going for me and that's all mine." He pressed the insulation to reseat it and felt a heavy weight. Sighing, he dug his car keys out of his pocket for the penlight aiming it at the bowel of the underside of his home. The light glinted. Metal. He leaned forward. Randy's other rifle! As he reached up to pull it out, his body twitched. Was this the gun Randy bugged him to use when they went hunting last month? Something about wanting his opinion on how well the gun worked. Randy never cared what he'd thought before. He sat on his heels thinking. *Randy, you jerk, are you trying to frame me for something? I bet only my prints are on this gun.* Would someone be coming after him? The cops maybe? In the tiny space, he squirmed out of his shirt, using it to carefully pull the rifle out. He stuffed the insulation back in place and crawled out backwards and stowed the goods in his trunk. He was soaked in sweat and shook from anger and fear. He drove out of the trailer park wondering what he was going to do now.

Washington, D.C: 1993–A lesbian was shot to death outside a gay bar by a man who had solicited sex from her. Macon, Georgia: 1993–Elizabeth Davidson, a twenty-five-year-old lesbian was shot to death in a bar; another woman was shot twice in the thigh. Two youths, aged fifteen and sixteen were charged with murder and aggravated assault.

Chapter Sixty-Four

"Willie, you were where? And with what woman?"

The man paled and threw himself at Vontana, ending up in a melodramatic heap on the floor, arms clutched around the agent's legs. He looked up at him, oblivious to the startled unease on the other man's face.

Once the snitch had been calmed down and pried off of Vontana, the agent laboriously pulled the confession out of him. "I been up all night! I'm real chawed up a'worryin' over this. I woulda told you last night, but you wuz sucha agger-pervokin ol' buzzard that I didn't rightly knowed what to do. It's the only thang I ain't told ya. I swear it on a stack of Bibles!" Willie whined and moved his arms around for emphasis. "But it wuz Randy's fault! I ain't touched a hair on 'er! I swear! That dang Randy tricked me! Told me his car wuz broke down, needed me to pick 'im up at the Klavern. His mouth's always cluttered wid' trouble. Said he'd give me fifty buckaroos to high-tail it down there. Ain't gave me a dang plug nickle."

"Fifty dollars! That should have clued you in immediately. Why the heck did you bother with him?"

"To play up to him. I knowed he wuz up to somethin'. You mighta needed to know 'bout it." Vontana was not a stupid man. He almost snorted his disbelief. Does Willie actually think he'd fall for that? No, Willie had wanted that fifty dollars and now he was back-peddling to save his sorry skin.

"The truth–or I'll beat the moss out of you!" Willie flinched like he expected to get punched. "On with it, Willie! Quickly!" The agent looked at his watch.

"Well, when I pulled up to the Klavern, I heard 'em all. It was a real send-up goin' on in there." Willie was animated, about to fly out of his chair. "Randy wuz cat-a-goglin drunk. That there slant-eye guy, I don't know who he be. Well, 'im an' Randy wuz passing words a'somethin' fierce. They wuz goin' after that gal left 'n right." He sniggered while boxing the air, his head moving back and forth in pretend blows. "Pow! Pow! She was a-squawkin' 'n cussin' right back at 'em. Mad enough to chew nails!" The rest came out in a down-home babble of fright and honesty.

"What else?"

"Randy called me yesterday." He coughed and sputtered like an old car.

"Willie, I'm glad you're *finally* being totally honest with me. I've got some questions for you, but I need to go into the next room to get something. You stay right here. Can I bring you anything? Water, coffee?"

"Coffee, cream 'n two sugars." Vontana was closing the door behind him when Willie called out. "An ashtray, too." The agent nodded, pulling the door again. "Oh, ah, do you, ah..."

"Spit it out, Willie," he snarled impatiently.

"I left so early this morning 'n I wuz so bumfuddled."

"Willie!" he warned.

"I saw some doughnuts as I wuz coming in. That'd be real nice. I'm so dang hungry my stomach feels like my throat's been cut." Vontana hesitated a few seconds in case more requests were made. "Well, Mr. Po-lice, take your foot 'n go."

"Ugghh!" whooshed out of the agent, breathy and frustrated, as he walked down the hall. "In one word–clueless."

"Hey, Vontana! Chocolate frosting!"

*   *   *

When Vontana burst back into the interview room with an older, blue-suited man on his heels, I was still cutting the circulation off Al's forearm. I dropped my hand quickly like I'd been caught. Reeling from my accusation, Al was lost in deep thought, leaving me to work the crowd. I stood looking at them looking at Al looking at the snitch through the two-way.

"Folks, meet my boss, Agent Hewson. Great news, Eason, and this is going to be interesting!" I had to hand it to Al, his poker face gave nothing away. He looked at me and I saw his eyes narrow slightly. I replied with a knowing look, sending thought waves that I got his message and I would keep my trap shut and watch events unfold.

"That man in there is my snitch." All heads turned to look through the glass like we hadn't been doing that for the last five minutes. "He's confessing."

"To what?"

"You tell me, Paloma." I looked to Al for permission. He dipped his head once, taking my hand for support.

"He's the third guy."

"Paloma, you were a bit harsh in your description of him. I never put him with the artist's image."

"Forgive me," I said, dripping with sarcasm.

"I'm going to interview him now. Would you like to hear?" Al's nod was more noticeable this time. Hewson stayed behind, turning a black knob on the wall speaker. Willie's sniffling came through clearly.

With his head Al indicated "go left", directing me away from Hewson. He leaned in and whispered, his eyes darting to check on the agent. "You had me going for a moment, Paloma. If he hadn't come back in here and told us about that guy in there, I would have believed you."

"I'm sorry. I've been in panic mode for so long." I still held out a bit of caution. Al's relief was all too apparent and I felt a tug of regret that I'd added to his distress about his agent friend.

Vontana was setting up a tape recorder while Willie sniveled and begged not to be arrested, convinced he would become a jailbird's love puppy by nightfall. Soon Vontana rapped a knuckle once on the window and Hewson dismissed himself.

I wanted to crack a joke, do something to ease the tension that was building inside me. I knew what was coming. I had fooled myself into believing that having told Vontana about the torture at the Klavern, the hard part was over. I hadn't realized what it would be like hearing it. And worse– someone I cared about was standing right beside me about to learn the intimate details.

Like all victims of crime, I'd spent a lot of time wondering what I could have done to prevent it. That surprised me. Studying crime all of my life, I guess I thought I'd be a bit more rational if I became a victim. I should know better. But reality was another story. My head told me one thing, my emotions, my heart wasn't believing it. And I worried, too, what my friends and family would think of me. I was no different than other victims.

I turned in a panic to Al. It had been stupid to agree to stick around. "Al, let's go! I've seen this movie. I give it a thumbs down. Let's talk to Vontana later." To Al's "you're crazy" look, I pleaded again. "I'm serious. Please! You don't need to hear this. It won't help you in your work and it won't help me at all." He was stone.

"Look, if it makes you feel better–it's not much more than the injuries that you've seen on me. They banged me around in the car, then in the Klavern. They tied me up. They burned me with ciga- rettes. They kept asking me how much I knew–about things I didn't know anything about. They wouldn't believe me that Lemond didn't have stacks of evidence laying around–or we didn't find it. They shocked the hell out of me, punched me, burned me some more. Okay. You've heard it. Let's go." I pushed his shoulder to turn him around to face the door.

"If you want to go, you can wait for me outside," Al said evenly. We locked eyes in a staring contest. He was working on a slow burn.

"I can tell Vontana that I don't want you here."

"You won't." I didn't know if that was comment or command.

"The hell with it. And the hell with you! What is it about men that when 'their women are injured', the only thing they can do is go cave- man and mark their territory. Here," I spread my feet further apart and pointed at them. "Go ahead and pee around me."

"Paloma, you're getting carried away. Just calm down. It doesn't help you to get upset," he said condescendingly.

"You're the *one* upsetting *me!* I detest being patronized." Al denied it. I gave up. I don't do well in confrontations of words and wills. My mind seems to blank out. Even more maddening is that the next day, I always come up with a few humdingers I could have tossed into the ring to make my point. But throw me in with some Klansmen and I can't keep the sarcasm from flowing. But that type of confrontation was different. It didn't concern matters close to home and heart.

"So Al, you're telling me that no matter how I feel about this. Look at me!" I waited until he complied. "No matter if I'm wholeheartedly asking you, begging you, and as my supposed friend, you won't leave with met?" He didn't answer.

Tears flooded my eyes. I did *not* want to cry! My voice always gets whiny and my annoyance at this habit make it even higher. I swallowed and gulped air until my throat felt ready for normal speech. I found the courage to tell the truth and lay it out for Al. "If you stay, it will rip my heart up."

His eyes narrowed again but our signals were no longer in synch. He held my gaze. "I'm sorry."

It didn't take much effort for the agents to get out of Willie the whole truth and nothing but. The questions started before I turned the doorknob. I could not look behind me as I left.

*   *   *

Al wondered how and why he seemed to momentarily take leave of his senses. What kind of buffoon was he? It just washed over him, this weird feeling of being out of control. His entire being seemed to burn with rage. It hit him as soon as he realized that the dirt bag on the other side of the window had been at the Klavern. Who was worse–the person who burns and beats up a woman or the one who stands around and does nothing to help her? He'd come across this so many times in his work, but he'd always handled it. Yes, this was different. Personal. But you'd think he'd have seen it enough so that when it happened to someone he cared for, he'd be her champion. But who was this, this putz that he was today? He thought of Aggie. If it had been her in that emergency room, the first time he saw her, the raw skin, blood, burns, cuts, bruises–the agony. He felt enraged just thinking about it! He needed to go and find Paloma. Apologize.

But he couldn't move. He wanted to know every detail, every move, every indignity Paloma suffered. And. Most of all. He wanted to hurt each and every one who'd participated.

Voices crackled thorough the speaker. He moved so close to the window that his breath fogged the glass.

"Who does Randy work for?"

"You know that."

"For the record."

"A guy named Swartzman, at the Gundersen plant."

"What does he do there?"

"Whatever Swartzman wants."

"Which includes what?"

"Following people, threatening them." Willie droned a long list of duties.

"And Richards?"

"Who?"

"Tom Richards. The Chinese-American."

"I gotcha! I guess he does too, but he ain't from 'round here. I only seen 'im last weekend."

"Why did Randy and Richards take Paloma to the Klavern?"

"Make it look like the Klan did it."

"Did what?"

"Ah, torture. And kill 'er."

"How did she get away? And get into the trunk of that car?"

"Randy started threatnin' that slant-eye wid' a pistol. They got into an upscuttle. Guns a'goin' off right 'n left. That's when I hot-footed outta there!"

"You left and did what? Went home?"

"Yep."

"Why didn't you call anybody about Paloma? Do something?" He didn't have an answer. Even Willie could recognize contempt. And Vontana wasn't keeping his hidden. It made him uncomfortable, sitting across from him and so close. But it didn't intimidate him as much as the look on the face of that girl in the Klavern. When Randy uncovered her head, she saw him standing there. Doing nothing. It was like she was seeing into his very soul. Knew how chicken-hearted he was. That one time they were hurting her and she just kept her eyes right on him. Even when she screamed, she just kept on staring at him. Never changed her expression. It was wrong what they did. While he just stood by. Too gutless to say anything, do anything. Except save his own hide. That girl knew that about him. And the look on her face followed him everywhere. Even in his dreams.

Vontana sighed wearily. "Go over it again. Every minute of your time at the Klavern." Willie licked his lips and while his hands shook, he talked of screams, how her body jerked as each shock was applied.

                    *   *   *

He was just behind that door. Spilling his guts. How can a gutless man spill his guts? He was telling those agents–strangers–more intimate details than I'd yet revealed to myself. I wanted to go kick his butt. I could've done it. That short, small punk. One scenario: I was pretty much Bruce Lee. Hands so deadly they'd be registered lethal weapons. Yeah. I'd make him beg for his life.

Droga! So that was what it was like to be manic. My whole body twitched. I needed a swim. Maybe Dixie and I could hit the beach in afternoon. Man, my legs were jiggling. If I sat out in the hallway like that, some agent would make me pee in a cup. I was vibrating like those desperate junkies around Fourth and Spring in downtown L.A. It scared me, the rage I felt toward that little fart. And for Randy and The Voice. I'd never experienced that depth of loathing. The loss of control, or the fear of it, was terrifying. The last time my life had gotten that dark was when my parents died. Then I'd gone to Aunt

Lilly's. And sank pretty low until Dixie's mom faced her down. Told my grandparents to get me out of there. If they hadn't...who knows?

I was in the pits of despair and what did I do? Dredged up all the painful episodes of the past! Conjured up a lot of useless what-ifs. Stuck that knife in, turned it. Must get some perverse pleasure in ripping up my insides again and again. I told myself to focus. Think of, of...happy. *Happy?* My ass.

Al was in there. I should have be mad. But I was so hurt. Depressed. Manic depressive. That's what that was. I should have lugged Heathcliff there with me. At least I'd have had something to do. I'd pop a CD in, blast that place out. Blast that guy in there who stood around and watched and did nothing. I needed heavy metal music playing *loud* to block all that out. I needed to calm down. The Voice's face. Kept thinking about him. Who he was. White Zombie? Nah, Motley Crüe's "Primal Scream." An appropriate choice. I toe-tapped the drumbeat to the song. The raging guitars a reflection of my emotions.

I walked across the hall to the Bias Crime Unit. I found Vontana's name plate, plopped down in his chair. My mind still wound up and jumping all over the world. Looked at that agent staring. Like I couldn't see him looking at me. Maybe he was trying to intimidate me not to sit there. Or wondering how I got those injuries. Both, probably. He *is* a cop. I should've snooped through the desk. That would've got him to–"Stop staring at me," I snarled and met his eyes directly. Embarrassed, he busied himself with a report. So bitchy, Paloma. Well, I had every right to be. What could I have done while I waited? Maybe I shouldn't have. I debated just taking off–not even telling Al where I was going. Not tell anybody. That'd show him. Show him how immature you are, Paloma. That guy was just behind that door talking about me. How they degraded me. I think I begged him. Begged him to stop. They didn't listen. Just like Al didn't listen.

The office door opened, a female agent tossed a file on the empty desk not bothering to close the door as she left. I read the black lettering on the door. Bias Crime Unit. Leave it to the government. I marveled how any normal citizen could find their way to the right office to report a crime. You're being stalked? That's threat assessment to you, madam. He spray-painted anti-gay slogans on the wall? Exhibited a bias to people of that particular persuasion? Heck, no. He beat the crap out of a gay. It's a hate crime, for crying out loud! And it doesn't stop there. You don't get shot by a gun with a silencer. It's a noise suppression device. I doubt victims care. I wondered what I'd do if I saw them–Randy and The Voice. I'd be sitting at a red light, look over. There they are. My burns were disgusting. The skin had puckered in a circle, like it bubbled up around the cigarette. They were oozing. I knew I was going to have scars. The whole world would stare at me for the rest of my life. I wanted to hurt them. Bad.

Janis Joplin now. "Cry Baby." Now there was a woman who could sing out her rage and agony.

What if I lost control? And then couldn't come back? Al would really dump me then. What would Dixie and her family say, do? That poor Paloma. You shoulda seen her before that stuff happened to her. My grandparents. It'd kill them. My leg. It wouldn't stop jumping.

What was taking so long? Why was I out there, not wanting to be, not feeling at all well, while a man who said he cared about me was in the other room doing the one thing that I begged him not to do? Meanwhile, he was ripping my heart out. I finally get up the nerve to express myself–which Al had been pestering me to do–and the very first time I lay myself on the line, I got slammed. Why didn't I tell him to leave with me now, or I'd never see him again? If I'd wanted to cool my heels, I'd have gone ice skating.

Because I was chicken. Pusillanimous. Word of the day. What if he'd said "fine"? Paloma, you know you're the type that the guys say, "Go. Who cares?" And they don't because they never call you to come back. No one wants me to come crawling back. Doesn't matter. Paloma doesn't crawl.

So. I was still there. No beach. No boat. No computer. I could've used Vontana's PC. My heart beat so fast it was more of a quiver. Maybe I was having a heart-attack, no that's a myocardial infarction, madam. As I giggled hysterically, it tapered off into a snort. That was attractive. There it went again. Babbling fool. I hiccuped and gulped air simultaneously. Then I was choking. Cough. Cough. Who can choke on air? That's supposed to *keep* you from choking. Well, leave it to me. If it's stupid, Paloma could do it. *Droga*, I was so hurt and confused.

* * *

It's odd, how successfully the mind can burrow itself away from the drama unfolding all around. Until Al hurled a chair across the room then flew out the door. I heard it hit from across the hall. Sitting at Vontana's desk, I was creating a chain from the paperclips I'd pilfered.

Scuffling from out in the hallway, then a sandwich of Vontana and Hewson, with Al the lunch meat in the middle, stumbled into the room. I added another clip without looking at them. I felt deadened, detached from it all.

"Don't, Al," Vontana ordered harshly. "He knows you. He won't talk if he knows he has an audience."

"That hick just stood there and let them touch her." Al's face flushed deeply.

The agent at the next desk gawked at me again. I knew he was thinking touch, as in fondle. And while Randy did attempt to rearrange my breast, The Voice had kept him focused on other things. I glared back at him brazenly. His eyes flashed as comprehension dawned that I saw what he was doing and that his thoughts were transparent. "Pervert," I snarled. He was smart enough to grab a stack of papers and beat it out of there. Go crawl under a food scrap, you cockroach.

Meanwhile, Al was shoved up against the wall, Hewson the thumb tack holding him in place. Vontana's hand was clamped over Al's mouth–an improvised noise-suppression device. "Take it outside, friend, if you can't handle it. That guy in there is telling me everything he knows–and for the first time. This is also the first time I believe he's not holding anything back, most importantly the truth." I stood by helpfully doing nothing. Taylor stuck his head in and asked if his partner needed help, seeming bewildered Vontana was working without him. He shut the door behind him as he left.

Al bellowed. "This all could have been avoided!" Vontana looked at me for support.

I saw all this from my peripheral vision so I could keep working those paperclips. I shrugged. Kept my head down. "This is a penis thing. I'm not equipped to handle it." I knew the men were all looking my way. I slipped on an extra large clip.

"You're forgetting Paloma's feelings in this." This I probably wasn't supposed to hear but Vontana's whisper carried across the small room.

Damn right! I wanted to scream it. Over and over. Damn right, he's forgetting! He's only in there hanging on to every word for his own selfishness. A moment of silence passed.

"Al?"

"Go," he spit out. They released him slowly. Al straightened his clothes while eyeing me. A lot of that going on this morning. I hoped he couldn't see me keeping tabs on him while the next clip was a blue plastic one, triangular. Let him think I don't care. I'm not hurt.

"Then, you said, Randy tortured her?" Vontana's voice seemed to boom out. Al's body grew rigid. Put it on the intercom, why don't you. Then you wouldn't have to talk so loud. Didn't they realize that this may be everyday fodder to them, but not to the victims? Shut the door before you continue your interrogation, stupid.

"Cigarettes," Willie reported. "For a long time, that girl didn't say nuthin' to them. She just sat there takin' it." A lot of that going around, too, I wanted to shout. Willie continued. "I mean it had to hurt. I could smell her skin burning."

"What happened next?"

"They wuz pissed she wuzn't showin' no reaction. The Chink used them paddle thangs. I thought when she yelped then, that would satisfy him. But it only made him, ya know."

"I *don't* know, Willie."

"I mean, he didn't, ya know, do it wid' 'er. But he shore wuz actin' like he wanted to. Weird boy, 'dat one! Randy told the Chink he wuz goin' to show 'im how to do it the real way, not chopstick style. What does that mean?" I couldn't hear the agent's reply. "He made fun of 'im, pullin' 'is eyes back at the corners, goin' 'ah-so, tank you ver-ly much'. And bowin' down." He laughed slightly. "Vontana, why does a whites-only group have a slant-eye workin' for them?"

"You'd be surprised what people do for money. I worked a case in Atlanta where a black man sold information to help the Klan. He wanted to get rid of a rival."

"That's the dangdest thang I ever heard!"

And that, thought Vontana, was why his partner, Taylor, was on Vontana's list of agents to clear or implicate.

Australia: A clause in the Australian Constitution prevented the government from aiding most Aboriginals directly. In 1967 this clause was removed by vote. A United Nations report of 1988 accused Australia of violating international human rights in its treatment of the Aboriginal people.

Chapter Sixty-Five

Enid let out an impressive shriek and ran to the TV.

"Y'all hush! They're talking about Randy." Bessie's Styling Salon became unusually still and silent.

"Turn it up."

"Shhh!" Enid hissed.

"I can't hear it." The patrons hissed in a group sounding like a den full of rattlers. The anchorwoman warned the next scenes contained violent content. The women replied with deep breaths. There was no audio to the clip, she apologized, but black and white and silent proved no detriment. They watched Randy enter a hotel room. Then his arm moved up. Enid grabbed a handful of Charlene's just-styled hair. She now looked like she'd walked through a tornado. Not a soul noticed. The tape froze on the TV screen so that viewers could get a good look.

It switched to a woman in bed, her face blotted out with that hazy square that magically follows as the image moves around the screen. They saw her arms raise up to ward off the horror. Freeze-frame. A chorus of disbelief sounded in the salon. Next, the gun fired, the women squealed and jumped like they'd been hit. The tape paused again and two other shots tore into her body. Randy turned, his features filling the screen. The women shrieked as if Randy himself was coming through the door.

"The woman has not yet been identified, nor has her body been found. The Savannah police, in co-operation with the Georgia Bureau of Investigation, are searching for this man, Randy Beamon." His face was shown above the anchorperson's shoulder as the camera moved in for a close-up. The description of Randy was kind, leaving out details of his usual viciousness and slovenly appearance. A telephone number was flashed next, and ended with the warning not to approach him.

As the station tuned back into the regular soap opera, the patrons of Bessie's Styling Salon were stunned.

"That poor woman!" Bessie said, meaning Charlene, Enid's customer. Enid had inadvertently destroyed her clients "do" in seconds. And after a hair weave, perm, special damaged-hair treatment, wash, cut, then style, Charlene's rear had grown numb during the three-hour treatment. Bessie's comment broke their freeze-frame.

The women switched into motion. Three women flipped the dinosaur head dryers down in tandem, the inverted bowls seeming to devour their heads as they dropped. The others chattered about what they were doing at the precise moment they saw Randy's face on TV. Bessie demonstrated exactly how she'd held the can of hair spray above Martha's head and how her finger froze, giving her customer an overdose of Salon Secrets. She expertly combed a light layer of hair over the spot, spirted it with spray, and assured Martha her expert maneuvers had saved the day. Those not under the hands of other hair masters paid testimony to Martha's lovely new style, gushing about Bessie's professional cover-up. Charlene shifted her weight to her left cheek, resigned to sitting at least another half hour.

*   *   *

Billy Ray sat in the blazing sun, car running to keep the air flowing. He felt like a lone duck during hunting season. It was only a matter of time until he found himself in the cross-hairs. The GBI was coming. Randy wouldn't know he'd turned him in, the agent promised. *Sure!* He was sitting in the car about to piss off the most wanted man in Georgia. Everything was okay. *Sure!* His dad wouldn't be mad that he'd backed out on the plans. He was biting his nails to the quick and killing himself slowly by chain smoking. He was okay. *Sure!*

He watched a car turn in, flash its lights twice. He replied in kind. A man stepped out and came toward him. As he got closer, Billy Ray's hand stopped in mid air, lips waiting for filter. *Shit!* The guy walking toward him was the same one who came out of the office building in Savannah one night when he was riding with Randy. The two had switched envelopes. The man had been fiery mad they'd come to his workplace. Randy, as usual, thought it real funny because...this agent's a WRF-er! Billy Ray dropped his lit cigarette, not caring where it rolled. He ripped the car in reverse, body sunk low, and drove away like a maniac.

Fifteen minutes later, in the southwest part of Savannah, Billy Ray drove into a shopping center and caught his breath. He spent five minutes scanning the cars entering the parking lot. He wasn't followed. He didn't think the agent had gotten close enough to see him. If he had, then the agent would tell Randy. Billy Ray was so relieved he didn't give his name or any other personal information to the GBI when he'd called.

Now what was he going to do? He couldn't think anymore. Everyone had gone crazy! He was gonna lose it if things didn't ease up soon. Billy Ray reached for a new pack of cigarettes from his glove box. Al's business card lay on top. He picked it up, flicked it against his fingers. Looking around the shops, he spotted a pay phone.

*   *   *

"I was meeting them and one of the agents is in on it." I listened on an extension as Billy Ray frantically described his aborted meeting.

"Are you okay?" Al asked.

"Yeah."

"Where are you?"

"Westside Shopping Center."

"Were you followed?"

"I'm pretty sure I wasn't."

"Do you know the agent's name?"

"No."

"I'm glad you felt you could trust me."

"I figured after what Randy done to that lady, she wouldn't be trying to sell me out."

"I'll bring a security man with me. We don't want any problems. The mall's on my side of town. I'll be there in fifteen minutes."

"What are you doing to do?" I asked as soon as we hung up and I'd raced into the kitchen.

"I'll have to make this up as I go along. If he's willing, I can bring him back here and we can talk to him."

Personal matters were left suspended. Al had returned home from the GBI office an hour ago. I'd called Dixie to come rescue me, leaving an hour before him. Al hadn't approached me since he'd come home, but he gave me meaningful glances. Brave soul that I wasn't, I kept acting like I couldn't figure out his facial codes, making sure I wasn't ever alone with him. Aggie had figured something out and one by one, she, Beverly, Clarice then Dixie had surreptitiously disappeared. Their efforts were wasted. A few minutes later, Billy Ray called.

"Do you have any photos of Vontana?"

He nodded. "Why?"

"For Billy Ray to look at."

He nodded again, his jaw set firmly. "He's not dirty, Paloma."

"Well, you'll know for sure. What about the other agents?"

"No. I don't see any others socially. When they help the Center, they don't get photographed because of their undercover work." He rifled through his desk drawer and showed me a photo. He and Vontana were on a boat, and Al didn't look like he was having a good time. "I was so seasick."

"You seemed okay on the *Katie*."

"I was for the most part, but I went prepared–patch and tablets."

"Do you need them every time?"

"Don't care to find out. It's a simple thing to do to keep from wanting to kill myself. Where is everybody?"

I held up a note Aggie had scribbled and tacked on the frig. "They're down at the lake."

"Please call her cell phone and get them back up here. I'd feel safer. You're only gonna have Gus." He went into the library and came out loaded. A few seconds later, Al and two guards drove away in a cloud of dust.

Soon the four women entered the kitchen after stomping their feet on the door mat, friendly grumbling about being left behind this

morning. As a peace offering, I made coffee and orange juice, serving
them in the living room while I relayed what had happened during our
meeting with Vontana, skipping details of Willie the Snitch, and Al.
I wrapped it up with details of Billy Ray's frantic call. As we
dissected the news, Al phoned.

"Vontana's not dirty. Billy Ray said it wasn't him they had visited
that day."

"I'm so glad for you, Al."

"Thanks, sugah. Billy Ray found a rifle and bowling bag under his
trailer that belongs to Randy. Vontana's out of the office. I'd like his
input."

"What about Hewson?"

"They're off together. I've saved the best news."

"I'm all ears."

"We've got the evidence to nail Randy acting under WRF orders for
Lemond's murder. You are finally proven right!"

"How?" I yelled in excitement, making whipping motions with my
hand to get someone's attention. I chastised myself for my celebratory
outburst. I had been right, but Lemond was still dead.

"Randy took photos of Lemond. He was in the building with WRF
letters painted on the walls. Randy asked for a bag he'd hidden at
Billy Ray's and believed he was so dominated or scared of Beamon,
he wouldn't look inside."

"*Idiota!* Billy Ray is learning he can fly by himself. Tell me
what's inside the bag, Al."

"Okay, curious Paloma. The most important find is money, about
thirty thousand dollars. Blood money, I'd guess. There's a hotel
room key, a tie tack of a computer, initials LAB on the back."

Before he could ask, I shouted. "Yes, it's Lemond's!" I had
everyone's attention now. "Lemond Arthur Branson."

"We're going to a place to talk. That's the way he wants it. He's
so scared, Paloma. The kid's heading for a break down."

"Be careful, Al."

"There's something else in the bag, sugah." I steeled myself. Al's
voice said to. "Three pictures of you. Two were, I guess, taken at
your home."

"I hope I was wearing clothes," I joked, using humor to hide my
concern. The real Paloma's skin hatched major goose bumps.

"Do you have a pool, palms and big, leafy trees?"

"Ah-huh."

"And a black swimsuit."

"Ditto."

"The last one is you looking pretty foxy in a white clingy dress.
You look awesome. I can't see any tan lines."

Without a thought I blurted out. "Eason, when I tan, it's the same
way all over."

*   *   *

Moonpie watched the news broadcast feeling an odd sense of pleasure. Randy'll get his due now. The GBI was looking for him. He'd do more time, she hoped, for murder than for rape. Not that anyone would believe her. She turned off the TV, scooped up her car keys and drove to Randy's. She wanted to be there when they hauled him off.

What she found at Randy's was the front door swinging in the breeze and a fine mess. She called out several times but wasn't surprised when she didn't get an answer. Someone else was looking for him, too. He was running scared and she knew just where he'd hide.

*   *   *

Swartzman finally had something that pleased him. Red was handling his job as intelligence officer with gusto. "Swartzman, Hughes just called a Klan meeting. I've got Willie covering that. Tom Richards has been up all day, just about recovered except that ass of his'll be sore for a long awhile. Grainger's still not back in town, never came back when that girl got outta jail. I've got a few men looking for him. Randy hasn't been spotted since the Klavern incident. Carl is watching his place. Moonpie just left there. Want us to stop her?"

"Not unless you see her helping him, although I don't think even she's that wacky. Excellent job, son. Excellent! Have Willie report directly to me." He called Camp Alpha, ordering them to the plant.

"Okay, Base, we'll be there in twenty minutes. You got a drill for us, boss?"

"Yes. It's time to test the men, see if you're worth what I'm paying you." He turned up the volume on the TV to catch the news. He patted the original tape marveling at the technology that made it possible. Such a tiny camera in that sprinkler head. The newscast made him smile, even though Mildred just announced the psycho he was watching on the news was now calling on the phone. Swartzman took his time answering.

"Whatcha want, Randy?"

"For someone so hot to get the diskettes, you sure took your sweet time getting to the phone! I've got 'em. Let's trade."

"For what?"

"The money you promised."

"Since when did you start keeping promises? Or is it everyone else who has to?"

"Stick to bidness, Swartzman. Ten thousand."

"And how are we supposed to accomplish this transaction?"

"My car's at the WalMart. Keys are under the driver's mat. Put the money in the trunk and take the diskettes with you. I'll be watching, but you won't be able to see me. If you screw up, I'll kill you."

"When?" He asked, not at all threatened by this stupid yahoo.
"Any time."
"Randy, have you been watching the news?"
"No, I ain't got time for that."
"Okay, I'll get right on this." He hung up and called Red.
"We've got two men who can watch his car at WalMart, boss."
"Good."

Japan: *"Blacks are like bad currency driving out good currency. It's like in America, when the neighborhoods become mixed because blacks are moving in. It ruins the atmosphere."* *Justice Minister Seiroku Kajiyama, comparing U.S. blacks to prostitutes in the Shinjuku district of Tokyo.*–Boston Globe 1/6/91.

"Moreover, Japan has become a highly educated and quite intelligent society. Much more so than America and [other countries]. In America, there are considerable blacks, Puerto Ricans and Mexicans and such. And on average it [the level of intelligence] is still quite low." *Premier Yasuhiro Nakasone, 1986, discussing intellectualism in Japan.*–Boston Globe 1/6/91.

Chapter Sixty-Six

When Wanda reached Hughes by phone, she let him have it good. Ending her long list of complaints, she griped, "I've messed up a good manicure punching the buttons on this phone! I told you not to turn that dad-burn thing off in case I needed to get you."

"Get me is right. Why're you so riled up?"

"Randy wants Billy Ray to meet him."

"Where?"

"If I'd listen to you, you jerk, I wouldn't have jack squat to tell you. I shouldn't even say anything now. That would sure teach you a lesson."

"Wanda, I don't have time. Please!"

"I guess I'm the only one that thinks I done sumpin' real smart."

"And what was that, sugar beet?"

"I listened to his phone call." Wanda related what she'd overheard.

"L-Log's Landing?" Hughes was so excited his stutter was in full force. Why that place–a creek that was a local swimming hole? Hughes wouldn't tell his wife why this was such good news.

This whole Randy mess had her so angry and she still didn't know everything that was going on. Wanda would not tolerate anything but getting her own way. But she couldn't even get her husband in one place long enough to zero in on him. And he'd sent the kids away so she couldn't use them to drive him crazy. She made sure to slam the phone down extra hard as she hung up. Wanda just had to have her own way!

*　　*　　*

The more Billy Ray talked to Al, the better he liked him. If Al didn't agree with something Billy Ray said, it never showed. They went down into the woods, a place Billy Ray had discovered and never told anybody. It was his thinking place. He spent many quiet hours laying under a tree beside the small brook that passed through the Willow Pea Cemetery and into the woods. Today Billy Ray was joined by Al and the watchful eyes of his security team.

Once Al convinced the young man to have the conversation taped, Billy Ray revealed his outings with Randy–mostly passing time away with endless driving to and from nowhere. Or evenings of bluster and beer which they called Klan meetings. After an uncomfortable silence, Billy Ray confessed about the hotel break-in and Randy taking shots of Paloma on River Street. After much hesitation and watching the stream gurgling past, Billy Ray blurted out the truth about Hughes' involvement in the Klan. "Dad's always bragging that all the men in the Hughes family have been Klan officials ever since the war." Al assumed Billy Ray was talking about the Civil War, but didn't bother to ask.

"Dad wants his sons, blood and-or adopted, to carry on the legacy. And then there's this stuff with Randy. He says I got to tell him what Randy says and does, and to play along with him. But I'm tired of all this, Mr. Eason. I want to live in peace! And I don't want no more to do with Randy! My whole life has been nothing but fighting and shouting. I'm thirty-two years old and ain't got nothing but a tin box to show for it. I want something better. And I want out of this town."

Al's questions drew out what Billy Ray thought might be his first steps toward his new life. For the first time, the boy-man thought it could happen.

"Mr. Eason."

"Al."

"Al, what's wrong with my father?"

"What do you mean?"

"We ain't never had a conversation like this. I learnt early on not to discuss what I wanted, just do what he expected. It was easier that way."

"Easier on everybody but you." One of the security guards approached.

"Mr. Eason, telephone."

"Who?"

"GBI.

Billy Ray freaked.

*   *   *

"Brother Willie, get the cross from the shed and take it to our meeting place–the future site of our victory."

"Okay. Hughes?"

"Imperial Wizard!"

"Sorry. Imperial Wizard, are we going after Randy?"

"Yes. Now get busy."

"Good," Willie said more to himself. He was madder than a hornet with Randy. The jerk had lied to him. Owed him money and promised to pay up today, but didn't. When they'd met that afternoon Willie hadn't known then the idjit was running from a murder rap. He could have been caught right along with him. Maybe with Randy gone, things would calm down. And he could stop running from place to place, snooping and telling lies every time he turned around. Trying to keep track of them all had wrecked him. He had to hurry with the cross, inform Swartzman of Hughes' plans, get in touch with Vontana and rejoin the Klan at Logs Landing.

Hughes turned to the group and spoke sonorously. "The Righteous Klans of Georgia, Klavern 26, has asked its members to uphold the honor and dignity it has maintained throughout its existence. We shall strike down the forces which are against us! Do we have the right?" the Imperil Wizard asked.

"Yes!"

"Do we have the power?"

"Yes!"

"Is God on our side?"

"Yes!"

"Let's do it!" The men grabbed hunting rifles, Rebel flags, pistols and ammunition before piling into two pickup trucks, their white robes billowing in the wind behind them like the weekend wash. They sang *Onward Christian Soldiers* for a their victory song as they drove to Logs Landing.

* * *

When Red returned to the camp hidden deep in the Chatham County woods, Swartzman had all WRF personnel loading firearms and ammunition into the trucks. The men complained at first. They'd just moved the heavy crates to this spot two days ago so that the GBI wouldn't find them at the Gundersen plant. Red had cut off their groans with a blazing look of rage. As he made his last report, he could tell Swartzman was pleased with his work. Red was in awe of his leader. The older man had anticipated what would happen during the last forty-eight hours and he had been correct. What an honor to serve him!

"Red, what we've been training for will be happening tonight. I'll address the men, get them revved up for the fight. I'm counting on you to be by my side. Help them finish checking the gear then join me."

Red carefully counted the contents in each crate, but hurried nonetheless in order to catch part of Swartzman's speech. The Chief was speaking enthusiastically, telling the men what had to be done, instilling courage and trust. Excitement filled the air. "The call to arms has sounded!" Swartzman said. "It is time the mighty WRF mobilized against the forces of evil in our country. The white race must be saved! The call to arms has sounded!" The men cheered.

"So, Chief, where are we headed?" Red asked as he joined his leader.

"Logs Landing." Red was surprised at the location, but he would never question his new hero why.

* * *

"Hang on, Bruce." Al tossed the phone on the ground and sprinted after Billy Ray. "What's the problem? Billy Ray! Talk to me." Al caught up and grabbed him by the shoulder.

"I don't want to go to jail! I told you that stuff so you could stop the violence! Stop Randy! Not turn me in!"

"That guy on the phone is a friend. I've known him all my life. He can be trusted. He was only returning my call just now. He'll help us. You've got to talk to them sometime. And you don't have to tell everything that you told me."

Billy Ray's face relaxed ever so slightly. "How?"

"I'll be you're lawyer."

"I don't have any money."

"You got a dollar?" The young man nodded. "We'll get the guards to witness our arrangement. You've hired yourself legal counsel." A bit more of the tension eased out of Billy Ray's body. But there was plenty more swirling around inside him. "The other things that you did–riding with Randy–I don't think you should worry. They want him, the groups and weapons. I'll be up-front with you on what the GBI is going to do–that is as soon as they let me know. You and I will *always* discuss things first." Billy Ray walked numbly back to the clearing. Al picked up the phone, Bruce still waiting. He told Al about the tape of Randy shooting Brice.

"That's where we've been, at the TV station where it was sent to, then back to the lab to analyze it. What's happening on your end?"

"Plenty. I'll tell you, but first I have to talk to my client. I'll call you right back." He sat on the ground and motioned for Billy Ray to do the same. He passed on the information about Randy on video. "Were you with him at the murder?"

"No!"

"I'll tell Vontana about the bag Randy hid at your place and meeting him at Logs Landing. You and I will figure out what to tell the agents tomorrow, okay?"

"Yes. Thank you." Billy Ray dropped his head toward his crossed legs and cried. Al left him alone for some time, then returned, putting an arm around his thin shoulders. With sundown approaching he was eager to call Bruce back but waited until his new client was composed.

"I-I-I don't want to go home. Would it be alright to go to my father's?"

"Just keep our meeting secret for now." Al watched the defeated young man make his way slowly back to his car. Alone, Al called Vontana.

"Client, huh? Your new girlfriend is opening up all kinds of things for you. I'm glad you called me back, Counselor."

"So am I."

"Now fill me in."

"I don't think we should even have Billy Ray there, Bruce."

"Why? Randy may not show his face without him."

"Remember Mutt Higgins?"

"Yeah."

"This is something like that."

"He's cracking up?"

"Uh-huh."

"I'll meet you at the Chick N' Chat. I'm on my way. Let's get Randy."

* * *

"Billy Ray just left."

"Why isn't he going to meet Randy?" I asked.

"He's falling apart," Al answered.

"So's Randy."

"Bruce told me about the tape."

"Al, you've stolen my thunder! Where is Billy Ray going–home?"

"His father's. When Randy calls him there, instead of Billy Ray going, he'll call me. Vontana and I are heading that way now so we'll be close by.

"You can't go after Randy just the two of you!" I cried. "And you're not even law enforcement."

"Sugah, I don't know what Bruce has planned, but we'll be careful. By the way, isn't this the same thing I told you a few times in the past few weeks?"

"I have no idea what you're talking about."

"Ha."

"Please, Al, call as soon as it's over."

"Promise. Here's Vontana now." Then he was gone.

* * *

"You stupid jack-ass fool! You ratted me out!" Randy roared over and over. Billy Ray had walked in the door seconds ago when Wanda announced he had a phone call.

"What?" He felt dazed, as if he'd received a blow to the head.

"You sold me out!" The conversation steadily degraded until Billy Ray's temper snapped.

"Enough, Randy! Or I'll hang up!" Randy quieted, except for panicked breathing. Billy Ray found comfort in the twist of circumstances. Now he was in control instead of Randy. Now Randy needed *him*. He laughed.

"What's so danged funny, B-Ray?"

"Nothing. What's your problem? I can't meet you if I stand here talking to you all night." As soon as Randy finished yacking, he'd call Al to report this conversation. He'd never had to meet Randy again. Ever.

"When you met me tonight, you was gonna have the boys from the plant waitin' to get me."

"What boys from what plant?"

"You tryin' to screw me over, ain't ya?"

"You talkin' crazy, ain't ya?" Billy Ray mocked Randy, but the other guy didn't seem to notice. If he did, for once he kept it to himself. "Tell me *calmly* what's happening so we can figure this out."

"I was at our meetin' place to scout it out and half of Rincon comes driving up, guns and equipment like the dang Army was invadin'. You sent 'em."

"Randy, I haven't told anyone. It's a public place. Of course there are people there. The guys with the guns are probably doin' a little huntin'. Of animals, not you. Let's get on with this."

"There you go tellin' me what to do again."

"You don't have anyone else stupid enough to help you so don't start that crap or I ain't coming." He felt empowered, wished he had time to tell Randy everything that disgusted him. He stayed silent giving Randy time to pick up his chin and wipe the surprise off his face.

"Meet me at the old homestead."

"That place is still standing?"

"Yeah, ain't nobody remembers it."

"But that complicates things. The Landing will be fine. You got spooked because you saw somebody you recognized."

"You're making me pissed, Billy Ray. Why don't you want to go?"

"It's just gonna take more time because I'd have to get a boat. And it's easy to pass. I ain't been there in years."

"Okay, then. Log's Landing. I'll be waiting. And you come alone. Two hours." Billy Ray hung up relieved. The GBI would get Randy and he'd be out of his life. He turned around. Wanda was staring at him opened-mouthed like an apparition was floating behind him. She doubled over moaning. Billy Ray knelt down beside her. She sat up suddenly and ran to the bar looking for her keys.

"What's the matter, Wanda?" He stood, grabbing her arm and turning her around. "What have you done?"

"I didn't mean to. Guys with guns. Waitin'. Oh, no!"

"Wanda, don't mess with this! You don't have any idea what's going on!" Her mascara ran down her face Alice Cooper fashion. "Where's Dad?"

"With his men."

"Where? At the Klavern?" He shook her when she didn't answer.

"First off. Then they will be going to Logs Landing," she finally said.

"How did you know?"

"I-I listened in." She tried to justify it. "He's my husband."

"Wanda, there are all kinds of people looking for Randy. Guys with guns."

"He killed a woman–it was on TV!"

"I know! There's no telling what Dad's gonna find when he gets there!"

"He was going to find out anyway from you," she whined.

"I wasn't gonna tell him!" She headed for the door. "Wanda, you can't go. You'll get yourself or someone else killed."

"I can't just sit here. We have to stop him before he leaves the Klavern. What have you done?" She repeated in an hysterical stream.

"Me? Don't go blaming this on me!"

"It's all your fault! You wouldn't tell me nothing. Why wouldn't anyone tell me?"

"Dad wanted it that way. I'll take care of it." he said quietly. "Don't I always take care of it?" She nodded and collapsed into his chest. He held the woman who had been more like a child than a parent to him. The woman who didn't want her own kids to call her Mom.

* * *

"You have to get Agent Vontana for me!"

"He's not available."

"Just tell him it's Willie."

"Sir, he's not in the building," the GBI agent said. "He's off duty."

"Then call him at home. He'll want to talk to me."

"Who are you?"

"I told ya. Willie."

"I meant what are you to him that he'd want to be bothered when he's off duty."

"Ah, he, ah." Willie didn't know how much he should say. He didn't want to set off Vontana. Even though Willie wanted to be free of the GBI agent, the money Vontana gave–no paid–him was good. And above all else, it kept his wife from nagging him about bills and wanting to know where every dime went that Willie put his hands on. This guy on the phone–he was an agent, wasn't he? He probably had civilian helpers, too. Maybe telling him would get this lard-butt into gear and Vontana would call him back quickly. He had to get back. He didn't want the Imperial Wizard to wonder what he was up to. "Ah, he ah, pays me sometimes, you know, to help him out."

"Oh, his snitch. Hold on." Willie hated that word–snitch. It implied something tainted. He held on for nearly five minutes. "He's not at home. Can I help you?" He didn't think Vontana would like him talking to anyone else, even though he had some hot news. He hung up the phone and went back to his truck. As a safety measure he nailed a red cleaning rag to the end of the large pine limbs hanging out the back of his truck bed and then rechecked the tightness of the ropes holding the cross in place. He drove to Logs Landing.

* * *

I'd been talking more on the telephone than a telemarketer on overtime. Each time it jangled everyone would look at me. Without discussion I'd be-come the answerer. I'd just placed the receiver down in the cradle when it pealed again. For variety, I didn't answer until the third ring. No one nagged me. I couldn't figure if they were stupefied from current events or mesmerized at my silly game.

"I need to speak with Mr. Eason. *Now!*"

"Ah...he's not here. Billy Ray?"

"Yeah. I got to talk to that guy! Everything's all messed up!"

"They've left to get Randy. This is Paloma, could I help you?" With a little more urgent prompting from me, he explained the Klan heading for Logs Landing with the WRF in pursuit. Al and Vontana walking right into the middle of it. I interrupted him once to tell the group.

Aggie crossed the room quickly, grabbed her tote bag and frantically dug inside. Cross stitch supplies were flung onto the floor like she detested the craft. She held up her cell phone and furiously punched numbers. "If the Klan runs into Al they'll do worse than hang him." She tapped her foot. "Al doesn't answer."

Billy Ray agreed to meet in front of the Community Center in Rincon. I plundered through Al's desk for Vontana's work number, leaving messages for him, then deciding to do the same with his boss Hewson. Hoping the agent on duty was as sincere as he sounded, I left cell phone numbers for call back. Aggie loaded weapons she'd taken from Al's hunting cabinet, placing them in the trunk and a few inside the car as I ran down the steps with my pack. Clarice and Beverly would stay behind to take the calls and pray.

Canada: Kitchener, 1992–Ontario police suspect arson at the home of Monna Zentner, an anti-Nazi activist who leads vigils outside of European Sound, *a Kitchener store that markets Holocaust-denial literature. Zentner had recently demonstrated against David Irving who had given a speech at the store. Irving, a British Holocaust-denier, was reportedly paid by store owner Michael Rothe, a known Nazi sympathizer. Banned from entering Canada due to a 1991 conviction in Germany of defaming the dead, he illegally entered the country through the U.S. Irving was previously arrested in British Columbia and given forty-eight hours to leave the country. He tried to cross into the U.S., but was denied entry.*

Chapter Sixty-Seven

At night in LA, you know where you are. The horizon shimmers like a million glittering candles. The ocean helps you track which direction your nose is pointed. Tonight it was as if we were driving thru a tunnel. Over-hanging tree limbs and moss obliterated the few street signs, and road-side lighting was rare. "The dark is going to be a problem," Dixie commented as we drove slowly through Rincon. "How much further, Billy Ray?"

"About three miles." Aggie picked up speed outside the city limits. I watched the headlights play eerie Balinese shadow puppets on the highway. A few moments later Billy Ray leaned forward. "It's about a quarter of a mile on the right," he said excitedly. "Slow down. You'll see a little clearing and a street light." Suddenly he beat on the dash. "Go! Go! Keep going!" His voice sounded like he was hyperventilating.

"What?" we all asked.

He ducked down into the seat. "Nothing."

"What's wrong?" I asked him.

"Nothing!"

"If you're hiding something from us, I'll beat you with this pistol then shoot you," I informed him matter-of-factly. Dixie was trying to get my attention with head and eye movements, probably telling me to make nice-nice, but I kept evil-eyeing him.

"Billy Ray," she said evenly, "please talk to us."

He sighed the woes of the world. "That was my dad's car." His voice was even, but heavy with sadness. "He's in the Klan."

"Maybe someone's borrowed his car," Aggie said trying to give the guy some hope.

He shook his head. "He's the Imperial Wizard."

"Wizard the Gizzard is your father? Geez, what do..."

Dixie turned around and glared at me. "Is there another way there?" She asked when she finished visually admonishing me.

"Yeah."

We turned less than a quarter of a mile later. The dirt road was so thick with trees, I didn't think it could get any darker. Dixie popped the headlights off and I learned once again things will always get worse. I could barely see the hood of the car.

"If we use the lights, we may as well get a bullhorn and ask them to come to us," she said and braked the car. "But we can't drive like this. Can we walk from here?"

"It's about two miles." We discussed solutions.

"Idiota!"

"Who, me?" Dixie asked.

"No, pal. I'm the idiot. Here." I stuck a hand in my pack and pulled out the night vision goggles. I looked through them before I passed them over. "These things are so cool."

"I thought you gave all the evidence to the GBI," Dixie scolded.

"You know how forgetful I am."

"And a good thing, too." Aggie added. Dixie adjusted the goggles then quickly drove off. I hoped we wouldn't run into unfriendlies. There was absolutely no place to turn the car around–the shoulder being a sheer three-foot ditch bordered by the woods. The road, more like a lane, wasn't wide enough for two car widths. I took out the night vision scope and cyclopsed the area.

"Paloma, you are a kleptomaniac."

"I try to do you proud."

Dixie snorted a reply. Suddenly she slammed on brakes and sent the car in reverse fast enough to give us whiplash. We all looked over our shoulders, straining our necks as if we all had the job of steering.

"There's someone at the bend in the road."

I snapped my head forward. "Where? What? Who?"

"I saw a small light."

"Did they spot us?" Aggie asked.

"Who knows. Now what do we do?"

"There's a boat launch three miles before the landing. We gotta double back," Billy Ray offered.

"How are we going to get to the landing–swim?" I groused unintentionally.

"There's a house right before it. A man keeps some boats there." Dixie was on the highway already doing eighty back the way we came.

We lost precious time doubling back, snitching two john boats and transferring equipment. Billy Ray tapped me when we were close to Logs Landing. We anchored and waded to the embankment. Fortunately, there was a small beach at the bottom of the slope and it was sand, not clay, so we wouldn't have a slippery climb to contend with.

So much for Paloma–slayer of the Four Horsemen. The plan was for law enforcement only. The series of calamities I'd survived hadn't gained me enough butt-kicking experience. I was designated in undemocratic fashion to stay up on the slope above the boats to play a beacon so Dixie and Aggie could find their way back, hopefully with Al in tow. I was at distinct disadvantage being unable to object loudly for fear of giving ourselves away. As we sorted our equipment, we suddenly heard voices. A huge cross lit up the area above the cove. The crackle of fire was like a signal. Five seconds later all hell broke loose, like the barricade against evil and madness had just been gutted, its poison free to ooze. I heard three successive *thooms* then Georgia's own earthquake began. Aggie and Dixie were mobile and ran to hide behind a tree. Billy Ray stood transfixed. I grabbed his arm and yanked him along, accidently diving on top of Dixie. The earth stilled but the fireworks had just begun. I wanted to giggle–the hysterical kind that bubbles up when fear is so evident. I gave the night vision goggles to Dixie. She slipped them on and went into cop mode, checking the territory.

"You see anything, Dix?" I asked.

"It all seems to be north of us," she reported over her shoulder.

"So far." Aggie interjected. "Billy Ray, does your father have rockets?"

"No," he said wide-eyed and stilted, like he was in a dream. "Rifles and pistols is all."

"That's good, at least. We only have to worry about big weapons from the WRF," Aggie said.

"That's bad enough. We've walked into a friggin' clash of Fourierist gone haywire," I negatively contributed.

A voice rose over the rounds of gunfire–a shout of pain and uncertainty. A man called out to a friend for help. He pleaded and questioned his fate to the whole forest, stone cold dread overtaking his voice. I silently willed for an end to his agony, a silence instead of his beseeching voice–for him to hurry up and die–then I felt amoral.

"Okay, gang. We're out gunned and out manned." Officer Hightower faced us, looking like a fly with the goggles strapped to her forehead. "No one has to do this." No one backed out of helping find Al and Vontana. I thought perhaps it was the moment to stack our fists on top of each other's and yell "all together now" or some such. The hysterical giggle still threatening.

Rebel yells tore through the night–chilling sounds from fevered men hopped-up for a kill. Dixie was intently searching directly ahead. I wondered which was worse–her having full view of the night, or me crouched behind her in near blindness and ignorance. We crawled toward the edge of the embankment. Taking turns with the scope and goggles, we watched the chaos unfold.

The cross still burned bright, lighting up a small corner of the darkness. But the rest of the night was ink black and we wouldn't have known what was happening without the night-vision equipment to penetrate it. Men were running in 180 degree directions in the cove north of us. The Klan had come adorned in all their silliness. Six were struggling up the far bank, holding the bottoms of their robes like pioneer women running in long dresses. Para-militarily clad WRF men were chasing them. In the background, the tat-tat of gun fire was constant. I watched a fight around the fiery cross then donned the goggles and focused on the massacre in the opposite direction. It went full force another few minutes then tapered off. We waited in the calm. I became only aware of time. And it grated on my nerves like chewing a wad of aluminum foil with a bum tooth.

"Eason, don't come down here!" We three women almost dove toward the source of the sound. It was maddening, the dark.

"That's Vontana. Let's go!" I commanded.

"You can get killed. Wait!"

"You think I was going to charge down the hill?"

Dixie ignored my question and stood on her knees, intently searching ahead of her. Then her arms were flaying around like a Dutch windmill. Seconds later something plopped onto me. Taking her flying cues, I made the same motions and discovered we were playing hot potato with a fat, juicy moccasin who'd left his tree for the warmer ground. I sent it sailing behind me.

"Was that what I think it was?"

I couldn't answer Dixie, I was busy checking my undies.

"Aggie," Dixie spoke like she'd just jogged a mile. "I think this is your call."

When I braved a look, the game warden was using her rifle, dancing it around in the air to keep the snake's attention. She quickly picked up the intruder and whipped it in the air like Indiana Jones cracking his whip. That snake wouldn't bother anyone else. Ever.

"Wow," Billy Ray commented, respectfully. Indeed.

We belly-crawled forward–Dixie volunteering to be point man until we entered a clearing.

"There are four men in military garb down at the beach," she reported. "They have automatic weapons pointed to at least three other men. I can't tell who exactly. They're partially hidden by all these trees. One looked like Al's shape–his curly hair–but I can't be sure." Dixie was leaning so far over the embankment I couldn't see anything but her long legs and butt. "There's a boat under us."

"Now we're talking. What kind?" I asked.

"About a fourteen-footer, motor-powered. The guys are about five hundred yards due north."

"That's Logs Landing–the cove where Randy wanted to meet me," Billy Ray told us, jerking on my arm like a child.

Dixie didn't like my idea, but experience won out this time. With Aggie a deadly shot and Billy Ray familiar with local faces, they would head farther north to stir up a little trouble as I went into action. Dixie would cover me as I slipped into the boat.

I slid down the sandy slope and crept into the fiberglass tub. The possibility of getting my butt tattooed with 30.06 slugs made me unusually graceful and quiet. Flipping up the seats, I rooted around the bins and pulled out all the life jackets. I lined them against the hull and added the seat cushions next. I made the tank ready. Crawling around, I found the anchor line and hauled it in. Not pausing once to think how ridiculous this plan was, I turned the key.

It started after two more tries. I calmly handled the delay like I was out boating on my day off, not alerting a ton of hopped up men with lots of guns and ammo. Still crouching, I put the boat in reverse and gave it a hefty shot of gas. In the middle of the river, I made like a ground hog popping up out of its hole. I saw images of heads looking my way. Ducking back down, I steered the boat more or less toward them and goosed it forward all the way. I crouched down by the cushions and willed my body to relax. I heard gunfire. The boat rammed the shore and I rolled up so fast and hard I nearly knocked myself out on the hull and steering wheel before being smacked back into the boat.

Suddenly unsure if exploding gas tanks were reality or a bit of Hollywood, I stopped the engine with shaking hands. Again I could hear gunfire. Since pieces of the boat weren't being ripped up around me, I guessed the bullets weren't for me. I pulled the pistol out, rolled over the port side into the marsh. I felt like a fox in a hen house with a gun-toting farmer on my heels. I hid in the brambles.

The guy was almost on me as he crashed through, as surprised to see me as I was to see him. Death was easy for both of us. My hand went up automatically. A slight tensing on the trigger. Several bullets slammed into him. I heard a soft "oh" as he fell. It was so absurd that killing had been that effortless. Instinct pushed me on–someone else at the controls so I couldn't dwell on what had just happened.

Squatting down, I pilfered the dead guy for weapons. Four double banana clips for the AK-47. I could now shoot sixty-two times without reloading. And could finally see in the dark using his goggles. I manically swiped everything–slipping his knife in my pocket and pistol in my waistband. I slung the automatic over my back guitar style.

Suddenly someone crashed through the brambles and tripped over a log. He was regaining steps before he hit the ground.

"Paloma?" I stopped aiming at his head, bringing the gun down. "It's me!" We crawled quickly toward each other. "Over here. There's a small cove we can get into. Bruce should be here soon." I handed him the goggles, saw him moving and put my nose to his rear. A thundering boom sounded from behind–another rocket–and soon after a wave of river reached up and pounded us. Next the ground seemed able to slap me full body. Debris from the river clung like skin as the water drained away. Then I was in the cove fumbling for Al. "Paloma, I can't believe...it's..." I held him tighter. "Who...?

"Aggie." Pant. Pant. "Dix." Pant. "Billy Ray." I answered.

"Billy Ray?"

"Later."

"Did you?" He moved his head in the direction of the dead guy. I nodded, looked up and screamed. Al shouted Vontana's name as a body came diving into our tiny cove. He pushed my drawn hand away. I braced for the shot that never came.

"You are fired up, girl." Vontana said, seeming unfazed by nearly being shot. "I take back everything I said about you meddling in my territory." He gave my shoulder a squeeze. Vontana took the goggles and the automatic.

"Friends are up the slope," I said.

Vontana leaned half out of the cove, protected from view by the straw-covered limbs of rotting trees. "I think there are seven guys left, but don't take my word for it," Vontana told us. "How much ammo did you bring?" I relayed the inventory as I unloaded the pouch with the clips and passed them over.

"We didn't fire anything until I took my boat ride."

Al pulled me into him hugging tightly. "That maneuver saved our lives. We were able to get away." I admit I was proud of the stunt. "Okay, Bruce, what next?"

"Get up that embankment."

"Here," I said, handing Vontana my penlight. "Signal two shorts and a long. Dixie's above you."

He stuck his torso out and quickly back in. "Done. Okay, Al. You go first." Vontana told me how to negotiate the sliding sand and bullets. Run like hell seemed a good idea to me. We took turns checking the lay of the land through the goggles. I watched Al go up the side. Too quickly it was my turn. I clawed my way up like a crab on speed. Dixie grabbed me and pulled. She gave me her goggles. Now that I could see what had been happening around me, I didn't want to. Bodies littered the slopes and cove. I gave her the goggles and she moved closer to the edge. My brain registered no Billy Ray.

"He went to see if he could find his Dad." The men were in a group hug, hopefully devising a brilliant plan to get us safely out of here. When asked, we circled, shielding the glow of the penlight, as Vontana talked to us. Dixie looked up and gasped. I followed her gaze and saw a blob shape behind Al.

"Stabenski?" Vontana asked softly into the darkness.

"Hey!" Stabenski came closer and whispered. "What the hell is going on here? Hewson cleared me earlier today. When we got the call that you guys were here, he told me to give you a hand. But I didn't expect this. Are you okay?" He wiped his upper lip and slyly glanced around him. "Vontana, they arrested Kenwood tonight. At the airport with a boatload of money."

"Kenwood was dirty? He was a good investigator. How did you find us?"

"Her message," he nodded toward me, "said Logs Landing. Once I got here, it wasn't hard to figure out where. I followed all the shooting, saw Paloma in the boat and came over." Gunfire erupted again in the distance. "It's still like the fourth of July over there."

I believed Stabenski loved to hear himself talk. I was still chaffed at the way he treated me at Al's farm and would rather go it alone than have this pompous jerk help, but I was sure no one wanted my opinion right then.

"Hey, hey!" Billy Ray whispered, coming back unscathed.

Aggie went to him. "Well, child?"

"I didn't find my dad."

"That doesn't necessarily mean bad news," she said sympathetically.

"Yeah. But Randy's there–alive! He's down at the cove!" Suddenly, he tensed and pushed me aside. "What's your name?" I felt stabs of hot fear shoot down my neck.

Stabenski nervously licked his lips. "Hey, tell that Georgia cracker not to point his weapon."

"What's your name?" Billy Ray spoke louder, pushing the gun toward Stabenski.

"Keep quiet. Put the gun away, Billy Ray!" Al commanded.

"Is his name Evan?"

"Yeah, Evan Stabenski."

"He's the one!" The flash of gunfire was closer this time. Right from inside our group.

The irony of the increase in racial hostility in Western Europe is that the birth rate in countries like Italy, Germany, France and Britain is flat. A French government study suggests the countries may have to import immigrant workers after the year 2000.–Time 8/12/91

Chapter Sixty-Eight

I was blind-sided by a rugger named Al Eason. His strong hands tugged hard enough to rip my scapula as he threw me down the embankment and another body followed.

"*Bosta*!" Aggie exclaimed, in an accurate imitation of a Brazilian in distress, as she rolled over me. I began to claw my way back up when two long ski-like feet appeared, followed by the rest of Dixie, goggles still strapped to her forehead. Throwing my hands around my head instinctively for protection, I buried my face in the dirt. After we untangled, Dixie made slapping sounds as she cleaned herself off. I spit and griped.

"What happened?" It seemed like Aggie had yelled. The night had become that still.

"It was Stabenski who met Randy that night." Dixie blew away the sand on the goggles with quick puffs of air.

"I figured that much. No wonder the asshole looked so nervous. He was acting like he was at his first turkey shoot wearing a bulls-eye jacket," Aggie whispered. "What happened after Al sent me and Paloma flying?"

"Stabenski hit Vontana with his gun. I got a foot in the ribs when I intervened. Nearly took my breath away. Then Al chucked me over the side, too."

"That's our Al. Saving the womenfolk," Aggie said with a hint of anger.

Stabenski's voice sounded out breaking the stillness. "Randy, don't you dare leave without me! I got Eason." The boat engine started. We crept toward the cove.

"Is that Randy in the boat?" Aggie asked as she handed me her goggles to verify.

"This is the best quality I've seen in goggles. The detail is fantastic," I said as I peered into the night toward the cove.

"P, this is not the time for a technology review!" Dixie admonished.

"That's all I had to say. Geez. That's Randy, all right! Handsome, ain't he? The boat survived the crash. I'll have to work on that next time."

Dixie looked sharply at me, non-verbally saying there wouldn't be a next time if she could help it.

I continued on. "There's another guy with them I don't recognize." Stabenski came into my view, roughly pushing Al into the boat. "Al and Stabenski are at the cove now!" I watched the agent's hand rise then recoil from the shot he fired. The unknown man crumbled.

"Was that Al?" Aggie asked panicked.

"No! Another guy, with Randy." Aggie put a hand on her stomach, relief deflating her like a balloon. Dixie and I protectively braced her. "I'll get one of our boats," she said shakily. Aggie sloshed her way down the river where we'd tied off our craft. Dixie crawled up the embankment to check on Vontana and Billy Ray. They were gone.

It would be slower, more agonizing work, but we decided to use the quiet trawler motor and take turns paddling for added speed. With this plan we could follow Randy and not give away our pursuit and hopefully be able to hear if any danger was headed our way. We stowed our equipment and guns on the boat benches for ready reach as our eyes roved the banks, three sitting ducks, searching for trouble.

We came up with inventive ways to relieve our cramped muscles from paddling, Aggie keeping up pace with our rowing. I had just offered to drown because I couldn't force another stroke from my wimpy arms, when we finally heard the others up ahead.

"How much farther?" Stabenski asked.

"Ain't much," Randy crisply replied.

"That doesn't tell me anything," the agent snapped. "Damn woman messed up the engine with her heroics."

"We'll have to float in," Randy replied.

"I was going to sprout wings and fly."

We turned toward the bank and rested as we waited for them to go further. Eventually we heard Randy as he steered the boat to the left bank and tied it off. We did the same further back. Dixie quietly swam ahead to check out the situation. Aggie and I tried to find a shoreline, but there wasn't any at this part in the river.

"There's Dixie," Aggie pointed. I heard before I saw.

"They've gone into an old shack up ahead."

"Was anybody else there?" Aggie asked.

"I couldn't tell. But there is a small landing and some stairs to get to it." We used the overhanging trees like monkey bars and inched our way toward the shack. My arm muscles twitched in protest, making my grip weak. I tried to focus on something else. It didn't work.

"It's just on the other side of these trees," Dixie whispered.

"About time," I muttered. Dixie, having no gear, took ours to dry land. As soon as the pack was off my back, I sank into the water and floated deadman style to rest and get my muscles unclenched. We climbed up on the tiny dock. The terrain beyond was different here, a high cliff, almost sheer, loomed before us.

"There are earthen steps over here," Dixie told us.

We baby-crawled cautiously to the top. A single bulb hung from the sagging porch, and illuminated a run-down shack sitting on short pillars. The grass was almost waist high. We crawled forward. Suddenly, Al came stumbling out of the house, followed by Randy and Stabenski. Al fell, then tried crawling away from Randy's abuse. They took turns kicking and punching him as Randy strutted around him swinging a rope. At one end was a noose. In a theater of pain, we had a direct view of their beatings.

"We better do something fast," I whispered. "Randy likes to get to the point very quickly." The plan was for Dixie and Aggie to split up, each heading to a different side of the house. As usual, I'd stay behind in a lessor role to help get everyone back to relative safety.

Within seconds of Dixie and Aggie disappearing, two shots rang out. I was already inches from the ground, but closed the gap anyway, hoping the shots weren't coming my way. When I managed the nerve to look up, Randy was doubled over, bawling in pain. It was a nice change.

Stabenski was pulling Al behind the oak tree. I crawled closer. A shotgun-toting, huge woman loomed out of the woods and walked purposefully toward Randy.

"You," she said nudging the gun in Stabenski's direction. "Get off my property." Stabenski clutched Al close to him like skin and held a gun to his temple. They disappeared toward the river. I helplessly watched, unsure of what to do.

"Moonpie, you dumb bitch. You shot me," Randy whined. His sister replied by firing close enough to shut him up.

"You cuss at me again, and I'll blow your rotten pecker off." She raised the shotgun higher as she approached and whacked him on the side of the face. Randy crumpled. Moonpie picked up the noose and one of his arms, dragging him like a bag of garbage into the darkness at the rear of the property. Aggie trotted out of the shadows to follow.

Dixie ran hunched over to me. "Let's get Al." We moved toward the dock. Stabenski still threatened Al with the pistol as he ordered him to start the engine. "Paloma," Dixie whispered, "I'm going down there. You stay here. Not one sound and don't you dare move."

"I can help you."

"No! I'm more trained for this than you. Stay put. Promise?"

"Just go."

"Not until I have your word."

"Word."

*   *   *

Aggie peered through a space between two slats of the old shed where Moonpie had taken Randy. She saw the guy kneeling on a table, groveling and begging his sister to set him free. The noose was looped around his neck, the other end tied to something hanging from the ceiling. A contraption used to string up deer for gutting, Aggie realized. Moonpie was venting such deep, pent up emotions, she was frothing at the mouth. Aggie tried the door. Locked.

Above her, she noticed a missing board. Using a rusted paint can as a stool, Aggie stood and was able to reach the missing plank. She looked inside.

"I ain't gonna kill you, Randy. I only want you to admit what you done to me, then I'm gonna let them take you to jail." She hunched over while her body heaved.

"I ain't done a cotton pickin' thang to ya, you fat ol' pig! Exceptin' what you deserve." He continued his degrading, sexual invective at his sister. Moonpie pumped a round into the shotgun. That distinctive sound of the clicking metal was frightening enough to even silence Randy.

"You shut up, you evil moron! I hate you! I HATE YOU!" She shrieked.

Aggie knew she needed to intervene before things got further out of control. But the girl's mental instability combined with that shotgun was an added worry. Before she could make a decision, Randy, never knowing when to back off, set events in motion.

Moonpie had become still, seemingly calm with she stared out into space. Randy suddenly jeered at his sister, making childish faces.

Suddenly Moonpie came alive, giving him a resounding *slap* that sent his head reeling. "I shoulda knowed this would be a waste of time. You ain't never accounted for nuthin' you done before. Maybe I should just kill you." Something in her eyes must have sent a warning to Randy. He stiffened.

"No, don't, Moonpie. I'll listen to ya." He repeated it until the girl stepped away. She told it all, seeming to remember each movement Randy thrust upon her, in her. When she finished, Moonpie looked her brother in the eyes. She was depleted, her voice hushed. "Why, Randy? Why'd you rape me?"

"Rape you? Uh-uh! You better jiggle dat dumb brain a' yours. You been shakin' your stuff at me 'n every man since you knowed what a pecker was used for." She lunged at him. The old wooden floor split and swallowed up one of her legs. Moonpie fell against the table, her weight sending it crashing to the floor. She flopped over in a heap, buried her head into her arms and shrieked hysterically.

Aggie banged on the walls shouting Moonpie's name, running from slat to slat, pounding, pulling, trying to get inside. She found a weak board and ripped it out after three hard tugs. Reaching inside, she tried the door, all the while yelling at Moonpie. She took in the horrible scene before her.

"Help." It was a barely audible plea. The noose had tightened from the added weight when the table fell over, leaving Randy unsupported. With his legs, Randy was desperately trying to set the table upright. He found that on his tiptoes, he could loosen the pressure on his neck. But he was beginning to cramp and twitch. His foot slipped, the table skidded far out of his reach. His legs kicked out in blind purpose. His hands moved from the noose digging into his neck to the taunt rope above him, but he was unable to stop the slow strangulation. "Help. Me. Moon." She looked up just as his hand reached out toward her. She jerked back in panic. Whimpering like a wounded animal, Moonpie slid into the corner watching Randy struggle. His body made one last effort, a lurching epileptic-like seizure, then grew still.

Aggie whammed the door until it broke under her weight. She rushed to Randy lifting him up. She tried to hold onto him with one arm while searching for something to cut the rope. Aggie called out to Moonpie for help but didn't receive any. She balanced him against her and reached for the table. Suddenly she was flying forward, Randy ripped from her arms. Moonpie was screeching, running nowhere. Banging into walls, beating out at nothing. It didn't seem possible but her cries grew louder.

Momentarily stunned from butting against the wall, Aggie waited for Moonpie to spin off into another direction. The pathway clear, she hurried over to Randy, snagging the table on her way. She rested his legs on top just as Moonpie flew past, abruptly turned and charged at the small game warden. Aggie drew back and cold-cocked the deranged woman with a harsh left hook. Moonpie's head snapped back, stopping her in her tracks. Slowly she tipped over like a large bowling pin and smacked down onto the floor. *Finally* Moonpie was quiet. Aggie turned to Randy. She felt for a pulse but didn't find one. Tried digging the noose away from his neck but it was hopelessly embedded. It had been too long. Randy, too, had been silenced.

Aggie faced Moonpie. Coming to, the pathetic girl immediately began to move. She moaned. Her entire body bucked and quivered. Shrieks and wails tore her mouth open. She looked up at the older woman. Tears spilled from her eyes while she babbled and flailed at herself. Aggie stood by helplessly watching her, unable to approach. Eventually she grew still and Aggie sat down beside her. Moonpie lay her head on Aggie's lap. Her eyes appeared glassy, nobody home in there anymore. Aggie could think of nothing to do but rock the heavy girl as Moonpie continued babbling nonsense and sucking her thumb.

Russia: There are currently some four hundred anti-Semitic groups in Russia according to a report of the Inter-Ministerial Forum for the Study of Anti-Semitism. The groups accuse Jews and Freemasons of having ruined Russia. Anti-Semitic articles appear in the press with regularity.

Chapter Sixty-Nine

I used a sweet gum tree as poor cover, but soon felt itchy in the darkness doing nothing. As I stood up something brushed my ear, nearly causing me to cry out. I gingerly looked up. An old rope swing with a stick tied at the bottom dangled from a limb. I silently sighed in relief. Creeping to the edge of the cliff, I stared out into the dimness. A short while later I was able to make out a shadow on the other side of the dock. It was moving slowly and silently. Toward Dixie. My pal's back was to the shadow as she hunched down doing something. *Come on, Dix, time to look around you!* I scrunched down and clawed a hole in the ground. Scooping up a handful of turf, I molded the damp earth into a few small pellets and tossed them toward her. *Droga! Behind you!* Taking scant cover in the few bushes growing out of the cliff side, I tossed out more debris. The figure turned my way. I made like a statue. Seeing nothing, it continued to advance toward Dixie.

Droga! If I made too much noise I could get Dixie or Al hurt or killed. My brain raced to find a solution. The shadow crept closer to Dixie.

Some Tarzan-like impulse suddenly came over me. I grabbed the rope swing and ran. Ricocheting my feet off the sweet gum, I turned slightly to clear the brush and sailed out into the darkness hoping Dixie would see or hear the movement, look around her and spot the shadow. S*nap!* It was as loud as cannon fire in the relative quiet. I dropped like a diamond ring down the kitchen drain. I landed with a thud, pain–burning, hot snakey pain, worse than any I'd experienced in these months of maladies–made my left leg shimmy. I clutched my appendage as if that would take the hurt away. Trying not to alert the entire state of Georgia, I shoved a fist in my mouth and bit down, but sound drifted out across my knuckles.

"Aaaahhh! *Desastrado!"* I rolled over, my face burying into the sand. *Ajuda mi*! Help me!" I whimpered. A thousand curses churned in my brain.

"Paloma," Al whispered. "Get over here." In a haze I tried to move to-ward his voice but succeeded only in my mind. He grabbed my arms and pulled, both of us ending in a heap against the cliff.

"What happened?" Al asked anxiously as gunfire erupted from somewhere around us on the dock.

"Leg," I managed through tightly clenched teeth. Al just had to reach down and feel the hurting mass. I yelped. I replied with a string of four letter words–English. He ordered quiet.

"Where's Dixie? We have to find her."

"Thanks to you, sugah, she's okay. Me too. That's twice you've saved me. I need to find Aggie. And Stabenski. In the distraction he got away."

"You mean when I screamed."

"From the looks of things, anybody else would have done the same–or worse." He was shining a penlight over my leg. And he poked me again. His touch sent out a roar of nauseating pain. I went limp as a dishrag. "You're not shot," he reported, like big yippee! "It's broken."

"Thanks. I feel better now."

"Don't. I didn't say *how* bad." Al, the pragmatist, to the end. "Will you be all right by yourself?"

I nodded. "It's gonna hurt like hell with or without a party."

"Let's get you in the boat. For cover." Each uneven step Al took in the dark jarred me until my whole body was clammy and shaky. When he guided me down onto the boat seat, I collapsed weakly and slid onto the deck. I was useless to everyone.

"Paloma, I need you to hold the light so I can patch you up." I lay there like a dead dog. "Hey, come on. Focus! Paloma!" He lightly slapped my cheeks several times.

"Okay," I snapped testily, a bit of the fog clearing from my brain. I batted his hand away.

"Sugah, I've got to straighten the leg." He leaned me up against the seat as I illuminated my injury, seeing for the first time the extent of damage. Even in jeans, I could tell my leg was bent at an unusual angle. Just looking at it roiled my insides and I broke out into another duo of sweats and shakes. The heck with tough girl. I lay back and shut my eyes tight. First-aid he called it. Wreaking havoc was my description.

I fought to keep from vomiting. *"Droga*, Al! All we need is whiskey, a campfire, knife and a few tumbleweeds. Can't this wait for modern medicine?"

"No. There's bone sticking out of your skin. You're bleeding badly. I think straightening it will help or at least allow me to bandage you up."

"Do it fast." I'm sure he did, but it felt more like something used to in-duce confessions. Along with the bamboo shoots up the fingernails, the honey dip followed by ant bath, and a week in the two by two hot box.

"I need your pants out of the way."

"Al, this is not the time for hanky-panky." I weakly bantered, trying to lift my spirits, while Al fished in his pants pocket. Like a good boy scout, Al carried a Swiss Army knife. For some stupid reason, I wondered if it was the one that had the corkscrew and eating utensils. But I didn't have the energy to ask. Even with the blade, it was more like mutilation as he made one pant leg into shorts. "Here, sugah, help me make some strips." When I didn't move he grabbed my face and shook it gently. "Stay focused, Paloma. We need a tourniquet. You have to do something to stay awake."

"I am doing something. I'm laying here suffering." He gave the rest of my body a once-over, not finding anything worse to deal with. Al wrapped my leg as I worked on staying conscious. And not screaming out foul, bloody murder. Finally he was finished. I was completely drained. The slightest movement took a gargantuan effort.

He shined the light in between us. "Are you sure?"

"Go counselor. They might be in a jam."

"Keep a look out, sugah. There still are people around who wouldn't mind seeing you dead."

"They're getting their wish." He eyeballed me for a few seconds, kissed my lips, stared again. He started to say something, stopped, gave my forehead a peck then vanished into the darkness. I was abandoned. Alone.

I'm sure I dozed, or passed out. Occasional spits of gunfire made me jerk awake and sit up. But seeing beyond a few yards was impossible. The third time I sat up to check my surroundings I heard soft footsteps on the dock. They were sounding closer. A flashlight flicked off and on at brief intervals. I silently prayed it was Dixie or Aggie sent here by Al. I waited tensely. *Uh-uh-um.*

I almost screamed aloud. I could barely make out the form in the darkness as it neared. The tell-tale throat clearing of The Voice–Tom Richards. I reached for the gun in my pocket. Gone! *Puta que o pariu!* Calm down. Think! I beat on my pockets. Felt the knife I'd taken from the dead guy earlier at the cove. Moving clumsily, I slipped toward the rear of the boat and opened the knife. Sawing on the tie line, I set the boat adrift.

Richards ran toward me. I slid to the controls and tried the engine. Dead. Frantically scooting aft, I flipped up the seats, searching the storage lockers. My hand wrapped around something. An oar. As I pulled myself up onto the seat, the boat listed wildly. I turned. Richards had come up out of the water and was hanging onto the boat rocking it. I tried to balance myself in the pitch and roll. I whacked him with the plastic oar repeatedly until he disappeared under the water. I fell back, banging onto my damaged leg. I leaned over, head down to keep from passing out.

Movement. Water splashing. He rose out of the river like a sea monster. "I'm going to kill you!" he screamed. Richards swam after the boat as I futilely rowed. He caught up to me yanking the oar. My body jerked sideways. I shoved with everything I had, using the oar like a spear to knock him backwards. He snatched it out of my hands as he fell away. I flopped down onto the deck and searched the seat containers again. The trawling motor was tangled in anchor line. I frantically shook it and pulled. I leaned back letting my weight help me free it.

As Richards climbed the rear ladder, I threw the small anchor at him. He flung his arms out for protection and got wrapped up in the line. He struggled and splashed in the water. The anchor pulled him down, but he wasn't entangled enough to keep him busy for long. He was still a threat. We drifted on.

In seconds, it seemed, Richards was back. I struck him with the trawler. He fell, quickly resurfaced, still wrapped in the line, trailing behind me like a water skier. I dropped the trawler back into the bin, started sawing at the rope with the knife. The anchor came sailing at me. I ducked. It glanced off my shoulder and thudded onto the boat. I had to ignore the pain. Richards was back on the ladder–less than two feet from me. I yelped in surprise and fear.

He took a swipe at me. I grabbed his arm and gave him a shove. He fell off the slippery step and scrambled for purchase. I attacked, trying to separate him from the boat. As he knocked me backward, he climbed onto the ladder again. I got in a good head slam, zeroing in on his right ear. He slipped and banged fast and hard against the boat. Cursing and flailing, Richards tugged his arm. It had wedged down deep between the ladder and the stern wall of the boat. I took advantage of his predicament, carefully moving away from him, searching with hands and eyes for anything I could use for protection. Nothing! Moving back toward Richards, I crawled to the aft compartments. He was so close beside me it was unnerving. He continued trying to jerk free while heaping curses and death threats on me. I inched closer still. Raising up on my uninjured leg and arm, my other hand manically felt around in the storage unit for an improvised weapon.

Suddenly Richards jerked up. His arm was still trapped, but he'd managed to slide it higher up behind the ladder. He head-butted me, hitting my cheek with a painful *wham!* In the moon's glow I saw him tearing at his arm, roaring, pulling, and pounding. Throwing his whole body into releasing himself. I heard a pop. It sent Richards howling and cursing louder, as he blamed me for his damaged arm. Eventually he slumped over moaning and grew still. I didn't have long.

I thought of swimming for it. I was good, even with the bad leg. Any dangerous critters in the water that would be attracted to my wounded leg? Should I yell for help? It could get me shot. Each thought seemed to take precious hours–time I didn't have. Find something that would knock him out. Let him swim for it. I combed the last storage unit. Trash, lines. Life jacket. Trawler motor. It wasn't very sturdy but the trawler was attached to a long metal pole with a handle and clamp. It would have to do.

What now? Putter away from him at 5 m.p.h.? I cranked the small engine. It puttered then died. Suddenly the boat pitched. I went along with it, sliding into Richards, who had freed himself and was halfway into the boat. Then he was all over me–punching, grabbing, butting. By reflex I turned away. Mistake. Richards grabbed me from behind, his fist raining down and I couldn't do much but take it. With a handful of my hair he rammed my head painfully against the fiberglass surface. One time. Two. Three. Four. I smacked both of my hands down on his, flattening his grasp and taunt grip so I could flip around and face him. As he tightened his fist again, I used his outstretched arm to pull myself up onto my right knee then I leaned against the compartment for steadiness.

We were eye to eye. I felt the heat of his rage. Blood lust emanated from every pore. He cleared his throat. The sound mobilized me. I moved to punch him but slipped in the blood and water. He still gripped what was left of my hair. I was suspended in air, face down, my scalp burning. I reached up trying to rip my hair out of my scalp but he kept me flopping around unable to retaliate. I was drained. About to pass out. Fine. I would give up, succumb. Get it over with.

He flung me down, my broken leg taking the impact. The pain flared inside me. Then instinct kicked in. I was moving, propelled by an unseen force. *"Filho da puta!"* I caught him off guard by shifting my weight suddenly. My hand curled around the pole of the trawler motor. I swung it like a baseball bat. The thin aluminum connected with his temple, but with a head shake, he recovered quickly. My only weapon was now bent at a horrible angle.

I tried to crank it. Again. Again. Again. *Rrrmmm*! I goosed the engine. Richards brought h is arm around. Pistol almost in line to shoot me. *Survive.* The thought slipped into my mind, a brief surreal instant. "Aaaahhh!" I shoved the motor in his face, the blades coming to rest against bone while the gun fired twice. My mind and body worked separate from each other for physical and mental survival. I matched his screams with my own, his vileness with mine, terror matching terror. My mind whirled–images of him in my house, his destruction. His touch. Heinous laughter. At the motel. My fear. Hurt. Degradation. The Klavern. Torture. He was all about torture. I watched my hands holding the trawler, swinging it at him, felt the thrust and deep revulsion. Saw his haunting features no longer recognizable. I heard a nasal rasp from his flattened nose and sinuses. Heard him groan. Saw him shudder and fall overboard. He struggled in the water, first in racking motions. Then slower, winding down. Occasionally he grasped at the air, at life. A life that was, at last, no more.

1993: Massachusetts–Fall River: A Cambodian immigrant, Sam Nang Nhem, was beaten to death during an attack by a-bout a dozen men. A white man, Harold Latour, twenty-three, was charged with murder and committing a hate crime. California–Oakland: About twenty Asian gang members attacked five Hispanic sailors with clubs in an apparent racial assault.– Klanwatch.

Chapter Seventy

My recovery was slower, this time around. As soon as I'd gathered a bit of strength, I would be wheeled into surgery to repair another piece of my left leg. I didn't know if I should worry–why couldn't they get it all taken care of at once? After each operation, instead of getting better the pain from my left leg increased exponentially until pulling the bed sheet across it caused a weird searing pain that felt like someone was mashing hot ground glass into the appendage.

Grouchy old Doc Benson took pleasure, in typical physician fashion, to inform me how my Tarzan maneuvers caused several breaks and with too much detail, described how far up the leg one errant bone had traveled. He'd held up his hands demonstrating the distance in case my imagination was lacking. He scoffed at my complaints about worse pain, and once even suggested I was making it up, a product of whining indicative of the weaker female sex. While his bedside manner was gruff and condescending, his long-haired resident, Dr. Morgan, made up for it. I stared brazenly at him while he scribbled secret messages about my condition into a file while tucking errant blonde tresses behind his ear. He seemed to believe my complaints and did what he could for me.

My rescue in the boat was anti-climatic. Ascertaining that everyone was relatively safe at the Beamon shack, Al and a few agents had hunted for me several miles along the river. At first light, rescue workers began a full-blown search. Several hours later, a helicopter team sighted me in salt waters nearing the Atlantic Ocean. Richards, still entangled in the lines, had been dragged across an oyster bed where his body became anchored and stopped the boat from drifting further. The only good thing that psychopath did for me.

The whole mess, as southerners refer to such incidents, had more loose ends than the fringe on a king-sized bedspread. Aggie, Al and Dixie filled me in on what I'd missed at the Beamon shack. When Al left me in the boat and found the others, most of the excitement was over. Aggie was in the shed keeping Moonpie calm and they eventually got her to a hospital. She was now under intensive psychological care. "She has a long row to hoe," Aggie reported sadly. "Both legally and mentally. No one claimed Randy's body for burial. We paid for a simple casket from this anonymous donation that came into the Law Center." I nodded knowingly. My hacking of Gundersen computers was still a secret. Stabenski, proved that night to be the dirty GBI agent, was on the run. Vontana was busier than ever tying up several aspects of the case.

Guards were posted outside my room because of a backlash of threatening calls and hate mail. Klan and WRF sympathies were stirred and many who'd lost their jobs when the plant closed down in Rincon were looking for someone to blame. The town had been mulling over what they could do to recover. One idea was to use the plant for legitimate purposes, but nothing could happen until the GBI finished their tedious probe. There were a lot of people out of work, scared and mad. I couldn't blame them. But as some of the press coming out of Rincon stated, many of the townsfolk were angry that they had been duped and used.

"Howze Billy Ray?" I asked.

"He's handling things better," Al reported. "His father is asking to be placed in a protection program! He's swearing he can give hot information about the WRF and several Klans in Georgia, but Vontana doesn't think he has much of value to tell. Nobody else in the Klan is talking. Except for the dead, which were seventeen total, we have no idea how many of them were at Logs Landing from either group."

"Al, isn't it sadly ironic that those two groups–the WRF and the Klan–each standing for the survival of the white race, wantonly attacked each other– their white brothers? Destroying the exact type of group they each belonged to, each wanted to form more of! And all of the destruction and death at Logs Landing had nothing to do with a single minority. The supremacist groups were fighting each other for ultimate supremacy."

"Logic never figures into crime, especially hate groups, sugah. All the experts will be pondering over this incident for years to come," Al stated. All of us had been tremendously changed from that night of violence, and the previous incidents as well. Each of us were facing our own internal anguish that needed sorting out, to get it behind us. Fortunately, we had each other for support and understanding. Not everyone touched by the violence did.

"What else, Al?"

He thought a moment, then replied. "The woman Randy killed at that hotel has been identified as Sandra Brice. She was in charge of a woman's auxiliary of the WRF."

"They didn't miss a trick–recruited women, children."

Al nodded. "A man from the Gundersen plant, named Swartzman, has been arrested. Thanks to an anonymous source who'd sent me and Vontana copies of their financial records and other information. He, Vontana, was able to pin the leadership of the WRF on him. There's a good bit of useable evidence. The GBI arrested a man nicknamed Red, thanks to Swartzman. He swears Red's the man we really want."

"Well, they're all innocent."

"Every one of them, every single time." We smiled at each other. "Once they sort out the manure, they should have enough proof to nail the majority of them. They've been leaning hard on Swartzman. All but two of the WRF camps were clean when the local agents raided. The people were arrested and fined for operating a paramilitary camp."

"But that's all," I groused.

"It'll take time, sugah. Most of them are blaming it all on everyone but themselves. Mostly Randy and Richards."

"Of course they are. The dead can't speak."

"There's something else. Today Moonpie was charged with Randy's murder."

"No way! From what Aggie says, it wasn't really her fault. She's all messed up because of her brother. Al, you'll defend her."

"You're the new boss of Waving Girl?" We mugged at each other.

"Come, on, Al, She needs a good attorney. She shouldn't have to pay any longer for Randy's deeds. Otherwise, her brother is still winning."

He put his hands out, holding me back. "I'll check into it, sugah. I promise. She should get an attorney with experience in that type of case. But I'll make sure she's looked after. Now about you. How are you dealing with this whole mess?"

I was experiencing conflicting emotions about Randy. I didn't feel a bit of pity when Aggie told me how he gruesomely died. Then I worried that there was something wrong with me because of those feelings. Was I as bad as he? There *was* a black space inside me–a place where the events hung waiting to be exorcised. Sometimes the void filled with anger, other times sadness. I wanted the people involved to stand before their victims and a jury and admit their crimes. Especially Randy and Tom Richards. I wanted to hear the words "we find the defendant guilty". Have them alive to suffer behind bars for a long, long time. I wanted them to feel the weight of the death penalty and have their appeals drag on in court. Or did I? With those two fiends dead, everyone could now look to the future.

"It's okay what you're feeling–after what he did to you," Al told me, reading my mind. "And with all this," he waved his hand across the bed, "you don't need any more to worry about."

"*Droga!*" I couldn't articulate my feelings to Al. "I don't under-stand people like Richards and Randy."

"The hate?"

"They hate for just being born." Then I spoke quietly. "Richards just wouldn't stop. At the river, I became just as violent as him."

"No, sugah. Not anywhere close to it. What you did, you had no choice," Al assured me. He did what he could to help me with the aftermath. But what he couldn't do was quell the nightmares that had plagued me ever since I'd been forced to kill the two men that night.

*   *   *

Vontana swallowed another pair of headache tablets, chased down with cold coffee. There was nothing wrong with Stabenski's aim. He rubbed the lump on his face that the dirty agent had put there that night at Logs Landing. It ached like he'd just been punched yesterday. He checked the time on his watch.

"If it was my sorry ass, I'd be flying to South America," Taylor said again, still doubtful the agent would be in Jacksonville, Florida–a few hours from Savannah. And taking a train. He pretended to tie his shoe laces while he talked into a hidden radio to his partner Vontana, who was hiding behind an opened newspaper.

"I'm right about this one, Taylor. And we got a hundred dollar bet riding on it."

"When I take that fat ol' bill from you, Bruce, I'm going to that fancy country club in Savannah Beach. Gonna see if their service is any better than the Annapolis Denny's." Vontana chuckled. Until a few months ago, the country club had an all-white policy. The owners finally bowed to pressure from civic groups and the threat of losing money from several golf tournaments if a boycott was enforced. "Laugh all you want, Vontana. Today's the only day off I've had in three weeks. And where am I? Sitting in the hot sun with a fake beard that makes my face itch."

"You're gonna feel worse when *you* lose the bet," Vontana countered and dipped the newspaper slightly to scan the area for a few minutes. A bit later Vontana broke into a grin. "Heads up! Ten o'clock, Taylor." His partner looked, seeing Stabenski heading toward the train.

His arrest, with the help of Florida law enforcement went down quick and without incident. They were soon headed back to Georgia to enjoy what part of the day that was left.

"Come on, partner," Taylor said, as he handed Vontana five new twenty dollar bills. "Why were you so sure he'd be on the train?"

"I checked the schedules. That train is going to Los Angeles, the furthest he could get from Rincon."

"That still doesn't tell me..."

"Stabenski is afraid of flying."

1993, California: Rancho Penasguitos–An Hispanic migrant worker allegedly was beaten by two white men who taunted him with racial slurs. Lake Forest–A Korean store owner and his son allegedly were beaten by a white, black, and Hispanic after a customer argued with the Koreans over a purchase. Los Angeles–Two Asian Americans yelling anti- white slurs attacked a white man and a man of Hispanic and Asian ancestry. Sacramento–Black high school students beat a white youth.

Chapter Seventy-One

Shawn Munson watched the newscast with a growing sense of dread. "Who did they arrest from the WRF?" he screamed at the TV. "Get on with it!" It was two days later when he found out, this time from the newspapers. Swartzman's face looked back at him from the front page. Munson's plans, his dreams, were shattered. He'd never get the payment now.

"I'll get Swartzman and any one else who screwed with me," he vowed to the walls. He called his buddy at the Gundersen plant in Boston, the guy who'd recommended him to the WRF as equipment supplier. He had to leave a message. Waiting. All he's ever done is wait!

"Sorry it took so long to call you back. We've been walking on glass ever since the cops busted the Rincon operation," the Bostonian explained nasally.

"What about my money? Who's yanking my chain?"

"I'm telling you, the cash was transferred to Georgia."

"Then that Kraut squirreled it away."

"I don't think so."

"What do you mean?"

"We're still checking into it, but our guys tell us that Swartzman was shitting bricks when he found out there was no cash or stocks. He tried cooking the books to cover himself."

"Then who did it?"

"That's what we're looking into. Whoever it is, I'll personally wipe their hide all the way up from Georgia to Massachusetts and back down."

"Not if I get hold of them first," Shawn hung up, itching to vent his fury into a plan of revenge against whoever had wiped out Swartzman's–his–cash supply.

*   *   *

Billy Ray figured he'd developed an ulcer. Or maybe stomach cancer. He'd always kept his feelings locked in his gut which often caused him physical grief. But it had been burning, aching, gurgling, ever since the night–that night–with Randy and Moonpie. And it steadily grew worse. A stupid ulcer couldn't hurt this bad. He was all smoked out and tired of the taste of nicotine, but couldn't think of anything else to do instead.

Vontana opened the door of the interview room and waved to Billy Ray. His stomach twisted harder. "Our coffee must be getting to you. You look a little green. Are you ready to see your father?" No, but Billy Ray nodded. "Don't worry. He's cut a deal with the district attorney." Vontana gave his back an encouraging tap.

"Thanks, sir. For everything. Al said you'd be honest from the start." Billy Ray had noticed how these people–the GBI men, Al and his friends–treated people differently, especially women. He'd never known anyone like them and wished he could stay here, learn from them. For once he was spending time with good, trusting people. He hadn't known what he'd been missing.

"Hey, son!" Hughes grabbed him into a bear hug as soon as he walked into the room. "They treating you okay?"

"Yeah." Vontana shut the door and left them alone.

"We gotta talk real low. I bet they got the place wired up the wahzoo." Hughes pulled two chairs close together. He leaned over to talk.

"I cut a deal, B-Ray, so I'm coming out of this smelling like a rose." He sat back to show his broad grin, then leaned forward again. "As soon as we're in a new place, we can get the group up again. You'll like it now that there'll be new people."

"What group?" Billy Ray asked testily.

"The Klan. I'll make you Exalted Cyclops, since we won't have to worry about Barry making a stink. It'll all be fresh and new. It'll be great. You'll see!"

"Didn't you learn?" Billy Ray yelled and stood, tangling with the chair. He shoved it out of the way. "What about all the dead men at Logs Landing? Those guys didn't mean anything? They walked right into an ambush because of you!"

His father's face turned ashen. "You're a communist jew-nigger-loving fruit cake! A faggot. That's what this is about, ain't it? You're a homo and that's why you didn't want to stay in the Klan. You were afraid someone would find out. You never have had a girlfriend."

"Shut up! Just what was I supposed to bring a girl home to? A ratty trailer? A family like yours?" He banged his fist on the table. "You're getting a chance to start over, but you're already making plans for another Klan. You can't lead. You can't even run your own life!" He leaned against the table, suddenly drained of energy, and let the tears fall. "You won't always be this lucky. If Paloma or the GBI hadn't come along and broke the WRF case you'd be lynched by *your own boys*! You stole from them. You stole from the store. You took from me! Did you plan the Logs Landing stunt so that no one would be around to wonder what you did with all the Klan's money?"

"Someone has to save this country, prepare for the race war."

"There ain't gonna be no race war! You prey on helpless people, turning their minds so they can't think of anything except what you want 'em to. It ain't gonna happen, dad. And you're gonna get boxed in one day and then you're gonna be killed. Give it up. Please!" He clutched at his gut. The fire!

"Are you making your own deal? You are gonna sell out your old man, ain't you?" Hughes snarled.

Billy Ray shook his head hard. "You know me. You know I'd never–how could you even think that!" Suddenly, he knew the truth. "Are you saying that because it's what you'd do?" He nodded, answering his own question. "In spite of everything, I was moving with ya'll. And you know that."

"You're lying!" his father yelled.

"Me? You couldn't see the truth if it walked up and kissed you on the ass!" Hughes charged Billy Ray, clinging to his son like a leech. Vontana raced into the room with two agents in tow, quickly breaking up the scuffle. Vontana offered Billy Ray a hand up. The other agents shoved Hughes roughly into a chair and held him down while he cursed his adopted son.

"I'm ready to go now, Mr. Vontana," the young man said quietly. The agent led him out of the room, Hughes's rants following them down the hallway.

"Billy-Ray, he's been questioned off and on for over twenty hours. Once your dad calms down, see's your family..."

"Thanks for trying to make me feel better, sir. I don't have any family. I never met my real dad. My mama was a drunk and died during one of her binges. She walked in front of a car. When I was a little kid. " Billy Ray's voice came in a rush. "I want to get away from here. Alone. And as soon as possible. Any problem with that?"

"Any particular place in mind?"

"No. I ain't never been outside the state."

"With Carolina and Florida so close?" Vontana asked surprised.

"Nope. I been thinking about learning trucking. I could drive around, see some of the country, find a place to settle down. Then go to school for something else. I want a job I can build on."

"You can do anything, go anywhere," he said supportably. "People talk about starting over but you have the chance to really do it! You've got a clean slate."

Billy Ray attempted a smile, but it turned into a grimace. He doubled over in pain. Inside him burned a world of hurt.

*   *   *

Al had been in make-up mode from the moment I woke up in the hospital, sorry for his behavior at the GBI offices when Willie had confessed to being with Randy and Richards. When it was evident that I wouldn't be getting out of the hospital for awhile and as I grew more coherent after the surgeries and medications, he and my family were coming up with more elaborate schemes to help me pass the time and mend. The latest project was done in cahoots with Aggie and Dixie. While I was having some type of scan, the duo turned my room into a mock beach. The decorations were mostly tacky beach kitsch sold in the cheap tourist traps along the coast, but I smiled every time I woke up. My favorite was a coconut pod made into a pirate's head. It even had a patch over one eye. Jimmy Buffet tunes played and there was one of those CDs that played ocean sounds. Seagulls called, waves crashed, foghorns sounded.

Al arrived shortly after the mermaids had created their magic. He'd dressed in shorts and I got a peek at his muscular, tanned legs. He was sporting sun glasses, had a beach ball under one arm, a picnic basket in the other. We pigged out on boiled shrimp and crab. We chatted about nothing. I was feeling the best I had since stepping back on Southern soil.

"Al, no one's told me about Grainger," I said breaking the spell. "Were you able to get some dope on him?" His face was immobile and hurt as he increased his grip on my hand. Thank goodness the IV needle was plugged into my other paw. I shook it loose. It was a few minutes before he was able to talk. Even then, his tone was caustic.

"My *mother* hid him out until everything blew over! He's crying the blues now about being blackmailed into locking Dixie up! His family in danger. My foot! He hasn't been implicated yet. Him a victim! How could she know and still protect him?" The news saddened me. Since I'd met him, Al's demeanor held back his thoughts as he searched for the truth from others. But today, they bore his grief, leaving him uncharacteristically vulnerable. The breech between Al and his mother had become as wide as the Mississippi.

"Come here, Curly," I ordered. He scooted his chair closer and leaned over the bed rails. "Didn't someone tell you that your face could freeze this way?" I massaged his cheeks and forehead trying to help the storm pass. He took my hand and held it against his face and closed his eyes. "Who's guarding the door?"

"Gus," he replied.

"Tell him to keep it private for a while." When Al came back, I pulled him around to my uninjured side and made room for him in the bed. I cradled his head against my chest as we lay together, CD ocean waves crashing in the background. It was no boat or starry night but the time for healing was just the same.

1993: Pensacola, Florida–Michael Frederick Griffin, an anti-abortion protester, was charged with murdering a doctor who performed abortions. Wilmette, Illinois–Jonathan Preston Haynes murdered plastic surgeon Martin R. Sullivan because he believed the doctor was making non-whites look Aryan. He also confessed to a six year old murder of San Francisco hair-dresser, Frank Ringi, because he had bleached clients' hair.

Chapter Seventy-Two

"Reality sucks," Dixie told me after I ranted about the newspaper announcement that only a few Klan and WRF members were charged with major crimes. "There's not much proof of anything that happened at Logs Landing. They're all dead. Now shut up or change the subject," she ordered lightly. I'd begun trying to wean myself off of the crutches and was still ignoring the pain that never seemed to lessen despite the doctors' assurance. I spent my time at Aggie's, on the *Katie* with my grandparents, and trying to cheer Al. The long arm of the law wasn't long enough to nab Grainger. He escaped any charges of wrong doing and resumed his job as sheriff. Yeah, Dixie, reality sucks. Since the WRF was nationwide, it would be impossible to get all the members arrested for crimes perpetrated by their Rincon members. We didn't stop the WRF or the Klan completely, but we took the wind out of their sails. I admitted feeling smug about that.

On the day before Dixie flew back to LA, we had one final gathering, Carolina island style. For moving forward, mourning death, celebrating life. I didn't have a job to go back to, but Dixie did. I would follow her later.

Like the one-legged pirate I played in my youth, I managed to help Aggie and Papa catch enough seafood to feed an army. Dixie's family, Clarice's helpful neighbors, Lemond's Rincon friends, Waving Girl Law Center staff, GBI agents, Lester the Marshall who'd testified for Dixie, Ezeriah who'd found me in the trunk and even the judge who'd dropped the charges against Dixie, came in an assortment of vehicles, everybody drifting to Pop's backyard with arm loads of food.

Vontana and his family arrived last. The agent walked directly over to me and handed me a large yellow envelope. When I looked inside, my own face peered up at me. Al was right. I did look pretty hot in the white dress. Negatives were at the bottom. Another loose end tied.

"From Randy's things and Swartzman's office."

Geez, I had gotten around. At least in photo form. "Thanks." He shrugged and walked away. His daughter and wife were hanging onto Al like long lost relatives. It was heartening to see the bonds among the guests while strangers mixed, making new friends.

Al and Papa built a fire, setting the huge witches' cauldron on top of it for the Low Country cookout. I sat in a lawn chair and watched. Aggie framed another fire with cinder blocks and laid a thick metal rectangle on top. Laying oysters and clams on the surface, she covered them with wet burlap bags for steaming. I got the job of hosing the bags down at appropriate intervals, which I did right from the lounge chair. Aggie and I won the shucking contest and gladly ate every single one we'd opened in the race.

When the water in the pot was boiling, Al plopped in the net bag of shrimp boil–the necessary mix of seasonings–and followed with Clarice's homemade sausage and corn from his field. Shrimp and crabs were added last and soon after, the whole medley was poured over an old wooden table. Those around the table stepped back while the water drained over the side and in between the slats. After an appropriate interval, they all dove into the feast. An endless supply of casseroles, salads, homegrown veggies and desserts weighted down another table. Each item sworn to be the cook's best efforts and everybody's favorite.

"I should have worn my shorts with the elastic waist," I told Aggie as I tugged at the waistband for room to attack the plateful of desserts she offered me. My grandmother hovered, making sure I stayed off my leg. Tales were told, shenanigans exposed and jokes swapped. We watched Al and Papa standing to one side peeling shrimp over the table. Pop was a peel-as-you-eat guy while Al made little piles before he indulged. Papa discretely snuck some of Al's whenever he wasn't looking.

"Paloma, you come by it honestly," Gran told me watching my grandfather in action.

"Whatever in the world are you talking about?" I asked, knowing exactly what.

"Tomfoolery. Look at your grandfather. He's like a kid." Papa put a crab on Beverly's shoulder. She swatted at it absent-mindedly then screamed when her hand touched the creature. Beverly joined us all in laughter. Dixie sauntered over covering up a burp with a long slender hand. She picked at my desserts until I warded her off with one of my crutches.

"You don't mess with a woman and her sweets," I reprimanded Dixie and to Aggie I stated, "Papa made a good call."

"What do you mean?"

"Getting everybody together, Ag."

"Ag? That sounds ugly," Aggie commented. "If you insist on using it, I'll have to call you pigeon," said the plucky Game Warden. So Dixie had ratted, telling Aggie her irritating nickname–Paloma translates to pigeon in Spanish. Pigeon. I hate that. I'd find a way to get her back. "You're right, today's just the thing after all that has happened. Look at them. They're relaxed, getting back into the flow. Clarice and Bev are laughing. I haven't seen Al this at ease in weeks."

"Since he met Paloma," Dixie added, teasing.

"That Al is a right nice young man. You treat him good, Paloma."

"Yes, ma'am," I answered Gran.

"And he eats good, too," she added. The Southern stamp of approval. Gran lived in a simple world. All people were nice. She didn't know anyone otherwise. Simple. And that's how the day and evening went. It kept us all down to earth.

Hours later we watched the embers shimmer heat. Most people had drifted home or were cleaning up. I was a happy Buddha ogling everything from my chair, leg propped on pillows.

"Paloma." Al's tone warned of something serious. He took my hand and pulled it lightly signaling me to look at him. Firelight flickered on his face. "You won't come back, will you?"

I knew it was stupid but I said it anyway. "Of course I will. My grandparents are my family." His look was scolding. "Come on, Al. Can't this wait? This has been one of the best days I've had since I stepped off the plane."

"I'm sorry to bother you." He steamed off.

"Al. Al!" He came back, squatting down in front of me. I studied the smoking embers wishing they'd conjure up an oracle who'd give me an answer. At the least, something meaningful to say.

"I thought I was going to be the one to apologize from now on."

His smile was bittersweet, his look was again trying to penetrate my thoughts and feelings. "I'd like to get to know you better," he said finally.

"And I you."

"Kind of hard to do three thousand miles apart."

"Yeah." *Smooth and intelligent.*

"What do we do?"

"What do you want to do?" I sighed, throwing it back in his lap. He checked for eavesdroppers before he answered.

"I'd like you to be here–where I can be with you." He sat down on the ground and played with a few blades of grass. "What would you like?"

"Both." He knew what I meant. I felt immature for some reason, thinking Al more advanced in the relationship department. Maybe being married before gave him a leg up, or perhaps the ten or so years he had on me. "Can we see what happens in the time before I leave? You may be sick of me by then," I hedged. "Or something may happen that helps us decide."

He kissed me with his eyes. That old familiar desire to tap dance around matters of the heart snuck back inside me. "Al, please get me more tea." I held out my cup and rubbed my lips together. "The meds make me thirsty." He got up slowly, scooping up the cup on the way, not happy with the interruption. At the food table, one of Clarice's neighbors snagged him into a conversation and by the time he'd disengaged himself, Dixie had ambled over challenging me to a computer game. He stared across at us for a time while I pretended not to notice.

"You okay, P?" She asked, not taking her eyes off Heathcliff's screen.

"Super legal!"

"You may be very cool, but from the intensity of Al's scowl, it looks like you still have some unfinished business to attend."

"Yeah."

She scrutinized me, one eye closed. "Is that all you have to say?"

"Yeah," I answered sadly.

Oh, Great Spirit who dwells in the sky, lead us to the path of peace and understanding. Let us all live together as brothers and sisters.–Native American prayer for peace.

Chapter Seventy-Three

Handling crutches fairly well, but still feeling rough around the edges, I left Papa and Gran on their porch and drove to the Game and Wildlife Federation to say goodbye to Aggie. She was still waiting for word of her promotion and I insisted on her not leaving work to see me off. I didn't want anyone to do so. I hate airport scenes–not enough time to say what needed to be said or silly conversations to fill the time. I knew Aggie wanted to ask about Al and me, but I decided he could tell her want he wanted.

There hadn't been much *to* say, the counselor and I discovered. In so many essential ways we were opposites. His hands were for pulling weeds and mine were for hauling nets. And I just couldn't let go of L.A. We both had dreams, desires that were rooted deep down in our veins. It's hard to abandon something that's the core of your living, your identity. So we filed ourselves under "pending". Al was planning to fly to California next month after he wrapped up a case. I would miss him. I felt it already.

The last weeks on the island, I was kept in a state of bewilderment–expecting a desire to overcome me where I'd give up my friends, the boat, my house, my job, my goals, dreams, everything–to dash back into his arms. Prince Charming will sweep you off your feet. Nothing else mattered as long as you had your man. That was the story for girls growing up. My feet were still on the ground not knowing whether to go south or west.

I hobbled onto the plane, pain running up my leg with seething agony. I felt the tug of the island calling me back. Here was family, a warm cocoon of familiarity, stability, and simple, easy living. Soon the plane lifted in the air. I looked down on my beloved island, drinking in the palms, golf courses, roads, homes, storing them in my memory. They'd have to serve me until my next visit. I faced forward as the plane climbed and I felt the pull against my body as we sliced into the sky. To the lure of newness, an uncertain future, uncharted Western trails to blaze.

I dropped the seat back. I was drowsy and knew I'd soon be falling asleep. And with any luck, my dreams would be of new adventures, different experiences. And when I awoke? I'd be ready and waiting.

Don't miss Marisa Babjak's

second Paloma mystery

The Street Where Angels Fear to Tread.

Forthcoming late Summer 2004,

at booksellers everywhere.

The Street Where Angeles Fear to Tread

Polish-Brazilian Paloma is back in Seal Beach, California, and still reeling from a hasty departure from her dream job as a computer security investigator. Black-listed for employment with the top high-tech firms, and with mounting medical problems from a leg injury during her last investigation, Paloma takes a job as a computer analyst with the City of Los Angeles. Working across the street from her in Parker Center, the Los Angeles Police Department's headquarters, is her best-friend and policewoman, African-American Dixie Hightower.

Both young women are listless, their love-lives on the fritz, and a bit down on life in general. To lift up their spirits the pals set up a computer learning center for kids at risk.

When a precocious young prodigy befriends Paloma, the teen is searching for more than an opportunity to hone her computer skills. As Paloma hunts down a despicable network of individuals who prey on troubled kids, she is unaware of the dangers lurking just around the corner.

It's going to take more than her lock-picking and computer hacking skills, and even more than what Dixie, along with the Los Angeles Police Department, can do to save Paloma when she too, becomes lost on *The Street Where Angels Fear to Tread.*